WITH OR WITHOUT PANTIES

HOT COPS SERIES
Book 1

KAREN LIEVERSZ

SUGAR PUSH PUBLISHING

E-book ISBN: 978-0-6458556-0-9

Paperback ISBN: 978-0-6458556-1-6

Cover design by LJ at Mayhem Cover Creations

Edited by Kelly Rigby at Write with Kelly

Proofread by Jo Speirs at Nurturing Words

A catalogue record for this book is available from the National Library of Australia

Author Note

With or Without Panties contains frequent swearing and explicit sex scenes. It also touches on mental health topics, drug addiction, death, grief, and complicated family relationships that may be uncomfortable for some readers.

Please note, this book is written in Australian English, which differs in some instances from US English.

ı

To my beautiful rescue dog, Ruby, who showed that love heals all wounds.

And to my ever-patient husband, Eardley, for his unwavering belief in me.

Chapter One

Claire

The granny pants drape across my bed like a sadistic offering to the gods. An unsightly flag of surrender to any hopes of feeling sexy. What mother in her right mind gifts such a hideous pair of briefs to her daughter? On her twenty-eighth birthday?

A shiver runs down my spine. My mum. That's who.

What's worse, she thinks I should wear them to my job interview today at ECL Marketing. And what's even more appalling, I'm considering it.

A brief knock at my bedroom door is the only warning I get before it swings open and my mother sweeps in, flooding the room with the luxurious scent of Chanel N°5. My sister, Alexandria, follows. While Mum hides her curves behind an oversized black pant suit, Alex has them on display in a fitted navy-blue pencil dress and cropped navy jacket. Complete with a no-nonsense mahogany bun; she's the epitome of style and sophistication. Everything I'm not.

It's my fault they're here. I should never have told Mum about the interview. She was determined to lend me moral support. Apparently, that meant bringing my perfect sister with her. It's surprising Alex had time in her busy schedule. Which begs the question, what is she doing here?

Mum's hazel eyes widen as she takes me in, dressed in my white fluffy dressing gown. "Why aren't you ready?"

I fiddle with the belt on my robe and shrug. "I'm still deciding what to wear."

She glances at the pile of clothes on the bed, her gaze zeroing in on the underpants laid out in all their glory. She beams. "I'm so pleased you listened to me, Claire. The new underwear I bought for your birthday will give you extra confidence."

Alex follows Mum's gaze and stiffens. The haughty I'm-so-much-better-than-you expression on her face fades. Our eyes meet, and for a moment, we're little girls again, listening to Mum drone on about the importance of wearing clean underwear. Although in this case, cleanliness is a given. Good taste? Not so much. Alex presses her lips together and shakes her head. I give her a stiff nod. Yep. Our mother is certifiable.

Or am I the crazy one for considering wearing such ugly undies?

"Ah, Mum," says Alex. "How about we let Claire get dressed?"

Mum ignores Alex. Instead, she picks up the cute, pink embroidered dress lying next to the underwear. "You're not wearing this, are you?"

"Why not?"

Mum drops the dress and grimaces. "It's hardly very corporate, Claire."

I take a deep breath. If Mum had her way, she'd turn me into an Alex clone. "It's a marketing job, Mum. It'll look very smart teamed with a white jacket."

Alex nods. "And the colour compliments Claire's honey blonde hair."

Yes! I do a mental fist pump in the air. Thanks, Alex.

Mum's head snaps to my sister. She probably didn't expect her to defend me. I'm just as surprised. "This job interview is important. Claire needs to look her best."

Alex's phone, which is glued to her hand twenty-four seven, rings. She glances at the caller ID, her brows furrowing. "Oh. Sorry, I've got to take this. There's been a development in one of the high-profile cases I'm working on."

Alex strides out of the room. Show off. As if we didn't already know she's a hotshot lawyer. Mum's face softens into an indulgent smile. "I still can't believe Alex is a junior partner at thirty-two. Your father and I are so proud."

I bite my tongue. Of course they are. Alex was dux of the school and a university medallist. She even played hockey for Australia before giving it up to focus on her legal career. And to top it all off, she's married to another junior partner. My shoulders slump, a familiar hollowness filling my chest. Alex was always destined for greatness, unlike me. I barely got the marks to be accepted into an arts degree. As for sport, I feigned period pain at school as often as possible to get out of it. I slide the wardrobe door open and pull out a pair of stylish but sensible two-inch heeled white sandals. Anything higher and I risk tripping over myself at the interview.

"I'm surprised Alex could spare the time to come over."

Mum picks up on my snarkiness straight away, her lips pursing. "When I told Alex you were going for a job with ECL Marketing, she was very happy for you. She knows the CEO. They're on some board together."

Of course, she'd know him. I force a smile. "That was nice of her." I doubt that's the real reason Alex is here. Mum probably guilted her into coming. Not that I want her help. I can do this on my own.

I glance at the door, hoping Mum will get the hint. She doesn't. Instead, she hurries to the window and tugs at the sheer ivory curtains, ensuring there's no gap between them.

As if anyone's going to be peering through the tiny sliver of space.

"Your father and I only want what's best for you, Claire. We'd love nothing more than to see you settled down with a nice man and a good job."

I keep my face neutral and perch on the end of the bed. Mum's idea of a nice man is someone rich, and by a good job, she means something she can proudly tell her tennis club cronies about. Having a daughter who's a sales rep doesn't cut it, which is one reason I'm going for a marketing job. It's not what I truly want, but I need to prove to my parents that I'm not the loser they think I am. The other reason is the sales job is mind-numbingly boring, not that I'd ever admit it.

"Or ..." She clasps her hands in a rare sign of nervousness. "A nice man and babies. We're not getting any younger."

Babies? I haven't had a relationship survive longer than a month. A family is the last thing on my mind. I clutch my robe tighter.

Mum laughs at my discomfort, but there's sadness behind her eyes. It's not the first time she's hinted at grandchildren. I bet if she asked, Alex could pop out a couple of grandbabies and still make senior partner before her fortieth birthday.

It's time for Mum to go before she turns me into a complete nervous wreck. I point at the clock on my bedside table. "Mum, I need to get dressed or I'll be late."

"Oh, my. The time has gotten away, hasn't it?" She pecks my cheek. "I'll leave you to it. You concentrate on your job interview."

The bedroom door clicks shut, and I'm left alone with the suffocating fragrance of perfume, the weight of my mum's expectations, and the hideous undies.

I trace a clammy finger over the coarse cotton and shudder. I could pretend I'm wearing the appalling underpants, but I'm a terrible liar. Mum would see right through me, and I don't want to hurt her feelings. It's important to her—and even though we never talk about the day we found Granny dead on the toilet, huge white undies around her ankles, I know it had just as much impact on Mum as it did on me. It's why I'm slightly obsessed—okay, totally obsessed—with underwear. The problem is, our views on the subject couldn't be more opposed. Hence the repulsive pants she gifted me.

I swore never to put myself in a position where I could be caught dead wearing ugly underwear, and yet here I am, tempting fate. Then again, it's not like I've had any success doing things my way. Maybe it's time to take my mother's advice.

With trembling fingers, I drag the undies on. The fabric gobbles up my privates, hips, butt, and stomach until it's all the way to my waist, wrapping me in a garish bouquet. I swear the design contains more flowers than I've had kisses. I look like a garden with legs.

The pink embroidered dress is next, covering up the unsightly material. A check in the mirror confirms no visible panty lines. *Phew.* At least I'm rocking it on the outside. No one will suspect the disaster underneath. I breathe in.

Out.

In again.

It's only for a few hours.

What could possibly go wrong?

Chapter Two

Claire

I don't dare drive to the interview. My company car has GPS fitted so management can track our every movement and assure themselves we're not skiving at the beach instead of visiting customers. Fortunately, it's an easy bus ride to ECL Marketing's office in Parramatta. Both Mum and Alex offered to take me, but I waved them off. While I appreciate their support, the attention, and all that perfume, are overpowering. Not to mention, no grown woman wants her mother or older sister to drive her to a job interview. It makes me feel like I'm sixteen all over again. Besides, the short walk from the bus stop will settle my nerves.

Wrong.

I miss my stop and tumble off the bus at the next one. To make up time, I cut through a small park. The fluttering and squawking of lorikeets as they flit from tree to tree adds to the turmoil in my head, and a swooping magpie has me picking up my pace. It's like they know I'm wearing the ugliest underwear ever. But that's silly. Birds don't have X-ray vision. And even if they could see, they wouldn't care.

Gah! I'll never make it to the interview in one piece if I keep thinking stupid stuff. My fingers curl around the handle of my bag as if it were a lifeline. I count the cracks along the path. One. Two. Three … A flock of cockatoos screech past, disrupting my concentration. Now I have to start again! What is it with the birds today? A large white feather flutters in front of me, sending a shiver down my spine. Some say feathers are a message from angels, but given my luck and these ugly granny pants, it's more likely the devil's calling card in disguise. The sooner I get to ECL Marketing and relative safety, the better.

A cool autumn breeze picks up. I tug my jacket tighter, leaving the park behind me and step onto the road. A black SUV emerges from nowhere. It's so close I can see the driver's blue eyes boring into mine through the windscreen. Crap. I'm about to have a lot more than ugly granny pants to worry about.

I scramble back onto the pavement at the screeching of tyres. Smoke billows off the asphalt, clogging my nostrils with the acrid scent of burning rubber. Handbag clasped against my heaving chest, I stare at the space the monster vehicle now occupies. The exact spot where I'd stood only seconds earlier.

Work boots, with muscular legs wrapped in blue denim, step around from the driver's side. My gaze travels higher to an unbuttoned white shirt that does nothing to hide the black ink swirling over an impressive six-pack and pecs. Next is a military crew cut, but I barely register the fact. I'm trapped by the glare of icy blue eyes.

"What the hell were you doing, walking onto the road without looking?" The man's voice is a gravelly clap of thunder.

"Um …" My legs wobble.

Oh, God. Did I escape being run over, only to be beaten to death on the side of the road? I tense my core for fear of committing the ultimate embarrassment and wetting myself. Wearing these underpants was a terrible mistake.

"I ... didn't see ..." I blink back tears.

A bear-sized hand stretches towards me. I squeeze my eyes shut and flinch. This is it. I'm going to die wearing ugly granny pants. I'll be the butt of jokes for years to come once emergency workers and hospital and mortuary staff see them.

Gentle fingers clasp my shoulders. "Are you okay?" His voice lowers to a soft growl.

I open my eyes, expecting to see coldness. Instead, it's like looking into the sky on a warm summer's day.

"I think so." I gulp like a fish to stop myself from bursting into tears. "I'm not sure."

He pulls me into his chest and pats my back. A wave of heat sweeps through me at the spicy scent of his cologne.

"You're going into shock," he says.

Shock? I'm mortified. And a little turned on. What's wrong with me?

A tear slips down my cheek. I was stupid to think I could get away with wearing this ugly underwear without something terrible happening. What if he hadn't stopped in time?

The SUV guy gives me a gentle shake, snapping me out of my daze.

"Hey, miss, do you want to go to the hospital? You're very pale."

A wave of dizziness washes over me. "No, I'm fine. I just need to sit for a bit."

There's no way I'm going to the hospital. They might put me in a gown. See my unmentionables. There's still plenty of time for some terrible fate to befall me.

He squeezes my shoulder gently. "What's your name?"

"Claire."

"I'm holding up traffic, Claire. Can I take you somewhere?" He clears his throat. "You shouldn't be alone."

He doesn't seem as scary now his eyes have warmed up.

Still, he's a stranger, even if my treacherous body tingles at his nearness.

"That's kind of you, but I'll be okay in a minute."

"You're safe with me." He reaches into his back pocket and flashes a badge. "Detective Inspector Jake Matthews, NSW Police Force, at your service."

He also flashes a smile. It's the first time since climbing out of his vehicle, and it transforms him from potential biker thug to handsome cop saviour.

"I'm on my way to the station now. It's only a few minutes away. I can take you with me. You could rest there until you've recovered."

The shock of my near miss bounces around in my head. He's right. I shouldn't be alone. And there's no way I can go to my interview when my mind is spinning. But these granny pants ... What if something else goes wrong? What if we have an accident on the way to the station? Argh! What to do?

"I ... thanks, but ..."

I take a deep breath. Who am I kidding? I'm a mess. And he is a cop. I wipe clammy hands on my dress. "Yes. Thank you, Inspector. That would be good."

"Call me Jake." He opens the door and helps me into the passenger side.

I sink into the black leather seat, and he gives me another smile that on any other day would melt my panties, except ... argh ... I'm wearing ugly, inch-thick undies.

"Just give me a few minutes. I need to exchange licences with the guy who nudged the back of my SUV. It's only a scratch. But still ..." Jake buttons his shirt and closes the door.

What? I'd been so focused on my ugly underwear and Jake's delicious ink, I hadn't noticed a car had run into him. The memory of Grandma dead on the toilet, those ugly white undies around her ankles, flashes in my mind, and a wave of alarm shudders through me. I can't take another near miss. There's only one thing to do. I reach under my dress, wriggle the offensive underpants over my bottom and down my legs, and shove them into my handbag.

Better to be caught wearing no panties than those hideous things.

❧

True to his word, Jake's only gone a few minutes. The driver's door opens, and all that muscle and ink folds into the seat next to me. I gulp, heat prickling along my neck.

He places his hand on my forehead. "Are you feeling any better?"

I flinch at his touch. It's warm. Inviting. And so, so wrong. I clench my legs together. What if he discovers I'm almost naked in his SUV?

"You're flushed." His brows furrow. "Are you sure you don't want to go to the hospital?"

"No. Please. The police station sounds fine."

He stares at me for the longest time, grunts, and starts the engine.

Phew. I relax into the seat and close my eyes.

We haven't been driving for more than a minute when 'Push It' by Salt-N-Pepa blasts from my handbag. I fumble with the zip, the granny pants almost spilling out. I shove them to the bottom of the bag and grab my phone, heat burning my cheeks. The last thing I need is Jake getting a glimpse of them.

"Sweetie, I just wanted to wish you luck one more time."

"Thanks, Mum."

I peek across at Jake. He's watching the traffic, but I can tell he's listening. Not that he can help it. In my frazzled state, I've put my mother on loudspeaker.

"I won't make the interview now. I almost had an accident crossing the road. A police officer is taking me to the station to rest for a while."

"Oh, you poor thing," Mum screeches. "Lucky you're wearing clean underwear."

I can't believe she said that. A smirk tugs at the corner of Jake's lips. I jab my finger at the speaker icon, but the blasted thing doesn't respond.

"Yes, it is."

"Aren't you glad you chose the ones I bought for your birthday?"

"Yes, Mum." *Can this get any worse?*

"Well, it is, honey. You wouldn't want to be caught wearing something flimsy. Sturdy, cotton underpants are much better."

I stand corrected. It can get worse. Jake is outright grinning now, and no matter how many times I stab my finger at the phone, I can't get it off loudspeaker.

"Ah, I need to go." I sink into the seat. "I'll talk to you later, okay?"

"Sure, sweetie. Is the police officer married?"

"Mum! I'm going." I end the call, shove the phone in my bag and zip it closed. "Please don't say anything."

Jake chuckles.

"It's not funny. She … she's obsessed with …" I wave my hands in the air, my cheeks on fire. "You know …"

"It's okay." He turns and gives me the full weight of his blue gaze. "All mothers say things like that. It's no big deal."

"You don't know my mum. She …" I cross my arms and stare out the window. I'll make it worse if I try to explain myself.

He shakes his head and laughs again. Thank God he'll never know how hideous the granny pants are or that I'm no longer wearing them under my dress. The only good thing about being seminaked is it takes my mind off the missed interview. I can only hope they'll give me another chance.

§ð.

When we walk through the doors of Parramatta Police Station, two dodgy guys are arguing with three police officers at the front counter. From the rumpled state of their clothes and red-rimmed eyes, I'd guess the men have been arrested for drugs, but what would I know? This is my first time inside a police station. My biggest crime is walking into the path of a moving vehicle and ending up riding commando with a hot police officer.

Is that a crime?

It's beginning to feel like one as an air-conditioned breeze creeps up my dress.

The officers give Jake a respectful nod as he guides me past the counter, his hand a delicious fiery brand on the small of my back.

"Would you like a coffee?" he asks.

"I'd kill for a cup of tea."

He raises an eyebrow at me, and I slap my hand over my mouth. "I wouldn't really kill for one. I …"

"I'm messing with you, Claire." His eyes twinkle. "How do you have it?"

"White, please." We reach an open area at the end of the corridor, and I sink onto a sofa adjacent to the wall. It's surprisingly homely. There's a coffee table stacked with car and homewares magazines in front of it and a flat screen TV opposite.

Jake returns a few minutes later and hands me the tea, and I take a sip. Heaven. My mother always says there's nothing like a good cuppa to chase away your troubles. On this, we agree. On what counts as acceptable underwear to be caught dead in, not so much.

"Relax for as long as you want." Jake points down the hall. "I'll be in the office over there if you need me."

Now my nerves are less frazzled, I call ECL Marketing to apologise for missing the interview. It goes through to voicemail, and I leave a message for the HR manager. I'm sure they'll understand.

A heavy weariness settles over me. It's been a tough morning, what with nearly being roadkill and all. I kick my sandals off and lift my feet onto the lounge, smoothing my dress around my legs because … well, no underwear!

I scroll through my favourite architecture photographers on Instagram. It soothes my nerves to study the photos, and I learn a lot from seeing how others frame their shots. Photography is my passion, but there's no money in artistic endeavours, and therefore, they're a waste of time, or so my father drilled into me growing up.

With my focus on the phone, I'm caught unawares when warm breath fans my cheeks. I lift my gaze and stare into the sparkling eyes of a slavering chocolate labrador, his wet nose less than an inch from my mouth. He licks my face and turns his attention to my handbag, sniffing it with way too much interest. I grab the handle, and he barks—several yaps in quick succession.

Yikes. What the hell?

Two men stride into the room, one in uniform and the other in a suit. The guy in police gear looks fresh out of school, with pimples to match. The other one is older and attractive in a rakish sort of way. His eyes flicker with interest until he sees the dog at my feet.

"What's in the bag?" asks the older man.

"Nothing," I say. Too fast.

The one sporting acne steps closer. "So you won't mind if we inspect it."

I curl my hands tighter around the handle. "Yes. Yes, I do."

The older man steps closer. "I'm Detective Sergeant Greg Anderson from the NSW Drug Squad, and this here is Constable Dylan Longhurst and his sniffer dog, Milo. The dog's singled out your handbag. We need to check it for drugs."

My stomach churns. I can't let them see inside it. "That's not possible. I don't do drugs. Please, my name's Claire Thompson. If you look me up on your computer, you'll see I've never even had a speeding fine."

"Then open the bag for us."

"No, I can't."

Why is this happening? It's my worst nightmare come true. I glare at the dog, but his adoring gaze is glued to the officers, oblivious to the trouble he's getting me in. What is wrong with the stupid mutt? There are no drugs in my bag. Only horrible, ugly underwear.

Jake strides out of his office. "What's the commotion?"

Even though he's dressed casually, Jake has an air of authority that the other men seem to defer to.

The man in blue points his finger at me. "Milo here has detected something, sir, but the lady won't let us examine her bag."

"Is this why you didn't want to go to the hospital?" Jake looks me up and down, his jaw tightening. "You're on drugs?"

"What? No. That's absurd. I don't do drugs."

"If that's the case, you have nothing to worry about. Open your bag."

"I can't. I have personal stuff in there."

Jake cocks his head and studies me for a moment. "Would you prefer a female officer to inspect it?"

"Yes. No." I wring my hands in anguish. "I don't know." The last thing I want is for anyone, man or woman, to see what's in there.

Jake's face is all hard lines and not in a sexy way. "Claire. If you don't agree to the bag being searched, you'll be arrested for hindering a police investigation."

Why is this happening? Stupid granny pants.

"Okay." Tears well up in my eyes. "But can you be the one to do it?" I don't know why I ask for Jake, but the thought of anyone else rummaging through my bag makes my stomach churn.

Jake's gaze shifts to the other officers and back to me. "Alright, come into my office." His tone is harsh, the warm, gentle man who'd flirted with me earlier nowhere to be seen.

I trail behind him like a juvenile delinquent. "I'm embarrassed about what's in there, okay?" I stammer. "I don't understand why the dog picked on my bag, but it's not what you think."

Jake swivels, his blue gaze searching mine. And even though it's totally wrong, my naked nether region blooms as images of being strip-searched flit through my depraved mind.

He nods towards the desk. With shaking hands, I place my bag on top. Jake slips on gloves and grabs the metal zipper. I choke back a sob. Deep lines mar his brow as he watches me. He probably thinks I'm a nutcase and regrets not running me over.

I hold my breath as he pulls out my phone, wallet and sanitiser. He stacks them on the table as if he's got all day to do the search. Then reaches into the bag again. This time he removes two lipsticks, my leather business card holder and a tissue pack.

I gasp, letting the stale air in my lungs escape. There's only one item left. Jake's gaze snaps to mine and his top lip curls. But not in a sexy way. In an I've-got-you way.

His hand returns to the bag. When he withdraws it, my vision blurs and my brain turns to mush. I was wrong. There was one more item I'd totally forgotten about. All I see are iron bars, an orange jumpsuit and a cellmate declaring me her bitch. The dog was right. I'm carrying drugs.

"Can you explain this?" Jake's voice is soft, a slight tic in his jaw the only sign he's close to losing his shit.

"They're not mine," I whisper, shaking my head at the zip-lock plastic bag dangling from his fingers.

My legs buckle, and I grab the back of the chair to stop myself from crumpling into a heap on the floor.

His lips press into a thin line. "That's what they all say."

He takes another look at the plastic bag and the two white pills nestled at the bottom. His mouth opens like he's about to say something, and then he closes it.

"I mean it." I clutch his forearm. Not my finest moment, but I'm desperate. "I have a friend and …"

What am I doing? I can't dob Jules in. She's my best friend. Her husband would go berserk if he found out.

"Please. That's not what I was worried about. You have to believe me."

He peels my fingers away, his gaze raking my face like I'm some strange creature he can't fathom.

"Why are you so anxious, then?"

I glance at my handbag.

He doesn't miss the movement. "What else will I find?"

"Nothing."

I snatch at the bag, but he grabs it first.

"Ah-ah. Stand back."

I step away and cross my arms to hide the shaking. Damn it. If ever there was a time for the floor to swallow me up, it's now.

He digs inside, then freezes. His gaze darts from the bag to me and back again. The lines around his eyes crinkle, and he withdraws the multicoloured, waist-high, thick cotton granny pants. He holds them with both hands. They're huge. Even in his large hands, they're monstrous.

I cover my face. Forget Jules' pills. My humiliation is complete. Why did I choose the hot cop to uncover my dirty secret? This entire day has been one colossal nightmare.

Jake prises my fingers away from my face, his eyes warm.

"Is this what you're embarrassed about? The underpants in your bag?"

I peer at him through wet lashes and nod.

"I thought you were wearing them. That's what you told your mum."

I shake my head. "After the accident, I was scared something else might happen, and I'd be caught out in the hideous things. So, I took them off in your SUV."

He inhales sharply. "What are you wearing now?"

My cheeks burn as I avoid his gaze and focus on the buttons of his shirt.

"Oh." He clears his throat. "I see."

He hands the undies and plastic bag to me. "The imprint on these pills tells me they're Valium. Do you have the original packaging proving they were prescribed to you?"

Crap. As a sales rep for a pharmaceutical company, I'm well versed in the law and prescription drugs. "No."

His jaw tightens, and the heat in his eyes dims.

"But I promise you, they're not mine." So much for not dobbing Jules in. "They're my friend's. She borrowed them from her mum. I swiped them off her when I realised she was taking them without seeing her doctor. I meant to get rid of them but forgot."

My excuse sounds lame, but it's the truth. Jake searches my face, his blue eyes boring tiny holes into every cell of my brain. I try not to wriggle under his intensive gaze. Sweat trickles down my back and into my butt crack.

Jake grunts like he's decided I'm not lying. "Okay. I'll let it go."

A wave of giddiness rushes through me. "Thank you, thank you." Yay! No orange jumpsuit for me.

"But I'll dispose of the pills." He gives me a stern look. "And tell your friend that using medication not prescribed to her is *against the law*."

Heat flashes through my body. There must be something

wrong with me. I should not be turned on right now. Is it knowing he's a cop despite the casual clothes? Or the coiled strength lurking beneath the buttoned-up shirt? Or both?

"I will." I nod my head, grateful he's not pursuing it further.

He places a small black object in my hand. "I also found this piece of dried liver." His lips twitch. "I suspect that's why Milo took such an interest in your bag."

Damn. It must have fallen into my handbag when I was giving treats to Jules' new puppy last weekend. "Thank you."

"One more thing, Claire." Jake rubs the back of his neck.

I blink up at him. "Yeah?"

"I don't like the idea of you leaving alone without … ah … clean underwear. I'd be happy to escort you. Just to make sure you get home safely."

Chapter Three

Jake

No underwear. Hell!

The part of my brain being led by my dick itches to flip up Claire's dress and see for myself if she's naked. I back out of my office on the pretence of giving her privacy to compose herself. The real reason is I need to get a grip. Since when do I let a pretty face stop me from doing my job?

Greg and Dylan are sprawled on chairs at the round wooden table in our break room. Sweat prickles under my arms as their heads turn towards me. I don't know Dylan very well, but Greg's been my best mate since grad school. He'd never let me live it down if he knew I was attracted to Claire. He's been on my case for months to join the dating scene. But it's hard. Feels like cheating.

Greg pushes the newspaper he's reading to one side. "I thought you weren't coming in till lunchtime?"

I shrug. "My errands can wait. I was concerned about Claire after my vehicle almost hit her."

A glimmer in his eyes says he's itching to give me shit, but he sticks to business and nods towards my office door. "Find anything?"

I cross my fingers behind my back. "Nope. Nothing." Claire seemed genuine about the Valium tablets not belonging to her. Although, I've learned the hard way how good drug addicts are at lying and hiding their addictions. Prescription drugs are no less dangerous than illegal drugs when misused.

Am I letting attraction impair my judgement?

Greg eases further into his chair, legs crossed, arms behind his head, shrewd gaze drilling into mine. "Then why was she so uptight about us searching her bag?"

"Yeah? Has she got a sex toy in there?" Dylan rubs his hands together. "A vibrator or dildo?"

"For Christ's sake." I glare at him. "That's way out of line, Constable. Get your mind out of the gutter."

He jolts to attention, blood draining from his cheeks. "Sorry, sir. I wasn't thinking."

"No, you weren't. Show some respect." I pour myself a cup of coffee from the espresso machine. "I found a liver treat. Your dog needs retraining."

Greg leans forward, his head tilting to the side. "That hardly explains why she was having a meltdown over us searching the bag."

"Look, there was an item of a personal nature. I can see why she's embarrassed. I promised I wouldn't tell."

Heat creeps up my neck, and I tug at the collar of my shirt. I still can't believe Claire took her underwear off in my SUV. That she's been naked under that dress all this time.

The door to my office opens, and Claire steps out. She blushes an adorable pink as she finds herself the focus of three sets of eyes. Oblivious to the chaos he's caused, Milo runs up to her and sits at her feet. Her gaze snaps to me, bottom lip quivering while the dog prods her hand for a pat.

"It's okay," I reassure her. "He likes you."

"Oh. That's nice. I guess."

She strokes Milo's head. His eyelids flutter shut, and he nudges his face closer to her palm. My jaw clenches. I want to push him out of the way and take his place, feel those soft fingers massaging my scalp. Jesus, since when did I become jealous of a dog?

Dylan's face drops as he watches Milo with Claire. "Humph! I think you might be right, sir. Milo needs retraining. That's not proper behaviour for a police dog."

I choke on a chuckle, but Greg doesn't hold back, doubling over with a loud guffaw.

Claire blushes. "I'm sorry. I'll stop petting him."

"No, it's okay," Greg snorts. "It's too late now. Dylan will have to work on his obedience later."

"I should go." Claire straightens. "Thanks again for letting me rest here. I'll get a taxi and—"

"Whoa. No!" I'm standing in front of her in two steps. "I told you I'd take you home."

"I don't want to bother you." She talks to my feet, her cheeks still a pretty shade of pink. "You must have work to do."

"It's no trouble. Let me get my keys." I charge into my office, not wanting to give her time to call a cab. Or myself time to change my mind.

When I return, Claire has slipped off to the bathroom. Greg observes me with open interest on his face. He knows it's not standard practice. Bastard. Dylan avoids my gaze and fusses with Milo. Smart kid. Maybe there's hope for him yet.

"I shouldn't be gone more than an hour," I tell them.

"She only lives fifteen minutes away." Greg makes a show of checking his watch. "So, you should be back here in thirty." He scratches his chin, lips curling into a lewd grin. "Unless you're planning to do some further searching when you get there?" He shrugs. "See if she's running a drug cartel from the bedroom?"

I so want to wipe the knowing smile off Greg's face. Wait. "How do you know where she lives?"

"I looked up her details while you were rifling through her bag. That's all you searched … right?"

"Of course. I'm a professional. I'd never cross the line."

Greg's snide remark pisses me off. Sure, in my head, I've crossed it. And I let the Valium slide. Fuck it. Best to pull rank and shut this awkward conversation down.

"I don't need you to remind me of my responsibilities, *Detective Sergeant*. All I'm doing is ensuring a vulnerable young woman gets home safely."

The haughty indignation washes over my friend. He grins and nods. "Yes, *sir*. Of course, *sir*."

I grind my teeth, giving him my best 'fuck you' glare, but the grin is pasted on his face like superglue. At least Dylan has the sense to lower his eyes and pretend to be fascinated with his useless dog.

Claire returns from the bathroom, her gaze darting around the room.

"Is everything okay?" She nibbles her bottom lip, sending my thoughts in an inappropriate direction about what she would taste like.

There's something about Claire's golden bob that has my brain short-circuiting. With her slender neck exposed, I want nothing more than to run my tongue along the soft, smooth skin. Metallic green eyes, framed by the longest eyelashes I've ever seen, hypnotise me. Full lips …

A clearing throat cuts through my thoughts. Greg's grin has widened to comical proportions.

Damn! My head's screwed up. I give myself a mental shake. Lusting after a woman like this isn't me. I have a son. Responsibilities. I'm just doing what any decent person would do. Ensuring a young woman gets home safely.

"Everything's good, Claire. Are you right to go?"

She hugs the offending bag close to her chest. "Yeah."

§♠

I usher Claire out of the station and into the parking lot. She springs up onto the seat of my SUV before I can help her, tugging at the hem of her dress as it creeps up. It takes all my self-control to turn away from the long expanse of creamy flesh.

What is it about this woman?

I shut the door and saunter around to the driver's side, doing my best to appear unaffected. But the moment I sit in my seat, the walls close in. The vehicle's interior is too small, too tempting, knowing Claire's bare under that dress.

She gives me a shy smile, twisting her fingers in her lap.

"Here we are again."

"Yes." I buckle my seat belt and start the engine. A sweet floral scent fills the cabin. Claire must have sprayed herself with perfume while she was in the bathroom. I like it. It smells like a fresh spring morning. I wriggle in my seat to relieve the pressure as my dick twitches. It's going to be a long, fifteen-minute drive.

Claire directs me to a small subdivision off the main road in the leafy suburb of North Rocks. It's the perfect place to raise a family. Not what I expected of a woman on her own. Does this mean she isn't single?

I pull into the driveway and kill the engine.

"You've got a lovely home, Claire. Is it just you?"

I give myself a mental kick. Smooth. Real smooth.

"Thanks. Yeah." Her cheeks brighten and she unclasps her hands, smooths them down her legs. "The bank owns most of it, but one day it'll be mine."

She opens the car door. I jump out of the vehicle and bolt

around to the passenger side. Claire is halfway out before I can offer her my hand.

She hesitates for a brief second before taking it. Her gaze snaps up to mine when we touch. I swear there are sparks. Does she sense them too?

The moment her feet hit the ground, I let go, not wanting to creep her out. The sensible thing to do would be to get back in my car and drive away. I have no business getting involved with anyone. Not right now. But the last time I experienced such a powerful attraction was with my wife, Sally. What if it never happens again?

I ask the question hovering on the tip of my tongue before I lose my nerve. "Can I have your number, Claire?"

"Why?"

Shit. Have I misread the situation? Misread her? Am I the only one feeling anything? This is what happens when you haven't dated in years. I swallow, my throat dry like it's been sandblasted. "So, I can ask you out."

"Oh!" Her eyes widen.

I shuffle my feet, regressing to a gauche seventeen-year-old. "Only if you want to, of course."

She bobs her head up and down. "Sure."

She recites her phone number, and I punch it into my mobile.

"I'd better go." Claire pulls at the hem of her dress, reminding me, as if it wasn't all I'd thought about on the short drive, that she's naked underneath. "Thanks for dropping me off."

She gives me a brief wave and another one of those shy smiles, then hurries up the driveway and into her house.

I return to my vehicle and slump against the headrest, my heart racing. Did I do the right thing by asking Claire for her number?

Yes. No. I clench the steering wheel. Maybe.

What would Sally say?

My chest burns the way it always does when I think of Sally. She'd be the first person to say go for it, but how can I? Being with another woman still feels too much like cheating. I start the engine, take one last lingering look at Claire's house, and pull out.

Chapter Four

Claire

The door clicks behind me.

Oh. My. God.

What a day. Embarrassing and yet sooo sexy. Goosebumps ripple across my skin, a reminder of the electricity that flew between mine and Jake's fingers. I can't believe he wants to go out with me. He saw those ugly underpants. Felt them. And still asked for my number.

Or was it my lack of panties that he's interested in?

How do I tell?

I slip off my sandals, dump my handbag on the hall table, and pad along the polished floorboards into the open-plan kitchen. Everything is as I left it: breakfast bowl in the sink, unopened mail on the bench, pantry door ajar. It's one short step away from anarchy. Stupid granny pants. They scrambled my mind big time this morning. You'd think my mum would have tidied up while I was dressing. But no. Instead, she's placed a brochure on the table together with a hand-written note.

Wait. That's Alex's handwriting.

Claire,

If the interview doesn't work out, don't worry. I'm sure the right job is out there for you.

In case you're interested, I know of a firm that's offering scholarships for legal assistants.

Love Alex xx

I screw the note up and throw it in the bin. What is she thinking? Law is the last job I'd ever want. All Alex and my dad ever do is work, work, work. They're like robots. That's not me. And no way would I put myself in a position where Alex was lording it over me. No thank you.

I know she's only trying to help. I'm the one with the inferiority complex. But no matter how I dress it up, it still feels like Alex is rubbing my nose in my mediocrity.

I clean the dirty bowl and tidy up the mess on the bench before heading down the hall and to the bedroom. It's in an even worse state, the ivory quilt buried beneath a store's worth of clothes. A first for me. Again, those ugly underpants. They're like a virus, infecting the perfect order of my home. And mind. My breathing quickens at the chaos, and I busy myself with returning the discarded outfits to their rightful places in the wardrobe.

Once the room is tidy, I peel off my dress and bra and step under the shower. One of the drawcards when I bought the house was the renovated bathroom with floor-to-ceiling jade green tiles and a rainwater showerhead to die for. The warm water massages the kinks in my back. The police couch wasn't chosen for comfort, that's for sure. I soap up my breasts, the rich lather sliding against sensitive skin. My nipples harden, and all too soon, I'm thinking about Jake and those tats swirling over the type of muscles I've only ever seen on TV. Never in real life.

What would have happened if I'd invited him inside? With all the ink hiding under his shirt, Inspector Matthews might just have a naughty side. Would he have helped me into a clean pair of panties after an afternoon of fun without panties?

I shut off the water, along with my X-rated thoughts, and reach for a towel. There's no point getting my hopes up. A hot guy like Jake must have lots of women chasing him. I pad into the bedroom and open the top drawer. What I need right now is my favourite underwear to perk me up after that near miss—a pink lace G-string with cute bows on the sides and a matching bra with a similar bow between the breasts. Nothing awful can happen to me while I'm wearing this sexy lingerie. I drag on a pair of tights and a comfy T-shirt and run a brush through my hair to smooth all the wayward strands.

With order now restored, I snatch the granny pants out of my handbag and hover over the trashcan in the kitchen. Mum need never know … but I can't do it. She'd be hurt if she found out, and as annoying as she is, her actions come from a place of love. I walk to the adjacent laundry, open the lid of the white cane basket, and throw them in. I shudder. They shouldn't be anywhere near the rest of my clothes, contaminating them with their ugliness. But, for Mum, I'll keep them. Besides, if it wasn't for the unsightly undies, I wouldn't have met Jake, and that may turn out to be the best thing to happen to me.

I grab a bottle of sauvignon blanc from the fridge and pour myself a generous serving. I could have died. That's how I justify kicking back on the lounge to drink alone. Mum would never accept it as a good enough reason, but she isn't here to stop me. Or lecture me again on how lucky it was I'd been wearing the hideous underpants when I was almost splattered on the hood of Jake's SUV.

I take a sip of wine; it hits the spot, but I still feel unsettled. It's been the craziest day ever, and I need a distraction. So, I call the one person who can talk me down. As usual, Jules answers on the first ring.

"Hello, this is the local mortuary. How can we help you today?"

I choke. Of all the things to say, she chooses that? "Jules, you insensitive witch."

"Hey, girlfriend." She giggles. "What's wrong? You didn't like it? Don't think I have what it takes to be an undertaker?"

"I'm sure you could be anything you wanted. But I was almost run over, so your response is a little heartless."

"What?" she shrieks down the phone. "Are you okay?"

"Yes." I smile. "It was a close call, but it's all good. I'm enjoying an enormous glass of wine right now to help me recover."

"Do you want me to come over?"

"I'm fine." I shake my head, even though she can't see. "A really hot guy saved me."

"No!"

"Yes. Although, he was also the person who almost ran me down."

"No."

A full belly laugh grips me. I was right. Jules is the exact medicine I need after the disaster that was my morning.

"I kid you not. He was over six feet, packed with muscles and inked like you wouldn't believe." She squeals, and I yank the phone from my ear.

"You lucky girl. So, why are you talking to me and not still playing damsel in distress?"

"He had to go back to work. But guess what, he's a cop."

"No."

"Yes.

"No."

"Please, can you stop doing that?" I huff. "His name is Jake, and he's a detective inspector at Parramatta Police Station."

There's silence on the other end of the phone and then a piercing shriek. "Tell. Me. Everything."

So, I do. At least I tell her the parts that don't involve me taking off my underwear and a drug sniffer dog ratting me out. I should give her a bollocking for the trouble those pills caused me. But then she'd want to know what happened when Jake found them. I don't want to admit he let it slide. She'd question his motives. I'm sure he was just being nice. Exercising discretion. Isn't that what it's called?

As for those granny pants … I shudder. What a near miss. There's no way I can tell Jules about them. She'd ask too many questions. Questions I don't want to answer. She thinks she knows all my secrets. She doesn't. How do I tell my best friend I'm obsessed with wearing sexy underwear for fear of being caught dead in something ugly? I don't. The last thing I want is for Jules to look at me differently.

"So, are you going to see him again?" Jules asks once I finish blurting it all out.

"I want to. I was so hot and bothered I forgot to ask for his number. He's got mine, though. He'll call, won't he?"

"Well, if he doesn't, you know where he works." Jules giggles. "Or you could always rob a bank."

She's impossible. "Don't tempt me."

Chapter Five

Jake

The memory of Claire's perfume, her shy smile, and those damned underpants has me grinning like a schoolboy as I stroll into the station the next day. I haven't felt this type of vitality—like I can crush Sydney's underworld single-handedly—since I was a rookie. Two constables stop and stare as I walk past. Fuck. What am I doing? I don't stroll, and I sure as hell don't grin. I tone down my smile, nod at the pair, and make a conscious effort to march to the lunchroom.

I make a cup of coffee from the espresso machine and head to my office. The drab grey walls seem brighter as I imagine Claire standing in here yesterday. With no panties. I slam the cup onto the table, spilling it over the edges. Fuck. I grab some tissues and mop up the mess. I'm a fool for indulging in fantasies. If I dated Claire, I'd have to tell her about Sally. Would she understand? Or would she be out the door faster than a teen on ice?

I glance through the events of the last twenty-four hours on my computer. That takes care of the remnants of my good mood. Fucking drugs. I push out of my chair and stride into the briefing room. It's packed with over a dozen officers. There's a buzz of energy. But not the kind that charges a football stadium before kick-off. This is ugly. Dark.

Foreboding.

"Morning, everyone." I nod to the intel sergeant. "Please begin."

"Thank you, sir." She straightens her notes. "As you've all seen in the report, two males aged sixteen were found dead by the river at one this morning. Suspected overdose."

I grind my teeth. The commander's going to be all over me when he hears about this. "When are the toxicology results due back?"

"Tomorrow afternoon."

"Any leads?"

"Only a vague description of a van that may or may not be relevant." She purses her lips and glances at the door. "We're hoping Emily's event summary will give us some clues."

Greg raises his hand. "Ah, Em said she'd be a little late to the meeting."

I take a deep breath. Remind myself Emily Saunders is new and not used to our ways. It takes civilians time to adjust to the order of a police station.

A few minutes later, Emily races into the room, papers flapping in the air. "Sorry, everyone. I was finishing the analysis."

I tap my fingers on my thigh. "Was it worth keeping us waiting?"

A blush creeps up her cheeks, blending into the auburn curls scattered around her face. "I ... I think so," she stammers.

Fuck. The embarrassment in her eyes reminds me of Claire. Not good. I need to stay focused. Besides, it was a dick move to put her on the spot. She's proven to be a competent intelligence officer so far, although a little timid, which is why I shouldn't have been so harsh.

"Please, tell us what you've found," I ask, softening my voice.

She responds with a shaky smile. "There were four separate admissions to hospital last night. All believed to be drug overdoses and within a ten-kilometre radius of where the two bodies were located."

"Do we know their ages?"

"Three women in their thirties and a man in his forties."

Bugger. If it had been teens, I'd think it was a party gone wrong, and they'd simply taken too much. Then again, who's to say a bunch of adults weren't partying and overindulged?

"Thanks, Emily. That's great intel."

She beams at my praise, her gaze darting to Greg, who gives her a wink.

I make a mental note to have a word with Greg. Remind him of all the reasons he needs to stay away from women at work. He'd break the poor girl's heart if he set his sights on her.

I return my attention to the sergeant. "The greatest concern right now is if there's a contaminated batch circulating. Let's send some officers to the hospital for interviews."

She nods, and we move on to the rest of the agenda.

When the briefing finishes, Greg and I grab a coffee and head to my office. This is definitely a caffeine day. That, or take up smoking again.

I sink into my chair and rub my eyes. "Are we ever going to win?"

Greg flops onto a seat. "Probably not."

"What?"

He shrugs his shoulders. "You asked. We squash this distribution ring and another one'll pop up. It always does."

He's right. But it doesn't stop my determination to shut the fuckers down.

"The new civilian seems competent, even if she isn't punctual."

Greg raises an eyebrow. "You interested?"

"God, no." I shake my head. What's he playing at? As if I haven't noticed the way he looks at Emily. "She's too young. I'm just impressed with her enthusiasm."

"Yeah. She is pretty sweet." Greg raises his palm and grins. "But spare me the lecture. Even I can see she's too innocent for the likes of me."

He crosses an ankle over his knee, a gleam in his eye telling me not to believe a word he says. "I doubt she's much younger than the woman you took home yesterday. What was her name?" He scratches his jaw. "Claire?"

"Claire's not *that* young."

Is she? Fuck. I have no idea. I gulp my coffee and wince as the scalding liquid burns the roof of my mouth.

Greg tilts his head to the side. "So, are you seeing Claire again?"

"I'm not sure. She gave me her number."

"Yes!" He sticks his hand up for a high five. "You dog. Why didn't you tell me?"

I glare at him.

He smirks back.

I shake my head. "You're a pain in the arse."

"Right back atcha."

I ignore his stupid grin and open my laptop. "I asked you in here to talk work, not gossip."

"Yes, *boss*."

"Focus." I give him the bird as I scroll through the document on my screen. "I have a couple of questions about Alpha Pharmaceuticals."

"State-of-the-art facility. Three hundred employees. Obscene turnover."

I rub my tongue along the top of my mouth where I burned it. This is the problem with having a subordinate who's also my best mate. I swear Greg deliberately pushes my buttons to watch me lose my shit.

I cross my arms. "I haven't got all day."

"And you think I have?" Greg sniggers, ignoring my death stare. "They're planning to install additional security cameras and extend the drug-testing program to include office workers."

"Good. I'm certain the mysterious losses of pseudoephedrine from their factory are key to the meth filling our streets." I sip my coffee, taking more care this time. "If one of the staff is the thief, we'll catch them."

"We've also got approval to use a sniffer dog if we need one." Greg scrapes his chair back. "Will that be all, *sir*?"

"Almost. Arrange a meeting for me with the CEO of Alpha Pharmaceuticals." I smother a smile and wave at the door. "Now get out of here."

He gives me a mock salute and a wink and saunters off.

I finish the remains of the now tepid coffee, Greg's earlier comments still rattling around in my head.

Am I too old for Claire?

I check her out in the system—which feels uncomfortably stalker-like. She's only twenty-eight. I turn forty this year. Twelve years is a significant age gap, and something tells me the disparity in our life experiences is even greater. I spend all day rubbing shoulders with the dregs of society. Sometimes all night too. Not to mention, I have responsibilities I can't walk away from.

My chest aches at the thought of not seeing Claire again. But who am I kidding? A beautiful young woman like her could do so much better than me.

I grab my phone and erase her number before I can change my mind.

Chapter Six

Claire

I waltz into the office Friday morning like I'm the star actress in a Baz Luhrmann film. No one and nothing can wipe the smile off my face. Three days away from the office while I visited interstate customers has insulated me from my boss' frivolous demands and allowed me plenty of time to daydream about one sexy detective inspector. I still haven't heard from Jake yet, but it's only been a few days. I'm sure he'll call soon.

I sink into the seat at my desk and pull out my laptop. While it powers up, I check personal emails on my phone. ECL Marketing has replied.

Yes!

My pulse quickens. I glance around. There's only my colleague, Ashley, in the cubicle next to me, wolfing down a bacon and egg muffin and madly tapping on his keyboard. I open the email, and my good mood evaporates. Damn it. They're not giving me another chance to do an interview.

Resilience and punctuality are core values at ECL Marketing … *blah blah blah.*

I shove my phone into my bag. Unfeeling corporate scumbags. They don't care I was nearly run over.

So much for a new job. Looks like I'm stuck here for a while longer.

Ashley whispers from his cubicle. "Is the Unison account plan finished?"

Dread rolls through me.

Mr Liam *fucking* Andrews, aka my boss, read me the riot act last week. "Have the account plan for the Unison deal on my desk on Friday," he'd yelled. "It's worth five million dollars. We can't stuff up the negotiations." *Blah, blah, blah.*

But I'm sure he'd said the close of business. Didn't he?

I jump when the devil himself, so to speak, pokes his head through the doorway.

"Claire. My office. Now."

I bolt from my chair, racking my mind for a believable excuse. The bright daffodil walls are usually a source of inspiration. Not today.

Liam leans back in his chair, arms crossed, eyebrow arched. "Where's the plan?"

"Ah …"

"For heaven's sake." His eyes roll. "Don't tell me it's not done."

I bite my lip, drawing blood. "But I thought—"

He slaps his hand on the desk. "I don't want you to think, girl. I want you to do!"

I grit my teeth. *Girl?* He can't be more than five years older than me. No wonder his wife walked out on him six months ago. Condescending shit.

Liam wipes his forehead. He's sweaty, which is weird because the air-conditioning is set to an Antarctic temperature. "It's not good enough, Claire." He launches out of his chair and paces the room. "I'll have no choice but to give you a warning if your performance doesn't improve."

I might not be the best sales rep, but I'm not the loser he's making me out to be. Am I? I wet my lips and swallow to ease the dryness in my mouth. "I worked really hard to secure the Masters' account."

"And where did that get us?" His eyes bulge out of his head. "Margins were cut to nothing on the deal. We might as well have not won it."

I clench my hands in my lap. I don't know what's gotten into him. He approved the numbers. Said we had to win at all costs.

As he continues ranting about my performance, I focus on a glimpse of white singlet peeking out from his shirt. At some point, he's torn off his tie, claiming he's burning up. Not a surprise given all the hot air he's blowing. I can't take my eyes off that sliver of white. Who wears a singlet with a business suit? It's wrong. So wrong.

Fixating on Liam's underwear is the last thing I want to do, but I also don't want to hear how disappointed he is in me. It reminds me too much of my father's lectures. B grades were never good enough for him. He wanted me to get straight A's, just like perfect Alex. So, I ponder what else my boss is wearing under his suit. What has he teamed it with? White boxers? Or, God forbid, navy? No, he'd be a Y-front man for sure.

Do they even make those anymore?

I shudder. Liam's not an ugly man when he's smiling, but he's far from good-looking, especially when he gets a red spiderweb thing going with his eyes. I stare over his shoulder, his nasally voice a buzz of white noise. An MBA, economics degree, and company awards for excellence line the wall like some monument to how awesome he is. Or thinks he is.

"Claire, are you even listening to a word I'm saying?"

I bob my head up and down. "Yes." Nope.

He slumps at his desk. "The management team meeting has been brought forward to today, and they want to see the proposal for Unison."

Ah. Now Liam's behaviour makes sense, although he doesn't have to be a dick about it. All he had to do was tell me the time had changed. How hard is that?

"You've got until noon to get it together, or I'm pulling you off the account."

Over my dead body. There's no way he's using me as a scapegoat. And I'm not letting someone else take the credit for all my hard work. It's taken me months to get to this point. I've cultivated relationships at all six of their sites to understand what their needs are and how we can best deliver them. "Don't worry, it'll be ready."

I bolt out the door, relieved he stopped short of threatening me with a visit from Joyce—Bulldog—Massey, the HR manager. My ego still smarts after a run-in with her a few weeks ago when she pulled me up for arriving late three mornings in a row. The fact that I'd worked into the nights didn't count. So, I told myself no more taking work home. That's why the plan for the Unison deal isn't ready. But it's close. I thought I had today to complete it.

Ashley gives me a sideways glance as I slump into my seat. "Still in one piece?"

I nod. "Barely."

"You should have seen him before you arrived." A black curl bounces on Ashley's forehead as he gestures towards Liam's office. "I reckon he was seconds from stroking out."

"Yeah, he didn't look too healthy, but it didn't stop him from ripping into me. I'd better get cracking."

I tap away on my keyboard, pulling up the last pieces of data I need to complete the proposal. The opportunity to be involved in marketing was what attracted me to the role of sales rep at Alpha Pharmaceuticals, but the analysis has turned out to be way more tedious than I expected.

By midday, my shoulders are heavy boulders bearing down on the rest of my body, and a throbbing ache has taken up residence in my temples. I shuffle to the kitchen and make a cup of tea and a peanut butter sandwich. A few mouthfuls of both, and the pounding in my head eases.

On the return to my desk, I round the corner and slam into Liam.

"Argh!"

The half-eaten sandwich and tea fly across the carpet. Shit. A small paper bag falls at my feet. I scoop it up. Liam snatches it from my fingers and clutches it to his chest like it contains precious jewels and I'm a wannabe thief.

I suck in a breath at the feral look in his eyes. If anger alone could kill, I'd be nothing but ashes.

"Watch where you're going, Claire."

"Sorry."

He searches the floor with a narrowed gaze.

"Did you drop something else?" I ask.

"No," he snaps. "Is the Unison plan ready yet?"

I swallow, peanut butter sticking to the sides of my throat. "Yes, I just finished it."

"Good. That's good. The presentation is at one o'clock."

He storms down the corridor and into the men's bathroom.

What the hell crawled up his butt today?

I scrape the remains of my sandwich off the floor. This is not the first time Liam's lashed out. His moods have become increasingly erratic since his wife left him. Hopefully, he gets himself sorted out soon because one day, I'm going to lose it with him and say what I'm thinking, and I can't afford to do that. Not with a mortgage hanging over my head.

Liam asks me to present the proposal. Most likely so he can pin the blame on me if the management team hates it. But it goes better than expected. I speak without stumbling over my words, and the creative graphics I use to showcase the opportunities at Unison receive a positive response from the executives. Liam is calmer; the beads of sweat on his face have reduced to a pasty shine. I escape the moment the meeting finishes.

Ashley wiggles his eyebrows. "You survived."

"I did." I giggle. My body feels so much lighter now the presentation's over with. "Liam even complimented me."

"No!"

"Yes." I grin. "Proof miracles do happen. He was all praise in front of senior management. I hardly recognised him."

Ashley gives me a high five. "Well done."

I wave my finger at him. "Don't congratulate me too soon. You know Liam. He'll be back to his miserable old self next week." I've learned the hard way that praise is only fleeting.

I glance at my phone. There's still nothing from Jake. The confidence I've felt all week is waning. What if he doesn't call?

"Hold on a sec. You're holding out." Ashley tilts his head and squints at me. "Have you got a boyfriend?"

"What?" I look around to make sure no one else heard. "No. Why would you think that?"

"Because I haven't seen you glued to your phone that much since you dated the chemistry teacher."

"This is *nothing* like the chemistry teacher," I mumble. He had yellow teeth and dubious underwear. What sort of grown man wears Batman undies?

"Ah-ha! So, there is a new guy." Ashley pushes off his seat and hunches over me. "Spill. You know you'll tell me eventually."

Crap. I totally will.

I roll my chair back to escape Ashley's minty breath. "We only met on Monday. I don't even know if we'll go out."

"But you want to."

"Ashley."

"Claire."

I roll my eyes. Like Jules, he can be as annoying and tenacious as a terrier. "Yes."

Ashley ignores my personal space and leans closer. "So … what's he like?"

"Nice."

"C'mon, Claire." He stamps his foot. "I'm in between partners at the moment. I need to live vicariously through you, and with the dry spell you've been having, I'm dwindling away to nothing."

I press my lips together to stop laughing. "Alright. He's a cop."

"Kill me now." Ashley fans himself. "Please tell me he's hot."

I smirk. "Smoking."

Ashley flops back into his chair, grinning. "Awesome."

"You pair aren't paid to gossip." The shrill voice cuts through me like a sharp blade. Joyce—Bulldog—Massey stands in the corridor, hands on hips, practising her 'you're fired' stare on me. At least, I hope it's not for real.

"Sorry. I was debriefing Ashley on the presentation."

"And what do hot cops have to do with it?"

"Ah …"

"That's what I thought."

She waves her hand in the air with a cutting motion that suggests she would enjoy slicing me into tiny pieces if she could get away with it. "Back to work!"

I stare at my laptop, and bite my lip so I don't burst into tears. Or worse, say something career-limiting.

My mobile dings.

I pull it towards me, careful to keep staring straight ahead even though Joyce has stomped towards reception. It wouldn't surprise me if she had eyes in the back of her head.

Ashley: Ignore her.

Me: Why does she hate me?

Ashley: You're a hot babe, and she's an ugly bitch.

I glance across at Ashley. He gives me a wink.

The phone dings again.

Ashley: So, is your cop into handcuffs or more of a baton man?

By four pm, the office is as quiet as a library. Or a morgue. The executive team departed soon after their meeting for a long weekend of 'team building' on the Gold Coast, in other words, excessive drinking, eating, and golf. Those of us left behind were encouraged to take an early mark. But the down-side of being on the road for three days is I have a mountain of work to plough through.

"You still here?"

Yikes. I jump in my chair and bang my knee on the desk. "Shit. I mean, ouch."

Our CEO, Ben Green, smiles down at me with a warm expression. His dark grey suit hugs his stomach a little too snugly, but otherwise, he's in pretty good shape for a man in his late fifties.

"Sorry, Claire. I didn't mean to startle you."

"That's okay, sir." I rub the top of my knee. It stings like crazy. Thank God I was working and not fooling around on the internet. Liam has zero tolerance for using company equipment for personal use, even though the policy hand-book approves it. As long as it's not excessive or inappropri-ate. I don't know what Mr Green thinks about it. Today, when I presented to the executive team, it was the first time I've seen him in months. "Shouldn't you be on a plane, Mr Green?"

"I'm flying later tonight." He glances down the corridor. "I've got a meeting shortly. With reception gone for the day, I'll wait up there."

I nod because what else is there to say to the big boss? He seems distracted. Like he wasn't expecting anyone to be here.

Mr Green waves at my desk. "Don't stay too long, Claire."

"I won't. I'm nearly finished."

He strides down the corridor, and I slump into my chair. That was weird. He must be meeting with someone very important to stop him from travelling to the Gold Coast with the rest of the management team.

I return to my Word document. It's boring as all hell, but Liam will be pleased with the competitor intelligence and new leads I've gathered. The next time I glance at the clock— a massive digital display on the bright yellow wall—it's five thirty.

The laptop powers down, and I shove it into my bag. Stretch my neck. I've spent way too long bent over the keyboard. Oh, for a massage. I sling the laptop bag over my shoulder and walk down the corridor. The murmur of voices gets louder. It must be Mr Green's appointment finishing up.

I turn the corner and come face to face with Jake.

What the hell?

He stumbles backwards, looking as poleaxed as I feel. What's he doing here?

I open my mouth to ask him, but the words stick to my throat. The dark grey suit he's wearing makes him look very distinguished. Powerful. If I didn't know better, I'd assume he was another CEO.

I'm so focused on Jake, I don't notice Mr Green until he clears his throat. "Claire, I thought I told you to go home."

There's an edge to his voice. He's not happy to see me. What manager isn't happy to see their employee working late on a Friday?

Is he in trouble with the police?

Mr Green gestures to Jake. "This is In—" He clears his throat again. "Jake. A friend of mine."

Friend? My CEO is friends with the man I'm hoping to date? Kill me now. This cannot be good.

Jake's expression goes blank, and his gaze shifts above my head. "Nice to meet you again, Claire."

Mr Green's head whips from Jake to me and back again. "You know each other."

"Yes." Jake straightens his jacket, drawing my attention to his hands. Such nice hands. But he continues to avoid my gaze. That's when it dawns on me; he wasn't planning to call. While I've been thinking nonstop about him, Jake's already forgotten me.

Mr Green's phone rings. He lifts a finger. "Sorry, I need to take this. I'll just be a moment." He scurries down the corridor.

"How have you been?" Jake taps his fingers on the outside of his thighs.

It's sexy as hell, even though all I want to do is slink away and lick my wounds. "Good, thanks. And you?"

See, I can carry on an inane conversation with the best of people.

"Claire." His tone is apologetic.

I don't want to hear what comes next because I know it's going to be a rejection. I hold my palm up and look him in the chest. "Please." I lift my gaze. His blue eyes are as mesmerising as I remember. "Don't say anything."

He rocks on his heels. "I wanted to call."

"Then why didn't you?" I blink to stop tears from spilling over. It's not like he made any promises, except he did. He said he'd call. And he didn't.

"It was wrong to flirt with you." He reaches out and touches my wrist. The warmth is exquisite torture. "You're too sweet for me."

Too sweet? What sort of lame excuse is that? I stare at where his fingers burn my skin. He lets go and rubs his hands down his thighs, drawing attention to how well he fills out the suit pants. Damn him.

I can't let him see how much he's affected me; I have some

pride. I square my shoulders. "You heard Mr Green. It's time I went home. Bye, Jake."

I stride towards reception, head held high, my laptop bag swinging against my hip. In the foyer, I stop and take a deep, steadying breath. Damn it. I'd been so sure Jake was different from all the shitheads I've dated. Then again, I guess he is. He dumped me before getting into my pants. That's a first.

A flash of white stands out against the charcoal tiles near the entrance. I squat down and pick it up. It's a business card with Detective Inspector Jake Matthews splayed across the front. It must have fallen out of his pocket. I run a finger across his name. He's so much more important than me, a mere sales rep. It was naïve to think he'd be interested. I pocket the card. A little reminder of how I almost dated the sexy cop.

Chapter Seven

Claire

"Why did he ask for my number if he was never going to call?"

I gulp a large mouthful of sauvignon blanc and look to Jules for guidance. After Jake's cold shoulder, I was desperate for a friendly face. Jules didn't need to be asked twice, so now we're at the Albion Hotel in Parramatta, scoffing beer-battered fish and chips. We included salad to ease our guilt about all the fried food, but the greens remain uneaten. Green's an overrated colour, anyway. I don't even have a green matching set of underwear.

"I hate to say it, but maybe he realised he shouldn't have been flirting with you?" Jules purses her lips like she's sucking on a lemon. "After all, he is a cop, and he was in a position of power."

"But he called me *sweet*." I spit the word out. In any other context, I'd think it was an endearment. But not in this case. "What does that even mean?"

Jules shrugs. "He might have been trying to let you down gently." She picks up a chip, swishing it around in the tomato sauce like she's five years old, and pops it in her mouth. I shake my head. Food and alcohol are her answers to all of life's problems. Not that I'm in a position to judge.

"It's a shame carbs aren't good for us. I could live on them." She sighs and pats her stomach.

"I know what you mean." I pick up a chip and bring its salty goodness to my lips.

"You know nothing." Jules waves her hand at me. "I mean, look at you. You've got several inches on me and eat your body weight in chocolate, yet you're a perfect size ten. Please."

"I can't help my genes." I laugh. "Besides, I'd happily take some of your extra kilos if it made my boobs bigger. There's nothing sexy about a 10A bra size."

"Don't be silly." Jules slaps my arm. "You've got boobs. They're just—"

I pull the edges of my blouse open and peer down at my breasts. "Lost somewhere in my top, never to be found, despite wanted posters being put up all over the city?"

"Don't put yourself down. You're the complete package. If Jake isn't smart enough to appreciate you, then …" She squeezes my hand. "It's best he never called."

"You're the greatest, Jules. I can always count on you to pick me up."

Jules and I have been besties since first-year uni, thanks to a late-night bonding session over cask wine. I planned to prove to my parents I could make it on my own without becoming a lawyer by taking over the corporate world instead. Jules was destined to be Indiana Jones' female equivalent, uncovering rare artefacts in the deserted interiors of far-off countries. Unfortunately, reality hit after we graduated. The vast office, with floor-to-ceiling windows I'd envisaged strolling into each day, remains a mythical beast. I can't even see the outside world from my tiny cubicle. And Jules, well, she fell pregnant.

I nod my head at the empty bottle of wine. "What do you reckon? Should we get another one?"

"Absolutely." Jules leaps from her chair. "We're getting smashed tonight."

She swaggers off to the bar, long brown hair swishing from side to side with the sway of her hips. A group of rowdy young guys stumble into her path. She elbows her way through them, earning her a few scowls, but they must sense she's a woman not to mess with because they quickly back away.

I take a moment to check my phone.

Again.

Nothing. No missed calls. No texts.

I'd secretly hoped after seeing him earlier that Jake might ring me, despite what he said. The air sizzles when we're together. How can he not feel the connection?

I pull out his business card. It wouldn't hurt to have a cop's number programmed into my mobile. For emergencies. I create a new contact for *Inspector* and punch in his details.

My fingers hover over the phone. One text wouldn't hurt. Would it? But what do you say to someone who says you're too sweet for them?

I'll show him sweet.

I hold out my hand, take a photo, and hit send before I have time to change my mind. A smile curls on my lips. Who knew a simple text could be so rewarding?

Jules returns with our wine and the band starts playing. We kick back, sipping our drinks and enjoying the bluesy music. No more whingeing. Time to suck it up and move on. Who needs a man when you can hang out with your best friend?

It's midnight when we stagger from the table. The second bottle of sauvignon isn't feeling like such a smart move now. As for the couple of sambuca shots we drank afterwards—they're curdling with the wine and creating a growing rumble in my stomach. Yep. Poor decisions all round. Almost as reckless as walking into the path of a moving vehicle. I can only hope it all stays contained until I reach home. I suspect I have a date with my toilet bowl over the next few hours.

Several cops stand outside the entrance. My breath catches when I see the blue uniforms and flashing lights. Two men, staggering like they've drunk the pub's entire whiskey collection, are helped into a police car. A man in a dark suit stands away from the others, talking on his mobile phone. I peer harder through my blurred vision. Jake?

My heel snags on the pavement, and I stumble, jolting forwards like I'm going to belly flop into a pool. Except it isn't water underneath me but rough, unforgiving concrete. I squeeze my eyes shut and brace for the impact.

It never comes. Instead, I'm smashed up against hard muscle, a spicy masculine scent filling my nostrils. Firm hands grip my waist, and I float to the ground.

My eyes snap open to find Jake's calming blue irises inches from mine.

"Claire." His lips twitch. "We have to stop meeting like this."

My heart flutters, and then I remember … I texted him. And sent a photo. What was it? It seemed like a good idea at the time, but now I'm not so sure. I shake my head. Bad move. Everything turns blurry. I squirm in his arms, and he lets go.

My body sways, the growling in my stomach becoming more uncomfortable. "When you tell a girl you're going to call, you call." The words tumble out of my mouth. I wish I could say my voice is strong and demanding, but it sounds more like a drunk mouse begging.

Shutters slide down over his eyes, and flirty Jake disappears. In his place is Inspector Matthews, the stern police officer who searched my handbag.

I'm such a loser. Why can't I remember what I texted him? And why is he here? At least I'm wearing sexy panties. And a lace bra that pushes my breasts up and out. I gulp. What breasts? He didn't react at all when our bodies mashed against each other. He was as still and welcoming as a block of ice.

Disappointment bubbles up my throat, together with the wine, sambuca … the chips that tasted so good a few hours ago. Not so good now. I swallow, willing everything to stay contained. But no such luck. I stagger against Jake and spew the contents of my stomach all over his shoes.

Chapter Eight

Jake

I watch with horrified amusement as Claire throws up on my feet. She slumps, and I wrap my arms around her slim body to stop her from hitting the pavement. Her head lolls against my chest.

Christ! She's out cold. How much has she had to drink?

A constable rushes towards me. "Sir, do you want some help?"

"No, no. It's fine. I know this young lady."

He hovers near me, his gaze darting everywhere but at me and Claire. There's vomit on my shoes, trousers, and on my shirt where drool dribbles from Claire's mouth. When I saw her at Alpha Pharmaceuticals earlier, I was struck dumb. Literally, as I tried to remember why I'd thought it was a good idea not to call her. She took my breath away. Trite but true. She's not looking her best right now, but that doesn't stop a protective instinct from surging inside my chest.

The woman who staggered out of the pub with Claire shoves her face inches from mine, choking me with the fumes.

"You're not going to arrest her, are you? She's just a bit tipsy."

Tipsy? She's off her face!

"No. She's not causing a disturbance, although I'm not sure it's a good idea for members of the public to be vomiting on a police officer." My jaw clenches. "Are you a friend of Claire's?"

To her credit, she doesn't back down. Instead, her bleary eyes widen. "You're Jake."

A grin tugs at my lips. "Claire's told you about me?"

The woman balls her hands into fists on her hips and glares. I like how concerned she is, even if she probably helped Claire drink herself into oblivion.

"She wouldn't be this drunk if you'd just called." Her voice lowers, and I'm sure she whispers, "Arsehole."

I cock my head at her. "What did you say?"

She smirks and juts her chin. "You heard me."

I raise my eyebrows. "What's your name?"

She takes a step backwards. "Jules."

An ache starts in the back of my throat. It was rude of me to ask Claire for her number and not call. I don't know how she got my details, but I deserve the photo of a middle finger she sent me. And the one of her arse with the caption 'bite me'. Although, if that pic was meant to intimidate, it was poorly thought through. My dick's been at half-mast ever since I saw it.

"Well, Jules, I think the best thing is for me to take you and Claire home."

Jules glances up the street. "It's okay. I'm sure we can get a taxi."

"Really?" I pull Claire closer to me, my muscles straining against the dead weight of her body. "Even if you could lift Claire into a cab, I can't see anyone stopping for you. They aren't too keen on passengers throwing up all over their seats."

Jules looks around at the four constables stifling grins and a security guard hovering at the entrance. Dylan stands to the side, wide-eyed. Milo strains at the lead, his focus on Claire. Stupid mutt. There's something about her that has him forgetting all his training.

I shake my head. I'm no better.

"Okay. Thank you." Jules sighs. "It's not like we have many options."

Her response pisses me off. I'm a police officer, for Christ's sake. Surely that counts for something? "What are you worried about?"

She shrugs and casts her gaze over the woman in my arms. "Claire won't be happy you saw her this way."

"It's a bit late for that now." I chuckle. "I'm wearing her vomit."

Jules' cheeks turn bright red. "True," she mumbles.

I gesture towards my SUV parked a few metres away. I should have been home hours ago, but a late afternoon arrest of a two-bit dealer who sold coke to the deceased teens delayed me. Otherwise, I mightn't have seen Claire's texts until the morning. I recognised the pub in the background of her finger photo. Since she was clearly drunk, and for all I knew, alone, there's no way I could go home without satisfying myself that she was safe.

I ease Claire into the backseat. A pink silk blouse tightens across her breasts, so I'm extra careful to avoid touching her inappropriately as I clip her seat belt on. Thank God she's wearing jeans and not another short dress baring tantalising flesh. Her mouth drops open in a very unladylike way, and I gently close it. Her lips are soft. My dick twitches. Fuck. I swallow and slam the door.

Jules clambers into the front passenger seat. Her phone rings and she rummages through her handbag. "Yeah?" The colour in her face drains to a pasty white. "Okay. I'll be home in ten."

She ends the call. Her eyes are brighter, like she's had a double-shot espresso. "That was my husband. My daughter's got a fever. She's asking for me."

My opinion of Jules goes up a notch at the obvious concern in her expression. "No problem. I can drop you off first."

She glances in the back seat. Claire's still passed out, her head leaning against the window.

"I'll make sure Claire gets home safely."

Jules swallows several times. Shit. She'd better not throw up in my car. She gives me a sideways look. One that says she doesn't totally trust me. "Okay. But don't forget, I know where you work."

What the fuck? She's got some balls threatening a police officer. I grind my teeth. Remind myself these are two drunk women alone with a man they hardly know. Even though I'm a cop. Which apparently means nothing.

It's a short drive from Parramatta to Jules' house in Castle Hill. The roads are quiet, a blur of grey fringed by the soft glow of streetlights. We don't speak any further. Jules is a bigger woman than Claire. Probably the only reason she's still conscious and Claire's out for the count.

I park in Jules' driveway, and the light at the front of her house flicks on.

Jules slides out of the car. "Thank you." Her gaze lingers on the back seat before she slams the door shut and zigzags up the driveway. A man steps onto the front porch. Her husband, I presume. He wraps an arm around her waist. Even at a distance, I see her shoulders stiffen. Looks like trouble in paradise, not that it's any of my business. He raises his hand towards me. I flash my lights in response and reverse out.

When I arrive at Claire's house, I search her handbag for keys, unlock the front door, and carry her inside. She's still sound asleep when I lay her on the bed. The vomit has dried on her blouse. I gag at the smell of it. I consider taking her clothes off and leaving her in her underwear, so she'll be more comfortable, but I don't need to be a cop to know that's crossing the line. Besides, what if she isn't wearing any? I mean, I can tell she's wearing a bra, but what about underpants?

Shit!

I can't go there.

Instead, I unbuckle Claire's four-inch bright pink heels and drape the cover over her.

I should go home, but I convince myself it would be irresponsible to leave her alone when she's unconscious. I pull out my phone and send a text.

Mum, I'm caught up with work. Will be home in the morning.

It's after midnight, so I don't expect a reply. But I don't want my parents waking and worrying. I'm lucky to have their help raising my son. It was Dad who suggested Oscar and I move in three years ago. I wasn't sure how we'd go— two alpha males in a confined space—but Dad's surprisingly laid back and the biggest pushover when it comes to his grandson.

Oscar's five years old and already understands his daddy works odd hours. He's a good kid. Too quiet. Misses his mother. I miss her too. There's a hole the size of a football field in my heart, but life goes on or some shit like that. If it wasn't for Oscar, I'm not sure I'd bother.

My gaze wanders over the sleeping form of the woman who's been on my mind way too much the past few days. Perhaps there's another reason to bother. I tried to stay away from Claire, but fate has brought us back together. The way she makes me feel … hell, I'd be a fool not to give it a chance. But how do I do that when the door's still ajar on the last chapter?

Chapter Nine

Claire

Someone's jackhammering my skull. That's the only explanation for the torturous thump, thump, thump inside my head. I lift my hands and press against my temples, groaning at the effort it takes to move them. Why, oh why, did Jules and I keep drinking?

The crystal light shade on the ceiling shimmers down at me, confirming I'm in my bedroom. *Yay.* That's a good start. Sunlight spills around the edges of the curtains, stinging my eyes like salt on an open wound. *Ouch.* Not so good.

My mouth tastes like the inside of a toilet bowl. Not that I've ever stuck my head in a toilet bowl and taken a lick. But if I had, I'm sure this is how it would taste. Fur covers my tongue, and there's the odour of rotting food clogging my nostrils. I clutch my stomach to appease the storm brewing inside it. My silk top and jeans cling to my body. I must have passed out. Lovely! So much for being a mature adult.

"Morning sunshine, how are you feeling?"

What the hell? My gaze snaps to the door.

Ouch! A dozen blades pierce the tiny matter

masquerading as my brain. Just when I thought I couldn't feel any worse, there's Jake, looking healthy and edible.

Did I think edible?

Yeah. Even with the vomit coating my mouth and knives slicing into my head, I can appreciate the virile male specimen in front of me. He looks like he's stepped out of a *GQ* magazine, crumpled grey suit and all.

I groan. None of my fantasies had Jake seeing me while in the clutches of a massive hangover. "What are you doing here?"

His smile wavers. "I didn't want to leave you alone in case you needed help."

I press trembling fingers to my temples. "Please, what happened?"

He cocks his head. "You don't remember?"

"No. Everything's a blank after dinner at the pub." My cheeks burn. "Did we do anything?"

"No. Of course not." He shoves his hands into his trouser pockets. "You were out for the count."

I glance down at my top and note the dubious stain. Oh, no. "Did I throw up?"

"Yep." The right side of his mouth kicks up, exposing the cutest dimple. "All over my shoes and trousers. Some drool on my shirt. It wasn't pretty."

Heat flashes through me, and I jerk the quilt over my head. I can't look at him. Amongst all my romantic humiliations, and there've been a few, this is a new low.

He tugs the cover off and brushes my cheek with his hand. "It's okay. I've seen worse. Had more disgusting things splattered on me."

The caress warms my skin. It's comforting. "Sorry. I don't normally get drunk like that."

"Then why did you drink so much?"

My organs flip-flop. There's no way I'm telling Jake I was

pining over him. I give him a tiny smile. "Sometimes Jules and I lose track of our drinks."

Not a lie.

He presses his lips into a thin line like he sees right through me. It makes me feel like a wayward teen, reminding me of the obvious age gap between us. "I'm sure you'll pay closer attention next time."

He glances at his watch. "I have to get to work. Do you have any Berocca? Paracetamol?"

I nod and then wish I hadn't. "Bathroom cabinet," I say, my voice as weak as a two-week-old kitten.

His jaw tightens. "I won't find anything I shouldn't, will I? Like Valium tablets in a plastic bag?"

Oh, God. I'd forgotten about Jules' stupid pills. "No." It hurts to talk, but the last thing I want is for him to think I'm a druggie. "They weren't mine, I promise you. I don't do drugs. Except for the legal, liquid variety." And how I wish I was a teetotaller right now.

His face relaxes, and he gives me a small smile as he swivels and strides out the door.

The raucous laughter of kookaburras filters in through the window. I sit up, ignoring the knives in my head.

Jake returns with a glass of life-saving vitamin B and the painkillers. A sigh escapes me as I swallow the tablets and empty the glass. I flop back onto the mattress, resisting the urge to pull the covers up. I must make a pathetic sight: hair poking up everywhere, foul morning breath, and last night's crinkled, vomit-covered clothes sticking to my sweaty body.

"Do you always work on Saturdays?" I blurt out.

He gives me a wry smile. "No rest for the wicked, I'm afraid."

"Oh. Okay." Wow. He must be dedicated to his job.

"Claire."

If I wasn't lying down, his voice would bring me to my knees. The way he says my name … it curls around me like a warm embrace, even as the jackhammers continue beating inside my head.

"I've got to go. Are you okay on your own?"

"Of course. I'm a grown woman."

He tilts his head, a gleam in his eyes. "You didn't look like a grown woman passed out on my backseat last night."

I glare at him. "A gentleman would pretend that never happened."

The glimmer fades from his eyes; cheeky cop recedes and serious cop returns. If I wasn't so hungover, I'd ponder these two different sides of Inspector Matthews.

"You're right. I apologise."

He moves towards the door, only to stop and turn around.

"I'm sorry I never called. I was nervous." He fiddles with his collar. "If you'll still have me, I'd like to take you out."

My eyeballs pop out of their sockets. Jake wants to see me. I haven't ruined my chances with him. I swallow a groan as shards of light burn my fully exposed retinas. Of course, it only feels like my eyes have exploded. It would be super creepy and messy if it was for real. I shake my head to clear the stupid thoughts from my brain and immediately regret it.

"Okay. That would be nice."

He lifts an eyebrow. "Only nice?"

My fingers dig into the sheets. Jake seems to be forgetting that he wasn't planning on calling me. "Are you really sure you want to take me out? Or would it be a pity date?"

"Of course not. You're gorgeous, Claire. Any man with a pulse would want to go out with you." A flush of red creeps up his neck. "It's just … my life is complicated. There's no excuse for my behaviour. I got cold feet."

My heart flips in my chest. I like his honesty. No pretending he hasn't been a douchebag. It's refreshing. I ignore the banging in my head and give him a small smile.

"No problem. We can start again. Pretend we've just met."

"I can't do that." He grins. "I'm prepared to forget the

vomiting, but not what happened at the station. I've seen a lot of crazy things as a cop but you and that underwear ..."

No! Heat sweeps up my neck and into my cheeks.

"Okay, okay." I wave my hands at him. "Please don't go there. Not while my insides are being battered to death in slow motion."

He scrubs his hand across his mouth. "Sorry." His eyes rove over me in a non-creepy, protective kind of way. "You get some rest. We'll talk later."

My eyes droop as I sink into the mattress and tug the quilt over my head. I'm never drinking again. Never. I could write a book on how to scare guys off with embarrassing acts. Except ... I pop my head from under the cover and stare at my bedroom door. Jake's seen me at my worst and still wants to see me. Go out with me. *Me.*

I mentally fist pump the air, my head wincing at the small act. My lips curl into a smile. A date. He's promised me a date.

🐚

I wake up around lunchtime. My head still hurts, but there's less hammering inside my skull, and the light doesn't burn my eyes when I open them.

It takes ten minutes under the shower until any semblance of humanity returns, the hot water washing away the worst of the ickiness. I throw on a flowing floral maxi dress. Forget the bra. Or panties. It's not like I'm expecting visitors. And I've never heard of anyone being caught dead with no underwear. Then again ...

I draw in deep breaths.

In. Out.

In. Out.

I hate the weakness that invades my every cell when I think about how I found Granny that day.

My hand hovers near my underwear drawer.

Even though the dress is a soft cotton, it scratches against my skin like a wire brush. I groan. Nope. I'll take the risk of no panties. Again.

I scroll through the messages on my mobile. Two were sent to Jake. What the hell? I zoom in on the picture from the second text and groan. Yep, now it's clearer—my pale pink thong disappearing into my butt crack. The toilet fixture is in the background, so at least I didn't bare my bum in public. I must have been so plastered because I have no memory of snapping that photo. I'm not sure how I even took it. Or how I'm ever going to look Jake in the eye again. No wonder he was so eager to bring me home.

There are also three missed calls from Jules and four texts.

Jules: How are u?

Jules: Claire, answer me.

Jules: Pick up the phone!

Jules: Ring me by 12 or else!!!

I brew a pot of tea, make some toast, and shuffle outside. The sunlight forces my eyelids to half-mast. Should have worn sunglasses. Azaleas in myriad shades of pink shield the old wooden fence where two magpies squabble. It would be serene if I didn't have the mother of all headaches.

I take a sip of life-giving fluid and hit call back.

The phone doesn't even ring once before Jules answers.

"Claire. Thank God. Where have you been?"

I shake my head and groan when the pain, now reduced from butchers' knives to paring knives, pierces my skull.

"I was trying to sleep off the worst hangover ever."

"Did Jake get you home safely?"

"Duh! Yeah. I'm speaking to you, aren't I?"

"Don't be a smart arse. You know what I mean."

I grit my teeth. "If you were concerned, you should have got him to drop me off first."

Jules lets out a long sigh. "I would have, but Mick called and said Riley had a fever."

Oh, no. I press my hand to my forehead. I'm a terrible friend. "I'm sorry, Jules. Is she okay?"

"Yeah. It's come down. She's sound asleep now. All worn out, the poor little thing."

"That's good." And lucky Jules wasn't comatose like me.

"I figured you'd be safe." Her voice lowers. "He didn't try anything, did he?"

"Jules." I laugh. "He's a cop."

"He's also a man with a dick."

I snort, spraying liquid out of my nostrils and all over my dress.

"Shit, Jules." I dab my hand at the wet smudge staining the bright yellow fabric. "Give a girl some warning."

She chuckles. "I have to say, Claire, he's as hot as you said he was."

"A second ago, you were carrying on like he might be a serial rapist preying on drunk women."

Laughter tinkles through the airwaves. "He still could be, but he's nicely packaged if he is."

I sit straighter. The conversation is disrespectful after how nice Jake's been to me. "He was a perfect gentleman." My stomach gurgles, and it's not all because of the hangover. "And he said he wants to take me out."

"Yay." Jules squeals down the phone.

The magpies flutter away. It's almost like they heard Jules scream, too.

"Ouch. Please, not so loud." I rub my aching temples.

"I'll let you go. But keep me updated on Jake."

The birds return and settle onto the back railing. "Don't worry. I will."

"Alright. Enjoy your lazy afternoon."

"Thanks, girlfriend."

I hang up and swallow the rest of my tea. The magpies

regard me with beady but hopeful eyes, so I rip up the remains of my toast and toss it to them. They swoop down and gobble it up.

"It's not much, but it'll have to be enough, guys," I say to them. "I'll feed you some of the good stuff later." When my head is less tender.

I spend the afternoon dozing in front of the television and watching *Bridget Jones' Diary* and its sequels. What single girl doesn't have these movies on standby for emergencies and chilling out? Together with Jules, they've frequently soothed my broken heart. My last boyfriend was particularly nasty when he left. Accused me of being *too neurotic*. Said my fixation on underwear—his and mine—wasn't normal. Hello? What man in his right mind buys his girlfriend a pink bra to go with red panties? I don't care if the store had run out of matching sets. It's just not done. Ridiculous. Not to mention, there's nothing sexy about a man wearing saggy underpants or torn boxers.

Or more dangerous.

I'm not the one with the problem. Good underwear is more than functional. It's a statement about who you are. It's your last line of defence against bad things happening. No one wants to be remembered for wearing ugly underwear. Like poor Granny.

I swore I was finished with men after that idiot. It's been nice not to worry about someone else's expectations or opinions. But I'd reconsider my single status for Jake.

Six o'clock ticks over. *Would he be finished with work?*

I wipe clammy hands on my dress and dial his number before I chicken out.

"Detective Inspector Matthews."

I fumble with the phone at the sound of his low growl. "Hi Jake, it's Claire."

"Claire. I'm glad you called."

The low rumble of his voice sounds like sex: two sweaty

bodies rubbing up against each other, soft moans and answering groans. My imagination is out of control. This is what happens when you've had no action in, like … forever.

"I hope I'm not interrupting anything," I answer, my voice a cross between Marilyn Monroe and Daffy Duck. I hit my forehead with my palm. I'm such a loser.

He chuckles. "Nope. I was just finishing up. You're sounding better than earlier."

Lovely. If he thinks that, I must have sounded like a Mack truck trundling over gravel this morning. "Yeah, I'm more human now, thanks."

"Great."

"Umm. So, how was your day?" I slap my head again. Geez, could I sound any lamer?

"Average. Although, I'm planning to ask this beautiful woman out."

The hopeful butterflies swirling in my stomach pick up speed. "So, you really meant it earlier?"

"Yep."

I can't believe a man as hot as Jake would be interested in me. "Is this because of the panties thing?"

I squeeze my eyes shut. What is wrong with me? Granny must be rolling in her grave by now. And if my mother knew, she'd be demanding I pay back all the fees for the fancy girls' school she sent me to.

"No. It's not." Jake half laughs, half groans. "As much as I appreciated the photo you sent last night, I'd caution you against sending half-naked pictures of yourself to people you don't know. Even people you do know."

My face burns hotter than a bushfire. I'd meant the incident in his SUV, not that stupid text. Is there no end to my embarrassing incidents with this man?

"So, what kind of date do you have in mind?" And why should it matter? I'd eat a boring green salad in the park with this hunk of hotness if that's what he wanted. And I hate salad.

"How about a movie?" says Jake. "And dinner afterwards?"

"What would you expect in return?"

I slap my palm over my mouth the moment the words are out. Why the hell did I say that? I'm not usually this forward with men.

There's silence; then Jake clears his throat. "Your virtue is safe, Claire. I don't believe in sex on the first date."

My ears prick up at that. "All guys want sex."

"True." His voice lowers to a sinful baritone—silk sheets sliding over naked skin. "But I'd rather get to know the lady first."

Lady? I've been called many things over the years, but never that. He's too good to be true. It doesn't stop me from saying yes, though. Because what if he's as good as he seems? What if he's the one?

Chapter Ten

Jake

I bang my head on the desk. *I don't believe in sex on the first date!* What bloke says shit like that? If Claire gave me the signal, I'd skip the main meal and go straight for dessert in a heartbeat. First date or not.

Or would I?

I adjust my trousers. Jesus Christ. What is it about this woman that has me behaving like a creepy, horny teenager? My father would cuff me around the ears if he knew. There's a responsibility that comes with being a police officer, but there's nothing honourable regarding my thoughts about Claire.

I bang my head on the desk again.

"What's going on in here?"

I lift my face. Great. Just what I need.

Greg struts into my office and closes the door, blocking out the chatter and clanging of plates in the lunchroom.

He kicks back in the chair across from my desk and chuckles. "You can't afford to be knocking your skull like that, Jake. You're missing enough brain cells as it is."

I give him the finger. "Yeah, yeah. Real funny."

The smile on his face widens. "Is this about Claire?"

I stiffen. "I take it Dylan told you what happened at the pub last night?"

Greg smirks. "Yep."

He brushes a piece of what can only be imaginary lint off his jacket because he's always immaculate. "So, things didn't go well after you took her home?"

"On the contrary, I'm taking her on a date." The moment the words slip out, I kick myself. He's going to be all over me like cops on a rowdy crowd.

"Wow!" His eyes widen, and his lips curl into a lewd smile. "You must have done a number on the poor girl while she was passed out."

My vision blurs. "What the hell? That's low. Even for you." I jab a finger at him. "Any suggestion of taking advantage of a woman is never funny."

Greg raises his hands in the air. "Sorry, sorry. I was out of line." His shrewd gaze cuts right through me. "I've not seen you this worked up over a woman in a long time."

"I tried to stay away from her." I shake my head. "But the moment I saw her at the pub last night, I was done for. She's just so ..."

His smirk returns. "Hot? Sexy? Fuckable?"

I clench my jaw. "Respect, Greg. Respect."

He chuckles. "Okay, okay. Sorry. I can see you left your sense of humour at home today."

"There's nothing wrong with my sense of humour. You're not funny. What if someone spoke about your sister like that?"

His eyes narrow and his lips twist like he's just drunk curdled milk. "I'd cut their balls off."

I stare pointedly at his groin.

He gets the message and crosses his legs. "So?"

"She's sweet."

Greg leans forward, his gaze piercing my soul. "Sweet as in the forever club?"

Fuck Greg and his questions. No matter how much I like Claire, I can't have a relationship with her. Besides, there are no guarantees of forever. He knows that. "I can't go there."

"Of course you can."

"No, I can't." I rub the tight muscles of my neck. "You know why."

Greg's eyes soften. "You deserve this, Jake. Sally would want you to be happy. You're too young to be a miserable old man yet."

"I'm not ready. I'm not sure if I'll ever be. It feels too much like cheating."

Greg slouches back in the chair, arms crossed. "When was the last time you had sex?"

I stiffen. "That's none of your business."

A shit-eating grin widens across his ugly mug. "I'll tell you how long. Eight months."

"How the hell would you know?"

"Because you went more than a week without biting everyone's heads off. The entire station could tell you'd finally got laid."

Jesus Christ. My sex life is no one's business but mine. That one-night stand still sends chills through me. My dick might have been happy, but it was a fucking disaster. Never again. "You're like a bunch of retirees. Haven't you got anything better to do than ponder my sex life?"

"Nope." He cracks his knuckles. "Not really." The stupid smile on his face fades. "Jake, you're not like me. You're a white picket fence kind of guy. You deserve to find yourself a woman to love and to love you. A wife to come home to at night. Someone to help you raise Oscar."

"He has a mother." My jaw clenches, and a flush of heat sweeps through my body. "No one can replace Sally."

"I'm not saying replace her, but you and Oscar both

deserve female companionship." He sticks his palm up. "And before you say it, your mum doesn't count."

I swallow the lump in my throat that's threatening to choke me. "It's hard."

He nods. "I know. But Claire's the first woman I've seen shake you up since …" He pushes his chair back, his gaze flitting to the closed door and then back to me. "I think you should see where it leads." He squeezes my shoulder, opens the door and saunters out.

Greg makes it sound so simple. It's not. I pick up the photo on my desk. It was taken the day Sally and I brought Oscar home from the hospital. We were so fucking happy that it's like a bullet to my chest every time I look at it. But I can't put it away. It reminds me of what it was like to be in love. To feel good about the world. To have a future. I need that reminder.

I place the frame back on the desk. Is it possible to have that again? With Claire?

&

A headache teases the back of my eyes as I update the notes from my meeting with Ben Green. We both agreed his missing stock must be an inside job. Only senior management and operations have access to the materials so that puts Claire in the clear. Which is just as well because my every thought is consumed with her sparkling green eyes, middle finger and bare arse.

My mobile phone rings. I scramble to answer, my gut plummeting into free fall when I see the name on the screen. A call from Squad Commander Peter Gordon on a weekend can only be bad. "Sir."

"Afternoon, Inspector Matthews." Peter's raspy voice barrels down the phone. "I've got an impromptu meeting with the commissioner on Monday regarding Project Lock-Out."

Damn. The last thing we need is the commissioner getting involved.

I switch programs on my laptop. "There are several persons of interest under surveillance."

"And the teenagers who OD'd? Any leads?"

Sweat beads across my brow. Thank Christ, he can't see it. "We've confirmed it was definitely cocaine, and it wasn't contaminated. Based on the grade, I believe it belongs to Leadbetter's cartel." The bastard who's been leading us a merry dance for several years now. Every time we get close to pinning a crime on him, he manages to slip through our fingers.

The commander grunts. "That's something."

"We've also got intel on three possible locations for Leadbetter's numbers man, Scudasi." I pull the file up on the screen. "A raid will be executed the moment we have a firm sighting."

Silence greets me.

"Sir?"

"I don't need to tell you the media are all over this, demanding answers."

My stomach sinks. "We'll catch them. It's only a matter of time."

"It better be." He sighs. "I realise it's a Saturday, Jake, but can you send me a brief report for my meeting with the commissioner?"

Commander Gordon ends the conversation, and I slump my arms on the desk. The only positive about the cocaine crisis, if you can call it a good thing, is it's deflecting attention away from the increasing meth problem on our streets.

The investigation continues to demand more and more from me. How do I carve out enough time for both Oscar and Claire?

Chapter Eleven

Jake

I t's official. I suck at dates.

Claire clutches my hand. "It's okay. I don't mind."

We squeeze through a spirited group of teenagers blocking the cinema doors and escape into the shopping mall. If I'd bothered to ring the movie theatre, or even google them, I'd have found out they were having a special night showing all three of the Bridget Jones films. And they were sold out. The only other options are some animated kid's movie, R-rated blood and gore and a B-grade science fiction flick. Not the sort of films to relax with on a date.

"We could always go back to my place?" Claire strokes my forearm and, like a switch being flipped, my dick springs to life. Although, it's been on constant alert since I picked her up. Tight jeans accentuate her long legs, while her shimmering gold top draws my gaze to her pert breasts.

"I want to give you a proper date."

"What if that's not what I want?" Claire presses closer to my side, making it crystal clear what she's suggesting.

I stop walking and wrap my arms around her waist. As

much as I ache to take her to bed, that's not who I am. "What if I think you deserve more?"

Her eyes widen. She seems genuinely surprised. It tells me a lot about the blokes she's dated in the past. Arseholes. "More?"

"Yeah." I nod. "Sex is easy. Getting to know someone beforehand is much more rewarding."

Claire nibbles on her bottom lip. "So, you meant it about not expecting sex on the first date?"

"Absolutely." The one-night stand eight months ago was a mistake I never want to repeat. "Surely, you don't think I'm after a roll in the sack and nothing else?"

"Well ..." She shuffles her feet.

Have I been sending the wrong signals? Making Claire think sex is all I want? "How could you think so little of me?"

"It's not you, Jake." She shrugs. "I have crappy luck with men. Not to mention I'm clumsy, in a dead-end job, and look like I need a good feed."

I bark out a laugh, although part of me wants to pummel the guys who've done a number on her self-esteem. "I don't know a lot about what you do, so I won't comment on your job. And I must admit that stepping in front of a moving vehicle wasn't one of your finer moments. But let's get one thing straight; you're not thin. You've got curves where it counts."

"But—"

I tap the tip of her nose with my finger. "And you're smart and funny."

She opens her mouth. Then shuts it. Her eyes glisten.

I check my watch. "Our dinner reservation isn't for another two hours. Do you want to go to a bar?"

Claire chews on her bottom lip. "I'm a bit hungry. How about ice cream?"

"Ice cream? Won't that spoil your appetite?" I squeeze my eyes shut for a moment. Could I sound any more like a dad?

Claire's pouty lips curl into a flirty smile. "You won't let me have the dessert I really want."

Holy hell. She's pushing my self-control to the limits. I whisper in her ear, "Only good girls get dessert."

Claire's cheeks bloom pink and I grin. Maybe I'm not so bad at this dating game after all. There's an extra swagger in my step as I steer her through the mall towards a nearby quaint café. The relentless black-and-white check theme—from the walls to the floor and even the tablecloths—is tough on the eyeballs, but the ice cream is the best I've tasted. We take a seat in the corner and order double sundaes—chocolate for Claire, strawberry for me.

Claire doesn't waste time when they arrive, lifting a spoon full of chocolate fudge ice cream to her lips and sucking it into her mouth. My pants tighten and I smother a groan. I should have taken her to a bar. Dessert just might be my undoing.

I need a safe topic to get my mind off my growing erection, and while I shouldn't be thinking about work right now, I'm curious to see if Claire suspects anything untoward is going on at her company.

"You mentioned your dead-end job. How long have you been at Alpha Pharmaceuticals?"

"Five years."

She makes it sound like a death sentence. "What does a sales rep do?"

"Manages accounts. Sells stuff."

Claire licks the spoon, sending a jolt of electricity straight to my crotch.

"That sounds interesting." I spread my legs to relieve the pressure in my jeans. "You'd get to travel around a bit, wouldn't you?"

"Yeah, but the focus is always on more, more, more. More sales. More profits. More kicks up the backside when things go wrong."

She slips another scoop of ice cream into her mouth.

Fuck. My balls are going to explode if she keeps this up. "Isn't that what sales is all about?"

"I guess so." She waves her spoon around. "I'm not cutthroat enough. Some of the guys love the thrill of the chase. You know? We call them hunters."

I chuckle. "You're not a hunter?"

"Hell, no. I'm more of a farmer. I cultivate the accounts. Develop relationships. I like to be in it for the long haul. The hunters are always looking for their next target."

Wow. My gut told me there was more to this woman than she lets on. And it wasn't wrong. If building long-term relationships is what she loves about her job, then it makes sense she'd want the same stability at home. The same commitment. She'd make a loyal partner. A loving mother.

Claire's shoulders hunch and the sparkle in her eyes dims. Work is clearly not a pleasant topic for her and reminds me I have a potential conflict of interest in seeing her. Although, as her CEO said, only operations and senior management have access to the drug precursors. Claire's too far down the food chain to know anything, let alone be involved in the theft. "That doesn't sound too dead end to me."

She cocks her head to the side. "I guess it appears more exciting on the outside."

"I can relate to that."

"How?" She straightens, stretching the silky fabric of her top. I grip my thighs, resisting the urge to reach out and see if her breasts are as firm as they look. *What the hell is wrong with me? I'm a grown man, for Christ's sake.*

She leans forward, elbows on the table. The flowing sleeves of her blouse slide up her arms revealing slim wrists I could wrap my hand around twice over. "I'd have thought police work would be exciting. Although a bit too dangerous for my liking."

Her blouse gapes, a hint of white lace teasing my peripheral vision. I tense at the effort to keep my eyes on her face.

"It can be." I mirror Claire's posture and lean closer; the din of the café is making it difficult to hear her. "But we spend a lot of time in front of computers on admin stuff."

"That must be tough if you prefer being out chasing the bad guys."

I chuckle. "Don't believe everything you see in the movies."

Claire's gaze darts to my sundae. "You've hardly eaten anything."

I grin. "I was enjoying watching you eat."

"Oh!" Her cheeks turn the same shade of pink as the untouched ice cream in my bowl.

My phone vibrates in the pocket of my jeans. I consider ignoring it, but years of being responsible override the little brain in my pants.

I pull out my mobile. It's Dad. Damn. He wouldn't call unless it was important. "Sorry, Claire. I'll just duck outside to take this." I scrape my chair back and hurry out of the café. "Hi, Dad. What's up?"

"We're on our way to the hospital, but don't worry; it's not serious."

My fingers clench around phone. "What happened?"

"Oscar tripped on the back stairs. Cut his arm. I'm sorry, Jake."

"Damn it. I'll meet you there."

"No, no. We can take care of him. You enjoy your date."

I rub my aching gut. What ice cream I ate is curdling like sour milk. "Dad, there's no way I could have fun now. I'll be there soon."

"Okay." He sighs. "Sorry, son."

"Don't be. This isn't your fault."

It's mine. All mine. Oscar's my responsibility and I've let him down.

I return inside. "Sorry to do this to you, Claire, but I have to leave. My son's been hurt."

Claire's eyes widen. "Son?"

Fuck. I was waiting to see where things went with Claire before telling her about Oscar. A child can be a deal breaker for a lot of people. "Yeah. Sorry. I didn't mean to blurt it out like that."

"That's okay." She places her hand on mine. "This is only our first date. We haven't had time yet to share all our deepest, darkest secrets."

The café noise dulls to a faint murmur, the ice cream a cold, thankless mass in my stomach. Secrets? She has no idea.

Claire must see something in my expression. "It's nothing serious, I hope?"

"I don't think so." I pull my hand away, missing her soft warmth. "But I need to get to the hospital."

"Of course. Would you like me to go with you?"

My throat constricts. A part of me wants her there because being with her feels so right, but it's too soon to be introducing her to Oscar. Especially when he's hurt and probably scared. He deserves all my attention. "No, it's fine."

I almost miss Claire's soft "Okay."

What a shitty date. I'll be lucky if Claire takes any of my calls after this monumental fuck-up. Then again, she said first date. So, maybe it's salvageable.

Claire's smile returns, albeit a wobbly one. "What about his mother? Will you tell her he's had an accident?"

My stomach recoils like I've been shot. Now is definitely not the time to tell her about Sally. It's way too soon. "No. She can't help him. Oscar's my responsibility. No one else's."

Claire must sense I don't want to talk about it. She collects her handbag and cardigan without another word, and we leave the café.

Like a coward, I'm grateful for her silence and concentrate on driving. We arrive at her house in no time.

"Thanks, Jake. I had a lovely night." Claire unbuckles her seatbelt and places a hand on my thigh. "Please call if you need any help."

Her floral perfume tickles my nostrils as she leans closer for a goodnight kiss. Our first kiss. A chance to show I both respect and desire her. And want to see her again. I turn, and our mouths collide with more force than I intended. All thoughts of Oscar and the hospital vanish as my blood pumps south.

Claire's soft, plump lips open and our tongues tangle. The sweetness of chocolate ice cream still lingers in her mouth. My hands roam over her sides and before I know it, I've pulled her blouse from the waistband of her jeans and my hand is snaking underneath. So much for my plans to behave like a gentleman.

Claire's moans encourage me further, and I cup one breast. Her nipple is a precious jewel beneath the fabric of her bra, and my dick punches against my zipper, demanding to be part of the action. When she nibbles on my bottom lip and thrusts her breast into my palm, I know I need to stop. I have no business making out with her like a randy kid in a car. She deserves better.

I wrench my head away, sucking in air like I'm drowning. Claire pants, lifting dazed eyes to mine.

I trace a finger down her cheek. "I …"

She grabs my hand, holding it to her lips. "Don't you dare apologise. Go to your son."

It's after midnight by the time I get home. Oscar's cradled in my arms like a newborn as I carry him into the house. Painkillers and excess adrenaline have taken their toll. He was so brave when the doctor sewed up the gash in his arm—six stitches.

I was numb.

He doesn't stir as I strip and dress him in pyjamas. I tuck him under the Superman cover and sink onto the mattress next to him. Framed by wavy dark brown hair, his cheeks are deathly pale. Thank Christ he's safe and sound in his bed.

"Do you want a hot chocolate, honey?" asks Mum from the bedroom doorway. Shadows haunt her blue eyes. She's aged ten years overnight, her hair a mess around her face like she's been dragging her fingers through it. Which I'm sure she has.

I shake my head. "I'm a big boy now."

She smiles and lifts one eyebrow. "Whiskey, then?"

My face cracks into a smile. "Nah. I'm fine."

Mum gives me the look only mothers have, the one that wraps around you like a warm blanket and chases away the cold. "I'm sorry about ruining your evening."

"You did the right thing." To their credit, Mum and Dad kept a straight face when I told them I was going on a date. My first one in years. They didn't ask questions. Gave me space. "Oscar's health is the main priority."

She hovers in the doorway, her gaze drifting between me and Oscar. Then she backs away, closing the door behind her. I pull out my phone and text Claire.

Me: Oscar's home, safe and sound

The cursor blinks. Warmth spreads across my middle. She waited up for me.

Claire: Wonderful. How are you? xx

Me: Exhausted.

Claire: OK. Will let you sleep. Thx for a lovely evening xx

A smile ghosts my lips as I put the phone down. Lovely evening? The date was an unmitigated disaster, but that kiss we shared—dynamite. Even the stench of hospital antiseptic can't wash the taste of Claire from my lips.

I smooth strands of hair from Oscar's forehead. I'm scared to let him out of my sight. After letting Sally down, I'd be destroyed if anything happened to him. He's so small and vulnerable. Reminds me a little of Claire, not that she'd appreciate the comparison.

I wait for the familiar pang of guilt to hit me. Instead of a fiery blade to the heart, it's a dull ache unfurling within my chest. Dating Claire feels right. But not the farce we had tonight. She deserves a proper date.

Chapter Twelve

Claire

Date night.

Jake said he was taking me somewhere fancy, so I've gone all out on my outfit.

I strut down the hallway in six-inch platinum heels, rocking a slinky black dress that's a little shorter than I usually wear, but hello, it's Versace, and I got it on sale. Seventy percent off. Bargain.

I'm wearing my third sexiest panties: a Calvin Klein lavender thong with delicate lace trim. If Jake gets to see them —and I so want him to see them—he should be suitably impressed without it looking like I've tried too hard. The bra matches, of course, because no sane woman would leave the safety of home in odd underwear.

The doorbell rings, and I stumble. Crap. This is what happens when I give in to the temptation of shiny new shoes. I smooth my palms down the dress and check myself in the full-length hall mirror. Whoa! Does that cleavage belong to me? It's not like I don't dress up and go out, but the super boost push-up bra was an impulse purchase. And now I'll be buying a dozen more.

I take a deep breath in and count to five. I don't want to stuff this up. I really, really like Jake.

Another long inhale and I turn the handle.

The door swings open and so does my mouth.

Kill me now.

Jake's dressed in black trousers and a lavender shirt. The same shade of lavender as my underwear.

It's destiny.

Purple is a brave colour for a man, but Jake pulls it off. I want to yank my dress up right now and check how closely his shirt matches the colour of my panties. Of course, I don't. That would be weird.

"Hi, Claire." His voice is smooth, like caramel and chocolate, melting my insides while his eyes darken to swirls of grey-blue as his gaze sweeps over my body. "You look stunning."

"Thank you," I gasp in a breathless voice. Not sexy breathless, but more like 'I'm going to pass out from lack of oxygen' breathless. "Please come in. I'll just grab my handbag and shawl."

He gives me his panty-melting grin, the one that has me wishing I'd worn no panties at all, except then I'd have nothing to soak up the moisture pooling between my thighs. I step towards the sofa, relieved I don't topple over in the shoes. I turn, only to crash into Jake standing inches behind me. My heels wobble as firm fingers curl around my arms, holding me upright.

Jake's heated gaze dips to my breasts for the briefest of moments, sending a flurry of goosepimples across my skin. The veins on the sides of his neck pulse like they did when he confronted me that day on the street. But it's not anger swirling in those blue eyes this time. It's lust.

A giddy sense of power sweeps through me. The kiss the

other night was too fleeting. I need more. Ever since Jake nearly ran me over in his SUV, I've wanted to climb him, run my tongue along the ink swirling over his biceps, yank down his trousers and find out if he's a boxer or briefs man. Or does he go commando?

What am I waiting for?

I wrap my arms around his neck and press my breasts to the delicious, hard lines of his chest.

His jaw tightens, and he rests his hands on my hips. For a moment, I fear he's going to push me away, but then he lowers his head, sky-blue irises promising me tomorrow, the next day, and the day after that. He feathers his lips across mine. I sigh at the scent of pine and cedarwood, the barely there contact. Electricity sizzles between us. Goddammit, he's killing me with gentleness.

I lick along the firm seam of his lips, enticing him to take the kiss further. He responds with a growl, his mouth opening and our tongues colliding. Coffee, mint, and all things man consume me. Never has a kiss been so intoxicating. I need more. So much more. Jake's fingers dig into my hips, bringing the heat of an impressive bulge flush with my belly. I wriggle closer. But Jake wrenches away from me.

"No," I protest, my heart pumping as if I've just finished two spin classes back-to-back.

"Shh …" He cups my face in his hands, a slight tremble in his fingers letting me know pulling back wasn't easy for him. He presses a chaste kiss on my forehead. "I'm doing this right. Even if it kills me."

"What do you mean?"

"If we keep kissing"—his lips twist upwards—"we'll never leave."

"Would that be so bad?" My face warms. I'm such a hussy. But seriously, who cares about eating? Or stupid rules about not putting out on the first date? Or, in this case, the second one. Not me. It's been too long since I last had sex. Food can wait.

"No." The fire in his eyes hints at a wild night with no sleep, but his jaw is set. "I promised you dinner, and that's what you're going to get. It's what you deserve." He thrusts his hands into his pockets as though he doesn't trust himself not to touch me.

Fresh moisture pools between my legs. Jake's respectfulness is foreign territory and hot as hell. He's the type of man Mum would say is a keeper.

"Alright, Inspector Matthews. Have it your way. But let me tell you, after that kiss, your chances of doing a panty search when you bring me home just doubled." I give him a flirty smile. "Assuming you know how to do one, of course."

Jake swallows, his Adam's apple bobbing. "If, and when, I conduct a search, I can promise you one thing." His breath tickles the tip of my ear. "It'll be very, very thorough."

Oh my. I resist the urge to fan myself.

"Such a dirty talker, Inspector Matthews."

Red sweeps across Jake's cheeks, and he steps away. "Sorry, Claire. I'm not usually this crass."

I press a finger to his lips. "You didn't offend me. I like seeing you a little unhinged."

He sucks in a breath, and the stubborn set of his jaw returns. "Come on, you temptress. Prepare to be wined and dined."

Jake rests his hand on the small of my back and escorts me out of the house.

Nothing could have prepared me for the black limousine swallowing up the driveway.

I grip the doorknob as if it's a life preserver. "What's this?"

"I told you I was going to treat you right."

O.M.G.

He's too good for me. I'll mess this up for sure.

Jake clears his throat, dragging my gaze away from the

monstrous vehicle and back to him. He rocks on his heels, the only sign he's nervously waiting for my reaction.

When he said fancy, he wasn't exaggerating. I straighten my shoulders. "Well, lead on, Inspector Matthews. The prospect of the night ending in a panty search just tripled."

Jake shakes his head and grins as he leads me to the open door of the limo.

"Good evening, madam," the chauffeur says with a small bow.

I smile like I do this all the time and slide into the limo. The dress creeps up to a dangerous height on my thigh. There's no flashing of panties. At least, I don't think so. The limousine's interior has two long seats in plush cream leather and a tinted screen that separates us from the driver. An ice bucket with champagne and two glasses sits in the middle, together with bright red strawberries.

Jake climbs in beside me. "What do you think, Claire?"

"I'm speechless. This is so much more …" I clasp my hands on my lap. "It's a bit much for a second date, isn't it?"

Jake averts his gaze and pops the champagne bottle. "After the mess I made of the last one, I wanted this date to be perfect." He hands me a glass. "Don't overthink it. Just relax and enjoy."

Enjoy? I can do that. But relax? There's no way I'll get through this night without making a fool of myself. I'll need to keep my wits about me.

We sit in silence, our fingers laced together, as the car purrs through the streets. Jake watches the passing traffic, sneaking glances at me but making no attempt at small talk. I'm grateful for the quiet. It gives me space to process everything.

In no time at all, we pull into Old Parliament House. I stifle a squeal. Jake beats the chauffeur to my door and opens it for me. I feel like the heroine in some historical romance, the horse-drawn carriage replaced by a limousine. Handsome nobleman replaced by a hot, gentlemanly cop. It's a world away from my last boyfriend, who thought free cocktail hour at the pub was a romantic evening.

We enter a private dining room set for two—a black leather sofa by the open fireplace, more champagne on ice, and a cosy table.

A server takes my shawl and ushers us to our seats. "Would you like a glass of Chandon?"

I nod, my brain still in sensory overload. I'm not sure I can do this. The restaurant reminds me of the places my father insists on taking us every year to celebrate Christmas. And every year, he castigates me for embarrassing him. Last year it was for spilling red wine all over another patron as she walked past our table. I'm pretty sure she was wearing Prada. Dad didn't say it, but I know he was thinking, *Why can't you be more like your sister?*

Jake pulls out my chair, resting his hand on my shoulder. "Are you okay, Claire?"

"Yeah." I give myself a mental shake as I sit. I'm not with my family now. I'm with Jake. A sexy man who thinks I'm worthy of a fancy date. I will not embarrass him. Or myself.

The waitress places an ivory linen napkin on my lap. Then Jake's.

"I wasn't expecting this. Thank you."

Jake winks. "I'm glad you approve." And just like that, my nervousness disappears. Mostly.

I take a sip of champagne because … yeah … I'm still a little edgy. The bubbles work their magic like they did in the limousine, and a warm glow envelops me.

"Tell me, Inspector Matthews, have you always been a cop?"

"Yep." He smiles, his eyes taking on a faraway look. "All I ever wanted was to follow in my dad's footsteps. One of my earliest memories is getting in trouble for drawing a pretend body outline on the brand-new, tiled kitchen floor with permanent texta."

"Oh, no."

"Oh, yeah." His smile widens. "Needless to say, my mother was *not* happy."

"And does Oscar follow in his daddy's footsteps?"

Jake laughs. "I'm afraid so. We have to keep all pens and textas under lock and key."

There's extra warmth in Jake's eyes when he talks about his son. Whatever happened with his wife, it's clear Jake dotes on Oscar.

I fiddle with the napkin on my lap. "It must have been nice to have a clear direction."

"You didn't?"

Jake's sharp. He's picked up on my wistful tone. I shouldn't be surprised. After all, he is a detective.

"Nope." I shudder. "My parents wanted me to be a lawyer. Like them. But I couldn't imagine anything more boring."

The waitress returns and places a plate of bruschetta in the middle of the table. I grab a piece. Grateful for the distraction. But immediately regret it. How the hell am I going to eat this without making a mess?

I cut it into two bite-sized pieces and almost fist pump the air when the first slice of bread slips into my mouth with no topping falling off. I stop myself—just. There must be a limit to how much crazy Jake can tolerate.

I bring the second piece to my lips, only to catch the heat in Jake's eyes. He looks one moment away from tearing off my clothes and throwing me across the table. A tingle zips all the way to my centre.

That's when it all goes sideways.

My hand trembles and the bruschetta topples … into my lap.

"Crap."

I bolt out of my chair, but that only makes it worse. Food caught by the napkin splatters all over my dress and onto the polished floorboards. I bump the table with flailing hands, and my glass of champagne crashes to the floor.

"Crap, crap, crap," I whisper, heat flooding my face.

Jake bounds out of his chair and grabs my arms. "You okay?"

"Yeah." I swallow the bitterness in my mouth as the bruschetta threatens to make a reappearance. I'd never be able to look Jake in the eye again if that happened. So much for trying to be sexy and sophisticated. Why did I ever think a klutz like me could go out with a gorgeous man like Jake?

"Claire, look at me."

Jake's tone is imperious as he forces my chin up to face him. A smile twitches on his lips.

My face burns. It must be as red as the tomato. "I'm so sorry, Jake. I'm hopeless."

"Hey! Don't be silly. It was an accident."

"Really? Look at the mess I've made, and it's only the first course."

He laughs.

"I should go."

"Claire, please don't stress."

He strokes my arms, his palms warm and soothing on my sensitive skin. "You're not the first person to drop their bruschetta, and you won't be the last."

I trace my fingers along the stain on the tablecloth. "I'm embarrassed."

"I can see that, but there's no need to be."

The waitress hurries into the room, her face a pleasant mask, as if guests are always throwing their food around and smashing glasses. She clears away the dishes and changes the tablecloth.

I seek the comfort of the wrought-iron fireplace, patting at my dress with a napkin. Smoke curls up the chimney, escaping the crackle and flicker of the flames. How I wish I could escape too. It was a mistake to wear my third-best underwear. I should have worn my absolute favourite to make sure nothing went wrong.

Jake's the first guy ever who's gone out of his way to impress me. I don't understand what he sees in me, unless it is just sex? At the beginning, I would have been happy if that's all he was interested in. But not now. The more I get to know Detective Inspector Matthews, the more I like him. The more I want a future with him.

§⁜

I suck in a deep breath.

Out.

In again.

My heart rate follows the breaths, finding a steady rhythm.

The wine stain is barely noticeable on the silk. Black was a wise choice because I can't change my clothes. And I wouldn't dare try to clean the delicate silk with water.

Jake hovers near the table like he knows I need a moment. Could he be any more perfect? Gah! I doubt there'll be another date. I'd better make the most of it.

I back away from the fire. "Why'd you choose this restaurant?"

"I wanted the night to be perfect." He smooths his hands down his shirt. "And I wanted you to think there was more to me than being a cop."

The adorable dimple in Jake's cheek makes a rare appearance, sending a wave of hormones swooning through my veins.

More than a cop? He's a detective inspector. That's pretty high up, isn't it? Certainly, a lot more important than a sales rep.

"Well, a notice for next time, bruschetta should be down there with tacos and spaghetti as a food unsuitable for first dates," I mumble.

He laughs and brings my hand to his mouth, placing a gentle kiss to the tips of my fingers. "Duly noted. But what about a third or fourth date?"

I swallow. Is he serious?

"You want another date with me?"

His smile broadens. "Absolutely. You'll have to do a lot more than drop a piece of bruschetta to scare me off. Remember, I've scraped your vomit off my shoes and shirt and yet …" He shrugs. "Here I am."

I scrunch my eyes closed. Hearing it like that, I can't believe he wants to date me at all. I'm a disaster zone. "No. I don't want to remember that. And you should erase it from your memory banks."

His deep-throated chuckle washes over me like a warm bath. "Not on your life, Claire."

My heart flutters. He's crazy. There might be hope for us after all.

We return to our seats. A splash of indigo peeks out from where the top button of Jake's shirt has popped undone. My thighs clench. I know from our first meeting how far down his chest they go.

"I thought cops weren't allowed to have tattoos?"

His fingers fly to his shirt. "As long as it's covered up when on duty, there's no problem." He fixes the button covering the delicious ink. "I got it during my rebellious stage."

"You?" Jake might have freaked me out when I first met him, but everything I've seen of him since screams respectability, not biker tattoos.

"Yes, me." He sips his wine. "I resented my father's expectation I'd be a cop, even though that's exactly what I wanted. So, I did a science degree first. To prove I could do it. I got the

Aztec design around my right bicep in the first year. By the time I finished uni, my back and pecs and the other arm were inked."

Wow. That's unexpected. "What did your dad say?"

"That it might come in handy if I ever went undercover."

I burst out laughing. "He sounds like a smart dad."

"Yep." He smiles. "The best."

The main dishes roll out, and I wet my lips with my tongue at the scrumptious aroma of melt-in-your-mouth lamb shanks and creamy mashed potato. Yummy. Jake gives me a sultry grin that sinks all the way to my core. Cheeky man. I lower my gaze and focus on the food. Otherwise, I'm likely to embarrass myself with another incident like the bruschetta.

When the waitress returns with dessert, she gives us a warm smile and places a dark chocolate mousse in front of us. "This is the last course. Would you like a port or a dessert wine to go with it?"

I shake my head. "No, thanks." I don't want any more alcohol to dull my senses.

Jake waves her away.

I slump back and pat my tummy. "I'm not sure I can eat anything else."

Jake's face drops. "What about dessert?"

"I want to, but I'm stuffed."

"I love watching you eat, Claire."

His gaze dips to my mouth.

"You make these delightful moans while you chew. Those lips of yours were made for kissing." His eyes darken. "And other things."

Oh my! There's a definite bad boy inside Inspector Matthews to match his ink. My nipples pucker and my core ignites. If I was a flame, I'd consume the nearby fire. In the past, other guys have sounded crude and disrespectful—just like their underwear—when they've attempted any kind of dirty talk. But Jake, with those hooded eyes, makes me feel special, like I'm his entire world. I want to rip off my clothes and give him that world.

I dig into the mousse with a spoon and lift the decadent morsel to my lips. Jake squirms in his chair, face tense. I suppress a smile. I hadn't realised how much power I could wield with one tiny utensil.

'The Devil Went Down to Georgia' shatters the sultry spell.

Jake groans; his face screws up like he's in pain. "Sorry, Claire, I need to take this." He bounds out of his seat and moves towards the fireplace.

The spoon slips from my fingers. I was only eating for him. And for me, because I love watching him come undone.

I ogle Jake's rear while he murmurs into the phone. It's a butt I want to dig my fingers into while he does filthy things to me. My panties are so ruined. I should have brought a spare pair. Then again, I could remove them. The look on Jake's face, if he did a panty search and discovered them missing, would be priceless. And let's face it, I'm so letting him do a panty search tonight.

Jake slips his phone into the pocket of his trousers and turns around. His blue eyes are dull, lips pulled into a frown. "I'm sorry, Claire, but I need to go."

My chest tightens. "What?"

"That was the station."

I hide my hands under the table, clenching them tightly. "But don't you have tonight off?"

"I do. But there's been a development in the case I've been working on." He shoves his hands into his pockets. "Believe me, there's nothing I want more than to take you home."

"Can you finish dessert first?"

"No." He shakes his head. "A car is on its way to pick me up. They'll be here in a few minutes."

All the food I've eaten sticks to the walls of my stomach

like glue. Am I reading him wrong? Is this a set-up and he got a friend to ring so he could avoid finishing the date?

I push my chair back and stand. Jake closes the distance between us and cups my chin. "I'll make it up to you."

His lips brush across mine. My mouth opens as if drugged, and our tongues dart out to greet each other. Exploring. Tasting. Entwining. It doesn't feel like he's trying to escape me. I skim my hands down his back and curl my fingers into his buttocks. The muscles flex against my palms, and if it wasn't for his arms holding me up, I'd slump to the floor.

Jake slides his hands down the sides of my dress, sending flutters of electricity to my core. He halts when he reaches my hips and pulls his mouth away from mine.

"Don't stop," I pant. "Now would be a good time to conduct that panty search, Inspector."

His fingers clamp around my hips. "I'm not sure that's a good idea."

"I am."

The silver flecks in his irises darken to charcoal. "What would I find?"

"It wouldn't be called a panty search if I told you." I flutter my eyelashes in a way I hope looks sexy. "You'll have to see for yourself."

He glances at the door. While we're alone in this private dining room, there's still a risk of the staff walking in and seeing us. I'm so hot for him, I don't care. Jake's eyes glitter as he returns his attention to me. Looks like he's on board, too. "In that case …" He cups my butt and kneads the soft flesh through the fabric. His hand burns through my dress like a branding iron.

All I can manage is a sigh. I can't think with his cock pulsing against my stomach like it's got a mind of its own. His palm slides towards the hem of my dress. I can barely remember to breathe, lost to the calloused texture of his fingers as they graze my naked thigh.

Jake jerks away from me, his breath heavy. The loss of his hand on my skin hits me as keenly as if I'd been thrust into a snowdrift. But thank God for his quick reflexes because a tall man looms in the doorway.

"Sorry to interrupt your dinner, sir."

Embarrassment quickly replaces the lusty haze. It's the officer from the station from when I had my little handbag incident. Greg, I think his name is.

"Yeah, I just bet you are." Jake's voice is gruff as if he's just woken up.

At least I'm not the only one affected by our kisses.

Greg nods his head at me. "Apologies, Claire. I wouldn't interrupt if it wasn't important."

Jake smooths his palms on his trousers. "It had better be good."

Greg smiles like a fox who's learnt how to open the door to the chicken coup. "It is. It's the break we've been waiting for."

"I'm sorry, Claire. I have to go."

Jake sighs and clasps my hands in his, pressing a kiss to my palm.

"The limo will take you home." He turns to Greg. "Can you give us a minute?"

Greg grins. "Sure. *Sir*."

Jake mutters, "Arsehole."

Greg sniggers and strides out of the room.

Jake pulls me close and suckles my bottom lip between his teeth before trailing kisses up my cheek. His hot breath fans the sensitive skin behind my ear. "Can I have a raincheck on that panty search?"

"Lavender," I blurt out.

He pulls away from me, his browed furrowed. "What?"

"My panties." I gulp. "They're a lavender G-string. The same colour as your shirt."

"You're killing me, Claire." He swipes a hand across his face, his eyes wild as a storm. He presses his lips to mine, searing them, then hurries out the door.

I stare after him, fire coursing through my veins. For the first time since I started stealing Mum's Mills & Boon as a teenager, I'm starting to believe I can have a normal relationship with a man. One who's seen me at my worst and still likes me.

Chapter Thirteen

Jake

Greg briefs me on the situation as we speed along the road, lights flashing but no siren, the streets a grey blur. The suburbs are like that. Families blending into the sameness of their houses, cars and two-point-five children.

"There was a confirmed sighting of Scudasi entering the house on East Street," says Greg. "That was at ten-fifteen."

I clench my hands. We've been planning this for weeks. Had the tactical unit on standby. "You're sure it's him?"

He gives me a sideway stink eye before refocusing on the road ahead. "Of course, I'm sure. I wouldn't have interrupted your date if I wasn't."

"Alright then."

"So, how was it?"

"How was what?"

"Come on, Jake." Greg huffs like a five-year-old, like Oscar. "You've been living a monk's life for the last three years, and Claire's hot. Shall I draw you a picture?"

My gut tightens. My own R-rated picture of Claire is

firmly implanted in my brain, and I don't want Greg thinking the same way.

"Very funny." I suck in a deep breath. "It was good. Better than good. Right up until the moment *you ruined it*!"

"Yeah, sorry about that." He chuckles. "But I knew you'd be pissed if you found out we'd caught the creep without you."

I rub my temples, a headache coming on. "You're right about that."

"Sooo …"

"It's none of your fucking business. Can we focus on cracking this drug ring?"

"We won't be at the location for another ten minutes." Greg changes lanes and breezes past a truck. "You sure you can't give me some details about your date? Anything?"

"Jesus, mate, you're worse than a dog. I like Claire. I probably would have gotten lucky tonight if you hadn't interrupted. I can't wait to see her again. Happy?"

"Yep." Greg grins. "About time you started acting like a horny bachelor."

My blood boils at the suggestion I'm just looking to get my rocks off with Claire. I might have carried things a bit far at the restaurant, but only because Claire affects me in a way no other woman has. Not in a long time.

I slap my palm on the dashboard, and Greg jerks his head towards me. "She's not like the women you bang and forget."

"Whoa." His lips stretch into a stupid grin. "No need to get personal. As you said the other day, she's sweet."

"Greg." I bite out his name between clenched teeth and ball my fists by my side.

He raises his left hand again, palm facing me. "Okay, okay."

The car lurches forward, running a red light.

I glare at Greg. He shrugs his shoulders. "We're in pursuit."

"Really?"

He laughs. "Our lights are flashing. It's our right."

I shake my head. "Bullshit."

Greg's always been an adrenaline junky. If I took my inspector hat off for a second, I'd admit to thriving on the thrill of the chase too. But it's not appropriate. I'm his superior, something we both tend to forget.

If it wasn't for the fact he's driving and it might cause an accident, I'd smack the smug look off his face.

Greg cuts the flashing lights as we approach our destination and slows down to the speed limit. I shove all thoughts of Claire into a box and shut the lid. I need to focus on the job right now.

Three unmarked police vehicles line the quiet, suburban street. Greg drives past and parks a hundred metres up the road.

I strap on the utility belt Greg brought for me, don a bulletproof vest and holster my weapon. I'm surprised Greg could sign the gun out for me, but I don't question it. Not tonight. Adrenaline surges through my veins. We need this arrest, if only to keep the commissioner off our backs.

The target house is nondescript red brick with manicured roses in the front garden.

It looks normal. Harmless.

Looks are deceiving. Even the most beautiful roses have thorns.

Greg and I walk up the driveway, six officers from the tactical team at our flank.

"I presume we've got a search warrant?"

Greg rolls his eyes at me. "Now, you ask?"

I smirk, then still my mind. There's no way of knowing what waits for us on the other side of a locked door. We step out of the way and let the team do their job.

"Police. Search warrant. Open the door!"

Scudasi himself opens up, cigar hanging from his mouth, doped glaze in his eyes. "What the fuck?"

He slams the door, but he's no match for the men who swarm in after him. Greg and I watch from the entrance, guns at the ready. Within seconds, Scudasi is forced to the floor and cuffed. He's been a slippery character to pin down. But now we have him, it's only a matter of time before we get Leadbetter. I saunter inside and step over his prone body.

"Nice to see you again, Mr Scudasi. It's been too long."

I glare at the piece of shit through the one-way mirror. A Cartier watch circles his wrist, and enough gold jewellery to sink a small boat hangs from his bloated body. The sneer on his face says he thinks he's walking out of here. He's in for a nasty surprise.

"Detective Inspector?"

I turn to the door. "Yes, Constable?"

"We're ready to go when you are."

I've studied the footage we received several times. Satisfied myself it's the loathsome creep in the interrogation room we see handing over drugs for money. Frank Scudasi's a known criminal. Right-hand man to Leadbetter, one of Sydney's major cocaine distributors. And yet we've never been able to get anything to stick. Until now.

Greg and I stride in and close the door firmly behind us.

I get the preliminaries out of the way, reminding Scudasi of his right to remain silent but hoping he'll be arrogant enough to slip up anyway. "Seems you've been caught with a lot of cash tonight, Mr Scudasi."

His lips curl into a smirk. "I'm not saying nothin' until my lawyer gets here."

I swallow hard. It's what I expected him to say. "We know

you're just the middleman." I force a smile. "Tell us what you know, and we'll protect you."

He barks out a laugh. "Yeah, right."

"You'll be lucky to see the outside of a jail cell for the next ten years. Is that what you want?"

"You have no idea who you're dealing with, Inspector." He leans forward, pupils dilated with the telltale signs he's sampled some of the filth he helps peddle. "If you care about your family, you'll drop it."

I clench my fingers into fists to stop myself from wrapping them around his neck. "Are you threatening an officer of the law?"

He raises his cuffed hands. "No, no. Of course not, Detective." Sweat drips off his forehead. "But Leadbetter, he's a mean son of a bitch. If he can't get to you, he'll go after the ones you love. I've got a wife and two kids. I'm not risking them for anyone."

A chill runs down my spine.

Scudasi glances at Greg, and then back at me. "Like I said, I'm saying nothin' until my lawyer gets here."

Greg raises his eyebrows at me. I press my lips together and nod.

"Fine," says Greg. "We'll resume this discussion later."

Two constables arrive to escort Scudasi to a holding cell. I return to my desk and switch on my laptop. I kept my cool in the interrogation room, but the truth is, I'm rattled. Leadbetter has eyes and ears everywhere. I'll need to ramp up security even further at home. And for Claire.

The next time I check my watch, the shadows outside the window are losing their battle with the approaching dawn. Thoughts of Claire's lavender thong splitting her arse into two perfect globes have me sprouting a semi. I'm tempted to call her. Pick up where we left off last night.

I pack up my desk and head out the door, renewed energy coursing through my veins. "I'm out of here."

Greg gives me a knowing look, which I ignore. He can't possibly know what's going through my head.

My mobile rings, and my heart sinks when I see who the caller is. My dick, which had been stirring at the memory of Claire's flesh beneath my fingers, deflates faster than a popped balloon.

Greg straightens, sensing the tension winding itself around me.

"Yes?" I answer on the second ring.

The nurse is all business. "I'm sorry to call so late, Inspector Matthews, but you did say you wanted to be informed immediately of any change to your wife's condition."

"Absolutely." Goosepimples race down my spine.

"Her temperature is up. We suspect a urinary tract infection. But don't worry. If it is a UTI, it's been caught early."

"Okay." That's nothing antibiotics can't fix. "Thanks. I'll be there soon." I slip the phone into my pocket. "I'm needed at the nursing home."

"Shit." Greg gets to his feet. "Is it serious?"

"Sally might have a UTI."

He tilts his head at me, his brown eyes searching mine. "Do you really need to go?"

I stiffen. "What?"

He shrugs. "It's not like you can do anything. Maybe you'd be best off going to Claire's place. Find comfort in willing arms."

"While my wife's ill?"

"Jake, she's already sick." Greg rakes his fingers through his hair. "You can't get much sicker."

I grind my teeth. Greg's right, but there's no ignoring my duty. "I'm still her husband."

"But she's no longer your wife in anything but name."

We stare each other off. We've had this conversation several times this past year as Greg tries to convince me to start 'living' again. But it's fine for him. He's not the one holding the guilt.

I give him a brief nod to let him know I hear him, but I'm doing this my way. My footsteps ring out as I stride along the empty corridor of the station towards the parking area. I rub my eyes as if that will brush away the fatigue clawing at my body. How can I ever explain to Claire that I'm still legally married? That my wife became addicted to prescription medication and had a stroke after overdosing on it three years ago, and has been in a vegetative state ever since? Would she still want to go out with me if she knew?

Even as I ask myself the question, I know I'm not ready to tell Claire yet. I'd forgotten how good it feels to spend time with a woman. To laugh. To flirt. And not just any woman. Claire. There's something about her that has me wanting to hold on and never let go.

Chapter Fourteen

Jake

Sunlight filters through the window, bathing the lounge room of my parents' house in a soft, warm glow. It's my childhood home and my home for the last three years. I couldn't have raised Oscar and kept up with the demands of my job on the drug squad without Mum and Dad's support. They've been my rock since Sally's stroke.

Oscar pieces together bits of Lego on the two-toned beige carpet. The wound on his arm is almost healed, although I keep a close eye on him for any signs it's hurting. He's advanced for his age. And way too mischievous to be left unattended when he's in building mode. The last time I made that mistake, he smeared Vegemite all over the rug in the dining room, saying it was a moat to keep out the bad guys.

"Dad, can you watch Oscar while I make a call?"

My father peers over his newspaper from the comfy recliner near the window, glasses perched on his nose. "Sure. Is everything okay?"

"Yeah. Just something I've got to sort out at work."

It's not like me to lie to Dad, but I can barely admit how I feel about Claire to myself, let alone explain it to him. It took all my willpower to leave her last night. If Greg hadn't picked me up, it's possible I would have ditched the job and taken her home. Finished off what we'd started in the restaurant. Never before, not even with Sally, have I contemplated shirking my duties for pleasure.

What's Claire doing to me?

I stroll to the bottom of the backyard and settle on a bench seat next to Mum's favourite, pink grevillea. Two magpies flutter from the nearby grass into the branches of the large gum tree and glare down at me like I've stolen their spot. I pull up Claire's number and hit the call button.

Just as I think it's going to go to voicemail, she answers. "Hello."

I swallow a groan. Her soft, breathy voice is all it takes to have my dick stirring. "Hi, Claire. It's Jake."

"I know. Your name came up."

I bang my head with my hand. "Of course. How are you?"

"Fine."

"Great." Jesus. I sound as gauche as a teenager with his first girlfriend. "Did you sleep well?"

The magpies tilt their heads as if agreeing I'm a lost cause. I glare at them, but they turn away as if I'm not worth their time.

"Yeah." Claire's voice lowers to a husky whisper. "Although I had some sexy dreams about a certain detective."

My chest puffs out at her admission, and I pull at the collar of my shirt. The sun has a sting in it this morning. "You did?"

"He was doing a panty search."

"I see." Fuck. She's killing me. "And what did he find?"

"I don't know. I woke up."

I launch myself off the seat and stride towards the back fence. I'm going to have a big case of blue balls if I don't get relief soon. I lean against the palings. "You're a tease, Miss Thompson."

"Sorry about that." She giggles. "Not sorry."

My dick presses against my zipper. If I left now, I could be at Claire's house in twenty minutes doing the panty check for real. But I told Oscar we'd go to the movies. I can't disappoint him, no matter how hard my dick is. And Sunday's out. That's the day I visit Sally in the nursing home. Given the latest development with her health, I can't ignore it.

I suck in a big breath. "I've promised my son I'd hang out with him this weekend. What about next Saturday?"

There's silence on the other end of the phone. Shit. Is she disappointed? I am, but I can't tell her about Sally. Not yet. It's too soon. And I'm a coward.

"Claire?"

"I'm here." There's rustling in the background. Is she still in bed? My dick throbs at the thought of her hair all mussed up from sleep, her eyes dreamy. I change positions in a futile effort to relieve the ache in my jeans. "Just checking if I'm free."

Of course. It's presumptuous of me to assume she doesn't have plans.

"You're in luck, Inspector. Looks like I have no hair washing or dentist appointments scheduled in."

"That's good." I chuckle. She had me for a moment. "Thanks for finding time for me."

"Always, Jake."

My legs buckle at Claire's words, at their warmth and conviction.

"Was your night fruitful?" she asks.

"Yeah." I smile. "I'm sorry our date was cut short." Curse Greg for being so diligent. "But it was worth it. We caught a key suspect."

"That's good. I'm glad."

Claire's husky voice isn't helping the hard-on in my jeans.

Breakfast will be ready shortly, and I need to calm down before I return to my parents and Oscar. "I'd better go. I can't wait to see you next weekend."

"Me neither."

I hang up and give my dick a few minutes to settle, then meander back to the house. My face hurts with how hard I'm smiling. It's like my muscles are still getting used to this new position.

My father and Oscar have moved to the table on the back deck. Both are heads down, colouring in pictures of dragons with crayons. They're wearing matching red flannel shirts and grey pullovers. It does something to my heart to see the growing bond between them.

Oscar drops his crayon and pulls on my father's sleeve. "Can I have a biscuit, Grandpa?"

Dad pats his hand and glances at me. "Sure. Why don't you ask Grandma for one?"

Oscar doesn't need any further encouragement, jumping off his chair and running inside.

Dad turns to me with eagle eyes. "Was that your date from last night?"

Heat surges up my neck and across my cheeks. "It's that obvious?"

He chuckles and shakes his head. "Let's just say I've never seen you get off a work call with that expression. And I hope I never do."

Of course, Dad sees straight through me. Even retirement can't shake a cop's senses.

"We could look after Oscar now if you wanted to see your girl again." Dad lifts his palms. "Maybe stay into the night?" His eyes sparkle and it has nothing to do with the sun.

I shudder. There's no way I'm talking to my old man about sex. "Thanks, but I promised Oscar we'd go to the movies. He's looking forward to it."

My father scrapes his chair back and clasps my shoulder,

his expression sombre. "It's been three years." Dad's fingers tighten, and he clears his throat. "It's okay to start living your life again, son."

He pats my back and wanders into the house. I remain frozen on the deck. The specialists have repeatedly warned me that Sally will never recover, but guilt chokes my veins. She's still my wife, the woman I promised to honour in sickness and in health.

Will there ever be a right time to tell Claire about Sally? And will she understand?

Chapter Fifteen

Claire

I slip into my cubicle with seconds to spare. How I love Mondays. Not.

I'd hoped to see Jake over the weekend, but he works long hours and needs to spend time with his son. I get it, but it still hurts. The kisses we shared on our date remain seared into my lips. I want more of those kisses.

Liam lurches out of his office, tie half-undone, eyes red like he's been on a bender all night. Or crying. Has his wife started divorce proceedings?

"Claire, can I see you for a moment?"

I nod and traipse after him. *What have I done now?*

He collapses into his seat and leans his elbows on the desk. "How's the Unison account going?"

Is that all? He won't catch me out this time. "It's on track. I'll have the first stage of the plan executed by the end of the week."

"Good." He wipes his brow. "That's good."

Phew. "Are you alright?"

"Yeah, yeah." He points to a folder. "Can you photocopy

these documents and return them to me?"

I blink. *What?*

"I know it's not part of your job description, but I need it done urgently. Sonya doesn't get in for another hour."

I pick up the yellow folder. Freaking hell. It's heavier than it looks. This is going to take forever. Then again, I'm not in trouble, so that's a plus.

Liam follows me out of his office and slaps five dollars on Ashley's desk. "Get me a coffee. Double espresso."

Ashley's jaw drops.

I smirk and quirk an eyebrow at him. Welcome to the club.

We amble down the corridor in silence. There's nothing like being treated like menial servants to dampen the mood. I turn towards the photocopier room while Ashley continues to the front door, his shoes dragging across the carpet.

Twenty minutes later, I finish the copying. Ashley sticks his hand out as I walk past. "Cujo should be feeling better now he's got his coffee."

"What?"

"You heard me." He sniggers. "C'mon, Claire, don't tell me you didn't think the boss looked like a rabid dog before."

"I might have seen a small resemblance." I hide a smile and enter Liam's office.

He jerks his head away from his screen. "Thanks."

I place the papers on his desk and turn to leave.

"One moment, Claire."

My muscles bunch up. *What more does he want?*

"HR are implementing drug testing today." He sighs. "Everyone needs to be tested."

"I thought it wasn't starting until next month?"

"Me too. The board requested it be brought forward."

"Can they do that?"

"Not officially. Training on the drug and alcohol policy should have been completed first." He straightens the papers on his desk, his gaze skittering around the room. "But it wouldn't look good if we pushed back."

"True." I've got nothing to hide. "When do we have to do the tests?

"Now. They're starting with the sales team. Joyce is facilitating it."

I cringe. Wonderful. They've brought in the bulldog. This should be fun. "Okay."

Joyce strides into Liam's office as if on cue, hair tied back in a severe bun, eyes almost as red as Liam's. Maybe they had a late night together? I shake my head. Nah. No way.

"Ah, Ms Thompson." Joyce's nose wrinkles as if my name is synonymous with an offensive odour.

She hands me a container.

I pull out a stick with what looks like a piece of plastic on it. "What am I supposed to do with it?"

Joyce smirks. "Suck it."

"What?"

Her nose does that wrinkle thing again as if I'm not worth her time. "Stick it in your mouth and suck until it becomes soft. It's so simple, even a child could do it."

I bite my lip. Retaliation would be career-limiting, and unfortunately, I still need this job. I stick the plastic thing into my mouth and suck. Rolling my eyes, I pretend it's a lollipop, or something yummier, even though it feels more like a tasteless sugar cube scraping the inside of my cheek. *Take that Bulldog!*

Joyce's eyebrows pinch together.

Any lewd thoughts I'd had about sucking on the plastic disintegrate when Liam pops a stick between his lips. I should receive a bonus payment for witnessing such an obscenity.

When the plastic becomes soft, like foam, I pull it out of my mouth and insert it back into the jar. Ms Massey gives me a pen so I can write my name on it. I hand the container to her. She flinches, glaring at it as if it's dog poop. I give it to Liam instead.

"Thank you, Ms Thompson." Bulldog waves her hand at the door. "Tell Mr Collins to come in next."

I return to my cubicle and tap Ashley on the shoulder. "Cujo and the bulldog want to see you."

"Ouch!" He groans and rubs the area as if I've punched him. Idiot.

"They've brought forward the drug testing."

"I knew I should have stayed home today," he grumbles.

An hour later, I'm drowning in customer delivery issues when a flash of blue strides past—a police officer. My thoughts immediately go to Jake and our date on Friday. How I can't wait to see him again and have him complete his panty search.

Then I come back to earth. Why are the police here? I turn to Ashley. He shrugs and throws his hands in the air.

We don't have to wait long to find out what's happening. Bulldog looms over me. "May we have a word, Ms Thompson?"

Ashley raises his eyebrows. I shake my head. I have no idea why I'm being summoned. My legs shake as I stand, even though I've done nothing wrong. "Sure."

The police officer, Mr Green and Joyce, all huddle at the end of Liam's desk, sucking oxygen out of the room and leaving me light-headed.

"Claire." Mr Green greets me with a sombre expression. It scares me more than any angry words Joyce or Liam could have thrown at me.

Joyce points to a container on Liam's desk. "Is this your sample?"

I lean forward and peer at the label. "Yes, it's mine."

"You tested positive."

There's no mistaking the glee in Joyce's voice. If she really was a bulldog, she'd be dancing around in circles with my half-chewed arse in her mouth.

My knees buckle and I clutch the end of Liam's desk to stop myself from falling. "That can't be true."

"I'm afraid it is." Mr Green's tone is grim, and his face is even more severe.

I'm frozen. I can't believe this is happening.

Mr Green gestures to the police officer, who stares back at me with zero expression. "This is Senior Constable Jackson. He's requested a sniffer dog which will be arriving shortly to check the premises."

"What sniffer dog?" Joyce purses her lips, her gaze flitting between Mr Green and the officer. "As HR Manager, I should have been informed there was going to be a search. This is highly improper, Ben."

"I know." Mr Green sighs. "But the board and I decided it needed to be kept at the highest confidentiality."

"What do you mean?" Liam loosens his collar, his cheeks blooming.

"We've had one too many incorrect stock counts over the last few months. Add a positive drug test to the mix ..." His charcoal gaze flicks to me. "I can't dismiss the possibility an employee has been stealing from us to manufacture illegal drugs."

Oh my God. The missing products must be the real reason Jake was here a couple of weeks ago. Is that why he asked me out? To find out what I knew? And now Mr Green thinks I'm the culprit. It's like I've walked into an alternate reality. I have no idea how my legs are holding me up. Has Jake been faking it?

Joyce glares at Mr Green like she's ready to launch an attack. She thinks she knows everything that goes on in the company. This must be eating her up. Mr Green tilts his head at her, his eyes narrowing. She backs off. I almost forget I'm the one with the positive drug test. Almost.

"Ahem. We're here."

My face burns like someone doused me in petrol and lit a match. It's Dylan and his dog, Milo. Milo's gaze zeroes in on me, and his tail thumps the floor. Great. Of all the sniffer dogs the police must own, it had to be that one.

"Mmm ..." Joyce's eyes glow, her annoyance at Mr Green seemingly forgotten as she focuses back on me. "The dog seems pretty interested in you, Claire."

I groan. Stupid dog. "That's because he knows me."

"You've been caught with drugs before?" Mr Green's expression turns to full-on angry mob boss.

Yikes. I clench my hands at my sides and shake my head. "No, no. It was all a misunderstanding."

Dylan gives me an apologetic smile. *Crap!* He lets Milo run to me, and the crazy dog jumps up and licks my hand.

I give him a pat. "We're just friends, aren't we, Milo?"

Officer Jackson's eyes widen. "Ah, you're *that* Claire?"

I nod and lower my gaze. Oh God, does the entire police station know who I am?

Dylan grins at the other officer and nods his head before turning back to me, his face all serious.

"Do you mind if Milo has a sniff around your desk?"

"Of course not." I lift my chin to show I have nothing to feel guilty about because I don't. But butterflies still swarm in my stomach. It's hard not to feel like a low-life when everyone's looking at me like I am one. "I've got nothing to hide."

"Even your handbag?"

Dylan keeps a straight face, but his eyes are twinkling.

How dare he make fun of me. My job is on the line. My life.

"Yes. If you don't mind seeing a few tampons. Maybe a condom or two." I throw the last bit in for fun, even though having root canal surgery would be more enjoyable than what I'm experiencing right now. It wipes the smirk off his face.

Mr Green gasps, and Joyce purses her lips together. What I said was out of line, but I don't care. They're both looking at me like I'm a druggie. I'm not. Liam's expression is kinder, but only because he's busy mopping sweat off his face. It's like he's sunbathing under the Caribbean sun. He really should see a doctor. It's not normal.

Dylan calls Milo and they leave the office. I move to follow, but Joyce stops me. "Let them do their work. How about you sit down and explain yourself?"

"Hold on." Officer Jackson holds up his hand. "This is a police matter now."

"It's okay." I ignore the trembling in my hands and stare Joyce in the eye. "I've done nothing wrong."

"Claire." Mr Green folds his arms across his chest. "The test was conclusive."

"There must be an error." I swallow, my throat more parched than an archaeological dig in the Middle East. "You can check my blood if you want. I don't do drugs."

I have nothing to fear this time. No granny panties stashed away. No hot cop muddling my brain. Milo won't find anything, and there has to be a rational explanation for the test result being wrong.

Dylan returns five minutes later. My muscles tighten at his grim expression. He looks above my head, avoiding eye contact.

"Claire, would you mind coming with me?"

Liam's eyes widen, and fresh sweat breaks out across his forehead. "Is there a problem, Officer?"

Dylan waves us to the door. My hands shake as I follow him towards my desk, where Milo sits at attention. Dylan points at the cabinet. "Can you unlock it, please, Claire?"

My stomach drops at his tone. I fumble for the key in my handbag and open the top drawer, revealing two pens, a stapler and my toiletry bag.

"Can I look inside?"

"Sure," I say with more bravado than I feel. "But you won't find anything."

Milo sits next to him, panting at my cosmetic case. Stupid dog. Dylan unzips it. His entire body tenses and mine does the same.

Inside are a couple of brightly coloured tampons and—what the hell—a bag filled with white powder.

"No. That's not mine. I've never seen it before." My voice squeaks as panic sets in. Even though it's the truth, I sound guilty as hell.

Constable Jackson grabs my arm. Not hard, but firm, making it clear I had better obey him. Or else. "Claire Thompson, I'm arresting you for being under the influence and in the possession of illicit drugs ..."

My mind blanks out. I don't understand how this is happening. Ashley's bottom lip drops to the floor. Dylan's jaw is rigid, but his eyes are soft. Sympathetic.

I shake my head, tears welling in my eyes, my legs buckling beneath me. "It's not mine. There must be some mistake."

Dylan strokes Milo's ears and gives him a treat, no doubt congratulating him on ruining my life. "Is there anyone you'd like us to call?"

"No."

Hell, no. Mum and Dad would be gutted. Jules is at work and Jake ... He'd been so disappointed when he caught me carrying that Valium, although he believed me when I said they weren't mine. I can't expect him to trust me a second time, especially when this stuff looks illegal. All my hopes of something happening between us are gone. Shoved up someone's nose by the look of the white powder in my bag. Or injected into their veins. How would I know? I don't do drugs.

Chapter Sixteen

Jake

Squad Commander Peter Gordon and the commissioner file out of my office but not before issuing the usual threats to crack the case or else. I rub my face and roll my shoulders back. Fucking drugs.

No sooner am I rid of the bosses, then young Emily, the intelligence officer, knocks on my door.

"I've just emailed you the reports you asked for, Inspector Matthews. Sorry they're late. The computer was playing up this morning."

I press my lips together. Her analysis would have been useful in my meeting, but there's no point taking it out on her. Not after my superiors have already used me as a punching bag. "Thanks."

Emily mumbles goodbye and runs straight into Greg. He steadies her by gripping her shoulders. I don't miss the gleam in his eyes as she slips past him. Goddammit. How many times do I have to warn him she's off limits?

"Excuse me, Jake." Greg's expression becomes unusually

serious, like he's come from a funeral. It has the hairs on the back of my neck rising.

I cock my head at him. "What happened to sir?"

He gives me a small smile that doesn't reach his eyes. "I'm standing here as a friend, not your subordinate."

"Okay. That sounds ominous." I wave him in. "What's going on?"

He shuts the door and rakes his fingers through his hair. "Shit, Jake. I don't know how to say it."

Dread pools in my gut. I've never known Greg to have trouble speaking his mind. "Then just spit it out."

"Claire's been arrested."

"What?" I bound out of the chair.

Greg grabs my arm, stopping me from racing out the door. "Wait. Let me tell you what happened."

My heart thumps against my ribcage. "Is she alright?"

"Yeah." He nods. "A little shaken, but fine."

"Was she in a car accident?" Adrenaline pulses through my veins. "Did she cause it?" I've witnessed firsthand Claire not watching where she's going.

"No. Nothing like that."

"What, then?"

"She failed a workplace drug test and was found with what looks to be a small quantity of cocaine."

The blood drains from my face. No way. "What the fuck?"

"Sorry, I wish it wasn't true, but it is." Greg stares at the floor, avoiding my gaze. "As you know, Alpha Pharmaceuticals reported further losses of pseudoephedrine last week. So, when we got a call from their CEO that an employee had tested positive, I sent Dylan and Milo to inspect the premises. They found the drugs."

I clench my fingers into fists. "Why am I only finding out now?"

"You were in a briefing with the commissioner." Greg

swallows, his Adam's apple working hard. "I didn't dare disturb you."

There's something he isn't telling me. "What else?"

Greg squeezes my arm again. "Four grams were found, so technically, Claire's looking at trafficking charges, not possession."

I slump against my desk. There must be some mistake. "She's a bit out there at times, but she doesn't seem the type to do drugs, let alone deal them. Was a second drug test done?"

"Yep." Greg nods, a ghost of a smile flitting across his face. "While it'll take some time for the blood results to come back, the good news is she tested negative in a urine test."

"Thank Christ." It's not proof of her innocence, but it casts doubt on the original workplace test. Although, if she'd gotten high after I dropped her off on Friday night, the drugs could have been nearly out of her system.

"If it's any consolation, Dylan said she looked shocked. She let him inspect her drawer without protest. Not like she was with her handbag here at the station."

I hang my head. My breath constricts. It's too much to take in. There has to be another explanation. "Do you think someone could have planted them?"

"I guess a colleague could have looked to offload their drugs." He shrugs. "It wouldn't be the first time. We'll know more when fingerprints check it."

Greg hovers near my desk. "Are you alright?"

I scrub my face with my hands. Nope. Not even close. "Has she been interviewed?"

"Yeah." Greg nods. "She declined her right to a lawyer. Insisted she had no idea where the drugs had come from and then broke down. The officers took pity on her and halted the interview after ten minutes."

I pull myself upright. "Where is she now?"

"In the holding cell. It's her first offence, but since it's trafficking, not just possession, and the custody sergeant is in one of his 'take no prisoners' moods, bail's been set at five thousand dollars."

"Shit!" I swipe the papers off my desk and thump my fist against it. Red stains my vision. The first woman I've started to care about since Sally and this happens? "Has she phoned anyone?"

"Nope." Greg shakes his head and takes a step backwards like he doesn't trust my mood. And he shouldn't. "She said she has no one to call."

An image of Claire all alone does something to my heart. Guilty or not, there's no way I can abandon her.

Greg clears his throat. "I know you really like this woman, but you've only been on two dates. It's not too late to walk away."

His words are weights punching at my chest. He's right. So, why do I want to smash his face in for saying exactly what I'd say to him if our positions were reversed?

"Calm down, Jake." He raises his palms. I'd never punch anyone in anger, let alone Greg, but I imagine my expression is a bit feral. I certainly feel it. "You know as well as I do Commander Gordon will lose his shit if he finds out the woman you're seeing is an alleged drug felon."

Fuck. He's got me there. But none of this makes sense. I've been investigating drug runners for several years now. I've lived through Sally's deception. Even though I've been thinking with my dick, I still would have picked up the signs.

Wouldn't I?

Then again, I let the Valium slide when I first met Claire. She's so different from Sally. I'd convinced myself there was no way history could repeat itself. Now Claire's caught with illegal drugs. *Am I a blind man walking here?*

I shove my hands into my pockets. "What do I do, Greg?"

"If you're not going to walk away from her, then I'd get her out of here and deal with the commander later." He rocks on his heels. "You don't want your girl spending the night in the slammer."

"I don't want my girl being a drug dealer."

Greg squeezes my shoulder. "I admit, it doesn't look good. If she's innocent, we'll figure it out."

I switch off my laptop, and clear my desk. Operate on autopilot, my thoughts disconnected from my body. If Claire's guilty, I need to cut ties and cut them quickly. I can't go through this again.

When I arrive at the cells, Claire's misery is a melancholic violin tune wafting in the air. Huddled in the corner, the corn yellow of her jacket shines like a diamond in the dreary grey cell. Fuck. She doesn't belong here. I hope to Christ she's not guilty. "Claire."

Her head shoots up, and my heart breaks at the agony in her pale face.

"Oh, no. Not you." She hangs her head, her sobs ringing out even louder.

I straighten my jacket. Not quite the reaction I was expecting. I motion to the constable with me, and he unlocks the cell, leaving us alone.

The anger that had been racing through my veins like a Formula One car crashes to a standstill in the face of Claire's despair.

I kneel beside her. "You can go home now."

"No, I can't." She sobs. "I don't have enough money for bail."

"I've paid it. You're free to go." Some people might say I'm crazy for paying a five-thousand-dollar bond for a woman I've only known a few weeks. But innocent or guilty, there's no way I could sleep tonight knowing she was stuck in here.

Her head snaps up, gorgeous green irises shimmering. She snorts and rubs her nose, looking the worst I've ever seen her, and that's saying something.

"I didn't do it," she says.

My muscles tense, my stomach screwing itself into a tight ball. Fuck. I want to believe her. Her eyes are red from crying, but they don't have the telltale signs of a drug addict. There's no bruising, no hazy gaze. But there's no getting past the drugs hidden in her cosmetic bag. I clench my fingers into my palms and ask the question that could end our relationship before it's barely begun. "Tell me the truth, Claire. Were the drugs yours?"

"No. Definitely not." She maintains eye contact, a fresh tear teetering on the edge of her bottom eyelash.

The knot in my stomach unravels a little. She sounds sincere. But drug dealers are some of the most accomplished liars I've ever met. So are users. They're experts at fabricating stories. The one time I fell for lies was when I was emotionally invested. Like now. I smile, although my insides remain frozen. "Then you have nothing to worry about."

"But Dylan found them in my drawer. My locked drawer."

"I know."

Her bottom lip trembles. "You believe me?"

My throat stings like I've been breathing in exhaust fumes. "I want to."

Claire bursts into fresh tears.

I help her to a standing position and hug her against me. I won't lie. No matter how much I wish her to be innocent, I can't ignore the evidence. But I'll be dissecting it with the largest magnifying glass I can find, and if there's any hint Claire's been set up, there'll be hell to pay.

Her wailing tugs at my heartstrings and pulls me away from murderous thoughts. I rub circles on her back, and eventually, the sobs turn to hiccups, sniffles, and then blessed peace.

"Shall we go?"

She nods.

I wrap my arm around her waist and lead her through the back of the station to the car park, avoiding the peanut gallery out front. The few officers we pass give me a respectful nod and avoid gawking at the dejected woman nestled under my arm.

I tuck her into the passenger seat and plug in her seat belt before climbing into the driver's side. She's docile, like a lamb, the entire time. It scares the hell out of me. It's not like her. If Claire was guilty, she'd be playing up to me. Wouldn't she? Trying to get me on her side. Instead, it's like she's given up.

My hands clench the steering wheel as I manoeuvre out of the car park, a headache thumping behind my eyes. Rain splatters onto the windscreen. Claire huddles against the door of my SUV, staring out the window. A deep ache settles in my chest at the pitiful sight.

The rain intensifies, and I flick the wipers to maximum speed. Focus on the wet road ahead. Numb my feelings to the woman next to me.

Do I believe Claire and fight for her? Or do I walk away?

With Sally, the answer had been easy. She was my wife. The mother of my child. Of course, I'd fought to save her from her addiction. I've only gone on two dates with Claire. We haven't even had sex yet. It should be easy to pull away. But it isn't.

Chapter Seventeen

Claire

I fumble with the door lock, tears blurring my vision. Jake said nothing on the trip to my house. The silence cut through me more than if he'd ranted and raved at me.

I'm beyond embarrassed. I want to curl up, just me and a bottle of wine, and shut out the world. Forget about everything. The drugs. Mr Green's disgust. Bulldog's smug smile. There's no way Jake's going to want anything to do with me now. He's obviously only helping me because he's a good guy and I'm a pathetic charity case.

His hand curls over mine, and he takes the key. "Let me."

He opens the door and guides me inside like I'm a child. Is that all I am to him? A stupid child?

"Thanks."

He grunts and shuts the door.

My breath hitches. I want to be alone, but I don't. "Aren't you going back to the station?"

"I'm finished for the day."

"Oh. Well …"

Why's he still here?

"How about we get you cleaned up? You'll feel better after a shower."

"You don't need to stay." I hate the way my voice sounds. All needy, like a toddler clawing at mummy's legs.

He squeezes my shoulder. "I want to."

His eyes are warm. Worried. And something else.

I shuffle down the hallway to my bedroom. He doesn't follow. A part of me wants him to. Wants him to strip off my clothes. My panties. Pound into me until the day feels like nothing more than a bad dream. But that's never going to happen now. He didn't say he believed me. He said he wanted to. There's an ocean between those two statements, and my breaking heart sinks to the bottom of it.

I shrug out of my jacket, black pants, and top and drape them over the end of the bed. They'll need a serious dry clean to remove the stench of jail. My underwear is next—scarlet lace bra and panties. Fitting colour for a fallen woman.

The shower perks me up a little, and I slip on a long sleeve maxi dress over a black silk panty set I bought at Victoria's Secret last year. The silk is soft and velvety. Comforting.

I head towards the tantalising aroma of onion and garlic and stop in the doorway, mesmerised by the sight of Jake standing at the stove, stirring a pot.

Pain slices through my chest. The scene is too domestic.

"What are you doing?"

He turns, a small smile on his face, the grim expression from earlier gone. "What does it look like?"

My stomach flips. Maybe he's not going to ditch me?

"Why are you cooking?"

"You need feeding." He points at the fridge. "I hope you don't mind me raiding your supplies. I'm making spaghetti bolognese."

Tears prick my eyes. He's too perfect. "You didn't have to."

He gives me a stern look.

I throw my hands up. "Okay, okay, you wanted to." My mouth waters. I haven't eaten since breakfast.

His smile broadens, and he returns his attention to the pot. "It won't be long now."

Silence is our companion again while we eat. It's not as awkward as in the car, but it's a world away from the banter we shared on our date a few days ago. Jake's gaze is warm when it rests on me. Drawing me closer. Giving me hope he'll believe in my innocence.

He cups my chin in his palm. "Do you want me to stay for a while? I could ring home and let my parents know I'll be late."

"No. I'll be fine. I'm a grown woman." I cross my fingers at the lie. I'll be a bucket of tears the moment he walks out the door. "You should get home to Oscar."

"You sure?"

"I'll be fine, Jake. I've got work in the morning …"

Wait. *Do I?* They can't fire me, can they? After all, it's supposed to be innocent before proven guilty and all that.

I scramble from the table and dig my phone out of my bag. Two texts. One from my boss, the other from the bulldog.

Bulldog: Your employment is terminated. Come to the office to return the car keys and sign the paperwork. If you're in jail, then nominate someone to come in on your behalf.

Ouch. Straight for the jugular.

The text from Liam is a little nicer.

The Boss: Claire, I'm sorry about this. Please bring a bag to collect your things.

I stare at the screen, not realising how hard I'm squeezing the phone in my hand until Jake prises it from me.

"May I?"

I nod.

He scrolls through the texts, his face hardening.

"I'll come with you."

"You don't have to."

"Yes, I do." His voice is all steel. "You need someone with you."

I'm numb. How will I get another job? My reference from Alpha Pharmaceuticals will be as helpful as used toilet paper. If I can't find work, I won't be able to afford my mortgage. I'll have to sell. I'll be homeless. And I'll end up living on the streets. Wearing the same pair of panties day in, day out. My parents will disown me. I'll have to turn to prostitution to eat. The room spins. Argh!

"Claire?"

I try to open my mouth, but it's too heavy to respond, my body a lump of lead. Three images of Jake flicker in front of me.

"Fuck!" Jake sweeps me up in his arms and carries me into the bedroom. That wakes up my sluggish limbs.

"What are you doing?" I squeak.

"Putting you to bed."

"Jake!" As much as I want to have sex with him, I don't want our first time to be like this. With me freshly bailed out of jail. Then again, who says I'm ever going to see him again? Will this be my only chance?

The vein at Jake's temple throbs, and his eyes turn a grey-blue. "Claire, you need sleep. Nothing more." He tucks me under the covers and pulls the blanket around my neck.

I sag into the mattress, uncertain whether I'm relieved or disappointed that he's such a gentleman.

He brushes a few stray hairs from my face. "I take it your company car is still at the office?"

"Yeah."

"Okay. I have to go home now, but shall I pick you up at nine tomorrow morning?"

I nod, blinking back tears. I can't face work on my own. And there's no way I can tell my parents. As for Jules, she's likely to go all mumma bear on my boss or Bulldog and deck them if she comes with me. The last thing I want on my conscience is Jules ending up with a record. Best to take Jake's help while he's still willing to give it because I can't see him sticking around if he doesn't believe in me.

Chapter Eighteen

Claire

I wake from a crazy dream where chocolate labradors were racing through my house, sniffing out bags of white powder and depositing them at Jake's feet. I love dogs and hope to adopt one in the future. But if I do, it'll be a very different breed.

An incessant thumping disturbs the quiet. Is Jake back? I check my phone. I've been asleep for a couple of hours.

A headache lingers behind my eyes from all the tears. I haul myself out of bed and run my fingers through my hair, then hurry down the hallway. It's dark outside, and when I open the door, there's no one there. I step onto the porch and immediately regret it. The breeze is chilly, and so is the expression on my mother's face.

"Mum?"

She rakes her gaze over me, lips puckered in disappointment. "What in God's name are you wearing?"

I smooth my palms down the fabric. "A maxi dress. It's comfortable."

She narrows her eyes. "That's no excuse for wearing black

underwear under a light-coloured dress. I can see everything."

Oh, God. She's unbelievable. "Come inside." I usher her into the house. Stupid outside lights. That's what I get for buying the highest wattage—burn your retinas—globes.

She walks in, back ramrod straight. "I'll make a pot of tea while you sort yourself out."

"Mum. I'm not going anywhere. It doesn't matter."

"Of course it matters. What if someone else had called on you? For goodness' sake, Claire, I thought I'd brought you up better than this."

"Fine. I'll change."

The back of my neck prickles as I storm down the hallway. Mum's right. Spending time in a jail cell has muddled my brain. I open the drawer and the granny pants she gave me for my birthday wink up at me. Ugly pants. They're bad luck. Or are they? If I hadn't been wearing them, I wouldn't have been distracted and I wouldn't have stepped onto the road. Jake and I would never have met. I'd never have known the firm touch of his hand, his drugging kisses, or the passion in his eyes.

But what's the point of tasting heaven only to have it torn away from you?

I stroke the fabric.

It's scratchy.

Suffocating.

Soul destroying.

A bit like my mother sometimes. Gah! She's picked the worst time to drop in. I shove the granny pants to the back of the drawer and pull out dusky pink panties with lace edges and a matching bra.

I return to the kitchen, bracing myself for another lecture. My mother's specialty.

She gives me a once-over and groans.

"What now?"

"I can see your bra strap."

Dammit, she's impossible. "It's not that bad."

She shakes her head and tsks me. "No wonder you haven't found yourself a nice man yet."

"Mum. Please." I really don't need this right now.

"Alright. I'll say no more about it."

She pushes a cup of tea in front of me. I take a sip. Mum means well. Under normal circumstances, she'd never find me in anything but meticulously coordinated clothes with matching panties and bra. Today's an exception, what with ending up in jail and getting fired.

Mum's eagle eyes zero in on Jake's business card pinned to the fridge with a small magnet. Wrinkles line her forehead, and her pupils become shadowy pools of worry.

"What's this?" She pulls the card off and waves it at me. "Are you in some kind of trouble?"

"No, no. Of course not." I cross my fingers. Lies.

She tilts her head. "Then what are you doing with a policeman's business card?"

I swallow. Crap. I can't tell her we're dating. She'll be planning our wedding when I may not even see Jake again after tomorrow. "He's a friend."

"Since when do you—" Her eyes widen, and her lips break into a smile so wide it brightens the entire room like a supernova. "Is this the nice officer who looked after you when you were nearly run over?"

My insides play a game of Twister at my mother's hopeful gaze. "He's just a friend, Mum."

"Piffle sticks." She shakes a finger. "You could never lie. Have you gone out with him?"

"Mum!"

"You have." She rubs her hands together, looking like a cross between a wicked witch and a fairy godmother.

"Two dates. That's all."

"But there'll be more?"

Damn, she should work with Jake. Even a seasoned detective would struggle to beat my mother's interrogation skills.

I sigh. "I'm not sure." The chances of Jake asking me out again are about as high as bulldog Joyce telling me she believes I'm innocent and Liam nominating me for salesperson of the year.

"Oh, don't be bashful. I'm sure he'll want to see you again. I had a good feeling when I talked to you the day he gave you a lift. There was a catch in your voice."

"That's because I was nearly hit by a car."

"A mother knows."

She leans across the bench and clasps my hands. "I knew when I bought those underpants for your birthday, things would look up."

"What?" My mouth drops open. It's pretty clear where my craziness comes from.

"I've seen the flimsy scraps of lace and silk you buy. A woman needs to cover the goods. All the fun is in unwrapping the present. If you leave it half exposed, your man's got nothing to anticipate."

The expression on Mum's face is as serious as it gets, unless she's at a funeral. Does she honestly think those horrid granny pants would appeal to men? How the hell was I ever conceived? Poor Dad. I bet he became an expert at unwrapping his gift as fast as possible. My mother has an attractive figure hidden underneath the loose clothes she wears, so it would have been worth it once he got past the granny underwear.

Argh! My eyes. My brain. I do not need thoughts, let alone mental pictures, of my parents in any state of undress, or worse … having sex. I have enough issues to keep a psychologist busy for years without adding to them.

Mum places Jake's business card back onto the fridge. "I'd better get going. I only dropped in because I was nearby and couldn't wait to tell you the news. Your father and I are having a big bash to celebrate our thirty-fifth wedding anniversary."

"That's wonderful." I do my best to sound happy for her, but it's hard when I have no idea if I'll be free or locked up. "It's only a couple of months away. Is that enough time to get organised?"

"Yes. Plenty. We've just booked a beautiful Spanish-style hacienda in the Hills district. It'll be perfect."

"Is there anything I can do to help?"

Her eyes narrow into a cunning expression I know too well. It's the one she gives when she extracts promises out of me. Promises I don't want to make, like wearing those ugly granny pants.

"You can bring the nice policeman along as your plus one."

"Mum."

"That's all this old lady wants."

"Please." I roll my eyes. "You're only fifty-nine."

"I'll be old soon enough, and there are still no grandchildren to comfort me in my twilight years."

Blood rushes to my head. I've lost count of how many times we've had this conversation. She should badger Alex. She's the one who's married. But she's also the one with the high-powered job. It's like Mum's resigned herself to me being a disappointment career-wise and thinks all I'm good for is popping out babies.

She must realise I'm about ready to blow because she pecks me on the cheek. "Let me know how things go with your police officer."

I close the door behind her and stomp my feet like a toddler. She makes me so mad. This is why I couldn't go to her and Dad when I was arrested. She may not say it outright, but she thinks I'm a failure. They both do. I need to get these drug charges dropped before they find out. I'll never be able to look them, or my sister, in the eye again if I'm convicted.

Chapter Nineteen

Claire

M y mind is a swirl of debris swept up in a tornado as I climb out of Jake's SUV. He clasps my hand and guides me into Alpha Pharmaceuticals, his warmth calming my shot nerves. Sonya, the receptionist, flips bleached hair off her face, thrusts out her boobs, and gives Jake a bat of false eyelashes.

"Claire's here to collect her things." Jake doesn't muck around, his tone a warning—*don't mess with me.*

Not that Sonya gets it. She giggles and flutters those eyelashes again. "I'll call HR." She picks up the phone and whispers, "Claire Thompson's here." She murmurs something I don't catch before hanging up. "Ms Massey said to wait. She'll be with you shortly." She turns her greedy gaze onto Jake. "Is there anything I can get you?"

Jake gives Sonya an icy glare to rival the Antarctic pole. "No, thank you."

Her expression drops, and she purses her lips. "Fine."

Ha. Take that, bitch.

While Jake hasn't said he believes me, I'm grateful he

offered to be here today. I feel less alone. Less like a hopeless loser. Less like a criminal out on bail.

Joyce—Bulldog—Massey keeps us waiting fifteen minutes before she swaggers through the door in tight black slacks and an oversized multicoloured shirt. I choke back a giggle. The granny pants my mum gave me would suit Joyce.

"I'm glad to see you haven't lost your sense of humour, Ms Thompson."

Joyce is no different to Sonya, her pupils dilating as she regards Jake like a prize piece of beef.

"Good morning." She falls short of batting her eyelashes. "Mr …"

"Detective Inspector Matthews," responds Jake.

"Oh." Joyce's hand flies to her chest. "Sorry to disturb you, Inspector. We would have waited to sort out Claire's termination papers if we'd known she was still in jail."

Liar. That's not what she said in her text.

Jake glares at her like she's the scummiest criminal he's ever laid eyes on. His expression is so scary I could kiss him.

"Claire was released yesterday afternoon. I'm here as a friend." His voice is low and gravelly.

"I see."

Joyce's gaze flits between me and Jake faster than a butterfly's wings.

His eyebrow quirks up. "I believe there's some paperwork for Claire to sign?"

"Yes, there is." She glares at me, a scowl forming on her lips. "This way."

We follow her down the corridor.

Ashley whisper–yells, "Claire!"

He bolts from his chair, his gaze darting between me and Jake like he can't decide which one of us to hug. Jake makes the decision for him by wrapping his arm around my waist and tucking me into his side.

"Are you okay?" asks Ashley.

My cheeks burn as I sense the eyes of the entire office boring down on me. "Yeah, I'm fine." I'm not, but what else do I say?

"What's going on out here?" Liam staggers from his office. He looks worse than I feel. The spiderweb thing from yesterday is still staining his eyes, and the shadows have travelled halfway down his face. He nods his head at me. "Claire."

"Liam." I squeeze my fingers into fists. I won't cry.

Jake stiffens. "I don't believe we've met."

Liam's eyes widen as he takes in Jake's towering form. "No. I'm Liam Andrews. Claire's boss." He sticks out his hand. "That is … I was."

"And I'm Detective Inspector Matthews."

Jake ignores Liam's hand. Instead, he stares at him. Like, full-on stares the way a dog does before it lunges without warning and rips out your throat.

Liam swallows and takes a step back. I don't blame him. I would too if Jake looked at me like that.

"I'm here to support Claire," says Jake with a deep, menacing voice. "To make sure she's treated fairly."

Liam pulls at his collar and mumbles something about that being a good thing.

Jake turns to Joyce. "Is your CEO, Ben Green, in?"

"Yes." The lines between her eyes deepen. "I believe so."

"Excellent. I'd like to speak with him." Jake gestures down the corridor. "Shall we go?"

Joyce bites her lip. Anyone else and she'd be giving them a serve for ordering her around, but Jake has an air of authority that demands submission. "Of course, Inspector."

"Collect your things, Claire." Jake squeezes my hand. "I'll be back shortly."

"Okay." What the hell is he doing?

Liam studies me as if I'm some mythical creature he can't figure out. "I'm sorry it ended like this."

I blink away tears. "Thank you."

He gives me an awkward smile and returns to his office.

I slide into my seat for the last time. My laptop and screen are gone. Tears prick my eyes. I will be too, shortly.

Ashley whispers in my ear. A proper whisper this time. "So, is your boyfriend working on the case?"

I shake my head. "He's not my boyfriend. He just feels sorry for me."

"Riiiight." He fists his hands and pumps them in and out. "And by sorry, you mean he fucked you senseless last night?"

"Ashley!" I glance around to see if anyone heard, but there are no heads peering over the other cubicles.

He grins and leans back in his chair. Sips his coffee. "He's as hot as you said he was."

"Well, it's not doing me any good."

"Claire, please don't worry." Ashley sets his cup on the desk and squeezes my forearm. "This whole arrest thing is ridiculous. No way those charges will stick. I'm sure it'll all be cleared up in a few days. Then you can demand compensation from the company and find a better job elsewhere."

I wish it was that easy, but having my rights read to me and being marched into the police station has done a number on my confidence. I turn to my desk drawer. The top one is partially open. Dylan didn't close it after finding the drugs yesterday. My cosmetic bag is missing. He took that as 'evidence'.

I pluck a lone tube of lip balm from the drawer. "Jake tucked me into bed last night like I was five years old."

"Really?" Ashley's eyebrows climb his forehead. "Maybe I have a shot with him."

I slap his arm. "He's not gay!"

"Are you sure?"

"Yes." At least I think so. He seemed to be into the kisses we shared on our two dates. "He's just not real keen on making out with an alleged drug trafficker."

Ashley's smile drops to a frown. "You're not a dealer."

I slam the top drawer shut. "I know. But how do I explain the plastic bag?"

"I don't know. Someone could have planted it there."

"But who?" I lift my head to the ceiling as if the answer might be there. A fancy new smoke detector winks at me, but nothing else.

"I'd lay money on Liam." Ashley snorts. "Then again, the way old Bulldog's been on your case, I wouldn't put it past her either. She has a master key to all the locks."

I've never had someone openly loathe me as much as Joyce does. Still …

"Joyce is such a stickler for the rules. I can't imagine it being her."

I tear the company vision statement off the partition wall, rip it into tiny pieces, and throw them into the bin. It's a childish act of defiance, but it feels good. "I don't know what to think of Liam. He's been weird ever since his wife left him. But to set me up? That's a horrid thing to do."

Ashley glances around the office, then leans closer. "He's got all the hallmarks of an addict, Claire."

"What? I thought he just has allergies."

Ashley pats the back of my hand, a lopsided grin on his face. "Ah, you innocent."

I bat him away. "I'm not a child."

He rakes his gaze over me. "I can see that. So, can your hot detective. If I liked women, you'd be—"

"Very funny." I cross my arms and glare at him. He chuckles and downs the rest of his coffee.

Could it be Liam? He doesn't have a key to my drawer, so he'd have to steal it from Joyce.

Damn it. I don't know what to think anymore.

I slump my elbows on the desk, tears welling up in my eyes. "I won't miss this place, but I'll miss you."

"I'm gonna miss you too." Ashley's voice drops to a husky whisper, and he rubs his eyes.

I slide my photos into a small bag, along with the expensive pen my parents gave me at graduation and a coffee cup from Jules with *Kiss My Arse* scrawled across it.

"What about this pic?" Ashley points to a photo of Sydney Harbour at dawn pinned to the partition between our desks. It's one of the first panoramas I took with my SLR.

"Nah. You keep it. A present from me." I zip up the bag. "That's it."

Five years of my life reduced to one small gym bag.

Jake's timing is impeccable. He strides towards me, Joyce on his heels, dabbing at her nose with a hanky. She's as bad as Liam. The company needs to do something about the poor-quality air-conditioning. Or could Ashley be right? Is it more than allergies? Are they into drugs together?

Jake takes my bag. "Let's go."

My mouth drops. "But don't I have paperwork to sign?"

"We can sort that out later, Claire." Joyce's right eye twitches. "Go home and rest. It's been a terrible ordeal for you."

If my eyes weren't connected to their sockets, I'm sure they'd be rolling around on the floor about now. Joyce has turned from rabid bulldog to fuzzy golden retriever. I glance at Jake, but he gives nothing away, his face like stone.

"Okay. Ah, thanks, Joyce." I hug Ashley. "Bye, buddy."

"Bye to you too. And please don't stress. I'm sure it'll work out." He winks, but he isn't looking at me. His gaze is trained on Jake.

I roll my eyes and give him a playful shove, even though my insides are tied in knots. His cheekiness is one of the few things I'm going to miss about Alpha Pharmaceuticals.

Chapter Twenty

Jake

My police radar went off the moment I met Claire's boss and HR manager and has kept up its annoying ding ever since. Ben Green conceded Claire was unlikely to have anything to do with the missing chemicals and agreed to hold off on her termination until an investigation is completed into the drugs found in her drawer. Thank fuck. I pull into Claire's driveway and set the car in park. The streets are empty, but the curtains of a neighbour's house stir. No secrets in this little suburb.

Claire's eyes tear up as she grabs the door handle. Damn. There's nothing I want more than to drag her into my arms, but I don't trust myself to let go if I do.

"Sorry, but I have to get to work." I clasp her hand and kiss her fingers. "I'll call you at lunchtime."

"Okay. Thanks for going with me." Her voice is small, like a baby bird.

My protective instincts hammer at me to stay, but I have a meeting with the squad commander that I can't be late for.

I let her hand slip from mine. "Anytime."

With tears sliding down her face, she bolts out of the car and up her driveway.

Fluffy clouds drift across the sky. I clench the steering wheel, my knuckles turning the same shade. The colour of cocaine. Ice. Heroin. All the drugs that destroy young lives. My gut tightens as I reverse and head for the station, dialling Greg's number on my hands-free.

"Jake, what's up?"

"I need a favour." He leaves me hanging with nothing but the sound of the engine in my ears. "Greg?"

"Please don't tell me it's something illegal for your girl."

"Of course not, you idiot." I grit my teeth. Now is not the time for his brand of humour. "And I've told you before, you're not funny when you say shit like that. Not ever."

"Okay, okay. No need to get your knickers in a twist." He sniggers. "What can I do for you?"

"Find out if the fingerprints team has gone over the bag of coke that was in Claire's drawer."

"That's hardly a favour." He grunts. "They'll be doing that as a matter of course."

"True." The traffic lights change from green to orange, and I hit the accelerator. "But I want the results the moment they're available."

"Your turn to spit it out, Jake. I know you're chewing on something."

I sigh. This is why we work well together. "I want to know everything there is to know about Claire's boss, Liam Andrews, and her HR manager, Joyce Massey."

"I see." His voice climbs an octave. "No problem. Catch you when you get in."

"Sir," I say.

"What?"

"You forgot to call me sir." I press my lips tight to hold back a chuckle.

"Yes, *sir*," he says, followed by a muttered, "Fucker," and the line goes dead.

I smirk. He's not the only one who can give out shit. The diversion eases the knot that's been wrapping itself around my internal organs all morning. I'd bet my badge Claire's innocent and I'm going to prove it.

§**.**

When I return to the station, I find Greg sitting on my desk with a shit-eating grin that tells me I'll like whatever he's got to say.

"Hey, boss."

"What happened to fucker?"

He grins. "You heard that?"

"You know I did."

"It's an endearment." He shrugs. "Like 'boss'."

"Sure, it is." I roll my eyes and shut the door. "Get off my desk."

He slides off the table. "Fingerprints have dusted the bag."

"And?" My muscles tense like I'm about to chase down a criminal.

"They got one good print." He sticks up his right thumb. "A thumbprint."

"For fuck's sake." I glare at him. "Are you going to get to the point or keep carrying on like we're in some second-rate crime show?"

He winks. "You're cute when you're riled up."

I lunge at him.

"Okay, okay." He chuckles and jumps back. The fucker. "The print isn't Claire's."

Air rushes out of my lungs, and I sink into my chair.

Not Claire's.

Thank fuck.

Although it doesn't mean she's in the clear. It could belong to the source or a friend.

I look at my phone. There's nothing from Claire, not that she said she'd ring. But I can't help worrying about her. It doesn't sit well that she's all alone after having to collect her belongings from her workplace. "Have they run a match?"

"Of course." Greg slides into the chair across from the desk. "Nothing came up, but given the size of the print, the consensus is it most likely belongs to a man."

"And the cabinet? Did they find the same print there?"

"Sorry, Jake." He shakes his head. "Those all matched with Claire, but that's to be expected, given she uses it every day. And if the HR manager or her boss planted the drugs, they'd have to be pretty stupid not to wear gloves."

"You're right." But it would have made Claire's defence a lot stronger if a different print was found on her drawer. "Can we get fingerprints from all the staff at Alpha Pharmaceuticals?"

"Working on it." Greg taps his leg. "We need to tread carefully. Internal Affairs would have a field day if they thought we were giving Claire special treatment because of her relationship with you. Not to mention, Commander Gordon would go ape-shit."

I flop back in my chair and try to relax my muscles. "That won't be a problem. I know how to keep my personal and work lives separate."

The quirk of Greg's eyebrow says he doesn't believe me. "Good. Because it wouldn't go down well if it became known you were bonking her."

My jaw clenches. I should have seen this coming. "Bonking? Really?"

"What do you want me to say?" He smirks. "Fucking? Shagging? Doing the nasty?"

"Sometimes you're such a child."

He laughs. "Since no funny business has been going on

beneath the sheets or against any hard surfaces, it'll make it easier for you to prove your professionalism."

How the hell can he know that? "What makes you think I haven't …" I shrug. "You know."

"And you call me juvenile." Greg chuckles. "You can't even say the word."

He sticks his forefinger in the air. "One, you're a 'wait for the third date' kind of guy before making any moves on a woman."

I jerk forward. "Hold on there—"

"Two." He lifts his middle finger. "You'd tell your best mate." He points at his chest. "That's me. And thirdly"—he waves his hand at me—"it's clear you haven't had sex yet because you're still walking around with a giant stick up your arse."

My teeth hurt from clenching them too hard. "Tell me again why we're friends?"

"I keep you grounded, Inspector." He crosses his arms and gives me a smug look. "Can't have you slapping too many tickets on yourself."

"Yeah, yeah." I jab my finger towards the door. "Get out."

"Sure thing. I'm going … *sir*."

I bolt out of my seat to clip him around the head, but he clasps my forearm, his brown eyes glittering. "Don't worry, Jake. If someone's set Claire up, we'll catch them."

"That's the thing." A theory's been doing the rounds of my brain for the last couple of hours. Dare I put it into words? I swallow to moisten my mouth. "What if this isn't about Claire?"

Greg lets go of my arm and rocks back on his heels. "What do you mean?"

I perch on the edge of my desk. "The first woman I take out in years is caught with drugs soon after. Coincidence?"

Greg stills, and I can almost see the cogs of his brain clicking over. "It's a long bow."

"True. But we know Leadbetter's got his fingers in meth as well as coke." It's a crazy idea, but not outside the realms of possibility. If there's one thing I've learnt in this job, it's to weigh up all the evidence, no matter how tenuous.

Greg shakes his head. "If it's true, it means Leadbetter's keeping tabs on you."

"Yep."

"Jesus, Jake. If that's the case, you need to be extra careful."

"I'd never forgive myself if Claire got hurt because of me." A familiar sharp blade pierces my chest as I pick up the photo on my desk. "I still can't forgive myself for what happened to Sally."

"That wasn't your fault."

"I know. But it doesn't stop me wishing I'd been more vigilant." I clamp down on my molars. At this rate, I'll need false teeth before my next birthday. "I need to get back to work. Thanks for telling me about the fingerprint."

Greg closes the distance between us and lays his hands on my shoulders. "Not. Your. Fault."

He leaves without saying another word, closing the door behind him with a gentle click.

I return to my chair and open Leadbetter's file. Not my fault. He's right, but it doesn't stop the guilt from squeezing my heart. I'm a cop. I'm trained to see through lies, and yet I still failed Sally. The only way to protect my family is to cut off the source and put scum bags like Leadbetter behind bars.

I pick up the phone, my gut a swirling cauldron of fear, doubt, anger. "Hey, Dad."

"Jake. Is everything alright?"

I smile at my father's tone. Straight into police mode, like he never left. He always could smell blood in the water long before it appeared.

"It might be nothing, but I don't want to take any chances. Not with Oscar. Or you and Mum."

"You want extra security?"

"Nah, I think we have enough." There are cameras stationed around our house. An alarm is set up to ring the station if triggered. It seemed overkill when I had them installed, but I've learnt to take nothing for granted. "Just be extra vigilant."

"Always, son." His voice lowers. "We'll keep a close watch on Oscar. Don't you worry."

I hang up, the churning in my stomach settling. Dad was a formidable cop in his time. And his mind and body are still in the same great shape as the day he retired. He'll pick up on anything out of place.

As for Claire, I scroll through my contacts and pull up the security company I use for home. They'll be able to suggest a few measures to keep Claire safe without scaring her. I'm not even going to consider staying away. She'd assume I'd abandoned her. I can't do that to her. I can't do that to myself.

Chapter Twenty-One

Claire

"I can't believe Alpha Pharmaceuticals sacked me." The tissue in my hand crumbles. "What happened to innocent before proven guilty?"

"They're arseholes," says Jules, making herself comfortable on the couch. "They don't deserve you."

I sip my tea and pull another tissue from the box. "After Jake talked with Mr Green …" I bite the inside of my cheek to stop the tears from flowing. "I thought they'd wait until the police finished their investigation."

Jules hands me a chocolate. "So, what did Jake say?"

I pop the Lindt ball into my mouth, although its deliciousness is wasted on me at the moment, and duck my head. "I haven't told him yet."

Jules taps my chin, not letting me hide. "Why not?"

I squirm. "It's complicated."

Jules's lips flatten. "Did he dump you?"

"No, but …"

Damn it. How do I explain to her that I don't want to be Jake's charity case?

Jules snatches my mobile off the coffee table.

I scramble to grab it off her. "Hey, give that back."

"Nope."

She pushes me away and unlocks my phone. I really need to put a different security code than 0000 on it. I slump into the lounge. There's no stopping her when her mind's made up.

"Three missed calls?" Jules looks up, her brows knitted together. "I don't understand. Why haven't you rung him back?"

I stare at the rug under the coffee table. It's an abstract print I bought from IKEA a couple of years ago. Bright and cheerful. Nothing like my life.

"He doesn't believe me," I whisper, choking on the words.

"What?"

"He said he *wants* to believe I'm innocent. Not that he does." I gnaw at my bottom lip. It would be so easy to accept whatever crumbs Jake wants to throw my way, but I'm tired of men not doing the right thing by me. "I think I deserve more than that."

Jules hands me the phone. "Yes, you do." She wraps her arm around my shoulders and gives me a hug. "I'm so sorry, honey."

I shove another chocolate into my mouth to erase the bitter taste of disappointment. When Granny died, Mum and I ate an entire box of chocolates together. It's been my go-to ever since when life sucks. Which is all too often. But today, the yummy goodness does nothing to brighten my mood.

Jules' eyes light up. "We could always go out. Get trashed."

I shake my head. That's Jules' answer when things get tough. "As tempting as it is, I don't want the inevitable hangover that will go with it. Or to add to my reputation as a druggie."

Jules slaps my arm. "You're not a druggie!"

"Yeah, try telling that to my old boss, Bulldog Joyce, and …" I squeeze my eyes shut. "Jake."

"Didn't you just say you deserve better?" She passes me a tissue. "He's not worth any more of your time. Or tears."

"Thanks for taking the afternoon off, Jules." I dab my eyes. "I needed a friend."

"That's what besties are for." She pats me on the shoulder. "Besides, I'm worried. Who would want to set you up? And why?"

"I don't know." I wring my hands out. "It's been doing my head in. I get on okay with most people. Except Joyce. She's hated me from day one."

"Mmm. And she and your boss both had access to the drug test you did."

"Yep. And Joyce seemed thrilled I'd been caught. But why? Hating me isn't a reason."

"Arseholes don't need one."

I unwrap another chocolate ball. "As much as she loathes me, I can't imagine Joyce being into drugs or being that malicious."

"Have you told your parents?"

"God, no." I jerk in the chair, sending chocolates and wrappers flying. "I'd get a triple serving of 'I told you so'." Dad would lecture me on all the reasons I should have studied law instead of following my own path. He was wrong. I would have been like a pile of dog poop next to the shining gold star of my sister. But he's right about sales. It was the wrong choice for me. Not that I'll ever admit it to him.

"Claire." Jules gives me the no-nonsense *Mum-look* she gives her daughter. "I bet your dad could get to the bottom of it."

"No." No way I'm exposing myself to his censure. "I'll find my own lawyer."

"Why wouldn't you ask him for help?"

I sigh. "Because I don't want him to see me as a failure."

Jules grabs my shoulders and shakes. "This isn't your fault."

I try to pull away, but she's got quite a grip on her. "I know. But—"

"Claire, these are serious charges." She releases me. "You're going to need good legal representation."

"I'll find someone." I rub my arms. "Can we not talk about this anymore?"

Jules closes her eyes. Great. Now I've disappointed my best friend. She opens them again, her irises a warm brown, just like the chocolate. "Of course. I'm sorry if I was a bit rough."

"Don't be." I wave her away. "You're just looking out for me."

I screw up the tissue and throw it with the collection growing on the floor—a testament to my misery. "You don't need to stay. I'm going to crank the music up and clean. I'll be fine."

Jules cocks her head. "You sure? We could always watch a movie?"

"Nah. I don't think I can handle watching Bridget Jones or Elizabeth Bennet get their happy endings." The usual essential viewing for broken hearts. "Please. Go home and take care of your house." I give her a smirk. "It needs it."

Jules huffs and crosses her arms. "We can't all have floors we can eat off. Just wait 'til you've got kids."

Jules' harsh tone catches me by surprise. "But you love being a mum."

"I do. But it's hard work." Jules' lips purse. "So's marriage."

Whoa. Mick might be a workaholic and a little judgy about our drinking, but he worships the ground Jules walks on. "Is everything okay?"

"It's nothing." Jules jumps to her feet. "I'll leave you for now. But you should reconsider asking your dad for help."

"I'll think about it." I push off the lounge and kiss her cheek. As soon as I get myself sorted, I'll dig deeper into what's troubling her. "Thanks again for coming over."

As much as I hate admitting it, Jules is right. I need a competent lawyer and fast. But there's no way I can call my father. There is one person who could help. I pull out my phone and scroll through my contacts. Should I?

Damn it. I can't sit here and do nothing. As annoying as my perfect sister is, she's damned good at what she does. I tap on her number.

"Hello." Alex greets me on the first ring. Her tone makes me feel like I'm five years old and she's reprimanding me for touching her notebooks.

She seems distracted. I'm tempted to hang up, but she'll know it's me from the caller ID on her phone. "Ah … how are you?"

I should have thought this through a bit more. How do I ask her for a referral without incriminating myself?

"I'm about to walk into a meeting. What do you want?"

Ouch. She can be so abrupt at times. "It doesn't matter. I'll talk to you later."

"Hold on." I hear a mumble, silence, and then she's back on the line. "What's going on? You hardly ever call."

Her tone softens and tears prick at my eyes. We may not have much to do with each other anymore, but there's still the unspoken sister code.

Alex isn't a criminal lawyer like Dad, but she's got connec-tions. "Can you keep a secret?"

"Claire." Her tone is all business, and I can imagine her rolling her eyes at me. "I'm a lawyer. I keep secrets for a living." There's a shuffling sound like she's walking. "Are you in some kind of trouble?"

"Sort of."

"Define sort of."

Crap. I chew on my bottom lip. Am I really going to tell her?

"Promise you won't say anything to Mum or Dad."

"Claire." Her voice gets louder. "Just spit it out."

I clench my fingers so hard that the nails bite into my palms. "Promise."

"Fine. I promise. Swear on the bible." She whispers, "I'll even pinky swear."

I smile even though tears are sliding down my face. That's the sister who always had my back growing up. In primary school, she threatened to sue a boy when he made fun of my braces. Yep, that's right, sue, not punch. Even then, she wanted to be a lawyer, just like Dad. Instead, I was preoccupied with drawing and painting—a waste of time, according to my father.

I take a deep breath and put it out there. "I've been arrested for drug possession and trafficking."

The line goes quiet. The chocolate in my stomach congeals. A roar like a jet engine sounds in my ears.

"Alex?"

"Are you guilty?"

My vision bleeds red. How dare she. "No. Of course not."

Calling her was a mistake. I should have just looked up lawyers on Google.

"Where are you now?"

"At home." I wipe my wet cheek. "Look, don't worry about it. I'm sorry I bothered you."

"Claire, stop. You're not bothering me. I really have to go to this meeting, but when I'm finished, I'll make some calls for you. In the meantime, no speaking to the police without a lawyer present."

"Okay." A bit late now.

Alex hangs up. A part of me is still in shock that I told her.

Then again, she's not a bad person. It's not her fault; I hate how perfect she is at everything she does.

I wipe the beads of sweat dotting my forehead. That's one item out of the way. Now for finding another job. My shoulders slump. There's no way I can face seek.com today. It's not like the problem is going anywhere. It'll be there tomorrow.

Then there's Jake.

As attracted as I am to him, I can't be with someone who thinks I'm a drug dealer. He's either hoping to catch me out with something incriminating or he's after sex. Either way, I have my pride. As I told Jules, I deserve better.

Chapter Twenty-Two

Jake

I arrive at Claire's house and kill the ignition. A dull ache lurks behind my eyes, thanks to the arseholes at Alpha Pharmaceuticals. They followed through with sacking Claire. So much for Ben Green's assurances he'd wait for due process to be carried out. He lasted three fucking days. Pressure from the board, out of his control, so he said. Claire must be devastated.

So why hasn't she returned my calls?

I rub my temples. I wish I had good news to take the sting out of her termination, but I don't. There's been no match for the fingerprint found on the plastic bag containing the drugs. The lab isn't even sure it's a man's print now. Idiots.

Dusk cloaks the street as clear blue skies give way to grey. An evening breeze stirs up the leaves on the ground. Another month and winter will be on us. Music blares from Claire's house, assaulting the peaceful neighbourhood. My heart pumps along with the pulsing base as I walk to the front door. Movement through the window catches my eye. I push the bushes aside and peer through the glass.

What the hell?

Claire jumps and gyrates to Halestorm's 'I Get Off' like she's partying in a nightclub. The only reason I even recognise the song is one of the junior constables is obsessed with the band and has a habit of polluting the lunchroom with it when she thinks I'm out. Still, I can appreciate the way Claire's body sways to the music. The black leggings she's wearing leave little to the imagination, as does the tiny crop top that strains against her perky breasts. I adjust my trousers. Now is not the time to get horny.

A rustling sound alerts me to company, and I swivel towards the road. A dog sniffs at the grass on the nature strip while an elderly man picks up the dog's business with a black plastic bag, his gaze firmly on me.

Shit.

I straighten and nod at the guy like I'm not a peeping Tom. His eyes widen, but he continues on his walk, sneaking backwards glances at me. It's times like this I wish I wore a uniform. Then again, knowing how these small neighbourhoods work, news of a cop scoping out Claire's house would spread faster than a glass of red wine on a white rug.

I knock.

No response. Not surprising, given the screeching music.

The main door is open. Only the screen door stands between Claire and me. I try the handle. It turns. Fuck. I need to talk to her about her personal security and installing an alarm system.

I enter the foyer and stand in the doorway to the living room. Claire's back is to me, her butt wiggling to the music and sending a rush of blood to my groin. So much for my fears that she's been sitting alone, drowning her sorrows. Dancing is a much more productive way to ease tension. Although I can think of an even better one. I cut that thought off before my dick gets hold of it.

Claire spins and stumbles, letting out a shriek. "Jake!" She glances past me. "How did you get in?"

"The door was unlocked."

"Damn." Her face, already red from dancing, deepens to a crimson hue. "I don't usually forget."

"I'm glad to hear that. You can never be too careful." Especially now. But I don't want to scare her.

She rushes to the phone on the glass coffee table, tripping over her feet. The music stops. Thank Christ.

I move further into the room. I'd expected weeping after Claire's termination. A broken woman. Not this vitality. I've underestimated her. Although the puffy, charcoal smudges under her eyes suggest she hasn't had much sleep, if any.

"Why didn't you tell me Alpha Pharmaceutical terminated you?" The question comes out more gruffly than I mean it to, but I'm pissed she hasn't returned my calls. I'm the one she turned to when she was arrested. I'm the one who supported her when she went to her office the next day.

"You've already done enough," she mumbles to the floor and edges away from me.

I rub the back of my neck. She's giving off enough chilly vibes to start her own ice works. I don't understand. "Have I done something wrong?"

"No." She shakes her head, but it's obvious she's lying.

I shove my hands into my pockets and rock on my heels. It feels like we're on opposite sides of a wide chasm. "The guys at the station are working hard on your case. We'll figure out who framed you."

Her head snaps up. "You believe I'm innocent now?"

Shit. Is that what's bothering her? "Yes. I do."

I extend my arms. She's so slim. I want to wrap myself around her and protect her from the entire world. "Can I give you a hug?"

She bites down on her bottom lip and backs away. "I'm all sweaty from dancing. Would you like a drink?"

"Sure." I shove my hands back into my pockets. Okay. No hugs. "That'd be great."

She slips on a jacket and leads me into the kitchen area. Through the window, an outdoor spotlight illuminates the huge backyard and large gum tree against the back fence.

I lean against the benchtop. Try to play it cool. "I have to admit, I'm surprised to see you so upbeat."

She gives me a wry smile as she pulls a bottle of mineral water and a box of chocolates from the fridge. "I considered drowning my sorrows in wine after signing the termination papers, but I cleaned the house instead."

"Good on you."

She shuts the fridge door with a bump of her hip. "Alpha never appreciated me. They can go to hell."

I smile. Such fire. Nothing like the woman I found in the cells on Monday. Still, I wish she'd called me.

I prop myself on a stool at the island bench. Several loose photos lay side by side on the shiny granite: a lush backyard, stunning marble bathroom and a bedroom kitted out in ivory and lace. It's too easy to imagine Claire laid out on the bed, her hair tousled from sex. A glazed look in her eyes that I put there. My dick twitches.

Fuck. I scrub my fingers through my hair. What am I thinking? I came to check on her. Not jump her bones. "These pictures look like they could be on the cover of a home magazine. Did you take them?"

"Yeah." Claire shrugs as if they're nothing and slides a chocolate into her mouth.

I pick up the photo of the backyard. It's safest considering my dick has moved to half-mast. Claire sighing over the chocolate doesn't help either.

"They're very professional shots."

"Thanks. If I don't get another job soon, I'll have to sell." She snatches the picture from me and stacks it with the others. "Plus, I need to pay you the bail money."

Christ no. I can afford it. "Don't worry about that. It's not like I won't get it back."

"I guess. Thank you." Blood wells up on her bottom lip where she's been worrying the hell out of it. "But I still have a mortgage to pay."

"I'm sure we'll get you cleared before you have to make any drastic decisions." I swallow the lump in my throat. I'm not sure at all. The evidence is circumstantial, but in my experience, it's possible a jury could convict her on it. "Have you got a lawyer?"

"Yeah." She slips the photos into an A4-sized envelope. "My sister put me onto someone."

My fingers clench and unclench at my sides. I thought she might be missing me, like I'm missing her. I thought she'd appreciate some moral support. So much for my deductive powers. I'm way off. "I'm glad you're doing okay. I guess I should go."

"Wait."

Claire grabs my wrist, her green eyes like molten gems. "Why don't you stay for dinner? We could order Chinese."

My dick interprets Claire's suggestion as 'let's have sex'. Fortunately, my brain is still engaged and sets the wayward appendage straight. Claire's mood is jumping around so much that she's giving me whiplash, which is perfectly understandable after what she's been through. She's vulnerable right now and needs a friend. Not a horny arse trying to get into her pants.

I clasp her arms and pull her against me. "I'm not having duck feet."

"What?" She looks up at me with a cheeky smile. It loosens something inside my chest. "Ew. Who orders duck's feet?"

I tap her nose. "It's a delicacy in China."

"Yeah, well, we're not in China." She pulls away, opens a

drawer and takes out a menu. "I'm sure the local Chinese doesn't offer duck's feet."

"You're probably right." I take the menu from her. No way I'm letting her pay. "Shall I ring them and place an order?"

Claire's smile reaches all the way inside my heart and squeezes. I'm in dangerous territory and wouldn't have it any other way.

"I'll have satay chicken and vegetarian spring rolls." She sashays around me, her fingers brushing my arse. She covers her mouth and yawns. "Give me ten minutes to freshen up."

I tap her backside. "Coming right up, my lady."

She struts down the hall, wiggling that delicious derriere, no doubt to torture me. Little minx.

I order the Chinese. Tiny flutters start up in my stomach. Does this count as a third date?

After fifteen minutes, there's no sign of Claire. I wander down the hallway. The shower's not running and her bedroom door is partially open.

I knock. "Claire, are you okay?"

Silence.

My gut twists. What if someone had entered her house while she was dancing in the lounge room and lay in wait? What if she's been attacked while I sat oblivious in the dining room?

I shove the door open and come to a standstill. Claire's curled on top of her bed, a fluffy white towel wrapped around her, wet golden strands sticking to her cheeks. My heart does a funny leap. She's out for the count. And after what she's been through this last week, I'm not surprised.

I brush hair off her cheek and kiss her forehead. "Claire, wake up."

She mumbles something incoherent and snuggles into the mattress. It's adorable. And it looks like I'll be eating alone.

I scoop Claire into my arms and pull the covers back. With one deft move, I remove her towel and tuck her under the sheet. I'm treated to a flash of creamy flesh, but I refuse to dwell on it. Perving on a sleeping woman is a line I'm not willing to cross, no matter how much my dick suggests otherwise. Claire settles against the pillow with a sigh, and my heart kicks again. I seem to be making a habit of putting her to bed. A habit I could get very used to.

Chapter Twenty-Three

Claire

It's been two weeks since Alpha Pharmaceuticals terminated me. Two weeks since Jake said he believes I'm innocent. Two long weeks of not seeing each other.

At first, I feared Jake was having second thoughts. After all, it can't be good for his image to be seen with an alleged drug trafficker. But he promised it was because of an unprecedented workload due to the case he's working on and backed it up by ringing me every night, spoiling me with flowers and responding to my sexy lunchtime texts. For a man who's never sexted before, he's getting the hang of it quite nicely.

Tonight, the wait is over, thank God, which is why I'm staring at my lingerie drawer. Nothing feels right for our date tonight. Date number three.

My phone dings.

Jake: Sorry, Claire, but the commander has called a meeting. Not sure how long I'll be. You okay with takeaway?

Damn. That man works too hard. He needs something to look forward to.

I slip off my dressing gown, pull on a skimpy rose bra and snap a photo. This should perk him up.

Me: Will this help ur meeting go faster?

I hit send.

The cursor blinks.

And blinks.

Crap. Have I gone too far this time?

Jake: What have I told you about the dangers of sending revealing photos?

I shake my head. He's so sexy when he gets all bossy.

Me: I'm a naughty girl and need to be punished?

I include a handcuffs emoji, press send and wait.

And wait.

He responds with a hand. My knees buckle. Oh my! Is he planning on spanking me?

I drop the phone and return to the dilemma of what panties to wear, my body thrumming with anticipation.

A cheeky, rose bikini pant to go with the bra I teased him with? A sultry, red silk thong and matching balconette bra? Or virginal, white lace boyleg and no bra?

What would Jake like?

Stupid question. Jake's a man. All he cares about is what's underneath the panties. I make my decision and slide a burnt-orange bamboo-wool shift dress over my head. It's so light against my skin it's like wearing nothing. A squirt of perfume, a swipe of lip gloss, and I'm ready. Although, it seems pointless to coat my lips since I'm planning on Jake kissing it off soon.

The lip gloss is long gone by the time Jake struts up the driveway, plastic containers in one hand, a bunch of roses in the other. A flood of moisture pools between my thighs. Police uniforms are hot, but there's something about Jake in a suit that has my knees buckling. Or more likely, the man beneath the suit. Maybe we should skip dinner and go straight to the part where he strips off my dress, backs me up against the wall and pumps into me while he's still clothed?

Jake reaches the doorstep, twinkling blue eyes sending a flush of heat through me that chases away the chill of the evening breeze.

"Hey, Claire." He pecks me on the cheek, lingering one heartbeat. Two.

"Hi," I reply, my voice breathless.

He hands me the bouquet. "For you."

"Thanks." More warmth passes through me, and tears prick my eyes. No one's ever given me flowers before.

The spicy aroma of Thai curry hits my empty stomach. "I guess we should eat while it's still hot."

After all, I'll need the energy for what I've got in mind tonight.

He answers with a smouldering expression that scorches my nether regions. It seems I'm not the only one affected by our long-distance foreplay. His lips press against mine, coaxing them apart. I sigh into his mouth as our tongues entwine. A tingle runs down my spine and deep inside my core.

Jake breaks the kiss and runs his free hand along my arm. "You're cold."

No, I'm burning up. I shut the door while Jake shrugs off his coat. I swear drool almost slips from my mouth as I admire the ripple of his shirt across his chest and abs. He gives me a wink. I toss my head at him as if I'm not quivering with anticipation and retreat to the kitchen with the flowers and food.

We settle ourselves at the dining table. Jake pours two glasses of wine while I open up the containers. Coriander and chilli waft from the dishes, sending my tastebuds into overdrive.

He circles my wrist. "Wait."

Dark, brooding eyes imprison mine. I'm not that hungry after all. Dessert is looking more and more enticing.

He raises his glass. "To you, Claire—a strong, beautiful, sexy woman."

My heart flutters. A girl could get used to this sort of attention. I raise my glass, fingers trembling. "And to you, Inspector Matthews, a very naughty, handsome cop."

His lips curl into a delicious smirk. "You've seen nothing yet, babe."

I gulp my wine. The promise in his eyes is sinful. Decadent. It takes all my willpower to stop myself from straddling him. But I know he wants to do this right. Dinner first. Then sex. I hope. So, I dive into the dishes, scooping several servings onto my plate. Jake does the same.

It feels right sitting together like this. Like we've been a couple for years, not one month.

"So, how's your big case going?" I ask between mouthfuls.

"Slow."

I tap the table to get his attention. He glances up from his food, his expression guarded.

"That doesn't tell me anything."

"I can't talk about it, Claire." Jake puts his fork down and cups my cheek. "And even if I could, I wouldn't want to. It's nice to relax with you and forget everything for a while."

"Thanks." Heat creeps along my collarbone. He's doing it again. Making me feel special in a way I've never felt before.

"We're also working on your case." His thumb rubs along my jaw. "But again, I can't say anything."

We eat in silence, except for the chewing that sounds like a Great Dane tucking into his dinner after being starved for several days. I wish I could say the noise is coming from Jake, but it's not.

I attempt to slow down. Close my mouth. Eat like a lady. But even the thought of my mother's disappointment, if she saw me now, can't stop the small sighs of appreciation falling from my lips.

"This is soooo good, Jake. Thank you."

"The pleasure is all mine." He grins. "I love watching you eat, Claire."

He reaches across and wipes my cheek. "You have a bit of sauce there."

"Oh. Thanks."

Jake's finger stops midway to my mouth, his blue eyes a hazy swirl.

I drop my fork. "I'm full."

"You sure?"

"Yeah." I smooth my hands on the front of my dress; pray I've read all the signs right. "I'm hungry for something else right now."

His gaze dips to my breasts. "Me too."

My thighs squeeze together at his husky voice. I pull away, needing a moment. It's been too long since I last had sex. I'm scared I'll mess it up.

"Claire, there's no pressure."

He clasps my hand. "If you're not ready, we can take it slow. Nothing needs to happen tonight if you don't want it to."

Slow? I rub my thumb along the top of his hand. That's the last thing I want.

"No. I'm okay. I wouldn't have said I'm hungry for … you know."

Geez, now I decide to be coy? What a loser.

"I'm scared I'm not good enough for you," I blurt out.

Jake's brow furrows, and he tilts his head like he's trying to figure me out. "Hey, c'mon." He squeezes my hand. "Where's this coming from?"

"You're a cop. And not just any cop, but a detective inspector." Warmth creeps up my neck and along my cheeks.

Me and my big mouth. Why do I have to admit my insecurities? Why can't I accept he likes me? Wants me?

"Yeah. I'm also a grumpy pain in the arse." He chuckles. "Or so Greg reminds me every other day."

A giggle bubbles up my throat, the doubts slinking away. Jake's so easy to talk to. Even easier to look at. And he makes me wetter than any other guy I've ever gone out with. I wriggle in my seat. I should have worn the boyleg panties. They would have given the most protection. I'll soak through my dress at this rate.

Still, I need a moment to gather my courage, so I scrape my chair back and pull my hand from Jake's grasp. "Would you like some coffee?"

His face drops for a moment, and then his smile returns. "Sure."

Jake stacks the plates while I retreat to the kitchen and prepare the coffee. I don't know why I'm playing hard to get. I want to have sex with him. And that's the problem. I like him. Too much. I don't think I could handle a broken heart to go along with my tattered career.

When I enter the living room with a coffee for Jake and a hot chocolate for myself, Jake is kneeling on the floor, flicking through my CD collection.

"You've got quite a range here, Claire."

"Yeah. I like to think I'm well rounded."

"I must admit, I feared we'd have no music in common." He picks up a CD. "And yet you've got Tab Benoit. I wouldn't have taken you for a blues girl."

"What can I say? I like different tunes for different moods."

"What song would you pick for now?"

"That's easy." A quick scroll through my phone and I select Chris Isaak's 'Wicked Game' on Spotify.

Jake's eyes widen when the music croons out through the Bluetooth speakers positioned around the room.

"CDs are old technology, Jake." I smirk. "Just like—"

"Ah, ah. I'll show you old, young lady." He crooks a finger, his lips curling into a deliciously wicked grin.

I step forward and stand in front of him, my body trembling with anticipation. He's still on his knees, his face level with my crotch. His fingers skim the bottom of my dress. I close my eyes, hiding from the searing intensity of his gaze.

He falls to his knees. "Claire, look at me."

My eyes snap open.

His hand slips under the hem. It's warm against my skin. Firm. Strong. And I never want it to stop touching me.

"Do you want me to keep going?"

I groan. "I'll die if you don't."

He grunts. "Me too."

His fingers continue their journey up my leg, a slow, sinfully torturous meander like they've got all night to reach their destination. The dress slides with his hand until Jake reaches the spot I've been longing for him to touch.

Chapter Twenty-Four

Jake

I choke when my fingers brush against feathery softness. "No panties?"

Claire grins down at me. "I couldn't decide what to wear."

Moisture pools onto my middle finger as it glides through her cleft. The pressure in my pants is all-consuming. I have to taste her. I slide her dress up further, revealing delicate pink lips peeking through silky golden hair.

Claire worries her bottom lip with her teeth; it's a delectable mix of nervousness and lust. I hold eye contact as I inhale her musky scent and flick my tongue along her seam. She arches her crotch into my face, her head tilting back.

"Look at me," I growl, fingers digging into her arse.

"God, Jake." Her eyes glaze over with desire. "It feels so good."

"It's going to feel a lot better, babe. I promise."

I lick her again, edge my way between the soft folds and tap her clit. She groans and my tenuous control snaps. I bury my tongue inside her and lap at the sweet juices.

Claire grabs my head and holds me in place, enveloping

me in her musky scent. It's intoxicating. I want more. Need more. Will explode if I don't have more.

I close my lips around her clit and suck. Her hands tighten on my scalp, and her head falls back. She's incredibly responsive, and my dick aches to get in on the action.

"Oh, Jake …"

Claire bucks against my face, her breathy moans making my dick even harder. I knead her butt and spread the cheeks apart. She squirms but doesn't let go of my head as I continue to lick and suck the bundle of nerves that has her losing control.

"Jake, holy fuck!" she screams, her body softening against me as her hips continue to shudder.

Watching Claire come undone is the sexiest thing I've ever seen. I want to draw it out for as long as possible, so I lap her clit with gentle strokes of my tongue.

She whimpers. "No more, Jake. Please, no more."

I breathe in her spicy scent one more time, then stand and wrap my arms around her waist.

"I like your choice of underwear tonight," I murmur in her ear. "I'm thinking it should be standard."

She presses against me, her body still trembling in the aftermath of her orgasm. "Half the fun of wearing nice lingerie is having it stripped off."

I couldn't agree more. But she'll get no complaints from me. It's hot as hell knowing she's been naked under that dress. "Then why didn't you wear one of your lacy numbers tonight?"

"I wanted to surprise you." She flutters her eyelashes. "Show you what you missed out on by not doing a full body search the first time we met."

God, this woman makes me laugh. "You certainly did that."

I wince when her hand slides down and palms my dick. "Jesus, Claire."

"Do you need a little relief, Inspector?"

"You have no idea." I grab her wrist as she fumbles with my zipper. "Nah, ah! Let's take it to the bedroom."

"The floor too hard for you, old man?"

I spank her arse and hoist her over my shoulder.

She lets out a squeal. "Ouch!"

"We'll see who's too old, you cheeky woman."

I drag my mobile phone out of my pocket and throw it on the lounge, then stride down the hall with Claire giggling and my dick throbbing in my pants. Nothing is going to interrupt us this time. Not the station. The nursing home. Not even Oscar.

I throw Claire on the bed.

The unbearable hardness of my dick and balls tells me I won't last long. Except for that disastrous one-night stand, I've gone three years without sex. It took me a month of showers to scrub the greasy feeling of guilt from my body after that encounter.

For a moment, Sally's brown eyes flash in front of me, and then they're gone. My past. Replaced by sparkling green. My future? This is more than a fling with Claire. What exactly, I don't know. But I'm determined to explore it.

Claire's sultry gaze dips to my crotch. "Is that a gun in your pocket, Officer, or do you just like the view?"

I adjust myself and grin at the O she forms with her lips. "You'll soon find out."

I grab a condom from my wallet and stalk towards her.

Claire drags off her dress and lays back on the mattress, giving me a front-row seat to her glistening pussy. "You should have brought your handcuffs."

My dick jerks. Fuck. I can see her tied to the bed. At my mercy.

"Next time. I don't want to wait a second longer to be inside you." I kick off my shoes, then tear at my shirt, eager to get the constricting material off.

Claire inhales sharply, her hooded gaze roaming over my body.

My chest expands. I work hard to keep in shape, and the lust swirling in Claire's irises right now tells me my efforts are appreciated.

"I can't wait to lick your tattoos. From top"—her gaze drops to my groin—"to bottom."

I jerk my zipper down, nearly severing my dick in the process. Tears fill my eyes, but I ignore them and shuck my pants onto the floor. My socks follow.

"Whoa!" Claire lifts onto her elbows. "I didn't pick you for a boxer brief man."

What? I look down at myself. "They're just jocks."

Her face becomes all serious like she's entered an interview room. "Ah, no, they're not, Jake. They tell a lot about a person."

"Really?" Laughter bubbles up, but I keep it contained. While Claire's obsession with underwear is odd, it's also adorable. I don't want to make her feel uncomfortable. "And what's mine say about me?"

She tilts her head. "Charcoal grey suggests conservative and reliable. That's not a surprise. But boxer briefs? Especially Calvin Klein? Screams sexy!"

I grin. "So, you like?"

"Oh yeah. I like." Her head bobs up and down. "A lot."

Her eyes darken like she's ready to orgasm over my briefs. What will she be like when she sees the goods?

My swollen dick springs free from my jocks, pre-cum dripping from the tip. It's been denied for too long.

Claire scrambles to a sitting position.

I press her back down onto the bed. "Ah, ah. Don't move."

She licks her lips. "But I want to taste you."

"Not this time, babe. I'll embarrass myself if you put your mouth on me."

Her eyes sparkle, and that delicious mouth curls up into a smirk. Wicked woman.

"You like seeing me uncomfortable?"

"No." She nibbles on her bottom lip. "Well, sort of. It's nice to know I can shake that iron control of yours."

Control? That was lost the moment our gazes collided through my windscreen the day I nearly ran her over.

My fingers tremble as I rip the condom packet open and roll the latex onto my dick. I lower my body over Claire until we're chest to supple breasts. Throbbing groin to wet heat.

I pull back and latch onto one of her hard pink nipples.

"Jake!"

I peer up and see Claire's glazed eyes focused on my mouth. "You like that?"

She throws her head back and moans. I suck on the little nub, and she wriggles beneath me. My dick pulses. Fuck. Much more of this and I'll be coming all over her.

I let go of the nipple and pepper kisses up her chest, along her collarbone and across her jaw. Our lips meet in a barely there kiss that sends sparks in all directions. The house could catch on fire, and it wouldn't touch the inferno building between us. My dick nudges her entrance. She's hot. Wet. And I'm shaking with need. Time to make her mine. I slip my tongue into her mouth and tilt my hips, sliding in all the way to the hilt.

Claire's inner walls clamp down on my dick, trapping it in her warmth. Fuck! What a poor substitute my hand has been. I rest my forehead on hers. Steady my breath.

She scrapes her nails lightly down my back. "I love the way you feel inside me."

I grin. I like the way she makes me feel. Period. "That's a relief because I'm planning on spending a lot of time there."

She pinches my arse and bites my bottom lip. "Fuck now, talk later, Inspector."

I chuckle and pull out, then slide back into her. Our lips collide, and I inhale each breathy moan as Claire arches against me. Beads of sweat break out on my brow. Taking it slow had been the plan, but Claire's sweet heat is all-consuming. My movements speed up.

I lick the edge of her earlobe. "Sorry, babe, but I'm not gonna last much longer."

She nips my cheek. "That's okay, I'm … ooh, ah …" Her eyes roll back in her head. "God, yes!"

Claire's orgasm rips through her, squeezing the living hell out of my dick and hurtling me into my own explosion of fireworks. I pant, holding most of my weight up with my arms so I don't crush her. The spicy scent of sex and sweat envelops us.

If only we could stay like this forever.

She peeks up at me from behind those long, long lashes. "Wow!"

"Agreed." I press a soft kiss to her lips. "Wow!"

I roll over and dispose of the condom in the bathroom. When I return, Claire's spreadeagled on the bed, a goofy smile on her face. "So, that was a record."

My balls wither, and the semi I'd been sporting dies a quick death. Shit. I know I didn't last long, but still …

"In what way?"

"I don't think I've ever come so hard before."

Thank Christ! I scrub my fingers through my hair. "Really?"

"Yeah, really. And you can wipe that smug smirk off your face."

There's no way I can stop smiling now. "That was nothing. Next time I'm gonna make you come so hard you forget your name." And I forget mine.

She giggles. "I'm going to hold you to that, Inspector."

And she does.

Three more times.

I wake with my erection nestled in the crack of Claire's arse. She wriggles against it. Fuck. I wish I could stay, but sunlight peeks through the window, telling me it's time I returned home. I can't remember the last time I slept so soundly. Then again, I can't remember the last time I spent half the night making love. A twinge of guilt spreads through my chest, but I push it away.

I nip her ear. "What are you doing?"

She presses against me. "What do you think?"

I pump my hips, allowing my dick to slide between her cheeks. We both groan at the friction.

It would be so easy to slip into Claire's warmth. I press a kiss to the top of her head and wrench myself away.

She rolls onto her back, letting the sheet pool at her waist. "Get back here, Jake."

"I can't." I allow my hungry gaze to soak up her creamy breasts and hard, pink tips. She's not making it easy for me. "I need to go. Oscar will be wondering where I am."

"Oh. Of course." Claire's bottom lip wavers. "Oscar's very lucky to have such a good dad."

I drag on my underwear and trousers. "I'll make it up to you. I promise."

With a saucy grin, she dips her hand beneath the sheet and strokes herself. "You'd better."

My dick twitches with disappointment as I let myself out of Claire's house. The cool breeze fans my face, but the heat within keeps me warm. I feel twenty years younger, my body so light, it's like I'm walking on air.

Chapter Twenty-Five

Jake

Oscar squints, his eyelids heavy until he realises it's me. "Daddy!"

I drag him out of bed and squeeze him to my chest. "How did you sleep, little guy?"

"Good." His small arms curl around my neck. "Where were you?"

"I had to work."

"All night?" he asks, his eyes a wide-open book of trust.

"Yeah." I tap him on the nose. "All night."

"Work? Is that what it's called these days?"

Mum leans against the doorway in jeans and a red cashmere jumper, a grin the size of Sydney Harbour Bridge on her face.

My cheeks warm, and it's like I'm fifteen again. "Mum, I'm not going there with you."

She laughs. "I don't want you to. Believe me." Her expression softens. "It's good to see you happy, Jake. You've got a sparkle in your eyes that hasn't been there in too long."

I grin. I'm not surprised. My body is humming all over. Good sex will do that to you.

Oscar wriggles out of my arms. "Daddy, can we have pancakes outside today?"

I ruffle his brown curls, so much like his mother's that darkness almost overwhelms the light. Almost. "Sure. And maple syrup, if we have some?"

"Of course there's maple syrup," Mum scoffs. "I'll whip up some pancakes while you boys get yourselves ready."

Oscar zooms around the room. "I want to be Superman today."

"Okay. But it's chilly outside, so you'll need a jumper."

"Aww, Dad. Superman doesn't wear jumpers."

"How about a cardigan? You can pretend it's a special cape."

Oscar grumbles but doesn't resist when I hand him a red button-down.

I strip out of my suit and pull on jeans and a pullover. Even though I live with my parents, this is the first time I've spent the entire night away from Oscar for any reason other than police business. That's why Mum's beaming.

The moment we enter the backyard, Oscar darts towards the liquid ambar tree at the rear of the yard.

"No climbing," I shout after him. "And be careful of your arm."

He waves his hand at me and continues running until he reaches the foot of the tree and flings himself onto the ground —his version of Superman flying. I wince as leaves scatter in all directions. He has no fear, which is both good and bad.

Sunlight dances across the branches of the old tree, dissipating the fog. The red of Oscar's cardigan disappears in a leafy sea of bronze and fire as he rolls around. It's the perfect scene, missing just one thing. Claire. It's time to introduce her to Oscar. To my parents.

My stomach lurches. Shit. Am I ready for that?

And what about Sally?

A shiver ripples through me. For the first time, that question doesn't rip my heart out and smash it onto the ground. Sally and I are married in name only. And all the medical experts, and they've been a few, tell me she'll never recover from her vegetative state. So, what am I waiting for? I have nothing to feel guilty about. And if Sally could talk, she'd tell me to go for it. To be happy. Make a proper home for Oscar.

I turn at the crunch of leaves. Mum drapes an arm around me. "He's a good boy."

"Yeah, he is. I couldn't have raised him without you and Dad."

She rests her head on my shoulder. "You'd have found a way."

I nod, but I'm not sure I agree with her. Being a detective isn't a nine-to-five job.

Oscar's squeals and laughter burrow deep inside my chest as he continues to thrash around in the remnants of summer. Soon the tree will be bare, the leaves nothing but compost on the ground. Even though the russet-coloured foliage and the nip in the air tell me it's autumn, it's spring in my heart. Time to leave the past where it belongs and start living again.

Remnants of summer? Russet-coloured foliage?

I shake my head. Hell, I didn't know I had such poetry in me. I really am ready to move on. Even love again. Those are heavy thoughts. Mum hands me a mug of steaming coffee and returns to the kitchen while I sit at the wrought-iron table on the veranda.

My phone beeps, and I pull it out of my jean pocket.

Claire: Hey handsome, now we've mastered the 3 min sprint, are you up for a 5 min marathon?

I chuckle. Only Claire could make fun of my lack of control the first time and leave my ego intact. But she seems to be ignoring what came later in the night. I glance at the door. Mum and Dad are still inside. Good. The last thing I need is them getting a glimpse of these texts. I place my cup on the table and tap out a reply.

Me: Depends. Are you ready to have multiple orgasms without passing out on me again?

Claire: You'd better not be overpromising and unable to deliver, Inspector Matthews.

My pants tighten. Fuck. I love it when she calls me Inspector Matthews. It brings out a kinky side I never knew I had. The woman has no idea just how sexy she is. Or does she? I text a response and hit send before I chicken out.

Me: A cop never overpromises. If I tell you to come, you'll come.

"Here are the pancakes, honey."

Fuck. That was close. I shove my phone face down on the table and take the plates. "Thanks, Mum. Oscar, time for breakfast," I yell.

He's chasing an imaginary friend around and around the tree, probably a criminal, since he *is* Superman.

He stops, his torso swaying. "One minute, Dad."

"Now." My voice is soft, but the tone is firm.

His little body stiffens as if he's thinking of defying me and then he drops the stick and charges up the yard. Good. The last thing I want this morning is to correct his behaviour. See his happiness diminish, even for a second. Not when I'm feeling like the king of the world after waking up next to Claire.

I check my phone to see if Claire's responded to my text. I worry I took it too far. I'm still getting the hang of this sexting stuff.

A gif flashes up words with all the sounds Claire knows I want to hear from her—whimpers, screams, moans. I snigger. This is out of control. I'll never make it through breakfast at this rate. I type back a quick response.

Me: Got to go. Having breakfast with Oscar. Talk soon xx

I slip the phone into my pocket, groaning at the pressure in my pants. I've got a full-on boner now. Fuck.

"You okay, son?"

I jerk my head up. "Yeah. Morning, Dad." No way I'm telling him I've reverted to a teenager.

"Work's giving you trouble?"

"Ah, no." My body warms. "That wasn't work."

He gives me a knowing smile as he takes a seat. "So, I take it everything went well last night with your … friend."

I burst out laughing. "*Friend?* Really Dad?"

My father regards me with flinty blue eyes. The same blue as mine. "Your mother's right. You look good."

"I feel good. I like Claire a lot." My attention flicks to my son. He's stopped halfway up the yard, brushing leaves off his Superman suit. "I think I'm ready to introduce her to Oscar." And tell her about Sally.

Dad's eyes widen, and for a moment, I second-guess my decision. "That's a big step."

"Yeah, it is. But if I'm going to take things further with Claire, I need to know she'll be good with him." I rub the back of my neck. "Assuming, of course, it works out. It's still early days."

"Dad, look what I found?" Oscar scrambles into the chair next to me and hands me a white feather.

"Nice."

"It's an angel's feather."

"Really?" He's been obsessed with all things dragons and Superman lately. He hasn't mentioned angels before. "How can you tell?"

"Because it's white." He rolls his eyes at me. "Everyone knows angels are white."

I smile. Simple logic. "Of course." I hand the feather back to him. It's a foot long and in good condition. Most likely it's come from a cockatoo, but I'm not going to spoil the illusion.

Oscar runs his fingers along the silky ends. "Do you think it's a sign from God?"

My gaze snaps to my father. He's frozen, just like me. "I

guess it could be."

Large brown eyes, the same hazelnut as Sally's, sink into mine. "I wish Mum wasn't sick."

I swallow and clasp his tiny hand in mine. "I know."

My mother bustles out of the house, juggling maple syrup, strawberries and ice cream.

"Grandma, I found an angel's feather." Oscar thrusts the feather towards her.

She drops her load on the table and takes it from his outstretched palm. "It's beautiful."

He beams. "The angels sent it for Mum."

Dad and I share another *oh shit* glance, but my mother handles it like a pro.

She gives it back to him. "I'll find a small pot. You can plant it, like a flower, and keep it in your bedroom."

"That's a great idea." Oscar clutches the plume to his chest. "It'll be like Mum's with me while I sleep."

I grip the edges of my chair. Where is this coming from? I thought Oscar was coping okay with Sally's condition. The counsellor thought so, too. Are we wrong? Until I'm sure, I can't introduce him to Claire. It would only confuse him. And if our relationship flounders, it could traumatise him further.

Mum gives my shoulders a gentle squeeze and kisses the top of my head. "Breathe," she whispers.

I take a breath, grateful for her composure.

Oscar chatters about Superman and bad guys, the feather seemingly forgotten, while he inhales his food. By some miracle, he doesn't choke. Normally I'd pull him up for talking with his mouth full, but not after what just happened.

Mum and Dad exchange a glance that tells me their thoughts are still on the feather. On Sally. On the numerous assessments completed by specialists that have warned me she will never wake up again. My appetite has vanished, the feather a reminder that, no matter how much I need to start living again, I can never truly leave the past behind.

Chapter Twenty-Six

Claire

Jules and I meander along Circular Quay, where the sparkling sapphire blue water of Sydney Harbour promises relief from the shadowy streets and tall buildings. Relief from the fears and disappointments of life. Maybe it's because I grew up in Western Sydney suffering through summer heat waves, but I've always found this merging of the harbour bridge and the bleached sails of the Opera House with the lapping waves calming. Not that I need any help to relax today. Jake gave me all the relief I needed last night.

I grab hold of a street sign and swing around it. My hand slips, but I regain my grip and save myself from an embarrassing and painful collision with the concrete below.

Jules chuckles. I ignore her. Endorphins still sing through my veins from Jake's sleepover; his taste on my lips, his scent licking my skin, grazes from his five-o'clock shadow burning the inside of my thighs. With each step, my silk Parisienne panties brush against my sated lady parts.

Is it wrong I didn't shower?

Normally, I wash any evidence of sex from my body as soon as the deed is done, eager to erase all memories of the messy encounter. But with Jake ... hell, yes, it was messy, but God help me, it was a good messy. The best I've ever had. It was more than sex. It was making love. There's no other way to describe it. With other guys, I've always felt they were going through the motions to get me off, and missing the mark, so they could get their orgasm. It was different with Jake. He seemed to enjoy the journey as much as the destination. It sounds corny but true. And it didn't hurt that I came harder than I've ever come before.

The sun's rays dance on the waves, bopping and twisting with the gentle swell. It reminds me of the ticklish sensation of champagne bubbles up my nose, and that's how we end up sitting at the Opera Bar with a bottle of champagne instead of a chai latte. It's not like I always drink at lunchtime. Today is different. I'm different. Good sex will do that to a girl. And Jules is happy to oblige me.

I sip my champagne while Jules pops a couple of pills into her mouth.

"Headache? Or did you pull something on the walk from the bus stop?" I snigger. Jules is as fit as I am, which means she's in need of a serious exercise plan.

She nods, but her eyes slide downwards. What the hell? She's lying to me.

"Jules." I reach my hand across the table. "Please don't tell me that's your mum's Valium."

"Jesus, Claire." She bangs her glass on the table. "It's just painkillers."

"Okay, okay." I raise my palms. "No need to get all stroppy."

"Sorry." She gives me a small smile. "I might be a bit dehydrated. It's unusually warm today."

"I'm sorry, too. I shouldn't have jumped to conclusions."

Although, I'm not so sure I have. Jules' reaction was over the top. And it's not that warm. She's hiding something from me, and I'm certain it involves Mick. I'll let her avoid the topic for now, but I'll get to the bottom of it as soon as I get this horrible drug business over with.

Jules kicks off her three-inch boots and massages her feet. "We wouldn't have had to walk so far if we'd caught the train instead of the bus."

Sweat trickles under my arms. Jules knows I don't do trains. "It's a gorgeous autumn day. Perfect for a nice walk in the sunshine."

Jules gives me the side eye.

"Don't say anything." I raise my palm. "Please."

"Fine." Jules shakes her head and sadness creeps into her eyes. "One day you'll trust me enough to tell me. After all, I'm supposed to be your best friend. Aren't I?"

"You are." I grab her hands and squeeze. I could say the same thing about whatever's going on with her and Mick. "I'm sorry, Jules. Some things are just too painful to talk about."

"Alright. I won't say anything more. Today is about forgetting the crap and celebrating all the good things in our lives." She lifts her glass. "Like you getting laid."

I grin and clink my glass with hers and take a sip. Yes, sex with Jake definitely deserves celebrating.

"Claire. Is that you?"

I choke on my champagne at the unexpected voice and jerk my head up. Ashley's cheeky face peers down at me. Warmth spreads through my chest at the sight of my old colleague.

"So, this is how the unemployed spend their time." He plonks himself into the chair.

Jules does a double take. Ashley has that effect on people. His clothes are a little tight: charcoal pants hugging muscular thighs, a light blue long-sleeve shirt stretching across bulging pecs. And he has an aura about him that turns women's heads. He'd have them all over him, except he prefers men.

"I've got to live it up while I can." I give him a fake pout. "Who knows when I might find myself wearing orange overalls and cleaning bathrooms with a toothbrush?"

"Claire." Jules gasps. "That's not funny."

Ashley's smile drops. "I agree."

I look down at my clothes. "You're right. I don't have any orange underwear to match."

Jules rolls her eyes. "Since Claire's too busy worrying about her prison wardrobe to remember her manners, I'll do the honours." She sticks out her hand. "I'm her best friend, Jules."

They shake. Ashley's eyes twinkle. "Hi, Jules, nice to meet you. I'm Ashley, Claire's … ah, ex-colleague."

"Do you want to join us?" asks Jules.

Ashley gives an exaggerated bow of his head. "I thought you'd never ask."

"You're already sitting, smarty pants." I punch him in the shoulder. "I've missed you."

"I've missed you too. Liam's an even bigger pain in the arse since you left. Without you to pick on, I've become his bitch."

I arch my eyebrow at him. "Isn't that just a little sexist?"

"You know what I mean. He's got to be lording it over someone to feel like a man. That lucky someone is me." He waggles his eyebrows. "Now, if your fine inspector was the boss, well … let's just say I'd be happy to go down on my knees for him anytime."

A spray of champagne shoots out of Jules' mouth.

"Ashley!" I grab a napkin and dab it on my top.

His almond eyes widen in mock innocence. "Your friend's the one who spat all over you."

"You're impossible."

"Yes, I am. And you love me anyway."

"Yeah. I do." I scrunch up the napkin. It's only champagne. It won't stain my burgundy woollen blouse. I turn to Ashley, waving my hand at him like a flyswatter. "But note, I will cut you if you go anywhere near my boyfriend."

He leans back in his chair, a wicked grin on his face. "So, things are going well, then?"

"Yeah." My cheeks burn. "Really well."

"Good. You deserve it."

I cock my head at him. "That's it? You're not going to give me more shit?"

"Nope. I'm happy for you. You've had too many deadbeats. He looks like a keeper." Ashley taps my cheek. "So, wipe that frown off your face."

I paste on a smile. "There's still the little problem of my drugs charge."

Ashley's expression switches from silly to serious. "If anyone can find the evidence to clear you, it's your boyfriend."

❦

A depressing echo greets me as I kick off my shoes and shut the front door.

Home.

My haven.

The house I'll have to sell if I don't get a job soon.

Lunch with Jules should have perked me up. But all it did was remind me of the drug charges and my jobless state. I made light of it because I didn't want her to worry about me, but running into Ashley was a painful reminder of the mess I'm in.

I grab a soft drink from the fridge and plonk myself on the sofa. Ashley's the only person at Alpha Pharmaceuticals who keeps in touch. The rest of the sales team—let's just say, they're so fearful of catching my *drug cooties,* they couldn't unfriend me fast enough on LinkedIn.

Facebook beckons like the time-wasting seductress she is, but I show unusual restraint by opening up my laptop and heading straight for the job vacancies. No point feeling sorry for myself. I scroll through the ads, making notes of a couple that might be suitable. My pulse rate picks up when I see an opportunity with ACE Products, Alpha's main competitor. Not that I want the same type of job again, but I need the money more.

Two hours later, there's a lightness in my chest that wasn't there when I sat down. My resume is updated, and the cover letter finished: five years' experience with local and global accounts, responsible for fifty million dollars of revenue, secured new business worth over ten million dollars.

And alleged drug pusher.

Obviously that last bit isn't in there, but the allegation hides in the spaces between the words like a cancer. Although ACE Products wouldn't expect a reference from Alpha. Given they're fierce rivals, that would be awkward. Imagine if I got the job and won the Unison account? It would be the best revenge.

I save the documents and make a cup of tea.

An hour later, I'm back at my laptop, finger hovering over the send button, my stomach in tight knots. I swear it's twenty degrees hotter. While I'd be bored out of my brain, I have all the right credentials. ACE Products will be falling all over themselves to interview me when they get my application. Besides, the mortgage doesn't pay itself.

So, what am I afraid of?

I gulp the remains of my tea, attach my resume and press send. Then collapse against the lounge.

That wasn't so difficult.

The phone rings. My heart rate picks up as I answer—a purely visceral reaction to Jake's name flashing on the screen.

"Claire." His deep growl rumbles in my ears and settles between my legs.

"Hi," I squeak.

"Have you got plans for next weekend?"

"Besides washing my hair and trawling for jobs?"

He chuckles. "Yeah."

I smirk. Not that he can see. "Depends who's asking."

"What if it's the man who promised to rip your panties off with his teeth the next time he sees you?"

And just like that, my underwear is ruined. "In that case, I could probably make space in my busy schedule."

"Great." His voice smiles down the phone and enfolds me in a warm embrace. "How does a romantic weekend in the Blue Mountains sound?"

I squeal. So much for being coy. "Perfect!"

"The weather forecast looks good for bushwalking."

Walking?

I catalogue my wardrobe. Are any of my clothes suitable for traipsing through the bush?

"Claire, you still there?"

"Yeah. Sorry. I've only been to Katoomba twice. It sounds fun." For the mosquitos and leeches that will feast on my blood.

"You're in for a treat. The hiking trails weave through magnificent scenery. It's incredibly stimulating."

I tighten my fingers around the phone. Jake and I seem to have very different ideas on what counts as stimulating. "What about at night? Will there be open fires? Mulled wine?" My hold on the phone tightens even more. "A little nakedness?"

There's a grunt on the other end, then nothing.

"Jake?"

"Romantic implies wining and dining." His voice drops. "And lots of sex."

Heat floods my cheeks. "Oh. Good." Thank God he can't see me right now.

"And Claire?"

"Yeah?"

"I've changed my mind about ripping off your panties. Forget them. You won't be needing any."

Chapter Twenty-Seven

Claire

J ake is officially the best boyfriend ever.

The bed and breakfast he's whisked me away to clings to a clifftop overlooking the Jamison Valley. The scenery is breathtaking. I snap a few photos of nature's perfect canvas—shades of ochre against a backdrop of deep blue sky and green treetops—and put my camera aside.

My heart does a dance. Five stars. Five freaking stars! I feel like royalty. The bed covers are pulled back, little chocolates in shiny wrapping strategically guard the pillows, and a bottle of Moët chills in a nineteenth-century ice bucket.

I carry my toiletries into the bathroom, where a super-sized clawfoot bath beckons. Jake filled it before slipping out to give the owner our breakfast selection for tomorrow. Could he be any more perfect? Within minutes, my clothes are shed, and I'm lying in a tub full of bubbles, drinking in the black-and-white Art Déco features. A stained-glass window with roses and birds adorns the wall opposite, imparting an ethereal ambience to the room.

"Ahem."

Jake grins at me from the bathroom doorway like I'm a delectable morsel he can't wait to eat. At least I hope that's what he's thinking.

"How long do you think we're staying for?"

I chew on my bottom lip. Did I get it wrong? "The weekend. Aren't we?"

"Yep." He steps into the room. My turquoise G-string, the pair with little black bows on the sides, dangles from his fingers. "How much underwear do you need for two days?"

My face flushes. He wasn't searching my bag for drugs, was he? He said he believed me. "Were you going through my things?"

"Of course not. But it's hard not to notice all the flimsy scraps of lace and silk you've got laid on top of your suitcase. You must have a dozen pairs of panties and bras." He waves the thong and gives me a wink. "Besides, didn't I say you wouldn't need any?"

"I can't go hiking without them." I sink into the tub. "And I need options."

His lips twitch, but his eyes are steady. Searching. "Please don't take this the wrong way, but you seem to have a bit of an obsession with underwear."

I flick some of the bubble-soaked water at him, my stomach dropping. Damn. I knew it would come to this. It always does. Men just don't get it. "What do you mean?"

"Those granny pants when we met. Your wide-eyed appreciation for my underpants." He places the G-string on top of the linen basket. "The delectable scraps of nothing you wear."

"So? A lot of women like nice lingerie." They don't spend hours selecting what they're going to wear each day. I know that's not normal, but we all have our quirks.

He slips his fingers into his waistband. "It's unusual, that's all."

Jake's words cut a little, but I'm anaesthetised as he slides his boxer pants down his solid thighs. Oh, dear lord. I could never tire of looking at his naked body.

"Fine." I take a deep breath. "Call me nuts."

"Hey!" He shrugs out of his briefs, his dick jutting at me in salute. "I'm not judging you. I'm curious. That's all."

I cock my head, maintaining eye contact while I devour his nakedness on the periphery. "There's nothing wrong with me."

"I didn't say there was."

He prowls towards the bathtub and slides in, his head at the other end of the tub. My thighs open and he settles between them, the coarse hair on his legs tickling my delicate skin.

He's got that cop-like expression on his face that tells me he won't let this go until he gets an answer. So much for sexy times in the bath.

I let out a sigh and sink a little further into the water. Jake's already seen me at my worst, and yet he's still here. If anyone can understand my secret, it's him. Besides, a relationship needs honesty and trust to thrive. "I found my granny dead when I was eight."

His gaze, which had dipped to the space between my legs, snaps to my face.

"Jesus, Claire. I'm sorry. That must have been traumatic."

"Yeah. It wasn't one of my better days." Understatement of the century.

"I can appreciate how that would haunt you."

He rubs my knee with his palm. "But I'm not sure what that's got to do with underwear."

"I found her on the toilet." I focus on Jake's fingers and the gentle kneading of my leg. "Her dead body didn't bother me as much as you might expect. But I couldn't take my eyes off the huge, white underpants wrapped around her ankles. They were hideous."

Jake's irises twinkle and his jaw wobbles like he's about to burst out laughing.

My face burns. "You don't understand." It was a mistake to open up. I wish he'd never started this discussion. This is supposed to be a sensual soak. Not some comedy show where I'm the butt of the jokes.

"Sorry, Claire." He rubs my thigh with soothing circles. "It's just … only you could be cool with a dead body but distressed by the underwear."

"There was another time, too." Even though I want the conversation to end, I can't seem to stop.

I need him to know what makes me tick. Or is it the cop in him that has me spilling my secrets?

"What happened?"

Jake's blue eyes are softer than I've ever seen. I could lose myself in them forever. It gives me courage to keep going. "When I was ten, Mum and I were at the train station, and a guy exposed himself in front of us."

Jake's body stiffens.

"He didn't harm us." I stumble over the words, desperate to get them out before my mouth freezes. "He dropped his tracksuit pants, an ugly mustard colour, like diarrhoea gone wrong, pulled out his penis and waved it at us. He then turned, tripped over his trousers and fell onto the tracks." My chest tightens at the memory. I'd stepped forward, drawn like iron to a magnet, but Mum yanked me back. Thank God. "The train didn't stop in time."

"Shit."

He runs the back of his knuckles along my cheek. "That's something no child should ever see."

He's not wrong there. "I spent years in therapy."

"I've known trained cops who've never healed from witnessing violent deaths."

"The thing is, it wasn't the man's death that affected me. Not even seeing his genitals."

"What do you mean?"

I lower my head. This is not what I'd imagined when Jake suggested we soak in the tub together, but it's too late to stop now. He clasps my chin and lifts it until I can't avoid his perceptive scrutiny.

"It was his underpants." I gulp. "They were even uglier than the tracksuit pants: ratty, navy-blue Y-fronts that looked older than my granny when she died. They were horrible."

Jake strokes my cheek, his warm blue gaze seeing too much.

I close my eyes and shudder, the memory still as fresh as the day it happened.

"Everyone, my parents, the police, the psychologist, they all thought being exposed to the man's privates and then watching him fall to his death had traumatised me. They didn't understand. I was relieved the man died violently, that there would have been lots of blood to cover up his hideous underwear."

My eyes snap open at the fierceness of the words pouring out of me. The soft crinkle of soap bubbles popping is the only sound as Jake studies me.

Crap.

I should have kept my mouth shut. He's going to wish he'd brought his cuffs with him. And not for fun times, but to haul my sorry butt off to the looney bin.

"Wow, Claire. I'm not sure what to say."

I clench my hands under the water so he can't see them shaking. "You think I'm crazy?"

"No. But now I understand your preoccupation with underwear better. Thank you for telling me. Do you still see a psychologist?"

The gentle timbre of his words and the warmth in his indigo eyes stops me from losing it. He's not making fun. Still, I wish he'd never brought the subject up while we were in the bath.

"No. I didn't feel it was helping. If anything, constantly talking about what happened made me more determined to never be caught out like Granny or the man at the train station."

Jake drags my tight fist out of the water, coaxes my fingers open and clasps my hand.

"What about trains? How comfortable are you travelling on them?"

"I don't."

"What do you mean?"

Why does he have to keep pushing? Why can't he just drop it? I've trusted him with my fucked up obsession. Isn't that enough? I pull away from his grasp and pick up a cake of soap, hoping he'll get the hint that this is supposed to be a sexy bath.

"I hate them. I always drive or catch a bus."

"I see."

Jake takes the soap from me and massages my palm, his fingers firm, comforting. "I suspect you focus on underwear as a way of protecting yourself from the trauma of witnessing those deaths."

Huh? A tingle races up my spine. All the therapy I had as a child and no one ever said that to me. Then again, I'd never admitted my obsession to any of the psychologists.

"I guess. But with that logic, wouldn't I be scared of bathrooms?"

"Post-traumatic syndrome shows itself in many ways."

I pull my hand away. "I don't have PTSD."

"Maybe. Maybe not. But your preoccupation could be a type of obsessive-compulsive disorder. Both can develop in the wake of a distressing event. You could find it helpful to see a psychologist who specialises in PTSD."

A bead of sweat rolls off my nose. I swear the water's gotten hotter while we've been talking. I'm grateful for Jake's insightful understanding, but I can't discuss this anymore.

The water feels heavier, the steamy bathroom suffocating. My thighs quiver with the need to escape. I need a distraction to help put the memories back in their box, and since I'm naked in a bath with one very hot cop, the answer is obvious.

My nipples peek out from the bubbles as I slide up the bathtub. "I appreciate your impromptu counselling session. I really do. And I'll think about the psychologist. But can we leave my freaky past for now and get down to more sexy things?"

Jake's jaw tightens like he's got more to say, but then his gaze dips to my breasts as I hoped it would. "What did you have in mind?"

"I'm feeling very dirty after the long drive and could do with some help getting clean." I cock my eyebrow at him, giving him my best come-hither look. "And then a thorough inspection to make sure nothing was missed."

A deliciously wicked smile curls on Jake's lips. "You're in luck. Inspections are my specialty."

He slides the cake of soap along my leg, starting with the calf and working his way up my thigh.

With the intoxicating aroma of lavender and sandalwood filling my senses, I surrender to his ministrations, just like I surrendered to his questioning. Safe. Protected. And a little overwhelmed. I never thought I'd ever have the courage to tell another human being what I've confessed to Jake. There's only one reason I would open myself up to potential ridicule. I'm in love with him.

Chapter Twenty-Eight

Jake

Claire flops to the mud-caked ground, a massive camera dangling around her neck. "I can't go any further."

I skid to a stop. "Come on. It's not much longer now."

"That's what you said twenty minutes ago." She folds her arms across her chest and lifts her chin.

I smother a grin. She's adorable.

Several teenagers skirt past us, skipping down the steps, sniggering as they take in Claire sprawled in an awkward heap.

I squat down next to her. "You're making a scene."

She pouts at me, full-on pouts, and I can't help myself. I press my lips to hers. She opens and I explore her mouth, our tongues tangling in a slow, sensuous dance. My hands slide up and down the sides of her body. Her breath hitches at the contact, and she curls her arms around my neck. I can't get enough of this woman.

"Ahem." A gruff voice interrupts. "Excuse me, but could we get through?"

I jerk my head up. An elderly couple stares down at us,

bush walking sticks clasped in their gloved hands, kind eyes dancing. A sweet shade of crimson blooms on Claire's face. It reminds me of the strawberries we had for breakfast. Strawberries I'd plucked out of the bowl and hand-fed her. Strawberries that delayed our walk until late morning.

I jump to my feet, brushing at my cargo pants and willing my dick to calm down. Claire scrambles up as well, her head lowered as if the couple won't see her if she can't see them.

"Sorry about that. My girlfriend needed a breather."

The lady glances at her husband, her eyes twinkling with the kind of love that wraps you up and keeps you safe. It's the look my parents exchange every day.

She turns back to me. "That's alright. We still remember what it feels like to be your age. I'm sure that kiss helped with your girlfriend's rest."

A slow burn spreads across my face. "I must say, you both seem very fit."

The husband speaks up. "We've been bushwalking for the best part of sixty years. It's what keeps us young." He drapes an arm over his wife's shoulder and winks. "That and kissing. Looks like you two are on the right path for a happy life together."

They smile and continue down the slope with slow but steady steps, fading into the canopy of trees. It's a heartwarming sight.

Claire groans. "Oh God, I'm so embarrassed."

I squeeze her close. "Why?"

"Come on. You saw how old they were."

"Yeah, and they said they've been doing this for sixty years. How long have you been bushwalking?"

She rubs her lower back and stretches her neck. "About one hour and ten minutes."

"Then you're allowed to find it tough."

"What about you?"

"Ah, babe." I chuckle. "I jog a lot. Need to stay fit for the job."

Claire mumbles something I can't discern as she adjusts her small backpack.

"What was that?"

"I don't know what you see in me. You're all muscle on muscle while I'm skin on bone."

I grit my teeth. How can Claire not see how attractive she is? Every time we've gone out, I've mentally castrated at least a dozen men for looking at her with too much heat in their eyes. "Ah, ah. No putting yourself down. You have the prettiest eyes I've ever seen and a smile men would die for." I glance around to make sure no one is coming along the track. "And if we were alone, I'd show you exactly how much I love that body of yours."

She nibbles her bottom lip. "I don't feel very attractive right now."

"Do I have to kiss you again?"

Her lips twitch. "Maybe."

"Let's go." I peck her on the cheek. "I promise to give you the best massage of your life when we get back. Okay?"

I slap her on the arse when she grumbles about bossy cops. "Move it, Thompson."

"Or what, Inspector?" She sticks a hand on her hip. "You haven't got your handcuffs now."

A family inches their way down the trail, so I whisper in her ear. "I don't need them, but I promise you a spanking later if you don't get your cute backside moving."

Claire bats her eyelashes. "That's not much of an incentive to keep walking, Inspector Matthews."

I give her a mock glare. She giggles and darts ahead of me.

Her delectable behind sways from side to side in the fitted blue jeans. I smile so hard my face hurts. God, this woman! She makes me feel ten years younger. Twenty years.

Treetops and clear blue sky stretch in all directions, refusing to cower to a charcoal swirl of clouds to the west. Claire burrows her head deeper into my chest, one leg draped over mine, her soft, breathless moans having nothing to do with me and everything to do with the glass-walled skyway cabin and our distance above the ground.

I run my fingers through her sweaty hair. "You sure you don't want to take in the view?"

"Nope." She presses against me. Any closer and she'd be wearing my clothes. "Not safe."

"It's a spectacular sight."

She responds with a grunt.

I suppress a chuckle and return my attention to the scenery, or what I can make out, in between the people standing near the windows.

The elderly woman who had passed us on the trail approaches, her fingers gripping the rail tightly. "Your girl-friend scared of heights?"

I grin. "How did you guess?"

She answers with a smile. "I was the same when I was younger."

Claire peers out from the safety of my embrace. "Really?"

"Oh, yes." She gestures towards the glass. "On our first visit to the Blue Mountains, I couldn't stand at the edge of Echo Point and look at The Three Sisters without getting dizzy."

"What changed?" I ask.

She shrugs. "Time. Little wins with smaller heights." Her smile turns cheeky as her gaze flicks to her husband standing by the window. "Strong arms to hold me."

The cabin shudders. Claire squeals and shoves her head against my sternum. The elderly lady sways but holds her balance with ease. *Shit.* My father would take my gun and shoot me if he could see me now. "Sorry, ma'am, would you like a seat?"

She waves me away. "No, no. I'm fine. Besides, I think your girl needs you sitting next to her more than I need to sit down."

The woman returns to the window where her husband is taking photographs with what looks like the latest release iPhone. If I'm half as dynamic as the elderly couple when I reach their age, I'll consider myself lucky.

The cabin jolts again, and Claire claws at my jacket.

"Sorry, babe. I'll make it up to you." I nuzzle her hair, breathing in the tangy mix of strawberry shampoo and sweat.

"I'm the one who's sorry." She lifts her head, green eyes glistening. "I'm ruining our day."

"No, you're not." I feather my lips along her damp forehead. "But we'll stick to flat surfaces in the future. Maybe the beach next time."

She nods against my chest and mumbles so low I almost don't hear her. "Beach is good. Underwear will be safe."

I brace myself. "What do you mean?"

Her fingers bunch around the fabric of my jacket, and she slides her head towards me. I bend down and she whispers in my ear, her voice wavering. "I'm not sure I'm wearing clean underwear anymore."

I squeeze her arms and somehow manage to hold back a bellow of laughter. Given how Claire feels about the subject, the possibility of wetting, or worse, soiling her underpants, would disturb her even more than being hundreds of metres above the ground.

"We'll go straight back to the bed and breakfast when we land. Have a shower or bath. Whatever you want."

She mumbles what sounds like a *thank you* and returns her face to my chest.

My pulse picks up. This isn't how I imagined our weekend. Before we had Oscar, Sally and I enjoyed many trips trekking through the bush. I never stopped to think it might not be right for Claire. She's obviously gone along with it, for my sake.

I rub my palm in gentle circles across Claire's back. She isn't Sally. And I don't want her to be.

What do I want?

I want to tell Claire about Sally. I should never have let things get this far without being completely honest with her. That's a large part of why I arranged this weekend away. But after she told me about her grandma and that God-awful train incident, I haven't wanted to burden her with my secret. She has enough processing to do after sharing her traumatic experiences without me adding to it.

Or am I a coward?

I kiss the top of Claire's head and gather her closer in my arms.

One thing's for certain, I want her by my side. Even if she's curled into a sweaty, trembling ball. I want to protect her. Cherish her.

Shit.

Love her. That's what this constant ache deep in my chest is. I'm falling in love.

Chapter Twenty-Nine

Jake

"Scudasi is dead."

Greg looms in the doorway of my office, his body rigid, face giving nothing away except for a small tic below his left eye.

My fingers freeze mid-typing. After the blissful weekend in the Blue Mountains, I've been floating on air all morning. I even brought in some potpourri Claire insisted on buying while we were away. She said it would be good feng shui for my office. So much for clearing the room of negative energy. Greg's just dumped an A-bomb of it on me.

I drop my hands to my lap, heart pounding in my chest. "How?"

"Don't know yet." Greg closes the door. "The team are checking the cameras and records."

"Fuck!" I slam my fist against the table and bolt out of my chair. "Did someone get to him?"

"I'd put money on it."

"Jesus, we were so close to cracking this case."

Greg rocks on his heels. "There's still the information he gave us."

"And no proof except the statement of a dead man. A criminal." I rub my temples, a headache coming on. We'd convinced Scudasi to testify. Only a few trusted people knew. Do we have a leak?

I return to my chair. "When the media gets wind of it, Commander Gordon's going to mount my balls on his office wall."

"It's a temporary setback."

A tortured groan escapes my lips. "A fucking big one."

Greg sits across from my desk, legs crossed as if he hasn't got a care in the world. And he hasn't. It's not his career on the line. But I know he's seething on the inside. Same as me. He's just had longer to digest the information.

My phone dings in my pocket. Most likely, Claire. The heaviness cloaking me lifts a little. I wonder what naughty thing she's texted this time.

Which reminds me, as if I could forget. "What about Claire's case? Any development with the fingerprints team?" Her blood results finally came back. They were negative, but there's been no progress on the origin of the drugs in her drawer.

"I was getting to that." Greg's lips stretch into a smile large enough to rival Oscar when he's tearing around the backyard in his Superman suit. "Good news."

"You couldn't have started with it first?"

"Sorry." He shrugs. "When I got the call about Scudasi, it short-circuited everything else."

"Understandable." I wave my hand at him. "So, come on. What have you got?"

"There's been an unexpected development."

I straighten. "They identified the fingerprint?"

"Nope. I think that's a lost cause." Greg shakes his head.

"But Joyce Massey, the HR manager at Alpha Pharmaceuticals, came forward with some information."

I squeeze my hands together to stop myself from wringing his neck. "For fuck's sake. Spit it out."

His eyes twinkle. "No need to get your knickers in a knot."

Greg flicks something off his jacket. I swear he's stringing this out to watch me squirm. I glare at him. He grins back.

"Turns out there are a couple of cameras in the office."

"I don't remember seeing them."

"They're very inconspicuous. Look like smoke alarms. But that's not the fun part." His grin widens. "Ms Massey had them installed and activated before sending out proper communications."

All my muscles tense. "What the hell was she thinking? Surely, she knows it's an offence to film employees without their knowledge?"

Greg nods. "That's why she's kept quiet until now."

"She hates Claire. What made her come forward?"

"Turns out she has a conscience, and it's been having its own little dance party in her head at night, keeping her awake."

Sweat beads across my forehead. This could be the break Claire needs to clear her name. "And the cameras were on?"

"Yep. Ms Massey swears they'd only been switched on that day for *testing*. Then the business with Claire happened and she ..." Greg raises his fingers and draws quotation marks in the air. "Forgot to inform the employees."

My breath locks at the base of my windpipe. "The footage?"

Greg makes a show of dusting dirt off his jacket. "Even though it's been a while, she said it should still be available through the security company that installed the cameras."

Air whooshes out of my lungs. "Thank Christ."

Greg crosses his arms and gives me a funny look. The sort

where you know the other person is going to say something you don't want to hear.

"What if the video shows Claire with the drugs?"

My fists clench, and white-hot fire rips through my body. "It won't."

He cocks his eyebrow at me. "You sure?"

I grit my teeth. "Yes."

"Oh man, I should have realised sooner." Greg leans forward in his chair, a stupid grin on his face. "You got laid."

"Shut it."

"No can do." He shakes his head. "This is big."

I don't get a chance to respond. A quick tap on the door is the only warning we're given before it swings open and Squad Commander Peter Gordon strides in. If I thought I'd been furious when Greg gave me the news about Scudasi, it was kindergarten compared to the rage rolling off Commander Gordon. His eyes, two narrow slits of fury, bore into me.

The commander slaps a copy of the local newspaper on my desk. "What the hell is this?"

The headline sprawled across the top says it all: *Police Inspector in bed with alleged drug trafficker.*

Fuck. This is the worst timing.

"Stupid tabloids." Greg chuckles. "You can't believe anything you read in them."

The commander glares at him. "Out. I need to speak with Inspector Matthews in private."

Greg's head bobs up and down. "Yes, sir," he murmurs and scrambles to the door. It closes with an ominous click. How I wish I could follow him.

"Well?" Commander Gordon demands, his voice booming against the walls of the small office.

I straighten in my chair. Square my shoulders. If I show fear, he'll strip me down like a piranha until there's nothing left but my bones. "It's not true, sir."

He flicks a finger towards the photo accompanying the article. "Are you seeing this woman?"

"Yes, sir." I swallow. "But—"

"The article states she's been arrested for drug trafficking. Is that true?"

"Yes, sir, but—"

He grabs the paper and rips it up. "No buts."

Tiny pieces flutter to the floor, not unlike my career prospects right now.

"Do you realise how bad this looks, Inspector Matthews?"

"Yes, sir." I bite my tongue. Pushing back will only antagonise him further.

The commander drops into a chair. "This is a total cluster fuck, Jake."

I exhale a deep, painful breath. "I know it doesn't look good, sir, but Claire's innocent. Greg's found the evidence to clear her."

"It doesn't matter." He shakes his head. "The media's got the taste for blood. There'll be no stopping them now."

My heart sinks. He's right, but I still believe in the integrity of the process.

"I won't tell you how to run your personal life, Jake, but if your girlfriend's innocent, you'd better get the evidence sorted and her charges dropped. Fast."

I acknowledge him with a nod and take a big breath. Might as well get all the bad news out there. I keep my poker face in place and hope it's enough to stop the commander from firing my arse or pulling me off the case.

"It gets worse, sir."

His eyes bulge. "How can it get worse?"

"Scudasi was found dead in his cell this morning."

An ugly red hue spreads across Commander Gordon's

cheeks. "I'm not even going to ask how because if I do, I'll lose my shit, and neither of us wants that."

I swallow the lump growing in my throat. Will I end up demoted? Sent to a remote location? Fired?

The commander's jaw flexes. "Call a meeting for later this morning. I want every team member present and a full update on the strategy moving forward."

"Yes, sir."

The commander rakes his fingers through his silvery hair. "You have a month to crack this case, Jake, or I'll appoint someone else to lead it."

The room sways. Thank Christ. I still have a chance to prove myself. "Thanks, sir. I appreciate your support." And I mean it. I understand there's a lot at stake politically. "I—"

He holds up his palm. There's no defying the hand.

"It's the best I can do. I trust you to sort it out. But the commissioner will want someone to blame, and I'll be frank." He slaps his palms on the desk. "It won't be me."

The commander stands, giving me another one of his hard glares.

"Don't let me down, Inspector Matthews."

He leaves with a lot less bluster than he entered. I hang my head in my hands. There's no doubt in my mind Leadbetter's responsible for Scudasi's death. And the newspaper article has got that bastard's prints all over it. Would he go after my family? Claire?

I pull out my phone. "Dad."

"Jake, are you okay? We saw the front page of the paper."

"Yeah, I'm fine. Can you contact the security firm? We need to up the safety measures for Mum and Oscar. And Claire."

Chapter Thirty

Claire

The warm air of the shopping centre washes across my face, doing nothing to erase the heat that no doubt has my cheeks looking like they've been dipped in tomato sauce. It turns out walking with cramping muscles is hard work. I shuffle as fast as I can, my thighs and calves in the middle of their own little rebellion party after I forced them to climb down the mountain on the weekend.

I dodge two women and their prams, a group of senior citizens and three teenagers who should be in school. With each duck and weave, my muscles scream a little more. But I hurry on. Mum will be ringing any moment to find out why I'm late.

I reach the café, a homey Italian place with white-topped tables and lasagne to die for, and flop down on the seat across from Mum.

Her gaze narrows. "What on earth is wrong with you, Claire?"

I signal to the waitress, grab a napkin and dab my forehead. "I hiked with Jake on the weekend."

"*You* went hiking?"

"Yes." I laugh, but it comes out more like a snort. "I did. In the Blue Mountains. It was torture."

She chuckles, the lines around her eyes crinkling. "I'm not surprised. I didn't think you even owned a pair of shoes suitable for outdoor activity."

"Not really." I groan as I attempt to cross my legs. "I wore my casual sneakers. They have no support, but they're the closest thing I have to joggers."

The waitress arrives with a carafe of water and two glasses. My red face must have given me away.

"Thank you." I gulp down the water.

Mum rearranges the salt and pepper shakers. "Are you on the road visiting customers today? Is that why you were fine to meet me for lunch during the week?"

Oh shit. My stomach somersaults. At least it has athletic ability, not like the rest of me. I should have expected this. "I have the day off. Figured I'd need it after the weekend."

Her lips purse and her shoulders slump, disappointment flitting across her face. "I thought you stopped lying to me when you were seventeen."

I swallow, my mouth dry. "Ah …"

"Have you seen the local paper, Claire?"

"What?" *Where's this going?* "No."

"I see." Her expression softens as she pulls out her mini-iPad, runs her fingers over the screen, and hands it to me.

Sweat pools under my armpits. The picture is grainy, but it's me lying on the pavement near the skyway in the Blue Mountains, Jake with his arms around me. We'd just alighted, and my legs had chosen that moment to go on strike after the arduous hike to the bottom of the mountain and the death-defying ascent in a tiny glass cabin. Not to mention the loss of containment in my underwear that Jake and I agreed never to speak of again. It had all been too much. The headline above the photo is damning. I'm screwed.

"I'm sure this is a misunderstanding?"

Mum's voice is gentle, like I remember when she used to tuck me into bed at night as a little girl. She takes the iPad from me and slips it into her bag. Hands me a tissue.

"Yes." I sniffle. "And no." I blow my nose, proud of myself for not bawling like a baby.

She waits for me to say more. For an annoying mother, she's doing an awesome job of looking non-judgemental. I launch right into the details, not pausing for breath in case I lose my nerve. I tell her about the drugs at work, my positive test, and being fired.

"How did you get out of jail?"

"Jake paid the bail."

A ghost of a smile flits across my mother's face. "He must like you a lot."

"I think so." My bottom lip drops, and just like that, I'm a little kid desperate for approval from her mum. From Jake. "But he hasn't introduced me to his family yet."

She arches her eyebrow. "You haven't introduced him to yours either."

"It's not the same thing." I take a deep breath. "He has a son."

"Oh." My mother's eyebrows attempt to climb her forehead. Not an easy feat, given the Botox that's undoubtedly injected in her face. "How old?"

"Five."

"Your man's probably being cautious. He wouldn't want his son getting attached to someone too soon, in case it didn't work out." She inspects her nails—perfectly manicured and topped with pale pink polish—then drums them on the table. "What about the boy's mother?"

Good question. I confessed my secret to Jake, but I still know nothing about Oscar's mother. What am I afraid of? I need to stop dancing around the topic and ask him straight out. "She's not in the picture. I'm not sure what happened."

I pour myself another glass of water. "Jake doesn't talk about it. He lives with his parents, and they help care for Oscar."

"That's sad."

I wring my hands out, the newspaper headline still burning a hole in my retinas. What will Jake do? He won't want to introduce me to his family now.

The waitress reappears, a perky smile on her lips. Oh, to be eighteen again. "Can I take your order?"

"I'll just have an Earl Grey tea, thanks. I'm not real hungry …" My appetite went AWOL with those horrid headlines.

"Nonsense, Claire. You need to eat. You're skin and bone." Mum hands our menus to the waitress. "I'll have a decaf soy latte, and we'll both have the lasagne and salad."

Trust my mother to simultaneously criticise me and look out for me. But I guess some comfort food wouldn't hurt.

Mum leans across the table and whispers, "Are you okay for money, sweetie?"

I stiffen. Damn. This is one reason I didn't tell my parents. I want them to see me as an adult. Not a troubled teenager. "Yeah. As long as I get another job in the next couple of months, I'll be fine."

Lies. I have one more repayment on my mortgage and then things are going to get awkward real fast with the bank.

And what if I don't find a job? End up in jail?

"Make sure you call us if money gets tight. That's what family's for."

"Thanks."

The gymnastics in my stomach settles down. Confessing everything to my mother is easier than I expected. And oddly comforting.

Mum straightens in her chair, hazel eyes piercing mine. "So, what happens now with these charges?"

Crap. Sometimes I forget Mum used to be a lawyer. That she understands a lot more than she lets on.

"I've got a court hearing next month. Jake's team are looking into my case, but unless they find the real culprit, it doesn't look good for me."

She grabs my hand and squeezes my fingers. "Have you engaged a lawyer?"

"Yes." I pull my hand away from her. "No one you know."

"Claire!"

"I've got it covered."

"You should ask your father for help."

"No. Please, Mum. I'll work it out." I don't dare tell her Alex helped me. Dad would be annoyed that I'd gone to her instead of him.

But I'm a grown woman who can fix her own problems. I don't need to run to my dad for help.

Yet.

Chapter Thirty-One

Claire

I scramble onto the bus just as the door whooshes shut. The driver's gaze is fixed on his mobile phone, so he doesn't notice me being nearly squished in two. So much for safe driving. I slip into a seat, piling my few groceries beneath me. I glance out the window and spot a figure emerging from the bushes near the bus stop as we pull away. My heart rate skyrockets. I knew someone was following me. Damn reporters haven't left me alone since that stupid newspaper article on Monday.

A cockroach scuttles over the bags at my feet. Lovely. The sight of it would normally have me screaming and climbing the seat like my life depended on it, but all I can muster is a tiny shiver. I have bigger problems to worry about.

My lawyer was all depressing news when I met with him yesterday.

"There's a fifty percent chance you could be convicted," he'd said.

"But I'm innocent!" I'd yelled before jumping up and down like a toddler having a tantrum. Not something I'm proud of. He'd adjusted his glasses and tapped the file on his desk with his finger.

"I understand, Claire, but the circumstantial evidence is damning, and unfortunately, it's pointing at you."

It was a complete waste of five hundred bucks. So much for asking Alex for a recommendation. I get that my lawyer was trying to prepare me for the worst, but I don't want someone representing me who's not prepared to put everything they've got into proving my innocence. It felt like he was taking the easy way out. If Jake's investigation doesn't uncover the real culprit soon, I'll have to do what Mum suggested and ask my father for help. He has connections in high places and a reputation for winning against the odds.

I haven't seen Jake for five days, not since returning from the Blue Mountains. Only talked on the phone and texted. He hasn't said much about the newspaper article. Only not to worry. He's busy working on some big police operation and on my case. I swing from wanting to see him to deciding we should avoid each other until Monday's headlines are a distant memory. But it's Friday, and I miss him. Miss what we shared on the weekend.

I pull out my mobile.

Me: Hi Jake. Do you want to come over for dinner? xx

The cursor flashes. The bus rumbles along. My heart beats faster. I almost wish the cockroaches would scurry back. Anything to take my mind off the blank screen.

Jake: Sorry. It's going to be another long night at the station x

Damn it!

I squeeze my fingers around the phone. A horrible thought occurs to me. Is Jake too busy, or is he having second thoughts? Because I'm not a great catch right now. Mud sticks and I'm covered in so much of it; I could start up my own mud-brick factory.

My stomach rolls with the bus as it swerves around a

corner, and I cling to the armrest to stop myself from lurching into the aisle.

My phone dings again and I jump.

Jake: Work is crazy right now. How about lunch on Saturday?

Gah! My breath catches as another cockroach dashes past. This is ridiculous. I'm overthinking things and making up problems where they don't exist. I respond to Jake, trying to stay cool.

Me: Great. C U then xxx

I text Jules, and she agrees to meet me outside the local golf club. She arrives at the same time as the bus. I jump into her car, a hoodie pulled over my head.

She greets me with a raised eyebrow. "This is a bit clandestine."

I scowl at her. "Someone's been following me."

"Alright then." She tears away from the curb, tyres squealing as she runs an orange light.

I grab the seat to stop myself from jerking forward. "What the hell?"

She smirks at me, flecks of amber shining in her brown eyes. "I've always wanted to do that."

"There's no one chasing us now."

"You don't know that." She glances in the rear-view mirror, her smile fading. "Actually, I think there is a car following. Hold on."

She slams her foot on the accelerator and guns the sporty Mazda up the steep hill. I grip the seat, my heart racing as fast as the car as Jules takes a hard right down a side street. "Jules, slow down. You'll get us both killed." What is wrong with her? She's one of the safest drivers I know. But not today.

She gives me the finger, which freaks me out even more. "Both hands on the steering wheel."

She cackles and swerves to miss a fallen branch. I close my eyes. She's going to kill us. We'll be on the six-o'clock news, my name forever tarnished as an alleged drug trafficker. The only positive is I'm wearing latte-coloured, satin boyleg panties and a matching bra. So, no embarrassment for my dead body in the morgue.

The car slows, and I open my eyes. "What the hell were you thinking?" My voice trembles.

Jules brings us to a stop, the engine still running. Her pupils are wild, like dirty flood waters breaking the banks of a river. "I was thinking, what if there wasn't a reporter following you? What if it was someone from the drug gang who peddle that shit? They've seen your face. Your name. They could come after you. Silence you."

My blood freezes. "That's crazy talk."

"Is it?"

"Yes." At least I hope so. "I don't know anything, so why would anyone want to silence me? It's silly."

"I guess so." She shrugs. "Sorry. I watched this episode of *CSI* last night, and it was about a murderous stalker."

I shake my head. Jules is getting us both worked up over nothing. It's just her over-active imagination. I play punch her in the shoulder. "You watch too much TV."

❦

It's a short drive to Jules' house, and soon we're lazing on the back deck, wine glasses in our hands, watching her four-month-old staffy cross puppy doing zoomies around the yard.

I shake my head at the label on the bottle. "Chardonnay? Really, Jules?"

"Sorry, girlfriend. If I'd known I was going to rescue you from enemy territory today, I would have stocked up on your favourite poison."

I gulp a mouthful. It's a mellow, full-bodied oak. A pleasant change. But I don't tell her that. I screw my face up. "It'll do."

She shakes her head and pops a pill.

What the hell?

I bite my tongue. Literally. A coppery taste floods my mouth. But I can't help myself. I need to know. "What are you taking?"

Jules washes the tablet down with her wine. "Paracetamol."

Her nose twitches. She's lying to me.

I cross my arms against my chest. "By paracetamol, do you mean your mum's Valium?"

She shoves the plastic container into her handbag. "Don't make a fuss, Claire."

"In other words, it is." What's wrong with her? Is that why her driving was erratic? I can't believe she's still taking those tablets. And I can't believe she lied to me. "When we were at the Opera Bar, was it a pain killer you took or Valium?"

"Please, Claire." Her eyes glisten. "I'm not addicted or anything."

Damn it. I knew she was lying. "Why take them?"

I hate pushing her, but I loathe the fact she's taking the pills, stealing them, and then lying about it even more.

She shuffles closer, her gaze darting to the back door. "I think Mick's having an affair."

"What?"

Jules and Mick might have married because of her pregnancy, but they seemed to be in love.

She sculls her wine and pours another glass.

"He's been working ridiculous hours the last few months. Including weekends."

"That doesn't mean he's cheating on you."

"I know. But it's the little things. He's on his phone constantly, and when I ask what he's doing, he says it's work." She takes a swig of wine. "He's an accountant, not a high-flying businessman."

Jules is always so upbeat. I'm a terrible friend for not noticing something was wrong. I squeeze her hand.

She squeezes back, a tear sliding down her cheek. "That's why I take the Valium. It takes the edge off."

"Jules, drugs aren't the answer."

"I know. I don't take them very often. Please, Claire, can we not talk about it right now?" Her brown eyes implore me to let it go, but I can't.

"Promise me you're not taking that stuff when you're driving, or worse, when Riley's in the car."

"Of course not." Her eyes flash, and her fingers tighten around her glass. "I would never endanger my daughter."

That's a relief. Her honesty comes through in the fierceness of her words.

She sips her wine. "I've only taken one now because we're safely at home and Mick's picking Riley up from school today.

"Okay." I want to quiz her more, but Jules will only clamp up if I push further. Besides, she rarely grills me when I do stupid shit. Like the time I loaned money to my last boyfriend, against her advice, and never saw it again. I need to cut her some slack and change the subject. But it doesn't mean I won't be circling back to it in the near future. I love her too much to watch her go down the slippery slide of drug addiction. She'd never forgive herself if Riley got hurt because of it.

I click on photos and show her my phone. "What do you think?"

She scrolls through the pictures. "They're lovely, but that's no surprise. You keep a beautiful home."

"It's my fallback plan."

She arches an eyebrow. "What do you mean?"

A heavy band tightens around my rib cage. "If I have to sell."

It's the last thing I want to do. But my only other option is to ask my parents for help. I'd never hear the end of it. They'd lecture me on why I should have gone to university. Followed in their footsteps and become a lawyer.

"It won't come to that."

"If I don't get a job soon, I'll have no choice." I grab my phone from her. "Although, if I'm found guilty, I'll have bigger things to worry about."

"Jake will clear your name."

"This isn't the movies." I huff. "He can't go all Clint Eastwood for me. He's not above the law."

"No, he's not." She giggles, the lines around her face softening. The worry about her husband forgotten. For now.

She swirls the wine in her glass and takes a sip. "But you're innocent."

If only it was that simple. The newspaper article was damning. The ugly way it suggested Jake was compromised by his association with a possible felon, it was clear the local media had already passed judgement.

Guilty!

Jules cocks her head at me. I can almost see a lightbulb lighting up above her head.

"If someone was following you, why did you text me instead of seeking refuge at the police station?"

A lump sticks in my throat. "I didn't want to bother Jake."

Jules drops her glass on the table, her posture stiffening like she's about to launch into a series of kung fu moves. "Why not?"

"Because I don't want to cause him trouble at work." I gulp my wine. It tastes better with each mouthful. "You read those headlines."

I turn away and watch the puppy rolling on the lush buffalo grass. Not a care in the world. Safe and loved. I'd felt like that last weekend when Jake and I were in our perfect bubble. Now? I don't want to be a liability for him. Although, it doesn't mean I'm not counting down the hours until I see him tomorrow. Does that make me selfish?

Jules' little girl bounds through the back door, cute as a button in her school uniform.

"Mummy, I'm home."

Jules' face warms at the sight of her daughter, but not before she gives me a look that says she hasn't finished with our conversation. "Hello, sweetie."

Riley skips to Jules and wraps her arms around her waist. Jules sits her on her lap and kisses her cheek. They look so alike with shiny brown hair, button noses, and hazelnut eyes. A cramping ache fills my womb. Until now, my biological clock has been dormant, but it's easy to imagine a little girl or boy on my knee, Jake's blue eyes staring back.

Riley wriggles off Jules' lap and launches at me, smacking my cheek with a wet kiss. "Aunty Claire," she squeals.

"Hey, pumpkin." I hug her slim body and flick her ponytail. "How was school?"

"Awesome. I drew a picture of Mummy, Daddy, Zola and a pony."

I widen my eyes in mock surprise. "You have a pony?"

She gives Jules a side eye. "Not yet."

Jules' eyes narrow, but her lips twitch. This is not the first time Riley's mentioned a pony. "Not ever, young lady."

Riley grins, clearly not deterred. "Can I play with Zola?"

Jules nods, and just like that, Riley slips out of my embrace and runs into the backyard.

Mick appears in the doorway. He's a slender man with a shaggy mop of hair that always looks like it's a couple of months overdue for a cut. There's a possessive glint in his eyes as he focuses on Jules. It's not the look of someone unfaithful. There must be another explanation.

Mick's gaze roams over the empty wine bottle and chip packets. "Afternoon, ladies."

His expression is neutral, but the air thickens, and I swear the temperature drops ten degrees.

Jules lifts her chin as if daring him to say more. "Claire thinks a reporter was following her."

"I see." His brows furrow. "And what does the wine have to do with it?"

Jules' eyes glaze over. "Wine fixes everything."

His Adam's apple bobs as if he's not happy with her response.

I sigh. Now I've caused trouble for my bestie. It's bad enough my life is heading towards the rubbish tip. The last thing I want to do is drag her with me.

❧

I glide through the front door. Alright, I stagger. A bit. I feel like a naughty teenager being dropped off by a friend's father. Not that Mick wasn't polite. I've just had this epiphany that maybe alcohol isn't the answer every time life slips sideways.

There were no reporters waiting to jump me when I came home. Still, the eerie sensation of being watched prickles. Could Jules be right and the drug cartel is after me? I shake my head. Nah. She was being overdramatic. Still, it doesn't hurt to take precautions. I double-check the lock on the door and tug the curtains closer together.

My eyes are too tired to look at the tiny screen of my mobile, so I flop onto the lounge and turn on my laptop. I scan through emails first, my heart slamming against my ribcage when I see ACE Products has responded. I gasp for breath. It's only been a few days since I sent my application.

"This has to be a good sign. Doesn't it?"

I glance around the room as if someone's going to respond to my question. But it's just me and the four walls.

I open the email.

Blood rushes from my head like a massive tidal wave. It's a thank you, but no thank you.

I scroll up and down the message. I don't understand. I have the experience and the customer relationships. Hell, I have competitor knowledge they could suck out of me if they wanted to. Dammit. I slam the laptop lid down and pace the floor. They must have rejected me because of the newspaper article.

I grab my mobile and call Ashley to see if he knows anything. There has to be another reason. Otherwise, how will I ever get a job?

"Hey, Claire. Do you know what time it is?" he answers, his tone unusually curt.

"Yeah, yeah, wine o'clock." The frown on my face lifts.

"Beautiful, you've caught me at a bad time. I've got a hot date tonight. What's up?"

"ACE Products rejected me."

"What?"

My thoughts exactly. I grip the phone tighter. "I applied for a job last week, and they sent me a rejection email today. It was for the same role I was doing at Alpha Pharmaceuticals."

"Oh." Ashley's voice drops. "I'm so sorry, sweetie. They probably saw the newspaper article. Everyone's talking about it."

"Great. I'll never work in pharmaceuticals again." Not that I want to, but I also don't want to be unemployed. I curl my feet under my legs. "My life is over."

"Don't be like that." He tsks me. "You've still got your hot cop. Hell, I'd quit my job in a heartbeat if I could get me some of that candy."

I pat my flaming cheeks. "Stop imagining yourself doing unspeakable things to my boyfriend."

He chuckles. It's both evil and cheeky at the same time. "Oh, Claire, you little innocent. I'm imagining him doing unspeakable things *to me*."

My face burns, in part because Ashley still manages to shock me, but also because I know just how good Jake is at doing unspeakable things.

"I'd love to chat, but I really do need to get ready for my date. My man drought is finally over."

I'm pleased Ashley's going out. He's been single for too long. And I'm glad I called him. He has a way of making me feel better about everything.

I return to my rejection email.

Dear Ms Thompson,

Thank you for your interest in the position of Sales Representative. You have not been successful at this time.

Yours Sincerely

My heart shrivels. No one gets a rejection this fast. ACE Products didn't even bother with the usual, *we wish you well.* The only explanation is, I've been blacklisted.

My fingers hover over the buttons as I think about creative suggestions on where they can stick their stupid company. Fortunately, I haven't had enough alcohol to make that mistake. I delete the email instead.

Another message gets my attention. This one's from my lawyer, suggesting we meet again on Tuesday to discuss my court appearance. No way I'm wasting another five hundred dollars on that loser. Time to swallow my pride and text my father. He reached out to me the day the headlines broke, but I wasn't ready to talk to him. To admit failure.

I should call rather than text, but it's Friday night. And I'm wasted. I don't need a lecture from Dad about my drinking habits.

Me: Hi, Dad, sorry I missed your call. Are you free next week? I'd like to discuss my charges with you. If you're too busy, that's OK. xx

My phone dings. That was quick.

Dad: Claire, of course it's ok. Come home for lunch tomorrow.

Trust my father to dive straight in. But I'm seeing Jake, so

Dad can wait. It's not like anything can happen over the weekend.

Me: I'd love to, but I've got plans. What about Monday?

Dad: Done. Come for dinner.

My eyes sting. I expected my father to give me a hard time, but he made that easy. Then again, he might be saving the lecture for when I see him in person. I close my laptop and crawl off the lounge. What I need is a good night's sleep. Everything will look better in the morning.

Chapter Thirty-Two

Jake

I reach the front of Claire's house and wipe clammy hands on the back of my jeans. I've been up to my eyeballs with work this week. Even Oscar has suffered as I pulled all-nighters at the station. It's becoming the norm, and it's killing me. With each phone call, I've felt Claire pulling away. And I don't blame her. How can our relationship survive if we never see each other? And when the hell is the right time to tell her about Sally?

The door opens before I can knock. Claire looks edible, innocent, and ... wary. My chest tightens.

"Jake."

"Hey."

We stand, like two strangers, regarding each other for ten of the most awkward seconds of my life. It couldn't be more different from how we woke up together last Sunday in the Blue Mountains, our legs entwined.

I clear my throat. "Are you going to let me in?"

A blush creeps up her face. "Sure."

The moment she moves away from the opening, I drag her into my arms, slamming my lips against hers. *Real smooth.*

Her mouth opens, granting me access, and my tongue sweeps in. She tastes of chocolate, mint, and the elusive essence that is Claire. I nibble her bottom lip, my voice an unrecognisable growl. "Fuck, Claire. You're killing me."

She nips my lip, drawing blood.

I plunder her mouth again, her soft sighs wrapping around my dick and trapping it against the unyielding metal of my zipper. I ignore the ache in my heart, reminding me I'm still living a lie, and herd her into the hallway.

We tear our lips apart, our ragged breaths roaring in my ears.

Claire wets her bottom lip. "Do you want a drink before lunch?"

"What I want is to be inside you."

Claire tenses and ... shit, I've said the wrong thing.

She pulls away. I groan, missing the smooth touch of her skin. "A lot's happened, Jake. I think we need to take a moment to talk."

Fuck. She's right. I'm behaving like a horny arsehole.

"Do you think we should break up?" she whispers, a tear slipping down her cheek.

Fuck no. Is this what she's been thinking all week? My breath catches on the words hanging between us. "Is that what you want?"

"No." She wrings her hands out. "But I'm worried your career could be affected because of me."

"It won't be." I hope. I rake my fingers through my hair. She doesn't need to know how pissed off my commander is. "And, no. I don't want to break up with you." I'm in love with her, for Christ's sake.

Her eyes shimmer with unshed tears. "What if I'm convicted?"

"It won't come to that."

Tears well in her eyes. "I'm sorry, Jake. It's been a shitty week. Reporters have been following me. Mum and Dad know about the charges now. And my lawyer's on my case to plead guilty."

What the fuck? She needs a new lawyer. "How did your parents take it?"

"Better than I expected. And I'm going to talk to my dad about the charges next week. See what he thinks."

"Good." I'm relieved her family are supportive. I cup her chin with my palm. "We're getting closer to finding the evidence we need to clear your name."

I shouldn't get her hopes up, but I can't stand to see her looking so forlorn. She needs some good news. I don't give her details about the cameras in the office. That's confidential and still an unknown. There's been some technical glitch in retrieving the data, so computer software experts have been called in. They're optimistic they can retrieve the footage. I bloody hope so.

Her lips form a perfect O that has my dick banging its stupid head against my zipper again.

When her tongue dips out to lick her bottom lip, I swear I'm going to die from strangulation of my dick, or balls. Or both.

The shadows fade from Claire's eyes, and the tension morphs from combative to sensual. "I missed you."

Three simple words that burrow inside my chest and mingle with those other three words I've thought but have yet to utter. "I've missed you, too."

Claire's gaze dips to my crotch. There's no hiding the bulge. Her pupils dilate and her lips twitch. The cheekiness I've come to know and love rises to the surface.

"However will I repay you for working so hard, Officer?"

We should talk more, but she has sex written all over her beautiful face with those come-fuck-me eyes and pouty lips. No red-blooded man could say no to her not-so-subtle invitation. I push gently on her shoulders. Not too much force, but enough to get my message across.

Claire drops to her knees, hands reaching for my trousers. I swear there's a small drop of drool escaping her mouth.

I grab her wrist. "Gentle, babe. I won't last long."

"Trust me."

I shudder at the promise flashing in her sassy eyes.

She flicks the catch on my belt and unzips my pants, inch by agonising inch until my dick springs free. Jutting like a signpost. Directly at her face.

"Oh dear, Inspector, that looks very painful."

My fingers curl in her hair, yanking her head back. "What are you going to do about it?"

I love it when we play these little power games. It might seem like she's the one about to submit, but I don't kid myself. I'm the submissive—a writhing mess of testosterone bowing to her will.

Her answer is to lick from the end of my dick, down to my balls and back up again. A tortured growl spills from my throat. She nibbles around the mushroom head like it's a goddamn lollipop, murmuring what I can only assume is approval as she sucks the tip into the warm, wet haven of her mouth.

I jerk my groin towards her, keeping a tight hold on her hair. There's a muffled oomph from Claire, but she doesn't let go. Instead, she adds to the fire, cupping and massaging my ball sacs with her firm, soft hands and wicked fingers. My legs wobble at the unexpected contact, and my balls tighten. Fuck, she's good at this.

Claire hums around my shaft and continues kneading the sensitive flesh of my balls, her nose flush against my pubes. The vibrations strip the last of my self-control. My dick thickens.

"Claire, I'm going to come."

"Mmm …" She peers up at me, her eyes glazed over, and sucks harder.

My release hits me like a proverbial freight train, pulverising my mind and soul into a million tiny pieces.

Claire continues to lick me clean before sliding up my body and kissing me on the cheek. Her kiss is chaste, a total contrast to the wanton woman of seconds ago. My heart thrashes in my chest in a good way. This woman means everything to me. There's no way I'm letting her go.

"Your turn now, babe."

She nuzzles my ear. "I'm counting on it."

I hoist her in my arms and carry her down the hall to the bedroom. I must look a sight, zipper undone, dick at half-mast, flapping in the breeze. But it's not like anyone can see me. I throw her onto the bed, possessiveness cutting through me at the flash of white lace between her legs as she bounces on the mattress. Lunch can wait. I have another appetite that needs satisfying first.

Chapter Thirty-Three

Claire

I want to be a better person. Not just for Jake, but for me, too. That's how I find myself sitting in a psychologist's waiting room, an envelope-sized smudge on the wall trapping me in thrall for the last ten minutes. Is it the result of a toddler smearing their sticky, chocolate-covered hands across the tired beige paint? Or did a tradesman brush up against the surface with dirty pants? Then again, who's to say it isn't dried blood left behind after a patient went psycho waiting for their appointment?

Okay, I admit that last thought was a bit out there, but the reception area isn't conducive to peaceful thoughts with its pale walls, tired plastic chairs and fake pot plants. A couple of prints would brighten up the place. Make it more welcoming. Unless the intention is to be insipid and boring, in which case, it's a winner.

The digital clock clicks over another minute. Patience isn't one of my virtues. I guess I can add that to my long list of faults.

The door to the psychologist's room swings open, and a

short, balding man scurries out, his red eyes bulging from their sockets. If that's what he looks like after his consultation, I'd hate to imagine what he looked like before.

"Ms Thompson?"

The receptionist pops a piece of gum in her mouth, her head not even lifting to look at me. "Ms Daniels will see you now." She motions towards the closed door, her gaze on the screen of her mobile phone.

I lurch out of the seat, my legs like concrete pillars, and stumble through the door.

The psychologist smiles and strides towards me. Her hair is pulled back in a bun, tiny wisps falling across her face. My fingers itch with the urge to smooth those strands into place.

"Claire, nice to meet you. I'm Amy. Please." She gestures at a comfy-looking two-seater. "Sit down."

I perch on the edge of the lounge, still not certain I can do this, ready to flee if it all gets too much.

She settles in a wing-backed chair adjacent. "So, how can I help you?"

I shrug. "I'm not sure."

"Okay." She crosses her legs and taps her pen against a notepad. "Then what made you come here today?"

"Something my boyfriend said."

"I see." She nods. "And what was that?"

My stomach clenches, squishing the cereal I'd had for breakfast into tiny lumps. This was a mistake. I shouldn't have come. "Nothing important."

She scribbles again, then returns her attention to me.

I squirm in my seat. This is as bad as the police interrogation room.

"Are you sure?" says Amy.

I lean forward, almost toppling off the chair. My heart thuds and sweat breaks out all over my body. Even between my toes. This is why I hated seeing psychologists when I was a kid. They nod their heads and look at you with kind, knowing eyes. It didn't help me then, so why do I think it'll make a difference now?

"I'm screwed up. I just don't know how to fix it."

She smiles and does that nodding thing. "Why don't you start at the beginning?"

I know it's cliché, but it's like a switch flips. I trip over my words, telling her about Granny's underpants, the guy at the train station, stepping out in front of Jake's SUV in those ugly pants Mum gifted me.

By the time I finish spilling my secrets, I'm floating on air. I had no idea how heavy a burden it had been.

Amy tucks a curl behind her ear. "Thank you for sharing, Claire. It takes a lot of strength to open up to people. To yourself."

I feel naked sitting across from Amy. She's so put together, except for the strands of hair escaping her bun. I'm glad I wore my Heidi Klum royal blue bra and panties today. Royal blue is a colour that says sane and capable. Not nutcase.

"What are you thinking about, Claire?"

Heat creeps up my neck. "Ah … nothing."

She continues to regard me with a serene expression, one perfect eyebrow arching ever so slightly like she knows I'm lying.

I glance down. How did I get myself into this? "I was thinking about the underwear I'm wearing," I mumble, my voice projecting into the floor.

When my gaze returns to Amy's, there's no judgement. Only warm brown eyes staring back at me.

"And what were you thinking about them?"

"They're royal blue." I clench my fingers, the nails biting into my palms. "It's a strong colour. A colour that says I'm in control."

She scratches in her little notepad. Her gaze drifts above my head. "Unfortunately, we're almost out of time. I hope you've found the session helpful, Claire."

A rush of air escapes me. Talking with Amy has been cathartic but exhausting. "I have. Thank you."

"Good. Today was about getting to know each other and me gaining some insight into what's troubling you. Next week we'll explore deeper."

"Can you fix me?" I blurt out.

"You don't need fixing, Claire." She smiles and taps that pen again. "It's about helping you feel better about yourself."

I gape at her. Nothing wrong with me? Is she kidding? Did she not hear all the crazy words that spewed from my mouth for the last hour?

I scamper out of Dr Amy's office, relieved there's no one waiting in the reception area. My skin tingles beneath my blue jeans and woollen jumper. It's like my appointment with Dr Amy stripped me of my secrets, leaving me walking in my underwear for everyone to see.

The lift takes me to the lobby, and five minutes later, I'm settled in the back corner of a small café, a cappuccino in my hands. I whip out my phone and text Jake.

Me: I did it

Jake: Good for you. Are you okay?

I giggle at Jake's determination not to abbreviate words. I send him a smiley face. He wanted to come with me, but this was something I needed to do myself.

I sip my coffee, the buzz of caffeine and sugar hitting my veins. Tea is my normal go-to in times of emotional stress, but not today. Today I need the heavy stuff. My underwear obsession is a secret I've been carrying for almost twenty years. It's liberating to have two people who know about it. I feel like I can do anything. Like the secret was holding me back. And maybe it was.

My phone beeps and I grab it, my heart rate picking up when I see the caller ID, and not in a good way.

The Bank: Reminder. Your mortgage repayment is due on 15th June.

The coffee curdles in my stomach. I'm almost out of time. If I don't get sorted in the next month, I'll have no choice but to place my house on the market.

Or ask my dad for money.

That prospect doesn't scare me as much as it used to, but it's still a last resort. My father surprised me by not giving me any lectures when I saw him earlier in the week. He's organised some hotshot barrister who charges two thousand dollars an hour to accompany me to court. He said he'd take care of the bill. I didn't dare object. I didn't want to object.

I've realised there are times when it's okay to accept help. I want these charges behind me, so I can concentrate on my future. One I hope includes Jake.

Chapter Thirty-Four

Jake

Sweat pours off Claire's boss, his leg bouncing up and down like an out-of-control yo-yo. The illegal video footage was finally recovered, and with it, Claire's freedom. I can't wait to see her face when she finds out.

I study the cowardly shit through the one-way glass for a few more minutes, giving the urge to connect my fist with his pudgy nose time to dissipate. Cool and clinical is what's needed. Cop first; boyfriend later.

I stride into the interrogation room and prop myself against the wall. It kills me not to be doing the interview myself, but my relationship with Claire makes it impossible. It could jeopardise the investigation as a potential conflict of interest.

Greg settles into a chair across from Claire's boss at the small metal table. "Before we begin, Mr Andrews, I must inform you, you have the right to remain silent. This means you do not have to say anything unless you wish to do so and that anything you say may be recorded and used for evidence. Do you understand?"

Andrews glances at me, then back to Greg. My fingers curl into tight fists. I don't know if I'll be able to restrain myself if the prick refuses to say anything. Finally, he nods.

Greg places an envelope on the table. "Do you know why you're here?"

Claire's boss shakes his head, sweat flicking into the air.

Greg hands him a photo. The man's jowls drop to the floor like a drooling dog as he studies the picture. His spider-veined gaze lifts to mine. He knows there's no wriggling out now.

"Where did this come from?"

"All in good time, Mr Andrews." I point at the photo. "Detective Sergeant Anderson asked you a question."

"I … I can explain."

Greg crosses his arms and leans back in his chair. "Really? Then please." He gestures towards the photo. "Explain away."

Andrews wipes a trembling hand across his mouth. Before he even opens it to speak, I know he's going to spew more lies.

"I was covering for Claire. She left them in the unisex bathroom and … ah, I didn't want her to get in trouble."

Every muscle in my body tenses. Lying bastard. Greg cocks his head at Andrews, who looks away and picks at the skin around his ragged fingernails.

We say nothing. The ticking of the wall clock dominates the room. Andrews' gaze flicks to Greg, who remains still like a statue. Andrews glances at me. Then squirms and scratches his face. Stares back at the photo.

He leans his thick arms on the desk. "Sergeant, you have to believe me."

"There's more than a photo, Mr Andrews." Greg smirks. "There's a video. It shows you taking the drugs from your office and placing them in Claire Thompson's desk drawer."

"Video?" he splutters. "What video?"

"Cameras were installed without advising the staff." Greg leans forward. "They show *everything*."

Greg's bluffing. There are no cameras in the hallway, so it's possible Liam Andrews is telling the truth, and he took the drugs from the bathroom to his office. About as conceivable as me dancing around the station in a hot-pink tutu.

Andrews' eyes fill with tears before he slams his head on the desk, his body wracked with deep sobs. Greg uncrosses his arms and waits.

And waits some more.

Finally, Andrews lifts his head, snot running down his face.

Charming.

Greg nudges the box of tissues in the centre of the table towards the pathetic excuse for a human. Andrews grabs several of them and mops himself up. Blows his nose. I wince at the honking sound. I thought kids looked grotty when they had colds, but Oscar's got nothing on the lump of man in front of me.

"It will go easier for you if you cooperate with us, Mr Andrews," says Greg.

Andrews snuffles.

Greg takes it as a *yes*. "Where did you get the drugs?"

Liam Andrews' hand trembles as he dumps the used tissues on the table. "I can't tell you that."

Greg turns to me. "What's the maximum penalty for perverting the course of justice?"

"Fourteen years." I glare at the man who set up an innocent woman. My woman. "And fifteen years for trafficking."

Andrews' face pales to match the bleached-calico walls.

"If you cooperate, the courts will take it into account." Greg shrugs. "If you don't …"

A half sigh, half sob escapes Andrews' lips. I suppress a grin. We've got him.

Andrews shakes his head. "I don't know much."

"That's okay." Greg gives him an encouraging smile while I imagine slamming the creep's face into the desk and demanding answers.

"Just tell us what you do know. Where did you meet to collect the drugs?"

"The cemetery." Andrews blows his nose again.

Interesting. We didn't think the dealers hung out there anymore.

"What did your contact look like?"

Andrews shoves the used tissue aside. "I couldn't see him clearly. He always wore black pants and a dark hoody, pulled down low."

"Anything else?" asks Greg.

"Yeah. There was this one time." Andrews blinks, his eyes as blotchy as the first day I met him. "A car's headlights blasted us. I noticed a massive ring on his finger. It had a huge sapphire in the middle. It was an odd thing for a bloke to be wearing."

I feel, rather than hear, Greg's sharp inhalation. There's one man with a ring fitting that description. Terence Leadbetter.

Greg sits taller. "Are you sure?"

Andrews nods. "I'm sure."

I grind my teeth. Leadbetter's the boss. Why would he be dealing directly with a nobody like this snivelling coward? Something doesn't add up.

Greg continues. "Has he always been the one to give you the drugs?"

"Yeah. Why?"

"The container in Claire's drawer contained four grams of cocaine. That's a hell of a lot for personal use."

"I thought it was safer to purchase a larger quantity." Liam Andrews' ruddy cheeks turn even ruddier, if that's possible. "That way, I wouldn't need to go back as often to buy more. The guy gave me the creeps."

Bastard is lying. I ball my fists by my side to stop myself from launching at him.

"So, he didn't ask you for anything else, like ..." Greg steeples his fingers and tilts his head. "Stealing pseudoephedrine from Alpha Pharmaceuticals?"

Andrews' eyeballs bulge and sweat drips down his face. He swallows and chokes on his own spittle. Greg keeps steady eye contact. I cross my arms tighter. Wait for him to break.

Andrews lets out a huge sigh and rubs his eyes. "He threatened my family. I had no choice."

Yes. Finally. A confession.

"Of course." Greg softens his voice as if he gives a fuck about the deceitful bastard who framed Claire.

Andrews' gaze darts to me and then back to Greg. "That's everything. I swear."

I push off the wall. I shouldn't approach, but I need to know if Claire was targeted because of me. "Why Claire?"

Andrews' eyes go wide. "What do you mean?"

"Why choose her drawer to hide the drugs?"

"I don't know." He rubs his forehead. "I just grabbed Joyce's master key and shoved them in the first drawer I came to."

The lying snake. "Wouldn't her colleague Ashley's drawer have been closer?"

Andrews shakes his head, and his gaze flits around the room as if looking for an escape. No chance, arsehole.

Greg clears his throat and glares at me. Fuck. I'm getting carried away. I step back. We have our answer anyway. Andrews can't lie for shit. Claire was targeted. I'd bet my badge that Leadbetter told him to plant those drugs in her desk drawer.

"Are we done now?" asks Andrews as he mops his brow.

Greg smiles. "Not quite."

I open the door. Two constables enter.

Greg slides his chair back and stands. "These officers will formally arrest you."

"What?" Andrews' eyes widen to comic proportions. "I thought you were going to help me?"

"We are. The judge will be informed of your cooperation."

Greg leaves it at that. I want to say so much more to the piece of shit, but I can't. Any suggestion we've not acted professionally could backfire on me. And on Claire. I can't let that happen.

Greg and I debrief in my office, which means he slumps into a chair, and I pace the floor.

"You did well, Jake." He points his finger at me and winks. "I half-expected you to tackle Andrews."

"Funny." I stop pacing and rub my jaw. "I shouldn't have interfered. Sorry about that. But at least we know who's been stealing from Alpha Pharmaceuticals."

"Yep." Greg nods. "It's typical Leadbetter. Get someone hooked on drugs, then blackmail them into stealing for him." He presses his palms on his thighs and leans forward. "Your hunch was right. Leadbetter's watching you."

Greg's expression mirrors mine. Fear. Not for ourselves but for my family. For Claire. This is part of the job I'll never get used to.

I give him a tight smile. Leadbetter must perceive our investigation to be a serious threat. Which means we've got to find him. And soon.

❧

"Excuse me, Inspector?" A young constable hovers at the door.

"Yes?"

"There's a Mrs Andrews here to see Liam Andrews."

"She can visit him after the paperwork is completed." I dismiss the constable with a wave of my hand.

"Yes, sir."

"Wait!"

The constable stops midturn.

"Put her in an interview room. We'll have a quick chat with her."

"What's that all about?" asks Greg.

"Probably nothing, but there's no harm in interviewing Andrews' wife."

Greg scratches his head. "The preliminary checks we did on Andrews showed he was separated."

"Perhaps she's worried he won't be able to pay alimony?"

"Or he had nobody else to call." Greg chuckles. "Not the best way to win his wife back, if that's what he's hoping."

We enter the interview room; it's one of the few instances in my career where I'm struck dumb. Mrs Andrews is stunning: long raven hair, sexy red lips and a body that must have other women wanting to scratch her eyes out on a regular basis.

She bats her false eyelashes at us. "Where's my husband?"

Years of training hold me in good stead. Inside, my jaw has smacked the floor, but on the outside, I'm like granite. Greg isn't as smooth, scrubbing his face with his fist.

I gesture towards the chair. "Please have a seat, Mrs Andrews." I tilt my head. "It's still *Mrs* Andrews, is it?"

"Yes, yes." She waves a hand at me, an enormous diamond catching the light. "We're in counselling. Is my husband okay? He called to say he's been arrested."

"That's correct."

"Oh my God!"

My bullshit metre flies off the scale. She's as big a liar as Andrews. Maybe bigger. Talking to her was definitely a smart decision.

Greg takes over. "The charges are for possession and trafficking of narcotics."

"No!" Tears fill her eyes. "He would never be involved with drugs. It can't be true."

Her protestation is as fake as the soccer balls under her top. I'm sure of it. Greg catches my eye. He's grinning, not believing a word that comes out of her plastic lips either.

He nods at her as if he understands and gives a damn. "I'm afraid it is."

She dabs at her face with a tissue. "Can I see him?"

Greg ignores her question and points at her fingers. "That's a stunning piece of jewellery, Mrs Andrews."

For a moment, her mask drops, and her eyes reveal a well of trickery. The change is so fleeting, it would be easy to believe I'm mistaken. But I know I'm not.

She holds up her right hand. "This old thing? Yeah, it is beautiful, but unfortunately, it's only cubic zirconia."

"Really?" Greg leans forward. "It looks authentic."

"That's why I bought it." She pastes on a bright, fake smile. "It only cost a few hundred dollars. I get compliments all the time."

Greg smiles back at her, but there's no humour in his eyes. There's no doubt he's thinking the same thing I am.

I scroll through Liam Andrews' file in my head. He's thirty-three, wife is thirty-one. They have three children, a modest three-bedroom weatherboard house in Castle Hill and a Subaru Forester. Hardly the type who can afford a diamond of that size.

Greg taps the desk. "Did you have to leave work early to get here?"

"Yes." Her lips curl into the first authentic smile since she arrived. "My boss practically shooed me out the door."

"You must be relieved to have an understanding employer," he says.

She lifts those razor-sharp nails and inspects them. "I'm very lucky."

A young constable pops her head in the doorway. "Sir, Mr Andrews is ready to receive visitors."

Greg stands. "It looks like you can see your husband, Mrs Andrews."

"Thank you so much, officer." She bats her eyelashes at me. "And you too, officer …"

"Detective Inspector Matthews."

Her eyes widen. "You look too young to be an inspector."

"I assure you, I'm not."

She bats those ridiculous eyelashes before swaying out of the room, hips flicking from one side to the other.

Greg chuckles. "I'll get right on it."

I frown at him. "Right on what?"

"I presume you want me to review the background check that was done on her and her husband? And in particular, whether Liam Andrews has a life insurance policy?"

"That's scary." Laughter bubbles up. "We've been working together too long."

"It's not hard. There's no way that woman married for love."

"Agreed. She's got gold digger written all over her." The back of my neck tingles. "Question is, how did she afford that ring? Or did someone buy it for her?"

Chapter Thirty-Five

Claire

Curled up on my sofa, with a blanket draped over my shoulders, I sip a cup of tea and scroll through job vacancies. One advertisement keeps drawing me back—a property stylist. I have no experience, but that hasn't proved very useful for me when applying for sales jobs so far. The job's for a boutique real estate company. And the ad specifically encourages people without qualifications to apply, stating a passion and flair for interior designing is what they're looking for. The owner has a kind face. I could imagine working for her. Besides, what have I got to lose? I tap out an expression of interest, impressing myself with my proactivity and hit send.

My mobile rings and I scramble to pick it up when I see it's Jake. "Hi."

"Hey, Claire. Are you sitting down?" There's an excited edge to his voice that has every muscle in my body on high alert.

I place my laptop on the coffee table and press the phone to my ear. "Yeah."

"You're a free woman."

My fingers shake and the mobile slips onto the rug. Crap. I slide off the couch and scoop it up. The screen is still intact. Luckily it didn't fall onto the floorboards. Did Jake say what I think he said? "Sorry, could you repeat that?"

"The drug possession and trafficking charges against you have been dropped."

"Oh my God." My hand trembles so much I can barely hold the phone. "Thank you. Thank you. What happened?"

"Additional evidence came to light. That's all I can tell you at the moment."

"Yay." I stumble to my feet and spin in a circle. "I'm free."

"Yes, you are." His deep-throated chuckle goes straight to the juncture of my thighs. "I'm stuck at a formal function at Government House until later this afternoon. Will you be home if I swing by later?"

"Hell, yeah." My voice kicks up into a squeal. "I'll see you when you get here." And I'll have a special reward waiting for him.

࿔

Three hours later, I throw the door open, run down the three steps of the house, and fling myself into Jake's arms as a free woman.

"Oomph!"

Jake stumbles backwards, his muscular arms straining to hold me up as my legs wrap around him. "I take it you're glad to see me, babe."

His husky voice vibrates through my body.

"Thank you. Thank you. Thank you." I pepper him with kisses: his cheeks, nose, ears.

His fingers dig into my arms. "Not that I don't enjoy having your hot body pressed against me like this, but can we take this inside where it's less wet?"

Yikes. How had I not noticed the rain?

I mumble, "Yes," and bury my nose in the crook of his neck.

Jake shuffles into the house, no mean feat, with me clinging to him like a monkey. But I can't let go. Never want to let go.

"Come on, Claire. Let's dry off."

I uncurl my legs and lower my feet to the floor. "Sorry. I'm just so happy." A blush creeps up my neck. I'm coming across way too clingy.

I grip his biceps, recognition weakening my knees. "You're in uniform."

"Yeah. I've come straight from an official function." Water drips down Jake's face, a grin twitching on his lips. "You like?"

I nod, my mouth suddenly dry.

Tattoos peek through his soaked shirt. He brushes damp strands of hair from my face. "You're wet."

"I'm always wet when you're around."

A groan escapes him and his mouth slams against mine. Our tongues tangle. His hands slide to my breasts, cupping them through my long sleeve T-shirt and flicking the engorged tips with his thumbs. I dig my fingers into his butt.

For the first time since Jake bailed me out of jail, I feel like his equal.

He growls, a possessive rumbling that sinks deep inside my core.

"I'm going to take you right here in the hallway if you don't stop kissing me, Claire."

"Would that be a bad thing?" My voice is husky, my vision hazy as I focus on the pleasure his fingers are giving me. My breasts ache to be free. For him to ravish them with his mouth.

He wrenches away, his eyes like a wild animal. "Let's get you out of these soggy clothes."

Yes. Please. He peels my shirt off. I shiver when the cold air hits me.

Jake's heavy-lidded gaze drops to my chest. My nipples are like pointy diamonds punching at the ivory satin bra. He flicks the catch with scary ease. I thrust my breasts out so he can warm them with his mouth.

He crouches in front of me, his lips curled into a wicked grin. Okay. Change of plan. Looks like he's warming me lower down first. I can work with that.

He makes quick work of the button and zipper of my jeans. I hop on each foot, helping him to ease them down my legs. Next is my thong. Then, my fluffy pink socks. I close my eyes, so eager for his mouth that I don't even care that my panties are discarded on the hallway floor.

But instead of the silky touch of Jake's tongue on my nether regions, I'm swung upside down, his hand slapping my butt.

"Argh! Jake, what are you doing?"

"Shower first. I don't want you catching a cold."

He carries me down the hall and into the bathroom. Places me on my feet.

"No." I scrape hair off my face and glare at him. "Sex first."

"How about a compromise?" He turns on the water. "Sex and shower at the same time."

The possessiveness in Jake's expression turns me inside out. I nod, not trusting my voice to do more than squeak. He strips off his uniform, those sky-blue orbs never leaving mine, even while he sheaths himself in a condom.

I wrap my arms around his neck and straddle him. He carries me into the walk-in shower. There's no more foreplay. I don't need it. What I need is Jake inside me.

We both groan at the delicious sensation of joining. He bites down on the sensitive hollow of my neck and pistons in and out with deliberate precision. With each stroke, the fear I could lose this man, a fear more terrifying than the drug charges had ever been, washes away.

"I love you," I murmur against his ear.

His answer is to recapture my mouth, his tongue plunging deep inside, mimicking the thrusting of his pelvis. A tingle of awareness ripples through my body and into my core.

The old me would have obsessed over Jake's lack of response, but the new me is confident in this connection we share. It's more powerful than anything I've experienced before. Jake might not have said the words yet, but I'm sure he loves me. And I'm never letting him go.

Chapter Thirty-Six

Jake

"Fuck, I've got a cramp!"

Greg chuckles. "I thought you were fit?"

"Yeah, yeah." I give him the bird. "For running and swimming. Not being holed up in a stakeout."

The sedan is roomy enough, but my patience is slipping after being stuck in the shadows for two hours. There's no grass, no weeds, not even rats in this secluded estate. The warehouse we're watching has been in our sights ever since Jessica Andrews turned up at the station.

Greg stretches his arms out beside me. "This was nothing when we were younger."

"Nope. But those days have long passed." I rub my calf muscle, clenching my teeth at the stinging pain. "I need to piss. The fucker better show soon."

"I hope your theory's right, Jake."

"Me too."

Andrews broke down in a second interview, giving more details on how he stole pseudoephedrine from Alpha Pharmaceuticals in exchange for drugs from Leadbetter. While he didn't incriminate his wife, we believe she's in on it as well. Helping to store the narcotics.

"You ever made out in a car, Jake?"

"What?"

He shrugs. "Just making conversation. Might take our minds off our old bodies."

He's right. I've never felt my forty years as much as tonight. "Once."

"Only once?"

"Yeah. With my first steady girlfriend."

He sniggers. "I bet you had no trouble contorting yourself in the car then."

"Nope." I grimace at the lingering spasms in my leg. "There was only one part of me aching then. And you?"

"Nah. But I made out near the river a few times. And the park."

"What?" I punch him in the shoulder. "How come I'm only finding out now?"

"Because I'm a gentleman."

I snort. "Sure, you are."

I check my watch. Nine o'clock. Claire's probably tucked up on her lounge watching a chick flick. Or on the phone with her girlfriend. I fire off a quick text.

Me: What are you wearing?

The little dots jiggle. My chest puffs out at the thought she's got her mobile out, waiting for me to text. I'm such a Neanderthal.

Claire: Didn't you warn me about sending sexy texts?

Cheeky minx. I tap out a message, aware Greg is rolling his eyes beside me.

Me: That was photos. Words are okay.

Claire: I'm wearing clothes.

Goddammit. She's such a tease.

Me: Take pity on me. I've been stuck in a car with Greg for hours. I'll never get the smell out.

She responds with a laughing emoji.

Greg punches my shoulder. "You're supposed to be watching for the suspect, not texting your girlfriend. Besides, it's rude to be on your phone when I'm right here."

I give him my finger. Again.

Me: Got to go. Greg's getting pissy.

Claire: Black silk nightie. Nothing else. Smiley face.

Blood rushes to my groin. Fuck.

Greg gives me a death stare. "You're acting like a horny teenager, Jake."

I grin. If it wasn't for his lips twitching, I'd think he was pissed at me. "That's because I feel like one."

He shakes his head and laughs.

But it's more than lust. Much more. "I'm meeting Claire's parents on the weekend. They're having a party for their thirty-fifth wedding anniversary."

Greg stops midchuckle. "Whoa. That's serious."

"Yeah. And then I'm going to tell her about Sally."

"I'm glad." Greg squeezes my shoulder, his eyes glistening. "It's about time. If anyone deserves a second chance, it's you, Jake."

Lights blind us as a car drives into the industrial complex where we're parked. We hunch down in our seats. I slip my phone into my pocket. Focus on the job.

The car stops outside the warehouse we've been watching, and a figure emerges, a hood covering the face. The head turns, taking in our sedan and another vehicle nearby. They've been parked in these positions for the last two weeks to give the appearance they belong here. The figure turns away, dismissing us as a threat, unlocks the door and slips into the building. The light inside catches his profile before the door closes behind him.

Greg rubs his hands together. "Bingo!"

"Yep. Leadbetter."

"How long do you want to wait?"

"We need to catch him with the drugs. If we storm the warehouse too soon, it may only incriminate Jessica Andrews. He could claim he had no knowledge of them."

Greg aims at the door with his phone, ready to snap photos.

Ten minutes later, light spills out of the building and Leadbetter slinks out. Jessica Andrews trots behind him, wearing a ridiculously short red dress and little else. She must have goosepimples on goosepimples in this cold. They're both carrying boxes which they place into the boot.

Leadbetter shoves Jessica against the back door of the car and mashes his lips against hers.

"Jesus!" says Greg with a gruff whisper.

"At least we can't see their faces." I chuckle. "I'd never sleep again if I had a visual of his tongue down her throat."

Leadbetter's hand disappears beneath Jessica's skirt, and Greg and I both let out muffled groans. Surely, they won't fuck each other in the parking lot of a deserted industrial estate? Deserted except for Greg and me and the tactical response team stationed nearby.

"This is gross."

Greg scrubs his eyes as if that will erase the porn movie in front of us. "Can we arrest him before he drops his pants and we're blinded by his sorry arse? Or worse."

I chuckle at his discomfort. I couldn't agree more. "Did you get clear photos?"

He grunts. "Of course."

I tap my bulletproof vest. "I expect he's concealing a weapon, so we need to tread carefully. He might use her as a shield."

I send the call to the tactical team hiding behind a skip bin. While Greg and I have been complaining about being stuck in the comfort of our car, they've been perched on bare concrete.

Leadbetter straightens, and his hands go to his belt.

"Ah, fuck, Jake. We *do not* want to see this."

Two tactical response members advance on the couple making out, guns at the ready. I calculate the distance. They should make it before Leadbetter shucks his pants.

I hope.

"Police. Don't move. You're under arrest." The officer's voice strikes like a viper in the deserted car park.

Leadbetter's hand thrusts inside his jacket, but the officer is quicker, blocking it and slamming him to the ground. Greg and I tumble out of the car with less finesse than we'd ever admit and converge, our guns pointed at Leadbetter.

The second cop grabs the flailing hands of a screaming Jessica and snaps handcuffs on her. The rest of the tactical response team converges on the scene.

Leadbetter's hauled to his feet. I can't hide the smirk on my lips as I confront him. His pants dangle low, revealing white underwear and a hairy gut spilling over the top. I smother a chuckle, imagining what Claire would make of it.

I snap my attention back to his face and grin. "Nice to see you again, Mr Leadbetter. It's been a while."

His eyes flash murder at me. "I got nothing to say."

"No problem." My smile widens. "I think the evidence will speak for itself."

I turn to Jessica Andrews and hold up the piece of paper in my hand. "Mrs Andrews, we have a warrant to search the premises."

Her face pales. She looks to Leadbetter. "Terry?"

"Shut your mouth. Not a word."

She flinches, her face dropping. By the looks of it, she's in love with the scumbag. Little does she know, but she's most likely made a lucky escape. People have a habit of dropping dead around Leadbetter. There's no doubt in my mind he got to Scudasi in jail.

I open the boot. "What have we here?" I glance across at

Leadbetter. He strains against the cop holding him but says nothing.

One box is open. Leadbetter must have checked the merchandise before bringing it to the car. I slip on a pair of disposable gloves and peel the top flap back. It's filled with plastic bags of white powder. Yes!

I motion to Greg, and we stroll into the warehouse. Despite the brisk temperature and the evidence we just found, my brow is slick with sweat. The future of my career and the safety of my family depend on a positive outcome.

Pallets upon pallets line the interior. With the help of a drug sniffer dog—not Milo because he's on a refresher course —we begin the arduous task of inspecting every package. Luck is on our side. After only twenty minutes, we find the narcotics hidden inside cases marked as tea leaves.

I do a quick count and shake my head. "Jesus, Greg, I estimate there's at least five hundred million dollars' worth of cocaine here."

Greg's mouth drops. "You're kidding me."

I glare at him. "I never joke about drugs."

His eyes twinkle. "That should keep the squad commander off our backs for a while."

As we return to the car, movement to my left has me whisking my gun out of its holster. Beady eyes stare up at me from a tiny furry face. Well, what do you know, there are rats living here, after all. I lower my gun. The rodent scampers off.

I roll my shoulders back and stretch my arms. Two years we've been working on this case, chasing the worst kinds of rats. It's going to be a long night at the station. But worth every minute. With Leadbetter in jail, my family will be safe. Claire will be safe, and I'll be able to call off the security firm keeping watch over her. It's time to tell her I love her. And come clean about my past. About Sally.

Chapter Thirty-Seven

Jake

The scent of eucalypts mingled with fresh rain wafts through the air on the lilting notes of a Latino band. From the black slate tiles and roaring fireplace to the wrap-around veranda extending into bushland, the venue is a world away from the city. Claire's parents chose well for their party. I only wish I'd had the chance to meet them before tonight. Introductions were friendly enough when we arrived, but the steel in Mr Thompson's eyes warned me to expect a grilling from him at some point during the evening.

Claire is a tempting vision in a flamenco-styled ruby dress. I spin her out, then pull her back in. The material fans around her, sending a pulse of energy to my groin. Her gaze dips to the offending area as if she knows exactly what she's doing to me. And she'd be right.

I wiggle my eyebrows. "Eyes up here, Miss Thompson."

Crimson floods her cheeks until her face resembles the colour of her dress. "If you didn't swivel your hips so much, my eyes wouldn't keep wandering."

"I could say the same thing about you." I drop my gaze to

her breasts. Creamy flesh peeks out from the sweetheart neckline. "That dress is doing a poor job of covering you up."

She runs her fingers across the bare skin of her chest. "I bought a new super boost push-up bra. You like?"

I tighten my hold on her. I hate that she's sensitive about her size. If only she could see the warm, sexy woman I see. I nuzzle her ear. "I'll like it even more when it's on your bedroom floor."

Claire's breath hitches and the song finishes. I gesture towards the veranda. My dick demands some alone time with her, even if it's only a kiss. We link hands and head outside, only to be stopped by her mother. Bugger.

"That was beautiful. I didn't know you could dance so well, Claire."

She giggles. "Neither did I."

"She's a fast learner, Mrs Thompson."

Her mum stares at me with a thoughtful expression. "Seems to me you're an excellent teacher, Inspector Matthews."

Claire squeezes my hand.

"We're going to get some air, Mum."

"Okay, dear, but don't be too long. We'll be doing speeches soon."

We escape to the veranda and the relative quietness of the shadows. I cage Claire up against the railing next to a large gas-heated lamp and inhale her floral perfume.

She nips my earlobe. "Are you enjoying yourself?"

"Too much." I thrust against her so she can feel how hard I am and murmur into her ear. "Watching you jiggle in that dress is pure torture."

"Claire, are you out here?"

Bugger. There's no mistaking the booming voice of Claire's father. I've never seen him in action in the courtroom, but I can imagine that tone scaring the shit out of his opponents.

Claire presses her face against my chest. "I don't suppose we could slip into the bushes?"

I pull away from her, smooth my shirt, and brush my knuckles along her cheek. "We can't hide forever."

"You'll change your mind if Dad gets you alone." She adjusts her dress. "You're the first guy I've introduced to my parents since I was eighteen. He's going to interrogate you like the scary take-no-prisoners barrister that he is. I'm surprised he's waited this long."

"You're forgetting something, Claire. I'm a police inspector. If I can handle my squad commander, I can handle a lawyer."

She shakes her head. "Don't say I didn't warn you."

"There you are." Claire's father looks us up and down as though checking to see if all our clothes are still where they should be. His gaze narrows on my chest and the ink peeking above the open buttons.

I step forward. "This is a very impressive party, sir."

His stern expression softens. "That's my wife's doing."

I chuckle. "Like mother, like daughter."

He gives me a tight smile and pins me with eyes the same green as Claire's but colder. Harder.

"I'm sure Claire can spare you for a little while." Mr Thompson gestures towards the door. "Come inside and have a whiskey. I've got some special reserve Laphroaig begging to be opened."

I turn to Claire. Her bottom lip catches between her teeth as her gaze darts between me and her father. It's sweet that she's worried about me. "Are you okay on your own?"

"Sure." She squeezes my hand. "I should mingle anyway."

I follow Mr Thompson inside. Red-hot coals simmer in the charcoal fire grate, throwing off a pleasant warmth that wards off the winter chill.

He opens the whiskey and pours me a generous glass.

"What are your intentions with my daughter, Inspector Matthews?"

My heart slams to a stop. *Shit.* Claire wasn't kidding. Her father's gone straight for the jugular.

A lump forms in my throat, and I swallow it down. Fear has no place here. "I like Claire, sir. A lot."

"You don't think she's too young for you?"

The blockage in my throat triples in size. "I did at first. But she's ..." God, what do I tell him? She's sexy as hell. Has me all twisted up inside. I can imagine her being my wife. Carrying my baby.

Fuck. Where did that come from?

Mr Thompson's gaze is steadfast. I'd never appreciated the similarity between police and lawyers, the ability to unnerve opponents with silence, as much as I do right now.

"She's not too young for me, sir. She's a smart, witty, caring woman, and I enjoy her company."

He takes a sip of whiskey and stares into the fire. "You have a son?"

Okay. Not what I expected. "Yes. I do."

He returns his gaze to mine. "The fact you stood by Claire through that messy drug business says a lot about you and your feelings for my daughter, Inspector. If your intentions aren't serious, then all I ask, as one father to another, is don't lead her on."

Christ. Claire's dad doesn't pull any punches.

"Sir, no one can be sure where a relationship is going to end up, but I can assure you, I'm very serious about Claire."

Mr Thompson's eyes narrow, deep grooves furrowing across his brow. "Does she know about your wife?"

My shoulders tense, and the hairs on the back of my neck stand up. *Fuck. Fuck. Fuck.*

"I'm not judging you, son." Claire's dad places a hand on my shoulder and gently squeezes. "But I think Claire would have said something if she knew, and from the look on your face, it's obvious you haven't told her yet."

"I ..." *Fuck.* "How do you know?"

His lips curl into a self-effacing grin. "I'm a lawyer." He shrugs his shoulders as if that says it all. "I wanted to understand more about the man my daughter has fallen for."

Of course. It's not like it's a secret. I was surprised the media didn't dredge it up when they splattered Claire and me over the front page of the local paper. "It's not an easy thing to tell someone, sir."

"No, it isn't. But the longer you leave it, the worse it will be."

"I know."

He slaps me on the back. "I'll say no more, Jake. But if you haven't told Claire the truth about your wife in the next week, I will. It's not fair to keep her in the dark. From what I understand, you've had more than enough time to explain it to her."

He's right. I should have told her before now. There's always been a reason to wait—Oscar, Claire's arrest, my fear. But now it'll look like I've been keeping secrets from her. Lying. Which is exactly what I've been doing. "Thank you, sir. I appreciate your understanding." I sip my whiskey, the burn down my throat doing nothing to warm the shiver up my spine.

"I can see you're an honourable man, and you're good to Claire. I don't want to ruin that for her." He knocks back the amber fluid and leans closer. Flames dance in his eyes. "But don't get me wrong, Inspector Matthews. If you hurt my little girl, I'll hunt you down and make you pay. What the newspapers did to you will look like pre-school compared to what I'd do to your career."

My balls shrivel in my pants. I should call Claire's father out for threatening me, but I don't blame him. I'm not sure I'd be as lenient if Claire was my daughter. Mr Thompson is a well-known barrister. For some reason, I hadn't made the connection. I thought Claire was on her own, but I couldn't have been more wrong. She wants to make it on her own, without her parents' help. My chest swells with pride.

"Honey, you men are looking very serious over here." Claire's mother glides up and links her arm with her husband.

He smiles a full-on smile that says he's very much in love with her, reminding me of my own parents. "Jake and I got talking shop."

She slaps him on the chest. "This is a party, Martin."

"Sorry, love." He grins. "But when you throw a cop and a lawyer together, we can't help ourselves."

"Well, I won't let you talk work all night. This is a gorgeous band, and we haven't had one dance yet."

I smother the smirk that twitches at the edges of my lips. Mr Thompson might be a formidable barrister in the court-room, but it's clear who's in charge at home. And it's not him.

He groans but doesn't resist when his wife pulls him away. "Remember what I said, Jake."

I nod, acknowledging that I'll do as he asks. I'd already planned to tell Claire after her parents' party anyway.

I nurse my whiskey, the glow of the fire washing over me.

Will Claire be as forgiving as her father?

Chapter Thirty-Eight

Claire

My sister makes a beeline for me the moment I re-enter the function room.

"There you are." Alex kisses my cheek. "Where's your handsome policeman?"

I roll my eyes. Of course, she'd be more interested in a police inspector than her unemployed flesh and blood. "He's talking with Dad."

"Ouch." She screws up her face. "Is that a good idea?"

"There wasn't much choice."

She laughs. "I guess not."

A champagne server approaches us. I grab a glass and chug half the contents down. Family functions are always uncomfortable. Too many successful people making me feel like a failure. But with Jake on display, it's doubly nerve-racking.

"Thanks for keeping my secret."

"That's what sisters are for. I'm sorry the lawyer I recommended didn't work out. Luckily you didn't need him anyway." Alex sips her red wine and smiles. "You look happy, Claire."

"I am. Things are going well with Jake."

"An inspector is quite a catch."

"Yeah." Jake's title shouldn't matter, but it carries weight with my family.

The music slows to a rumba, and my parents take to the dance floor. Dad's got two left feet, but Mum doesn't seem to mind as they sway side to side out of time with the music. What's he done with Jake?

Alex glances across the floor to where her husband is in deep conversation with two other men. If my memory is correct, one of them is a judge and the other one is a senior public servant. "Sorry, Claire, I know it's a party, but I've got some business to discuss. Talk later." She air kisses me and glides across the room.

I shake my head. Thank God I never followed in my sister's footsteps. In Dad's. There's more to life than work.

I spot Jake trapped near the fireplace with two of my aunts. He nods and smiles at them, his gaze darting around the room. As I get closer, I overhear Aunty Beth telling him about the day I peed my pants in the supermarket. Lovely.

I swoop in, clasp Jake's hand and glare at my aunty. "I was five years old."

Aunty Beth chuckles. "And such a cutie."

"Claire, look at you," says Aunt Mary. Her gaze travels up and down my body. "I swear you get taller every time I see you. And thinner."

"Thank you. I see you're both getting to know Jake."

Aunty Beth winks. "He's a fine young man."

"Yes, he is." I squeeze Jake's fingers tight, wondering how we can escape my well-meaning but suffocating aunts.

We're saved by the bell.

"Quiet, everyone. Quiet!"

My father stands at the front of the room, microphone in hand, Mum by his side.

Damn. I should have brought tissues. I just know I'm going to cry.

Dad launches into his speech. It's the usual topics, thanking people for coming, telling a few 'old married couple' jokes. Then he moves on to how they met.

"I first met Rachel thirty-eight years ago when she started as an intern at the same law firm I was working at. Both of us would get so flustered when we were in the same room as each other that I once handed her my hanky and told her it was the file she needed to prepare for court."

The room erupts into laughter.

Dad's face sobers, but light glitters in his eyes. "Love has a way of sneaking up on you. One day you're a single man, enjoying all the freedoms of bachelorhood …"

Mum nudges him with her elbow and glares.

He flicks a strand of hair away from her face, a smile curling on his lips as he returns his attention to the audience. "And the next day, your toothbrushes sit side by side on the bathroom sink, a toddler is interrupting you at the worst possible times, and your belt buckle no longer fits in the same notch."

There's a snicker across the crowd, and several people nod their agreement.

He grabs Mum's hand and brings it to his chest. "I'm a better person for having married you, Rachel. Thank you for loving me."

Sighs and clapping fill the room. The hum in my ears drowns it out as tears stream down my cheeks. Jake's arm curls around my waist, and I bury my head in his shirt. Inhale his spicy scent. Melt into his comforting strength.

My parents couldn't be more different and yet love binds them together. Could it be the same for Jake and me? I love him. And I'm a better person for having met him. For the first time in my life, I dare to believe I can have the sort of love Mum and Dad share.

෪

Jake's quiet in the taxi home from my parents' party. I worry my father has warned him off with the proverbial shotgun, but he assures me that hasn't happened. With my head against his shoulder, I drift to sleep to the gentle lull of the engine.

I don't stir until Jake carries me through the front door and into the bedroom. He removes my dress and underwear with an odd mix of reverence and efficiency. He says nothing and I say nothing back, the silence binding us more completely than any words. I shiver at the intensity in his expression.

Jake removes his clothes with the same methodical care he removed mine. I lick my lips at the ink swirling up chiselled abs and pecs, the proof of his desire jutting between his legs. I'm suddenly wide awake as he lowers himself over me and nestles between my thighs.

His tongue flicks out and licks across the seam of my lips. He sucks on my bottom lip, nipping it, then soothing it with his tongue. I return the favour, licking the lingering hint of whiskey from his breath. Jake peppers kisses down my neck and breast. I arch up as he latches onto the hard bud of my nipple and suckles. With each pull of his mouth, a fresh gush of moisture pools between my thighs. I wriggle my hips, begging for relief.

After what feels like hours of sweet torture where my nipples are slaves to the fiery brand of Jake's mouth, he releases them. He hovers at my entrance, hooded gaze on mine, then enters, inch by glorious inch, until he's buried inside me. I memorise every line on his face: the furrows between his eyebrows, the glazed desire in his eyes, his flushed cheeks.

Jake makes love to me slowly, like he's savouring an expensive shiraz. I burn beneath his ministrations, bucking against him to hurry up. He refuses to be rushed, pressing my hands above my head and into the mattress as he surges in and out of me, his blue eyes piercing my soul.

The room soaks up our grunts and groans. There's still no need for words. Only actions—the gentle sway of two bodies moving as one. Jake still hasn't said *I love you*, but his body tattoos the words into mine with every thrust. My orgasm rolls through me, a rumbling earthquake that exposes the very foundations of my soul. Jake shudders, biting my neck and spills inside me.

My inner walls continue to pulse with delicious after-shocks. I run my palms up and down Jake's back, hugging him closer. He continues to move inside me, riding out the remnants of his orgasm. A languid sense of peace envelops me, as does the salty scent of sex. Jake captures my mouth with his, our tongues coming together in a sensual rumba, the dance of love.

Jake rolls us to the side. His cock softens and slips from my body.

That's when I realise.

No condom!

I'm on the pill, so there's no risk of pregnancy, and I trust Jake to be clean. But he's always so careful about using protection. It surprises me he's slipped up. I'd dwell on the significance more if my mind wasn't a haze of sated lust.

He presses a chaste kiss to my lips and wraps his arms around me, pulling me into his chest. I slide one leg between his so we're fully entwined. That's how we fall asleep. One body. One heart.

Chapter Thirty-Nine

Jake

The distant din of the coffee machine filters into my office.

White noise.

I've never noticed it before. I do now.

The fluorescent bulb above my desk floods the room with harsh white light, making everything appear more artificial. Even the live pot plant in the corner.

I latch onto the memory of Claire's soft flesh beneath mine, her sweet, breathy moans, my answering grunts. Only, it doesn't soothe me, just reminds me of the one critical detail she still doesn't know.

I shut down the laptop and shove it into my bag. Each movement is mechanical. My body knows what needs to be done, even if my mind has retreated into that place minds go to when reality becomes too much to bear. I've seen it happen to new recruits when they witness their first deceased person.

I pull out my mobile, fingers at the ready despite my twisted insides. What do I say? I was going to tell Claire about Sally tonight. Damn it. Why didn't I say something on

Sunday like I was going to? I shake my head. Because we were both drunk on sex and I didn't want the outside world to interfere.

Me: Sorry, something's come up. Will call tomorrow. xx

She texts back straight away.

Clare: No prob. RUOK?

No. I'm not okay. *Fuck!* I need to bury myself inside her. Forget, just for a little while, that life is shitty. But I can't call her. Not like this.

Me: Yeah. Just some things I have to take care of.

Greg strides into my office. "I came as soon as I got your message."

His brown eyes are a melting pot of concern. My legs buckle, and I grip the edge of the desk to stop myself from stumbling. I shouldn't be worried about showing weakness in front of him. After all, he's the first person I called after triple zero that awful night three years ago when Sally collapsed. He had to pry me away from the stretcher as the ambos carried her from the house. It wasn't pretty.

"Thanks." I rub my fingers down the sides of my neck. "I'm not sure how long I'll be gone, but the doctors don't think she'll last the night."

"Don't worry about anything." Greg keeps his voice soft. Neutral. "We'll take care of things here."

I zip up the laptop bag. "You can call me if you need to."

"I won't be calling." Greg crosses his arms and glares at me. "You're on compassionate leave. Forget about the station."

My fingers tighten around the handle of my bag. "I need work, Greg."

"No." He grasps me by the shoulders, his brown eyes boring into mine. "What you need is to concentrate on your family. Sally is what matters right now."

I stare back at him. I'm a stranger in my body. "My chest feels like it's going to implode." I pull away from him and rub my mouth. "I didn't expect it to affect me like this. It's not like I didn't know she was going to die."

"While there's life, there's hope, Jake. Even when there isn't any. That's just the way we're hardwired. But death …" Greg rakes his hands through his hair, lifts his gaze to the ceiling, then back to me. "Death is final. You can never fully prepare for it."

My vision blurs. He's right. And if I don't leave now, I'll be sobbing on his shoulder like a little kid. I give him a terse nod and bolt out the door.

ॐ

Death permeates the palliative care room, its icy tentacles curling around the figure swaddled on the bed: white on white. It's like being lost in a blizzard.

Sally's breaths echo in the tiny room, except for those moments when she stops breathing altogether. Moments my breath stalls and a vice clamps down on my ribcage. But the heart monitor continues to blip, and soon enough, she sucks in another breath.

"Oscar drew a picture for you yesterday. He said it was of the three of us at the beach. There was a dog as well. I didn't have the heart to tell him you're allergic to dogs."

My throat is hoarse from talking. Rambling. I like to think Sally can still hear me. That my voice brings comfort. After all, I've been speaking to her like this for the last three years. In the past, her eyes would sometimes open and there'd be a flicker of awareness. Now, there's nothing.

"I'm sorry you won't see our son grow up, but I promise he'll never forget you. That he'll know how much you loved him."

I swipe at the tears rolling down my cheeks. What I won't tell Oscar is how Sally didn't want him at first. That she'd never wanted children. I won't be sharing that little detail.

She came to love him. That's all that matters. If only depression hadn't sucked her into a spiral of self-destruction. If only I'd realised how fragile her state of mind had been. If only …

Fuck. I told my parents I wanted to do this alone. Now I'm not so sure.

I kiss Sally's cheek. Wipe my tears from where they drop onto her face.

"I love you, Sally. I'll always love you." And I will.

We had many good years together. But she's my past and Claire's my future. Which explains the ache deep inside my chest—the ugly rodent of guilt gnawing at my soul. How can I declare my love to my dying wife while being in love with another woman? What sort of man does that make me?

Greg would say, a normal man.

A man with needs and wants. Desires.

If mine and Sally's positions were reversed, I'd want her to be happy. To find someone new. And she'd want the same for me, too.

It's been over twenty hours since I rushed to Sally's bedside. Twenty hours of watching her breaths become more erratic. Twenty hours of wishing she could be free and simultaneously feeling like the worst husband in the world for wishing her dead. Because there's no cure for the catastrophic stroke Sally had three years ago. Death is the only way she can escape the frozen world she's trapped in.

I change positions, my arse going numb from all the sitting.

Without warning, Sally gasps and her eyes open wide.

I half rise out of the chair. *What the fuck?*

Her upper back arches towards the ceiling, the whites of her eyes rolling into the sockets. Then, just as suddenly, she slumps onto the mattress.

My heartbeats trip over each other as I search for the buzzer. Seconds feel like hours; then I have the remote in my hand. That's when it hits me. The green line of her heartbeat is straight.

Sally's gone.

I tighten my grip on her hand. Tears well in my eyes.

Tears for the life Sally never got to live.

Tears for Oscar, who will never know his mother.

Tears I've kept buried deep inside for three long, miserable years.

❧

A familiar arm wraps around my shoulders. "Hey, son."

I peel my head off Sally's chest. "Hey, Mum."

"How about you come and get a coffee? Something to eat."

Tears spill down my cheeks. Now they've started, I seem to have an endless supply of them. "I can't leave her."

Mum leans her head against my shoulder. "Jake, there's nothing more you can do now. It's over."

I release Sally's hand and tear my gaze from the bed. My mother's eyes glisten with tears.

I scrub my face, but it does nothing to stem the flow.

My heart aches. For Sally. And for Oscar. "It hurts so much."

"I know." Mum wraps her arms around me, and my tears fall faster. The last time I cried like this was when the doctors told me there was no hope for Sally and that I should get her affairs in order. My mother was there for me then, too.

A few minutes pass. Maybe more. Time doesn't seem to exist in this alabaster tomb.

Mum pulls tissues out of her pocket and hands them to me. I blow my nose. The sound reverberates around the room. Jesus, I sound like Oscar.

"Thanks."

She smiles. The smile mothers give to soothe the ache, heal the wound.

A throat clears, and I turn towards the door. My heart squeezes when I see Oscar standing next to my father, his bottom lip quivering.

"Daddy." His voice is soft. Uncertain.

I close the distance between us and squat down in front of him. "Hey, little guy."

He lifts his arms, his eyes shimmering. I pick him up and squeeze his small body into my chest. He smells of soap and powder. Hope and innocence. I wish he didn't have to see this, but the social worker said it's important. That it will give him closure. I hope to God she's right.

Mum and Dad slip out of the room, and I return to Sally's bedside. I sit on a chair, Oscar on my lap. He stretches a trembling hand out and touches the sheet. "Mummy looks so peaceful."

"She is."

Oscar strokes the fabric, his gaze riveted to Sally's face. When Sally fell ill, I'd wanted to shield Oscar, but the counsellor cautioned against it. So, each month, I'd take him to the nursing home where Oscar would show Sally pictures he'd drawn. Chatter about his day. Tell her he loved her. Each month my heart would break all over again seeing them together. Seeing Sally unresponsive. Oscar seemed to handle it better than me. Maybe because he has no memories of her tucking him into bed. Singing to him. Cuddling him.

"Is she really dead?"

Tears prick my eyes, and it takes all my police training to keep them from falling. "Yeah. She is."

Oscar nods. "God will look after her now."

I swallow the football-sized lump wedged in my throat. "He will."

Oscar slides off my lap. "Can we go see Grandma and Grandpa now?"

"Sure."

I don't know what I expected, but Oscar is stoic beyond his years.

I lean over the bed and press a kiss on Sally's forehead. "Forgive me," I whisper so that Oscar doesn't hear. "For failing you." For falling in love again.

I take Oscar's hand and head down the corridor to the hospital café. Mum sits at a table near the corner. I grab a seat and lift Oscar onto my knee.

He scrambles off and slips into the chair next to me. "I'm a big boy now, Dad."

I ruffle his hair. "That you are." I don't mention he was happy to be held in the hospital room just minutes earlier. He wasn't such a big boy then. Neither was I.

Dad arrives with four cups. My stomach rumbles.

Oscar giggles, his eyes wide like saucers. "What was that?"

My father hands him a hot chocolate. "I think your dad's hungry."

Oscar grins. "I'm hungry too. Can I have pancakes?"

Mum smiles. "They might not have them, but I'm sure we'll find something you like." She turns to me, her eyes narrowing. "When was the last time you ate, Jake?"

"Ah …" I pause and think. I've spent the last twenty-four hours in a daze. "Not since breakfast yesterday." No wonder my stomach is giving its own rendition of a garbage disposal at work.

Mum tsks me.

Dad kisses the top of her head. "I'll get some food. You relax, love."

I give him a smirk that would have gotten me a stern talking to when I was younger. I can't help it. The normalcy of the moment eases the pain in my chest. "You don't know what I want."

"I think I can work it out." He rolls his eyes and squeezes my shoulder. "It's not like it's the first breakfast this family's had together."

Oscar buries his head in a colouring book my parents had the foresight to bring. I wish I could bury mine just as easily.

I pull out my phone. The screen flashes with the last text Claire sent. At six-thirty this morning. Shortly after Sally died.

Claire: Hope ur morning is better xx

If there'd been any chance Sally might come out of her vegetative state, I would have never looked at another woman. But every single specialist I engaged, and there were many, gave me the same advice—she had zero chance of recovery. They hadn't expected her to live past the first twelve months, let alone three years. She'd been in a holding pattern, waiting to die.

But it was still cowardly and grossly unfair to hide the truth from Claire. I should have told her about Sally soon after we started dating. I can only hope she understands how difficult it was for me to reconcile my growing feelings for her with guilt for moving on, because I can't imagine my future without her in it.

Chapter Forty

Claire

When I opened my lingerie drawer this morning, black consumed my thoughts. And not sexy black. So, I chose a plain black boy-short that I usually reserve for heavy period days and a plain black cotton bra. Jake hasn't been responding to my texts. Something's wrong. Very wrong. I can feel it in every pore of my being as I hurry from the bus stop, a cardboard box tucked under my arm.

Droplets smash against the windows and trickle down the panes of the police station like dozens of tiny streams. Or tears. I step through the door, my hands shaking. Water drips off my bright pink raincoat and strands of hair stick to my cheeks. My leather boots will be ruined, but at least my jeans and jumper are dry. It sucks losing the company car and having to rely on public transport.

My palms are clammy and my pulse quickens. I haven't been back to the station since I was arrested. It'll take some time for all the ugliness of my arrest to fade. The ambience doesn't help. Grey and beige are not happy colours and should never be seen together. The police force needs to engage a decent interior designer to revamp the decor, or better still, they should build a brand new station.

The young constable at the desk smiles at me. "It's a bit wet out there, isn't it?"

"Yes, it is." I flick the hood of my raincoat off and place the box on the sandy-coloured bench. "I brought some muffins for everyone."

He eyes it with suspicion. "I'm sorry. We can't accept gifts."

"No, no. It's okay. I'm—"

"Hi, Claire."

I swivel and come eye to eye with a familiar face. "Constable Dylan, how are you?" Heat fills my cheeks. The last two times I've met Dylan, my world has been turned upside down. And not in a good way. At least his dog is nowhere in sight. "I bought these muffins for the station as a thank you for being so helpful these last couple of months."

"Thanks. That's very thoughtful." Dylan nods at the constable behind the desk. "Claire's a friend of Detective Inspector Matthews."

"Oh. In that case …" The constable's eyes light up, and he peels the lid off the basket. His eyes widen. "Chocolate chip!"

Dylan rolls his eyes as the officer pulls out a muffin and begins devouring it. I'm glad I stopped at my favourite bakery. Although handing out muffins isn't the real reason I'm here.

"Is Jake in?"

"No." Dylan grabs a muffin. "He's not back from the hospital yet. You can probably catch him there."

Hospital?

The blood drains from my face. Poor Jake. *Why didn't he call?* "Oh no, has Oscar been hurt?"

"No. It's his wife. She was rushed there yesterday."

What the hell?

My heart speeds up like I've snorted the cocaine I'd once been accused of possessing and trafficking.

Jake's still married?

Dylan's face blurs. He's borne witness to my humiliation twice before. I won't break down in front of him for a third time. I blink back tears, mumble a goodbye and race out into the street. Dylan calls after me, but I don't look back. A bus pulls up and I scramble in. The door swishes shut, and tears slide down my cheeks.

No wonder Jake never invited me to his place. Or to meet his parents. Or his son.

I've been sleeping with a married man. A married man with a child.

§&

Blessed numbness cloaks my mind as I stare at the passing traffic, seeing nothing. But my ears ring so loudly that I'm surprised people around me don't complain about the noise. Eventually the scenery becomes clearer, and the buzzing in my ears softens. My palms sting and I release my clenched hands to find my nails have bitten into the skin.

The bus approaches Westmead Hospital. Fate or coincidence? Dylan never said which hospital Jake's wife had been admitted to, but there's a good chance it's this one.

I clamber off the bus at the next stop, grateful the rain has cleared. The fog in my head has also lifted. I must have jumped to the wrong conclusion.

There must be a logical explanation. Perhaps Dylan meant ex-wife? Yeah. That makes more sense. I should have stopped and let him explain instead of racing off in a panic. I shrug off the raincoat and fold it over my arm. Fluff my hair. Then stroll into the emergency department, trying to look cool when inside every nerve ending is screaming.

Grey is the colour of choice in the reception area, but it's light. Bright. And unlike the police station's drab decor, it lifts my mood. I'm sure I'll find out Dylan was referring to ex-wife, not wife. There are only a couple of people waiting, and they don't seem too sick as they scroll on their phones.

"Can I help you?" asks the woman behind the reception counter.

"Ah …" Crap. I only know the surname and have no idea if this is the right hospital. I hold my head high. I didn't do sales for five years without learning how to bluff my way through a conversation. "I'm looking for Mrs Matthews. She was brought in yesterday."

The woman—Amanda Travis, according to her name badge—taps her pen on the bench. "Are you family?"

"No. Just a concerned—" What the hell am I? "Ah, friend?"

Amanda squints over her glasses at me. "Are you asking me or telling me?"

This was a bad idea. "I'm a *friend* of the family."

She lifts her chin and peers further down her pokey glasses at me. "Then I suggest you contact them. Only *immediate* family are allowed to visit."

The security guard shuffles closer. Great. The last thing I want is to find myself back at the station, arrested for causing a disturbance at the hospital.

"Thank you," I mumble and slink out the door.

What now?

I wander down the corridor. A cup of tea is what I need to pull myself together. Then I'll call Jake.

I stumble upon a café. It's warm and inviting, with thick wooden tables and black iron chairs. The display of cakes is mouth-watering, but there's no way I could swallow solid food. I order a pot of Earl Grey tea and slide into a chair in the corner. There's a large palm next to the table, partly shielding me from view. I take a deep breath and repeat to myself:

logical explanation. There's a logical explanation. Jake is not a cheater.

An older couple talk in hushed tones at the table next to me. Their eyes are heavy from lack of sleep, but there's a buzz of energy that tells me they're relieved. I guess that must mean whoever they're visiting is okay.

"How was Jake when you left him?" asks the man.

My ears prick up, and I stare at the menu, pretending to read it. Are they talking about my Jake?

"As good as can be expected," says the woman.

The man clasps her hand. "I imagine he'll be feeling lots of emotions."

"Yes." The woman lays her head on the man's shoulder. "He's a good husband."

Husband? My stomach threatens to relieve me of its contents. I press my palm against my abdomen. Oh God. Please don't be my Jake.

A nurse approaches the couple's table. "Sorry to bother you, Mr and Mrs Matthews."

My stomach heaves. I swallow to stop myself from vomiting. Matthews? It has to be Jake's parents. I peer through the palm leaves. Of course. The man has the same strong jawline and piercing blue eyes as Jake. It's a wonder I didn't notice straight away.

"It's no bother," says Mr Matthews.

The nurse continues. "Some paperwork was missed with Sally Matthews' admission. Would you mind filling it out?"

"Of course not." Jake's father takes the folder from the nurse. "Thank you."

I slide out of my seat, the tea forgotten, and hurry to the door. Mr and Mrs Matthews don't notice me. They're too busy reading the documents the nurse gave them. I stumble my way through the corridors until I hit the fresh air outside.

I suck in deep breaths, my lungs screaming with each inhale. There's no logical explanation that frees me from this nightmare. No escaping the truth. Jake's married. Our entire relationship has been a lie. A sharp pain pierces my chest and cleaves my heart in two.

I stride towards the bus stop, desperate to get home and hide in my bedroom and never come out again. How could Jake do this?

Why would he do it?

He met my family. He held his own with my father.

Why would a married man do that? Was it all a game to him? Have he and his friends at the station been laughing about the little piece of fluff on the side?

My mobile rings and I rummage in my handbag. I freeze when I pull it out. Jake. An hour ago, I wouldn't have hesitated to pick up. Now, do I answer or ignore?

Heat rushes through me and a flash of red clouds my vision. I'm sick of men taking me for a fool. Not anymore. This fluff has claws, and Jake's going to find out just how sharp they are. There's a reason I'm wearing my no-nonsense panties today.

"Jake."

"Hi, Claire."

His voice is ragged like he's been up all night. My heart aches to comfort him, but I ignore the stupid, naïve organ. "What do you want?"

"It's so good to hear your voice."

"Really?" I grit my teeth. I will not be fooled. Not again. "What's wrong with your wife's voice?"

He sucks in a breath.

Gotcha, you cheating bastard.

"I can explain," he says, his tone flat.

My heart wants to listen to him, but my head says no way. He had a chance to tell me about his wife. He chose not to.

"Are you married?"

"Claire …"

Silence follows. Is he going to answer me?

"It's not that simple."

His reply is a bolt of lightning to the tattered remains of my heart. "Married. Not married. It's pretty simple to me."

"Yes, but—"

I cut him off. "I have no time for liars. Or cheaters, Jake. I never want to see you again!"

I stab the end button on my mobile, tears streaming down my face. The bus stop is just ahead of me, but people are gawking at the crazy lady, aka me, so I continue walking past them and call the one person who's never let me down.

"Jules!"

"Claire, what's wrong?"

I blubber into the phone. "Jake … wife … bastard."

"Whoa. Slow down, Claire. I can't understand you."

I grab a tissue out of my handbag, blow my nose and take a few deep breaths. This is not the end of the world. I will not fall apart.

"Sorry, Jules. I don't know how to say it."

"I find the best way is to just *say it*!"

I swallow the bile in my mouth. "Jake's married." Pain radiates across my chest as I wait for Jules to answer. "Did you hear me, Jules? Jake has a wife."

"I heard you. Are you sure it's not an ex-wife?"

"Nope. It's definitely wife."

"Wow! How did you find out?"

"A constable at the station told me. Apparently, Jake rushed to the hospital yesterday to be by her side. That's why he cancelled our date." My stomach churns with each word. Is that why he wasn't always available on weekends? I thought it was because of Oscar, but it seems he also had a wife to spend time with.

I can't believe I trusted him.

"Oh, Claire. I'm so sorry."

I stop and rub my chest, trying to ease the bone-deep ache. Houses line each side of the street, the hospital long behind me. It's a quiet neighbourhood except for a howling dog. He sounds as bereft as I feel. "Not as sorry as me."

"Wait." Jules' voice rises an octave. "Everyone else knew he was seeing you even though he was supposedly still married?"

"It seems like it."

"That's a bit strange."

"Not really. I suck at relationships. I only seem to attract losers or bastards, or both." I rub my temples. A headache claws its way across my forehead. "I might need some of your mum's Valium, Jules. To dull the pain."

"Don't be silly. You don't need drugs."

And she does?

"You take them."

The rain returns, a fine mist coating the path in front of me. I can't be bothered with my raincoat, although my woollen jumper will get soaked. Maybe the rain will cleanse me of the hurt.

"Yeah. But I'm a lost cause." Jules sighs in a way I've never heard before. I don't understand why she hasn't confronted Mick about her suspicions he's cheating on her. "You're stronger than you think, Claire. You'll get through this."

"But—"

"Look. You're the one who told me to stop taking stuff that wasn't prescribed to me. You were right to do that. If you think you need something to help you through this, then talk to your doctor. But give it a few days or a week. You're still in shock."

"I guess you're right."

"I know I'm right."

Despite the pain in my heart, I smile. That sounds more like the Jules I know and love.

"Claire, tell me where you are, and I'll come pick you up."

"I don't want to be a bother." I hiccup as fresh tears slide down my face.

"It's no bother. Now, where are you?"

I chuckle at Jules' mum-like tone and give her the address. What would I do without her?

The sooner I get home, the sooner I can have a proper bawl. Release the tears bottling up inside. Put this all behind me and move on.

My phone beeps. Jake.

"Can you believe it, Jules? He's trying to call me again."

"I don't know, Claire. Surely, there's a rational explanation."

My heart screams for her to be right, but my head says I'd be a fool to believe anything he said. "Jules, I've just come from the hospital where I overheard Jake's parents talking about his *wife*. Not *ex-wife*. *Wife*."

Jules doesn't answer. Jake's call goes to voicemail.

"Jules, you still there?"

"Yeah. I was trying to think of a reason to give Jake another chance. Unless you want to tell him to go fuck himself again, I say ignore him."

"Agreed." The ache in my chest intensifies as the two halves of my heart splinter into tiny pieces. "I've had enough of lies. I'm done with him."

Chapter Forty-One

Jake

Fuck! Fuck! Fuck!
Why didn't I tell Claire sooner?

I step back from the table. Mum moves as if to follow. I shake my head and hurry away, dodging stragglers who seem to make it their mission to stand in my way. Can't they tell my life is crumbling? Then again, this is a hospital, so perhaps their worlds are also on fire.

My pace picks up as I march down the icy, grey corridor, looking for an exit. I need to get out of here. Clear my head.

The phone rings, and I grapple like a crazy man, pulling it from my pocket. A sharp pain lances through my chest. It's not Claire.

I stop and lean against the wall. "Greg."

"Hey, Jake. Sorry to disturb you."

"That's okay. Have you seen Claire?"

"No. But she's the reason I'm ringing. She swung by the station earlier."

My throat constricts. "Someone told her about Sally."

"Yeah. Dylan. He thought she knew. He realised after she

raced out like the devil was on her tail that she didn't. I gave him a reaming."

"Nah. It's not his fault." I hang my head. She must be hurting so badly. Why the fuck did I keep putting off telling her? Nothing good ever comes from concealing the truth. I should know that by now. My job's all about ferreting out lies. "I rang her. She doesn't want to see me again."

"Give her a couple of days to calm down." Greg's voice is an even baritone, the one he uses when he's talking down an agitated perpetrator. In other words, he's telling me I need to give myself time to calm down, too. Fucker is too astute for his own good.

I bang the back of my head against the wall. Claire seemed so final when she told me to fuck off. Not that she used those words, but that's what she meant. "Thanks for telling me."

"Jake."

Fuck. I'm in no mood to chat. "What?"

"Do you want me to talk to Claire?"

I close my eyes, blocking out the constant stream of people passing through the corridor and sneaking sideways glances at me. "No." That's something I need to do myself. "But thanks for offering."

I end the call and dial Claire's number. Again. And it goes to voicemail. Again. Fuck! I shove the phone into my pocket.

Greg's right. I need to give her time to settle down.

I push off the wall and stride through the hospital corridor towards the café, projecting a confidence I don't feel. All the white and grey and pungent antiseptic is poison in my lungs. Oscar spies me before I reach the table and launches himself against my legs.

"Whoa! Hold on there, little buddy." I lift him into my arms and squeeze him tight. "What's going on?"

He wriggles against me, and I loosen my grip.

"Grandpa said I had to go back home with him, but I want to stay with you."

I ruffle his hair. "I want that too, but I've got grown-up stuff to do."

He sticks his bottom lip out, considering my answer. "What sort of stuff?"

I force a smile. He's not letting me get away easily. "Boring stuff."

His nose scrunches up. "Like maths?"

I nod. "Yeah. Like maths." He's inherited his mother's aversion to numbers and her love of reading. I swallow the lump in my throat. She'll live on through him.

My father launches out of his chair with more grace than you'd expect of a man in his sixties. "How about you and I go to the movies, Oscar?"

Oscar's gaze flits between me and my dad. I wish I knew what he was thinking. "I guess so." He turns to Mum. "Are you gonna come too, Grandma?"

"No." She shakes her head. "Not today. Grandpa wants one-on-one time with his favourite grandson."

Oscar's little brows crinkle. "Aren't I your only grandson?"

She taps him on the nose. "Yes, you are."

Oscar seems happy enough with the response and wriggles until I set him back on his feet.

I clasp Mum's shoulder. "I can handle this on my own."

She grabs my hand, squeezing it tight. "I know you can. But you don't have to." Her eyes widen. "Unless you want Claire to go with you instead?"

"No. I need to do this by myself." And I need to do it now. Before I lose my nerve. I pinch the bridge of my nose. There are also others who need to be informed. "Would you mind ringing Sally's brother? He won't give a damn since he gave her up for dead three years ago, but he needs to be told."

"Of course, love. And I'll call her two aunts. They were flying up from Melbourne this morning. Such a shame they didn't get here in time."

"Thanks."

Sally's brother won't waste his time or money on his only sibling. He's an engineer on an oil rig in the Pacific. His priorities are making money, then blowing it all on booze and women. But her aunts will be devastated they missed saying goodbye.

Oscar clings to my trouser leg, his bottom lip wobbling. "I want to stay with Daddy."

Christ. I thought he was happy to watch a film with his grandfather. He's not making this easy.

My father gets down on his haunches. "Come on, Oscar. I've looked up the movies, and you'll never guess what's playing?"

Oscar releases my leg. "Superman?"

"Yep."

His eyes widen to saucers. "Can I wear my cape?"

"Absolutely." Dad hauls him into his arms and stands. There's a creaking of bones, but I'm impressed with how well my father moves.

Oscar twists and grins at me. "I'm going to see Superman."

"I heard."

Dad strides off, not giving Oscar any time to think.

"You're sure you'll be fine?" asks my mother.

I point my finger in my father's direction. "Yes. Now go."

Mum gives me a peck on the cheek and wraps her arms around me. I breathe in her lavender scent and thank whatever God there is, yet again, for blessing me with such supportive parents.

Once Mum's gone, I slump in my chair and gulp the remains of my coffee. Fatigue dances at the edges of my vision. I've pulled all-nighters for work, but it's nothing compared to the emotional roller coaster I've been on for the last twenty-four hours. It keeps bringing me back to the question, why didn't I tell Claire sooner? What was I afraid of?

I close my eyes as if that will blot out the truth.

I was afraid of losing her.

What a fool I've been. The time to tell Claire about Sally was when we were in the Blue Mountains. When she revealed her childhood trauma to me. Now I might have lost her forever.

Chapter Forty-Two

Claire

I stretch my arms out, wincing as over-used muscles and tendons scream their objection. Although no sound can penetrate the boom of my speaker as Halestorm belts out, 'I Am the Fire'. There isn't an inch of me that doesn't ache. Even the tiny muscles between my rib bones. That's what I get for washing, sanding, and painting my lounge room in two days. And nights. I thought it would exorcise the ghost that is Jake, but I was wrong. He's still in my thoughts every single second of the day. And night.

With hands on hips, I turn and survey my handiwork. Violet is a bold colour, but it works for the feature wall of my living room, bringing out the reds and greens in the abstract-designed rug. And it contrasts well with the soft grey of the other three walls. All I need now are matching cushions for the sofa and white plantation shutters. Although, given the dwindling size of my bank account, the shutters will have to wait. I drop my brush into the water bucket and secure the lid of the paint tin.

A familiar Mercedes pulls into my driveway. My stomach

drops. What are my mother and sister doing here? It's too late to close the curtains and pretend I'm not home. I switch off the music, trudge to the entrance and open the door as Mum and Alex alight from the car. My mother looks like she's stepped out of a day spa in a soft, knitted brown dress and Alex is as casual as she gets in designer jeans, a white button-up and a black coat.

I paste on a smile. They don't know Jake and I are over, and I don't want to go there with them. Not yet. It's too raw. "Hi, there."

Mum's gaze wanders over me, her eyes widening. At least she can't find fault with my underwear showing through, but the tracksuit pants and T-shirt I'm wearing have seen better days. "What in the world have you been doing, Claire?"

She's so predictable. But a lecture is the last thing I need right now. I usher them in. "Painting."

"Yourself or the walls?" asks Alex. Her perfect lips curl into a smirk, although there's a sparkle in her eyes that suggests she's not being patronising.

I shrug. "I might have splashed a bit on me."

"A bit?" Mum shakes her head. "It looks like you dipped yourself in it."

"These are old clothes. It's all good."

"Oh my God," my mother screeches and slaps her chest with her hand. Her mouth gapes open as she takes in my living room. "What in the world have you done?"

"You don't like it?"

It's a rhetorical question. Mum is a beige person, or its close cousins, cream and eggshell. The only splashes of colour in her house are the cushions, and they are so muted they might as well be beige, too.

She wipes her mouth. "It's a bit much, isn't it?"

Déjà vu hits me like a dagger to the heart, and I stumble backwards. Those were the exact words I said to Jake when he picked me up in a limousine for our second date. Tears prick my eyes. God, I miss him, even knowing he's a lying, cheating bastard. He thought he'd stuffed up our first date and was trying to make up for it. Said he wanted it to be perfect for me.

Is that what I'm doing here? Trying to make up for my shitty life by making my home perfect?

"I think it looks amazing." Alex steps past Mum. "It's so you."

My jaw clenches. Is she putting me down? "What do you mean?"

"It's vibrant. Overflowing with energy. I love it." She turns around full circle, taking in all four walls and the ceiling.

What the hell? Have aliens taken over my sister's body?

"It's …" Mum licks her lips. Wipes her brow. Cups her jaw with her palm. "Colourful."

"Are you doing the entire house this way?" asks Alex as she places her handbag on the couch.

"I'm painting the kitchen in violet. It'll pop against the white cabinets. But I'll have light grey throughout and then feature walls with different shades of purple in the other rooms." Alex is right, there's a buzz of energy in the room that wasn't here before, and it gets stronger as I imagine the rest of the house in a similar tone.

Mum continues into the dining room and perches on a chair. Alex and I follow.

"Shall I put the kettle on?"

"Yes, thanks, love. A tea would be lovely."

I escape into the kitchen, although it's hardly escaping when the living area is open plan. "So, what brings you both here?" I ask. And why the hell couldn't they ring and tell me they were coming over?

"I called, but you didn't answer," says Mum.

Oops. That's what happens when the music is turned up loud. I check my mobile. Two missed calls from Jake. That's eight calls since I told him where he could stick his married arse. I'm surprised and relieved he hasn't dropped by. And pissed he doesn't care enough to come and see me in person. It just proves he's been playing me.

But why keep ringing?

The one thing I have in common with my mother and sister is our love of tea. It's always been the family go-to in times of emotional stress, so I brew a large pot and set it on the table. I even find a packet of Tim Tams that hasn't succumbed to my voracious sweet tooth and place them on a plate. That's about as fancy as I get with entertaining.

"It's great to see you guys." Lie. "But why are you here?"

Alex smooths her hands across the wooden tabletop. "There's a job going at my firm. I thought you might be interested."

I bite down a retort. Bullshit. It's clear she's here under duress. Again. The last thing either of us wants is to be working in the same office together. Mum beams next to her. This has to be her idea. Goes to show, even with all her lawyerly success, Alex is as captive to our mother's 'loving ways' as I am.

"What sort of job?"

"Receptionist." Alex brushes an imaginary piece of dirt off her blouse. "But there's scope to become a paralegal if you wanted to get your qualifications."

I keep my expression neutral. How lovely. Not. Either way, I'd be a gopher for my sister and brother-in-law. And I'd be bored out of my brain. No thanks.

My face must give away more than I think because Mum narrows her eyes. "Now is not the time to be picky, Claire." She sweeps her arm to the side. "You obviously love this house of yours. Do you really want to sell because you can't afford the mortgage?"

My shoulders slump. "No, I don't." But I also don't want to ask my parents for help with my loan, which is just as well because it sounds like they wouldn't give it to me anyway.

Mum's expression softens. "We wouldn't leave you stranded, Claire. But you need to be realistic. You can't—"

"I have a job interview tomorrow," I cut in.

Her face lights up. "That's wonderful. Why didn't you say so?"

I shrug and wince as the over-used muscles protest at the sudden movement. "Because I don't know how it will go." Truth is, I've got a good feeling about it, but it's hard to get excited about anything when my heart is bloody strips of shredded muscle on the floor.

"Is it with another pharmaceutical firm?" asks Alex.

"No." And this is where it gets tricky. My shoulders tense as I prepare myself for their censure. "It's with a real estate agent."

Alex's poker face slips into place. Typical lawyer. Mum tilts her head, looking confused. "You're selling houses?"

"No. I'm going to get them ready for sale. The job is for a stylist and photographer." Assuming I impress the owner, Monica Reynolds.

There's a flicker of surprise in Alex's eyes, but she quickly schools her features.

Mum stares at me like I just told her I was taking up stripping for a living. "Is the salary enough?"

"Yes." I resist the urge to roll my eyes. "It'll pay my mortgage."

Alex glances towards the living room. "Well, if what you've done so far is anything to go by, I'd say you've found your dream job."

My insecurities bubble up. Is she sincere? Or will she go home and tell her husband what a loser her younger sister is? "You don't think it's frivolous?"

"Absolutely not." Alex sips her tea and glances at Mum. "We spent a small fortune on an interior decorator after we bought our latest house. Renovated the three-year-old bathrooms on her advice."

Oh, wow. I'd assumed my sister had come up with the horrid black and mustard theme herself and wondered for the millionth time in my life how we could be from the same womb and yet so different. "I didn't realise until recently that it was something I would enjoy doing. And be good at."

"You're more than good at it." Alex laughs. "If I'd known you were hiding such a talent, I would have asked for your advice. It would have been a hell of a lot more tasteful than what we got."

Alex's praise is a shot of adrenaline to my self-esteem. I know I shouldn't need it, but it feels pretty awesome to receive a compliment from her.

She crosses her arms and pins me with a shrewd gaze. "And yet, you don't seem thrilled about it."

Shit. Bloody lawyers. They see through lies worse than cops. I twist my fingers in my lap. "I've still got the interview to get through. They may not offer me the job."

"And what does Jake think, dear?" Mum asks innocently, but the gleam in her eyes tells me she's picked up on my lack of enthusiasm as well. Once a lawyer, always a lawyer.

My throat constricts, and tears prick at my eyes. I grab a biscuit. If ever there was a need for chocolate, it's now. "It's not his decision." I bite into the heavenly snack and choke. Shit. I cough and spray crumbs in all directions. Alex thumps my back, and Mum pushes my cup of tea closer. I take a sip, my eyes burning.

"Claire?" The softness in my mother's voice nearly undoes me, but I stay strong.

"We're no longer together."

The expression—you could have heard a pin drop—was made for this moment. Mum's jaw drops. Alex stares at the Tim Tam on her plate like her life depends on it. And I resist the urge not to bang my head on the table.

"Are you sure it's not just a misunderstanding?" asks Mum.

Laughter bubbles up my throat. Given the number of tears I've cried, curse words I've screamed, and chocolate ice cream I've eaten, I couldn't be more certain. I nod, not trusting myself to burst into a wave of hysteria.

"You both seemed so happy at our party last weekend."

I scrape my chair back before the tears fall. I *was* ecstatic. And very much in love. Even daring to think about a future with Jake. But I was a fool. "I don't want to talk about it, Mum."

I take the plate and my cup into the kitchen. Mum stands as if to follow me, but Alex intercepts, clasping her arm. "Come on. Claire will tell us about Jake when she's ready. How about we go so she can get cleaned up?"

Mum opens her mouth as if to disagree, but Alex urges her towards the front door. I give her a quick wave of thanks, although I'm not sure if she's doing it for me or herself. Either way, I'm grateful.

The click of the lock catching is all it takes for the tears to spill over. I crumple to the floor and allow myself to wallow in sadness. To remember the soft firmness of Jake's kisses. His strong, clever fingers. The captivating creases around his mouth and eyes when he laughs.

All lies.

My phone buzzes. I pull it out of my pocket and choke on a sob. Another text from Jake.

Jake: We need to talk. Please, Claire, let me explain. xx

I'm tempted to block Jake's number, but I can't bring myself to do it. Besides, we do need to talk. He owes me answers. But I'm not calling him until I'm stronger. Until I'm certain I won't break down. Which, at the rate I'm going, will be sometime next century.

Chapter Forty-Three

Jake

As I step through the doorway, silence blankets the lunchroom more effectively than any order barked out by Commander Gordon. Several constables and the bail sergeant swivel towards me, their gazes darting in all directions but at me. Heads bowed, they murmur their condolences and scuttle out of the room. The emptiness inside my chest intensifies. I just want this nightmare to be over.

Unlike the cowards who fled, Greg and the young intelligence officer, Emily, remain, making eye contact. And I wish they didn't. Emily's blue eyes shimmer and deep lines furrow across Greg's brow. Their chairs are pushed together, a newspaper spread out in front of them. It seems a little too cosy. Bloody Greg. He'd better not be going behind my back and fooling around with her after I told him not to.

Greg pushes off his seat. "What the hell are you doing in here?"

"I wanted to check a few things."

And unpacking the boxes in the garage became too painful. There's a reason I haven't sorted through Sally's possessions until now. It's too hard. When I opened the first box, her perfume hit me smack bang in the frontal lobe. The musky scent was the polar opposite of Claire's light floral fragrance. Guilt consumed me like a swarm of bees, its sting sharp and burning. It made me question, yet again, am I a terrible husband for falling in love with Claire while Sally lay in a vegetative state? Some days I think I am. Other days, I know it was right to allow love back into my life. But most days, it just feels like a shitty hand that I'm doing my best to navigate. And fucking up in spectacular fashion.

Greg must see the ache in my soul because he breaks protocol and yanks me in for a hug. So much for being his commanding officer. His warmth feels good, and I hug him back. Squeeze harder than I normally would.

He slaps me between the shoulder blades and pulls away, rubbing his jaw. "I thought you promised to shave after you nearly took my eye out with that beard yesterday?"

I give him the finger, making sure Emily can't see my juvenile response. This is why I came to the station. I couldn't wait for Greg to drop by this evening. He keeps me grounded, and I need his irreverent humour more than ever today.

"You should be at home."

"I won't stay long." I scrub my face. The three-day stubble is sharp against my palm. "I just needed to get away."

"Would you like a coffee, Inspector Matthews?" asks Emily.

"No, thanks. I just need a moment with Sergeant Anderson." I shove my hands in my jean pockets and turn to Greg. "You got time to walk down to the café with me?"

"Sure." He winks at Emily. Pink colours her cheeks. I grind my teeth. Damn it. Looks like I need to remind him, yet again, why he needs to keep his charms zipped up along with his dick when it comes to the women he works with.

Greg grabs his coat, and we stroll down the street to

Coco Cubano. As its name suggests, the café has a Cuban flavour with a warm interior and strong, flavoursome coffee. We slide into the only spare table tucked away in the corner. Vintage photographs line the walls, including a wedding couple. Fuck. The last thing I want to look at is a happy couple, even if the photo is over fifty years old.

The waitress struts towards us with purpose, her expression strained. Given the size of the crowd, I'm not surprised. She'd be run off her feet.

"What can I get you, gentlemen?"

Greg's tapping on his phone, oblivious to his surroundings, so I answer. "Double espresso for both of us, thanks."

"Anything else?"

"No."

She sweeps the menus off the table and carries them away with rigid efficiency.

Greg puts his mobile down. "Sorry. I was just rescheduling a meeting."

"You didn't have to do that."

"Yes, I did."

A lump forms in my throat and tears prick at my eyes. Shit. I've never been much of a crier, but I've certainly made up for it over the last few days.

Greg steeples his fingers under his chin. "Have you spoken to Claire yet?"

"No." I shake my head. "She still isn't answering my calls. Or texts."

He drops his hands onto the table. "Then why don't you drive over there? Clear things up once and for all. She can't avoid you if you land on her doorstep."

"I can't."

Greg opens his mouth, but I cut in before he can give me a lecture. "I'm not sure Claire will forgive me." I swallow as bile creeps up my throat at the thought of never holding her again. "I'm not strong enough to have her slam the door in my face."

Greg crosses his arms and gives me a steely glare. "I've never known you to be a coward."

"Back off," I whisper between clenched teeth. I regret seeking him out now. "From her point of view, she was sleeping with a married man."

Greg grabs my wrist. "For the last fucking time," he growls, "the only thing you've done wrong is not tell Claire the truth sooner."

"Exactly."

We stare off at each other like dogs through a fence.

A different waitress arrives with our drinks. We both lean back in our chairs to give her room.

"Here you go, gentleman." The woman grazes Greg's arm and bats her eyelashes at him. "Let me know if you need anything else. Anything at all."

I can't help but smile at her obvious flirtation. It diffuses the angst enveloping our table, the tightness in my muscles slowly releasing.

"We're fine for now." Greg winks.

She saunters away, her arse swaying more than it did before, shiny black hair floating around her shoulders.

"How come you didn't get her number?"

Greg shakes his head. "Now's not the time. I've got a friend who needs me."

"Just because my life is a mess doesn't mean you should stop doing whatever it is you do." Except when it comes to Emily. He needs to shut that shit down now.

His eyebrow lifts. "Whatever it is that I do? What the fuck does that mean?"

"Nothing." I sigh. I didn't seek Greg out to pick a fight, and I don't have it in me to give him a bollocking. He knows how I feel about him fooling around with women at the station. I reach into my pocket and pull out the ring that's been burning a hole since early this morning and place it on the table.

Tears sting my eyes. Sally didn't want anything fancy. No engagement ring. Just a simple plain twenty-four-carat gold band with the inscription *Forever*. Turns out forever was only ten years.

Greg's gaze dances around the room. He shuffles in his seat and clears his throat. I don't mean to make him uncomfortable, but he's my best friend. I can't imagine having this conversation with anyone else.

The voices of the crowded café dull to a meaningless buzz. I trace the circle with my finger. The metal is cold. Unyielding.

Greg tugs at his tie. "You're freaking me out a bit right now, Jake." He forces a laugh. "You're not proposing or anything?"

"Ha! Very funny. As if you'd be that lucky."

After Sally's stroke, I never imagined ever marrying again. That changed when I met Claire.

I rub the bare skin of my wedding ring finger. No hint of a tan line where my wedding band once sat. "There should be two rings."

Greg's eyes harden into burnt chocolate points. He knows where I'm going. "It's not your fault."

"Yes, it is."

I pocketed my ring the night I caved into Greg's attempts to get me laid. The one and only time I had a one-night stand. It must have fallen out. I searched the woman's apartment like a madman, to the point she threatened to call the police if I didn't get the fuck out. Thank Christ, I never told her I *was* the police. It was already humiliating enough. Greg and I searched the bar the next day. Nothing.

I should have taken better care of my wedding band. That's the bottom line. Now there's only one ring to hand down to Oscar.

I pick up the ring and hold it in the palm of my hand. The light catches the smooth golden surface. "If I'd been wearing it, Claire would have known I was married. I would have had to tell her about Sally from the start instead of hiding the truth."

Greg sighs. "She also might have done a runner when you started flirting and never given you the chance to explain."

"I still did the wrong thing by not telling her sooner."

Greg stares at me, the intensity of his brown eyes making me squirm. He taps the table near the ring, then pulls his hand back. "Yes, you did. But you can still fix it."

"Greg—"

"Jake." He raises his hand, a tic pulsing in his jaw. "Stop pussyfooting around. From everything you've told me, it's obvious that woman loves you. I bet my balls you'll be forgiven for keeping Sally from her once you explain everything."

Greg's got one thing right. I'm a coward. But will Claire forgive me? I need to have my head in the game when I see her. And that's not possible until I make peace with my past. Give the woman I once loved the farewell she deserves. Then I need to hope like hell the woman I'm in love with today forgives me because I can't go back to the way I was before I met Claire. She busted through the walls I'd built after Sally's stroke, and now I can't imagine my life without her.

Chapter Forty-Four

Claire

The Oliver Brown Chocolate Café is an unusual location for a job interview, but Monica Reynolds, the owner of the real estate agency, explained her office is being remodelled. The promise of chocolate does nothing to lift the heavy weight crushing my chest, but I need this job. So, despite the urge to wear black and more black, I've dressed for the part right down to a pair of fuchsia-pink cheeky Parisian panties and matching silk bra.

I may not feel like a winner right now, but I'm determined to look like one. With my head held high, I saunter into the café.

A stunning woman with a beaming smile rises from a chair. "Good morning, you must be Claire. I'm Monica." She shakes my hand, her shrewd gaze sweeping over me. Red hair splashes around her face in a fiery halo. With her navy pencil skirt, crisp white blouse, and matching jacket, she's all class.

"How about we order?" She glides towards the counter.

"Sure." I bite the inside of my cheek. My bright purple and yellow dress is too 'out there' next to the immaculate Monica, even though I teamed it with a flowing cream jacket. I thought it suited the job of a property stylist. I'm not so sure now.

Monica looks expectantly at me.

"Sorry. A mug of a hot chocolate, thanks."

"And I'll have a decaf soy latte," Monica tells the guy behind the counter. She taps her phone to pay and we return to the table.

"Thanks for meeting me here, Claire. I must admit, you've already surprised me."

Damn it. This is what I feared—confirmation I've made a wardrobe blunder. I should have worn my black pinstripe suit. Paired it with less flashy underwear.

I break out in a sweat. "In what way?"

"I adore those colours on you. They work beautifully with your complexion and hair."

Oh. She's impressed. Not disgusted. Yay!

"Thanks. I figured I should dress the part." Crap. What am I saying? My hands shake, knocking over the bowl of sugar sachets. Gah! I'm so clumsy. This is what happens when you desperately want something. You stuff it up. "Not that dressing in a suit isn't appropriate," I say in a rush.

Monica laughs. "It's okay, Claire. I like these power suits. They work for me. But I can't imagine you in one. You're dressed perfectly, just as you are."

I dig my hands into the tops of my thighs. Is she for real? I'd felt a connection when we spoke on the phone, but I never dreamed we'd click this well.

"So, tell me more about your current role."

My palms go clammy. "I'm in between jobs right now."

She raises a shapely eyebrow. So perfect it must be microbladed. "Why's that?"

Sweat drips down my back. Luckily, the wool will soak it up. "It wasn't right for me, so I decided to leave." They threw me out on my arse for a false drug rap. One that I've been cleared of, but mud sticks. Obviously, I don't tell her that.

"And what wasn't right about it?"

Yikes. She's worse than Jake. And Mum. I take a deep breath. "I'd expected more marketing when I joined, but it turned out to be pure sales." I glance at my lap and back at Monica. "It was boring."

Monica bursts out laughing. "Oh, Claire. I'm not surprised. From the little we've spoken, and after meeting you in person, I can tell that a sales job would have been slowly killing you from the inside out."

Wow. She gets me. Better than I get myself. I'm so glad I answered the advertisement. I'd thought it was a long shot, but what did I have to lose? Except time. And I have plenty of that at the moment. Especially now I have no boyfriend.

No lying, cheating, boyfriend.

My chest tightens. I don't want to get my hopes up, but I'm getting positive vibes from Monica. My brain goes into overdrive. Could I make a career out of decorating houses?

I clear my throat. "So, can you tell me a little more about what's expected in the role of property stylist?"

"Of course." She leans forward, her eyes dancing. "You would take over the styling of properties and jazzing up the furnishings, as well as taking photos for advertising. That allows me to step back and focus on sales."

The server arrives with our mugs. Foamy chocolate goodness swirls on top. I take a sip, but it might as well be dishwater. While the interview gets better and better, the heaviness in my chest constricts with each and every breath, Jake never far from my thoughts.

Monica continues. "I was very impressed with the photos you sent through with your application. Especially the one of the bedroom. Do you have it with you?"

"Sure. But it's only on my mobile."

"That's okay. Do you mind if I take a look?"

"Of course not." I tap on the photo icon and hand my phone to Monica. "There are a few others there too. Please feel free to scroll through them."

If there's one thing I'm proud of, it's my photography. Even my mum can't fault it. It's what gave me the courage to apply for this job.

"Ah yes, this one." Monica smiles. "It's a brilliant shot."

"Thanks." Her smile is infectious. Reminds me of Jules. "Although I'd have used teal, rather than aquamarine, for the throw rug."

Her eyes narrow, making her look all business-like, as she studies the IKEA mock bedroom scene I'd snapped a couple of weeks ago. I'd been imagining all the ways I could have my way with Jake on the wrought-iron bed. That was before I found out he's been playing me.

"Why's that?" she asks.

"Teal would pop more against the teak."

She nods, looking impressed, and I preen inside.

She scrolls to the next photo. One of a bathroom with a large bathtub and walk-in shower. "Ooh, I like this photo. You've made the compact area look very spacious. Well done."

I shrug and pick at my nails. Seeing the photos again is a knife to my chest. A reminder of how happy and ignorant I'd been when snapping these pics. Imagining myself and Jake in all sorts of wicked positions. "I just changed the angle of the camera."

"You have an incredible eye. These are amazing."

I straighten and smooth my hands down the front of my dress. "Thanks." I squirm, unused to praise.

"Oops. I've scrolled too far." Monica's smile widens as if she's having her own secret fantasy.

She hands me back the phone. A photo of Jake in his cargo

pants, T-shirt and jacket, posing against a tree in the Blue Mountains fills the screen. My ribcage threatens to crack under the heavy weight of sadness. He looks so handsome.

Sexy.

Perfect.

Was it only a month ago he whisked me away to Katoomba?

"It's my ex-boyfriend."

"Oh. I'm sorry."

I tuck my phone into my bag. "It's okay. It wasn't meant to be."

With a willpower I didn't know I possessed, I look Monica in the eye. Her expression is neutral, a warmth in her eyes wrapping around me as if to say, 'I get you, sister'.

She sips her coffee. "When can you start?"

I squeeze my fists in my lap to stop myself from leaping over the table and hugging her. She's barely interviewed me. "I don't have any qualifications." *Damn! Why am I sabotaging this?* If I pull it off, I won't need Dad's help to get back on my feet.

"Claire, the photos you showed me don't come from qualifications. They come from an innate ability. A gift. And you have it."

Heat creeps up my neck. "Thank you. You're too kind."

She laughs. "I'm anything but kind, Claire. But I like to think I'm fair."

I think of Liam and the Bulldog. They weren't fair. I hadn't realised how downtrodden I'd been at Alpha Pharmaceuticals.

"So, Claire, I'll ask you again, when can you start?"

"Next week, if you like." It should be enough time to stop avoiding Jake's calls and let him 'explain' why he thought it was okay to lie and cheat. Get closure.

"That's perfect." Monica grins. "I'll get your contract organised in the next couple of days. There's a gorgeous four-bedroom heritage home coming up in two weeks. It's a little rundown but has so much potential. I can't wait to see what you do with it."

She sticks her arm out and hands me a shiny, embossed business card. "Welcome to the team."

Chapter Forty-Five

Claire

The sun hangs heavily in the west by the time I make my way home on the bus. The clear blue sky hurts my eyes. Reminds me of Jake. He'd be so proud of me. If he wasn't a lying, cheating bastard.

I clamber off the bus and trudge the short distance home. You'd think I'd be walking on air now that I have a job. A new career. But it's difficult to muster much enthusiasm. A cold wind doesn't help, freezing my cheeks and nose.

A vice squeezes my heart when I see the car out the front of my house. *Jake?*

I slow to a dawdle, even while my pulse races. It's one thing to rage at him over the phone, but in person, I fear I'll either collapse in a puddle of tears or throw myself at his feet and beg him to take me back, despite the fact he's married.

I swear my heart stalls when I see Jake standing on my front porch. There's an air of defeat about him. His check shirt is crumpled and partly tucked into his jeans. As I get closer, the desperate look in his eyes nearly undoes me. I clench my hands by my sides to stop myself from reaching out.

"Hi, Claire." Jake gives me a tiny smile, shadows turning his irises a dirty blue.

I tighten my fingers around my handbag. "Jake." My voice is soft, with only a slight hint of a tremor.

"Do you mind if I come in for a few minutes?"

"Yes."

He flinches as if I've hit him and his shoulders slump. Damn it. Whatever this man has done to me, he's obviously been through hell these last few days. His wife must have been sicker than I realised.

I unlock the door and gesture inside. "Five minutes. That's all."

"Thanks."

My legs are like jelly as I dump my bag on the hallway cupboard and head into the living room. I glance over my shoulder. "Would you like a drink?" I may be angry with Jake, devastated at his deception, but I haven't lost my manners. My mother would be proud.

"Yeah, thanks." His face softens. "It's pretty cold out there."

I turn on the jug and make him some instant coffee. Even if I had an espresso machine, I wouldn't use it. Not today. He doesn't deserve the good stuff. I hand Jake his mug and fall back into the lounge, hoping I look cooler than I feel.

He perches on the nearby one-seater. Sips his coffee and winces. His Adam's apple bobs in what would be a comical fashion if my heart wasn't playing drummer in its own little rock band in my chest. "I need to tell you the truth."

"The truth?" A bit late for that. I bite the inside of my lip, the metallic tang filling my mouth. "You've been married to someone else while sleeping with me. That's the truth, isn't it?"

A vein at his temple throbs. "Yes, but—"

"Excuse me, Jake, but I fail to see how there can be a but to that statement." I inject steel into my voice. I won't be taken for a fool anymore.

"Claire, just hear me out." His voice is harsh, like when Milo first ratted me out with my handbag at the station.

How dare he be angry with me. I'm the aggrieved party here, not Jake.

"Okay." I cross my arms and lift my chin. "Go ahead."

He stands and shoves his hands into his pockets. Stares at the violet feature wall, shakes his head. Then returns his attention to me.

"Sally started taking antidepressants after Oscar was born."

I tilt my head and glare at him. "Sally?"

He presses his lips together. "My wife."

I already figured that, but I wanted him to say it. I scrunch my face up. "That's no excuse for cheating on her."

"No. It's not." He lifts his head to the ceiling as if he's looking for divine assistance. Good luck with that, buddy. God would be the last one to condone adultery.

"She became addicted to a cocktail of prescription meds."

I gasp. No wonder Jake freaked out when he found the Valium in my handbag.

Jake's face twists. "Yeah. I had no idea. Three years ago, I arrived home around six in the morning after being out all night at a triple-murder scene." He sucks in a breath, and it takes all my willpower not to jump off the couch and hug the tortured expression off his face. "I could hear Oscar crying in his cot when I opened the door. Sally was lying on the floor next to him, unresponsive."

My fingernails dig into the palms of my hands. My heart implodes for Jake. For this woman I've never met. For Oscar. It doesn't excuse his cheating, but I can't help but feel sad for him. "What happened?"

"It was touch and go for a while, but she survived." Jake rubs his palm across his head and down the back of his neck.

"She had a stroke. It paralysed the right side of her body. All the best specialists were called in, but there was nothing they could do. Within months she deteriorated to the point where she couldn't even communicate."

A chill races up my spine and along my cheeks as the reality of Jake's revelation sinks in. "She never recovered?"

"No." He paces the room, seeming fixated on the violet wall. "She's been in a vegetative state for most of the last three years. I was told there was no chance of recovery."

Oh God. How awful. Poor Jake. And his poor son.

"What did you do?"

"I sold our house, put the money towards a deposit at a nursing home, and moved in with my parents."

Tears slide down my cheeks, the effort to hold them inside lost to the sadness filling my chest. Suddenly black doesn't seem so black, but more like a disturbing shade of grey. I pick at my fingernails, drawing blood.

Jake stops pacing and squats in front of me. "I'm sorry I didn't tell you sooner, Claire. More sorry than you can ever know. You're the only woman I've ever considered bringing into my life ..." He clears his throat. "Into Oscar's life since Sally's stroke."

He seems genuine, but I don't know what to believe anymore. I swipe my knuckles across my wet face. "It's a lot to take in, Jake."

"I know." He reaches out to touch me, then pulls his hand back. "Please understand. While Sally may have died last week, she's been all but lost to me for the last three years."

Blood drains from my face. "She died?"

"Yeah." He straightens. "You didn't know?"

"No. All I knew was she was in the hospital." I hit rewind in my head, my stomach roiling as I remember my last conversation with Jake. "What time did she die?"

He gives me a sad smile. "Early morning."

Numbness seeps into my skin. Even when drugs were

found in my drawer and my drug test was positive, Jake was there for me. And what do I do when he looks shaky? He wanted to explain, and I didn't give him a chance. I bury my head in my hands. How did things get so complicated?

A fresh tear slides down my cheek and I brush it away. "I'm sorry I didn't take your calls."

"Don't blame yourself, Claire." Jake shoves his hands into the pockets of his jeans. "It was my fault. I should have told you long before now."

He wrings his hands out, his blue eyes searching mine. I want to clasp his hands and kiss away the pain. Tell him it's okay. But I can't. He should have told me he was married, even if that marriage was all but void.

"I need time to process this, Jake."

"I understand." He fiddles with his shirt, tucking it neatly into his jeans. "Please call me when you're ready."

He shuffles out the door. I shut it behind him and lean my back against it. Slide down until my butt hits the floor. I'm not sure how I feel about Jake's actions, but they're not as heinous as I initially thought.

What would I have done in the same position?

I rest the back of my head against the door and close my eyes.

I don't know.

Chapter Forty-Six

Jake

"We're not getting a puppy."

"But Dad …"

Oscar peers up at me through tear-stained lashes. The spitting image of Sally. Fuck.

"No. I won't tell you again."

I tug him along the sand, slowing my stride so his tiny legs can keep up. My heart might be shards of broken dreams washed out to sea, but I'm not a monster.

Crimson stains the horizon, streaks of flamingo pink spreading above it. Sunrise. Sally's favourite part of the day. No matter how dark the night was, she said there was always tomorrow. I scowl. Wrong. There's no tomorrow for her. Drugs and depression swallowed her light. As for me, I've screwed up my future with lies.

It seemed crazy to drive all the way to the beach in the middle of winter, but Mum and Dad were right. The chilly breeze kisses my cheeks and fills my lungs with fresh, salty air. It's exactly what I needed after the funeral yesterday. Not to mention quality time with my son.

Oscar tugs at my hand. "Can I make a sandcastle, Daddy?"

The hole in my chest collapses, and I gasp for oxygen. "Sure, son."

I've been wallowing for long enough. Time to man up. Be a father first, widower second. And boyfriend? I'm pretty certain I've fucked that one up.

Oscar drops to his knees, places a bucket onto the sand and digs with the plastic shovel. I kneel and scrape away the sand. His giggles melt some of the ice encasing my heart since Sally's death. We work side by side, moulding the towers and turrets. Finish it with a moat and a large stick to represent a flag.

Oscar jumps to his feet and throws himself into my arms. "It's perfect, Daddy."

I fall back on the sand and hug his small body to me, soap and sea salt mingling in a potent scent that has me brushing the moisture from my eyes. "So are you, Oscar."

A soft pant is my only warning before a ball of fur crashes into me. In one swift movement, I leap to my feet, Oscar secure in my arms.

"Sorry, I'm so sorry," shouts a familiar feminine voice. "Zola, come here."

The dog jumps at my legs, sharp claws slashing through my jeans and down my shin bones. I grit my teeth and swallow a curse.

Green eyes latch onto mine. It's like a shot of adrenaline. "Claire. You got yourself a dog?"

"No, no." Claire grabs the wriggly mutt and holds it by the collar. "This is Jules' puppy."

Oscar's wide-eyed gaze fixes on the dog. "Daddy, can I play with him?"

The dog stares back at Oscar, tongue hanging out of its mouth, tail whipping back and forth.

"She's great with kids," says Claire. "She only leapt because you were holding Oscar and it made her excited."

I find that hard to believe, but Claire's sporting puppy dog eyes I can't resist. And so is Oscar. "Are you sure?"

"Absolutely. Zola won't jump on him, I promise."

"Alright." I lower Oscar to the sand. "This is my friend, Claire." At least I hope she's still my friend. I hope she's still a lot more than a friend.

"Hi," says Oscar. He smiles at Claire, then turns a mega-watt smile on the dog.

I sigh. It's like Claire knew what Oscar needed even though she's never met him before. "Off you go, but don't run too far away."

Zola barks and play bows. Oscar squeals and takes off down the beach, the hyped-up mutt on his heels.

I turn to Claire. Denim jeans mould her long legs. A small smile escapes as I take in her new running shoes. She didn't have them when we went to the Blue Mountains, and while her purple puffer jacket hides the treasures underneath, they're etched in stone in my memory.

"What are you doing here?" I pinch the bridge of my nose. "I mean, how did you know I'd be here?"

"I rang the station and spoke to your friend Greg." Claire tucks her hair behind her ear. "He told me you were bringing Oscar to the beach today."

God bless my meddling best mate. I shove my fingers into the back pockets of my jeans to stop myself from reaching out and touching her.

She removes her backpack and places it on the ground. "I brought some meat pies."

My stomach rumbles. "For breakfast?"

She shrugs and gives me the faintest of smiles.

"It's not home cooked, but it is comfort food." She drags out a picnic rug and smooths it onto the sand. "Sit and eat. They're still warm."

I lower myself next to her, my heart thumping steadily inside my chest, because, yeah, it didn't get washed out to sea. It just stopped beating for a while. I inhale the jasmine scent of Claire's shampoo, and my body comes alive. She hasn't said she's forgiven me yet, but she's here. With food. And while her smile is faint, it isn't a scowl.

The sounds of giggling and barking carry across the sand. My pulse kicks up a notch. "Oscar, come away from the water," I yell.

He waves his hand at me and steers back towards the soft sand, the puppy hot on his heels.

Claire sets out the pies on paper plates. "What about Oscar?"

"Nah. Let him have fun. I promised him pancakes later, anyway."

"Okay. Well, there's an extra one in case he wants it."

Claire drowns her pie in sauce and hands me the bottle. "Want some?"

"No," I chuckle. "I'm good."

"It's un-Australian not to have tomato sauce on your pie."

She gives me a silly grin, and we tuck into the pies; mine plain, hers looking like a crime scene. God, it feels good to sit next to her. To feel like we're a couple again, even if we're not. Yet.

I keep one eye on Oscar. He and the puppy continue to chase each other in circles, their antics leading them closer to the shoreline again. They're on the border where soft dry sand gives way to compacted sand. My pulse quickens.

"Oscar, come back here!"

He pivots and runs towards me. Thank Christ he's an obedient kid.

I swallow the last piece of crusty pastry. Claire's right about the pies being comfort food. The tightness in my muscles eases after eating, although that could be more to do with Claire than the pie. I wipe a smear of sauce from the side of her mouth. Her breath hitches, her green eyes swirling. She doesn't swat my finger away. Instead, she grabs my hand and nuzzles it with her cheek. Her floral scent tickles my nostrils and I lean closer. Would she let me have a kiss?

"Argh!!!"

A high-pitched scream, more urgent than the earlier squeal, tears my attention away from Claire's lips. Fuck. The foamy swell spills up the beach further than it has all morning, swallowing Oscar's legs. He topples over. Adrenaline surges through me. I failed Sally. I can't fail Oscar too. I launch into a sprint.

It's a short distance, couldn't be more than twenty metres, but I pant like I've run a marathon when I scoop Oscar into my arms. The dog launches itself at me as if it also wants to be plucked from the water, sliding its impossibly sharp claws down my legs. Fuck. Not again. There's no way in hell I'm ever getting a dog.

Oscar squirms against me. "Daddy, what are you doing?"

"Saving you."

He huffs. "It was just a little wave."

"What did I tell you about going near the water?"

My voice comes out gruffer than I mean to, but my heart's still racing.

His chin wobbles.

Fuck. I close my eyes for a second and open them again. "Sorry, Oscar. I got scared."

"You?" His eyes widen.

My chest constricts. "Yeah, me. I don't want to see you get hurt." I wipe the wetness from his eyes. "I need you to stay closer to Claire and me while you play."

He nods and I lower him to the sand. He and the dog scamper off.

Claire nudges my side, her breaths laboured, cheeks red. She must have run after me.

I brush strands of hair from her cheeks. "Sorry. I'm a bit

overprotective." More like fucking paranoid about keeping my family safe.

"You don't have to explain." She clasps my hand and kisses the tops of my fingers. It's a simple gesture and gives me hope that I haven't lost her.

We walk back to where we'd been sitting and flop onto the sand. Oscar and the dog return to chasing each other well away from the water. My heart settles down. I overreacted, but Christ, if anything happened to my son, I'd never forgive myself.

I draw in a deep breath. "Thanks for coming."

Claire turns towards me, her eyes the colour of a freshly mown lawn. The colour of life. Hope. She weaves her fingers with mine. It's a simple gesture. One that reaches deep inside and massages my aching heart.

"You should have told me about Sally much earlier. I would have understood."

I look away and stare out at the ocean—waves crashing against the shore, churning up the sand.

"I wanted to. It's just … I didn't know how. I mean, starting off a conversation with, I love you, but I'm still married. But don't worry, my wife's in a vegetative state and won't ever recover, so it's not really cheating." I breathe in the salty, cleansing air. "Yeah, not sure you would have understood that. I sure don't."

Claire squeezes my fingers. "I'm sorry about her death."

I press my lips together. "She's at peace now."

We sit side by side, our hands entwined. Oscar and the puppy scamper across the sand. It's surreal how natural it feels.

Claire shuffles closer, a goofy grin on her face. "Jake."

"Yeah."

"You said you loved me."

I open my legs and she nestles between them, her arse pressed against my groin.

Love? It's not a strong enough word to describe how I feel about her. "I was wondering if you'd noticed that little slip."

She peers up at me, her bottom lip quivering. "I love you too." She drags my hand upwards until it cups her breast. "So much."

I shift position to relieve the growing pressure in my pants, but it's a lost cause. Despite the despair of the last week, or perhaps because of it, the familiar cocktail of lust and love surges through me. Claire's had that effect on me from the moment she stepped out in front of my SUV.

She pushes her arse against my throbbing dick. "Feels like you have a not-so-small problem back there, Inspector."

I squeeze her breast. She gasps and arches into my fingers.

"Two can play at this game, missy," I whisper into her ear.

Oscar's squeals carry across the sand, but I'm watching him and can see he's having fun and is well away from the water. Claire lifts her head, and I touch my lips to hers. It's a fleeting kiss. A promise. She kisses me back. And just like that, all that's wrong with the world is righted.

Until I pull away from Claire and find Oscar staring at me, his head tilted to the side, smile wavering.

Shit.

I slide my hand away from Claire's breast and onto her waist. The only woman Oscar's ever seen me embrace is my mother, and certainly not like this, with the woman between my legs. What will he do?

The dog licks Oscar on the lips. Oscar giggles and wipes his mouth. "Ew."

I chuckle. "Would you like to sit with me and Claire for a while?"

"No." He shakes his head. "I want to keep playing with Zola."

"Okay."

He doesn't need any further encouragement, taking off in a flurry of sand, the puppy on his heels. No doubt he'll have questions about Claire later. But she's already scored brownie points by bringing the dog with her. Smart move.

Claire rests the back of her head against my chest, and I bury my face in her hair, my gaze on Oscar and the dog. The golden globe of the sun peeks above the horizon. Maybe I can still have a tomorrow … with Oscar … and Claire.

Epilogue

Claire

Two years later.

"**M**um, Ruby won't stop digging."

I peg the last pair of panties onto the clothesline, a smile tugging at my lips. Seven lacy scraps of fabric—as Jake likes to call them—and seven of Jake's manly boxer shorts positioned side by side. A pair of red panties. Red boxer pants. Black panties. Black boxer pants. And so on. Proof of how perfect life has become.

My panties are larger than I'd like, but the lace and frills stop them from resembling Granny's pants. Not to mention, none of them are plain white or a patchwork of flowers.

"Mum, the hole's getting bigger."

"I'll be there in a moment, Oscar."

The counselling is helping. I no longer wear panties in the house; the fear of being caught without underpants in an emergency is outweighed by the delicious risk of Jake destroying the delicate fabric in his hurry to ravage me.

I still coordinate my underwear when I go out, though. There's no way any sane woman should leave their home unless their bra and underpants match. On that, Dr Amy and

I will have to disagree. But I now decide which panties and bra to wear in under five minutes. That's freed up several hours a week. Hours I can spend making love to my husband.

"Mum!"

"I'm coming, sweetie. Hold on."

I rub the taut, round smoothness of my belly. One more month and we'll be giving Oscar a little sister or brother. It can't come soon enough.

I waddle towards the back of the yard. The grass is lush, not a trace of any weeds, and the edges are immaculate. Since Jake and Oscar moved in, my whipper-snipper has never been worked so hard. I snigger. Neither have I.

Three magpies perch along the top of the fence.

"Enjoying the show?"

They tilt their heads at me as if they understand. Ruby, our rescue cattle-cross, whines and paws at the dirt beneath them. Her nose burrows into a hole big enough to cause Jake heart palpitations if he could see the mess she's making of his veggie patch.

A glimmer of white catches my eye. "What have you got there, girl?" I manoeuvre onto my knees and pull out …

Wow! A long cockatoo feather wrapped in a sealed plastic bag.

"No!" Oscar snatches it from my hands.

"Oscar!"

His bottom lip drops. "Sorry."

"Hey. What's wrong?"

"It's an angel's feather. For Mum." He stares at the feather clutched in his hand and back to me, his eyes shimmering. "My other mum."

Oh, no. Where's Jake? Oscar needs him. I need him.

Tears slip down Oscar's face. "I buried it."

My fingers itch to comfort him. "Why did you do that?"

"I don't need it anymore."

I hold my hands out to him, and he clasps his arms around my belly. "Why not, sweetie?"

"Because I have you." He sniffles. "And Dad."

"That you do, son." Jake strides down the back path and kneels beside me. Thank goodness he's home.

"I'm sorry." Oscar clambers into his arms. "I thought if I buried the feather, God wouldn't make Mum stay here to look over us. She could go to heaven."

"You've got nothing to apologise for." Jake's voice cracks. "I think that was very noble of you, Oscar."

My heart skips a beat. "Yeah, your dad's right. And maybe Ruby digging the feather up is a sign your mum would rather keep watching over you?"

Oscar cocks his head, a miniature of his father, except for melting chocolate eyes that are going to break hearts when he's older. The love I feel for him is overwhelming. Like he's my own flesh and blood.

"You think so?"

I nod my head.

His brow wrinkles. "You wouldn't be mad?"

"Of course not. Why do you think that?"

"Because some of the other kids say I can only have one mum."

My gaze shoots to Jake's. Yikes. His eyes glimmer, Adam's apple bobbing as if he's swallowing back tears.

"Well, they're wrong, sweetie." I brush a lock of hair from his face, my heart aching for this sweet little boy. "Some people are lucky enough to have two mums."

Oscar's eyes brighten, and his shoulders push back. It's like a weight has been lifted.

"I'll put the feather back in the pot next to my bed." He squirms out of Jake's arms and smacks a kiss on my cheek. "Thanks, Mum."

Oscar races into the house. His shadow, Ruby, scampers after him.

Jake's brow furrows as he glances at what used to be a neat row of carrots and now resembles an excavation site. "Damn dog."

I wrap my fingers around his forearm. "She's good for Oscar."

He grunts. "Which is why I put up with the mangy mutt."

"You adore Ruby."

His lips twitch. "She's growing on me."

Jake helps me stand, his firm hands lingering on my stomach. "Have I told you how much I love you, Claire Matthews?"

I tilt my head at him. "Mmm … it's been ten hours since I heard those words."

"Has it now?"

He nibbles my ear, his tongue curling around the shell, turning my legs to jelly. "Are you wearing panties?"

He's toying with me. "As if you don't know."

He growls, tracing a path down my cheek with his lips, his soft breath blazing a fire across my skin.

"You are the biggest tease, Mrs Matthews."

The magpies squawk as if that's enough lovey-dovey stuff for one day and flutter away.

I lick the seam of his mouth. "And you love it."

Jake's answer is to swallow my words, our tongues tangling in a slow, erotic dance. I stroke the hard plains of his back while he squeezes my butt. Even with my tummy bulging between us, we fit together perfectly.

He links his arm in mine and leads me into the house. We stop at Oscar's bedroom door. Painted in deep grey, with a bright red, yellow and blue Superman quilt cover adorning the bed, it's the only room that escaped my purple theme. The feather stands proudly in a pot of dirt on the bedside table. Oscar sits on the floor with his latest Lego set, Ruby beside him.

"Claire and I are going to take a nap," says Jake.

Oscar peers up, a piece of Lego in his hand. "Okay."

"Will you be alright, sweetie?" I ask.

He giggles. "I'm a big boy, Mum. I know old people need more sleep."

I smother a chuckle. Jake sniggers softly.

Jake shuts the door, and we continue down the hallway. He ushers me inside and closes our door. Flips the latch he installed when we quickly learnt Oscar sometimes forgets to knock. I loved the violet feature wall in the living room so much, I did the same thing in my bedroom. Our bedroom. It gives it a mysterious, sensual ambience. Perfect for making love to my husband.

"Finally." Jake presses me against the door and rests his head on top of mine.

I arch against him, my core aching for his touch, but my stomach is like a determined prison guard, keeping our private regions locked apart.

"You wet for me?" Jake whispers in my ear.

"Soaking."

He groans, licking across my lips. "We'll have to be quiet."

"We always are."

That's the only downfall of sharing the house with a curious youngster. Fortunately, Jake's parents love having Oscar stay overnight. They miss seeing him and Jake on a daily basis, but they're pleased to see their son and grandson happy. And while my parents weren't too keen about my career change, they've welcomed Jake and Oscar into the family. It might have something to do with Dad thinking Jake has the potential to be Police Commissioner one day.

Jake peels my dress over my shoulders. I shiver as the cool air hits my skin.

He brushes a finger down the seam of my pussy. "I love it when you don't wear panties." He slides the digit between my folds. I shudder at the brief contact. He brings his finger to his mouth. "Delicious."

His husky voice undoes me and my legs buckle, but Jake's powerful arms hold me up.

His attention turns to my breasts. I'd stay pregnant forever to keep the new and enhanced size. The super-sensitivity. Jake wastes no time unclipping my bra and latching onto a nipple.

I dig my fingers into his shoulders and bite my lip to stop from crying out. "That's so good. Jake."

He swirls his tongue around one engorged areola and then the other. It's an intoxicating mix of pain and pleasure as he sucks as much of the flesh as he can into his mouth.

I place my palm against Jake's groin. I'm rewarded with a jerk of his hips. Emboldened, I grip the top of his trousers and wrestle with his belt. His hand covers mine. "I can't do slow today."

"Then fast it is, Inspector." He's all talk. He hasn't done fast in months. Too scared of hurting the baby. Hurting me. I undo the belt, flick the button open, and slide his zipper down.

"Claire, wait." His hand rests on mine again. His cock pulses beneath my palm, sending a fresh wave of heat to my nether regions. "Maybe we shouldn't."

"I'm pregnant, Jake. Not injured."

"Yeah, but …"

I squeeze his cock. He grunts. "You worry too much, Inspector Matthews. Just fuck me already."

He bursts out laughing. "God, I love you Mrs Matthews." He caresses my belly with slow, smooth circles. "And I love this little tyke in here."

Jake's so sweet, but he's also torturing me. "Come on. Stop stalling."

"Fine." He chuckles and slaps my butt. "Assume the position."

"Ooh, I love it when you talk dirty, Inspector."

He points at the bed. "On your knees, woman."

Fresh moisture leaks down my thighs. I'm so primed for him.

I clamber onto the bed on all fours. Then rest my elbows on the mattress. Jake slides a pillow under my belly.

"Comfortable?"

"Yeah." And happy. So happy.

He kneads my butt with his fingers, skimming the area I need him most. Teasing me. His warm breath is the only warning I get before he licks me from clitoris to anus. My core clenches at the soft, wet touch on my sensitive flesh. I grip the quilt cover. "Oh God. So good."

He flicks his tongue across my clit a few times and then dips it into my entrance. I thrust my hips against his face. His fingers dig into my arse, holding me still. My core pulses as my orgasm looms. He seems to sense I'm close, returning his attention to the bundle of nerves. I explode, bucking against his mouth, and bury my face in the bed to muffle the screams.

Jake covers my body, his cock prodding my soaked entrance. I peer behind me. His sky-blue eyes latch onto mine and burn white hot as he slides into me. We both groan at the exquisite sensation of joining.

Despite his assertions, he couldn't go slow; Jake surges in and out of me with infinite care. Just like I knew he would.

Warmth seeps into my bones.

My heart.

My soul.

This is what it feels like to be loved and to love—with or without panties.

Coming Soon

With or Without Trust

Greg and Emily's story will be released in 2024. Get ready to watch Emily bring Greg to his knees.

❧

And if you're wondering what's going on with Jules, don't worry. All will be revealed. Eventually.

Sign up for my mailing list to keep up to date on the next instalments of the Hot Cops series, and as a bonus, receive your free copy of the steamy Hot Cops novelette 'Breaking the Rules'.

www.karenlieversz.com/newsletter

Breaking the Rules

My headlights slice through the morning mist, allowing me to see the road ahead without the need to remove my Prada sunglasses. The sunnies were an impulse purchase. One I'm determined not to regret. Hence, I wear them rain, hail, or shine. Or in today's case, in the fog.

I turn up the stereo and get the bass pumping with my favourite rap music to drown out the whine of my faithful old car, Lexi. She's not fond of travelling at the open road speed limit. Another few weeks and I'll have enough money to pay for a service. One that should have been done six months ago.

Visibility improves and field after field of green pastures zip past. I adjust the air vents and imagine I'm in a luxury convertible, wind blowing curls off my face, a sexy man by my side. It's better than dwelling on reality. On the unpaid bills stuffed in my handbag. The threats from the bank to sue me for loans that aren't even mine. The empty savings account my boyfriend left behind after he scammed me.

A Huntsman spider scurries across the inside of the windscreen. My heart explodes. *Shit.* Pressing back in the seat, I try to get as far away from the giant, hairy monster as possible. I reach for my cardigan on the passenger seat. It's not ideal, but it'll have to do. Before I can pick up the delicate fabric, the car swerves, and the spider disappears down a crack in the dash. I slap both hands on the steering wheel and narrowly miss veering into the gravel on the side of the road. My knuckles turn white. That was too close.

An annoying whine pricks at my ears, ruining the hypnotic thump thump of the music. Its pitch is higher than the usual rattling.

"Don't give up on me now, Lexi."

I'm still twenty minutes out of town. The last thing I need is to break down and have to call a tow truck.

A flash of blue catches my eye in the rear vision mirror. My stomach free-falls as if I'm flying over a dip in the road. Damn. That annoying noise is a siren. From a cop car.

My hands tremble. I've done nothing wrong. Have I?

I hit the brakes too hard and fishtail across the bitumen. My heart punches against my ribcage. I can't afford to write off my car. I ease my foot off the brake and Lexi straightens out. I touch the pedals more gently and swing her onto the side of the road

I slump against the seat, my entire body a wet, saggy noodle, and turn off the ignition and the head banging music.

Silence, except for the erratic beat of my heart pounding in my ears.

I suck in a deep breath. I'm okay. Lexi's okay. I think. And we didn't hit anything. The only tree in my vision is a gnarled monstrosity on the other side of the road. So everything's good. Except for the enormous, uniformed officer heading my way.

I wind down the window and look up, up and up. Wow! He's tall. And hot. Scorching. Molten chocolate eyes pin me to the driver's seat in a not so sexy way, but it doesn't stop me from appreciating the chiselled jaw, razor-sharp cheekbones and short brown hair begging to be messed up.

Moisture deserts my throat, no doubt heading south to my panties.

I channel Audrey Hepburn and tilt my chin at him. "Hello, officer." Unfortunately, my voice doesn't get the memo and the words come out with a squeak.

He regards me with unblinking eyes.

I swallow and lower my gaze. Looks like I might be in a little trouble. Stupid spider.

"Licence please," he demands with a deep rumble that further moistens my already wet panties. I rummage in my handbag and pull out my licence. He points at my face. "Take off the glasses."

I remove my sunglasses, suddenly feeling naked in front of this-six-feet plus wall of testosterone. His expression doesn't change. Then again, I'm not wearing makeup. The image of a sex goddess is in my mind only.

"Stay here." He swivels and saunters back to his patrol car.

I clench the steering wheel and stare at the road ahead. I can't afford a fine. Could my life get any shittier?

He returns a few minutes later.

"Step out of the vehicle, Miss Cameron."

His voice is as smooth as his chocolate eyes, sliding over my eardrums, across my breasts, between my legs. I squeeze my thighs tight. There's something wrong with me. The man's going to book me and I'm imagining having my way with him.

"Sure."

I fumble with the door and push it open. Stumble out of the car. The officer's gaze drifts from my head down the body-hugging Ralph Lauren dress I found in a second-hand store to the ridiculously high heels on my feet. In hindsight, they weren't the smartest footwear for a three-hour trip to the country.

His gaze returns to my face. "You were travelling at twenty-two kilometres over the speed limit."

"Impossible."

He arches an eyebrow.

"My car can't go that fast." Can she?

"I assure you, it can." He hands me my licence.

"Thanks." I lean into the passenger seat and slip it back in my purse, belatedly realising I've given him a perfect view of my butt. But the dress is knee length. It's not like I flashed him. Still, the thought of being bent over in front of the hot cop has heat rushing to my cheeks.

I straighten and turn to face the officer. His expression is as still as a lake at dawn. No hint of what he's thinking.

"Have you been drinking?"

"No!" I snap. "I never drink and drive."

His brown eyes bore into mine. "I believe you. Looks like you're just a bad driver."

He pulls out a notebook and starts writing.

No, no, no. "Hey." I grab his arm. "You can't book me."

And why is he writing a paper ticket? Isn't everything electronic these days? Not that I dare ask him.

His eyebrow lifts, and a smirk tugs at his lips. Bastard's enjoying my misfortune. "And why's that?"

"Because I can't afford it."

His smirk disappears into a thin line. "You should have thought of that before you broke the law."

"Please." My fingers curl around the hard muscle of his forearm. Holy crap, he's so firm. My legs wobble. And a hint of sandalwood tickles my nose. Would it be inappropriate to lean in and breathe against his neck? My friend, Jo's right. I've been too long without a man. "What can I do?"

He places his hand on mine, his eyes darkening to black pools. "What are you suggesting?"

Oh God. Kill me now. Did I just proposition a police officer?

"Not *that*." Whatever *that* is.

He peels my fingers off his arm. "I'm pleased to hear it, since any suggestion of coercing an officer of the law would add another offence to the list."

Our fingers brush as he gives me the ticket, sending a tingle of awareness straight to my core. He clenches his jaw and pulls his hand away like I might have given him cooties with my touch. Arrogant sod.

"I'm only booking you for the speeding. I'll let the broken tail light and the less than impressive rally car driving go." Is he making a joke? From the stern expression on his face, I doubt it. "But make sure you get this vehicle to a mechanic once you reach town."

"Okay." No way. Paying this stupid fine will have to come before I spend any more money I don't have. But I'm not telling Officer Grumpy that.

I climb into the driver's seat under his watchful eye. The disappointment radiating from him is worse than anything my dad used to subject me to when I was a kid.

The engine starts with a splutter and a puff of smoke. No. Not now, Lexi. Don't fail me. I pump the accelerator, give the policeman a wave, and pull away. My wheels spin in the gravel and dust and rocks kick up. Damn it. What if he regrets his decision to let me off on the other offences and stops me again?

I risk a glance in the rear view mirror. He stands with his arms crossed, his attention firmly on me, looking hotter than he has any right to look.

Want to know what happens next? Sign up to my newsletter for your free copy of Breaking the Rules.

www.karenlieversz.com/newsletter

Acknowledgments

There are so many people to thank for making this dream a reality because writing a book is so much more than writing a book.

Firstly, a massive thanks to my writing pack, Carrie, Emma, and Antonella. You have been my critique partners, beta readers and biggest supporters. You've been there for the highs and the lows. I couldn't have survived this publishing journey without you. Love you ladies!

A big thanks to my critique partner, Kat, who worked chapter by chapter with me on an early draft of With or Without Panties, and to Jan-Andrew Henderson, who reviewed it and gave me ideas to make it stronger. And thanks to all my beta readers, of which they've been many—Davina, Dannielle, Helen, Carrie, Emma, Antonella, Kat, and Michele. One of my favourite pieces of feedback was from my sister, Michele, who said, "It reads like a real book." 😊

I mustn't forget my local cop source, Terry, who allowed me to pick his brains on all things policing for this book and others in the series. Although, I may have left him a little scarred by some of my plot ideas. If you're wondering where the idea for the title came from … it popped into my head one day after many months of brainstorming during my evening walks with my neighbour, Mary-Ann. And many a plot hole was solved thanks to my beautician, Liz, who endured endless hours of listening to me rave on and on about Jake and Claire.

To Anne, Frances, Laura, Carolyn, and everyone at Fellowship of Australian Writers Eastwood/Hills group, thank you for your encouragement, friendship, and support as I navigated this journey from curious hobbyist to published author.

And a massive thank you to Romance Writers of Australia for the courses, networking opportunities and competitions that helped me develop my craft. I owe much to this wonderful organisation for where I am today as an author. With or Without Panties (with varying titles) was a finalist in the prestigious RWAus Valerie Parv Award in 2020 and the Emerald in 2022. Then, in 2023 it came third in the suspense category of the League of Romance Writers, The Emily.

I'm so fortunate to have found outstanding editing support in Kelly Rigby. She is the red pen behind the words. Her structural and line/copy edits were key to making this the best possible story it could be. The fabulous Jo Speirs then cast her eagle eye over the final product to give it a polish that makes it shine. Thank you ladies! This leaves me with my amazing cover designer, LJ. Thank you for your patience as I obsessed over every tiny detail. I love the cover so much.

None of this would be possible without support at home because, like many authors, I maintain a full-time job on top of my writing. Thank you to my husband for keeping the house running while I locked myself away with my laptop. For keeping me fed and hydrated. For forcing me to socialise on a regular basis with some turns around the dance floor. And to Juno, our kelpie/staffy, who ensured that I participated in at least an hour of exercise every day whether I wanted to or not.

Lastly, and most importantly, a huge thank you to you, my reader, for choosing to read *With or Without Panties*. Given the huge selection of books available, I'm honoured and humbled that you chose mine.

Thank you!
Karen xx

About the Author

Karen Lieversz writes contemporary romance and women's fiction with heat, humour, and a dash of irreverence.

A born and bred country girl, Karen spent her childhood making up stories and reading to the cows, who proved to be avid listeners. Drawn to the city lights, she now lives in Sydney, Australia, with her husband and four-legged trainer. When Karen's not glued to her laptop, you can find her walking her dog or kicking her heels up on the dancefloor.

Keep up to date with Karen's Hot Cops Series and other misadventures by following her on Instagram *www.instagram. com/karenlieversz* or join her mailing list at *www.karenlieversz. com/newsletter* to receive advance news on her upcoming books and exclusive content, as well as receive a copy of the free steamy Hot Cops Novelette 'Breaking the Rules'.

Please Review this Book.

If you enjoyed *With or Without Panties*, please consider leaving a review on Amazon or Goodreads. It would mean the world to this author if you did.

Printed in Great Britain
by Amazon

36258577R00199